Lagrange Calling

A Cuss Abbott Novel

Doug J. Cooper

CS THRIVES THANKS TO YOU

Also by Doug J. Cooper

Crystal Deception (Book 1)
Crystal Conquest (Book 2)
Crystal Rebellion (Book 3)
Crystal Escape (Book 4)
Crystal Horizon (Short prequel & sampler)

Bump Time Origin (Book 1)
Bump Time Meridian (Book 2)
Bump Time Terminus (Book 3)

Lagrange Rising (Book 1)

For info and updates, please visit: crystalseries.com

Lagrange Calling
Copyright © 2023 by Doug J. Cooper

Published by: Douglas Cooper Consulting

Beta reviewer: Mark Mesler
Book editor: Tammy Salyer
Cover design: Damonza

ISBN-13: 978-1-7337801-8-6

Author website: www.crystalseries.com

my sweetie wears
rose-colored glasses
what could be better
than that

Chapter 1

"Are we go?" asked Vincent Rogalski, his butt tightening in excitement and fear. He sat on the couch in his apartment, eyes glued to a hoverview display. On-screen, his two partners strolled down the pedestrian thoroughfare on Demeter's Deck 4, three blocks from Avium Pharmaceuticals.

The two wore gray pants and sweatshirts, hoods shading their faces. They'd just left Gator Pub, a raucous college bar filled with similarly dressed revelers. The city's population tracking system—POTS—had them listed as "unknown" but was gathering clues to correct the deficiency.

Vincent worked as a security tech on the civilian side of Lagrange's Community Patrol, the police force for the micro-nation floating in space between Earth and the Moon. POTS, a system that monitored Lagrange's public spaces, was his baby. His job was to keep it updated, fix any bugs, and coordinate with the enforcement side of Community Patrol to ensure it remained a potent and reliable resource.

In the lower right corner of Vincent's display, small icons signaled that two ID shields were on standby. His girlfriend, Abbi Gillespie, the gray sweatshirt on the right, had given him these ultrasophisticated programs, tools that made people "disappear" from POTS, a capability he hadn't realized was possible until he'd seen it for himself.

Though Vincent didn't fully understand the technology, a shield didn't just erase the record. Somehow it ensured the targets never got recorded in the first place. *Poof.* Like they didn't exist.

"It's go time," Abbi confirmed.

"See you in ninety." Vincent launched the shields, and Abbi and Darrell "Bridge" Hollenbeck, so named because he had a single continuous eyebrow that spanned his brow ridge, disappeared from his display.

At that moment, Vincent crossed the line from being a regular citizen to being an offender. From a guy who'd never been in trouble with the law to high-tech criminal.

He did it because Abbi, the love of his life, had asked him to. And because afterward, their coffers would be overflowing. Comforted by the fact, he popped the last dose of Pulse—an intensely powerful pleasure pill—into his mouth. As the drug flooded his system, he sighed from its warm embrace. A happiness. A fulfillment. A hug as arousing as one from Abbi. Certainly as addicting. She'd turned him on to the drug, and now both she and it were his obsessions.

He didn't have anything to do for the next hour and a half, and before he became too consumed by his pleasure, he set a timer to rouse himself when it was over.

Abbi and Bridge were about to enter Avium Pharmaceuticals and steal enough Pulse pills to last the three of them for years. Because of Abbi's fancy POTS shields, the cops would never be able to link any of them to the theft. It was the perfect crime.

He passed the time listening to music and sipping beer. Every so often he checked his display, confirming that Abbi and Bridge were not among the identified.

They'd rehearsed it over and over. The two would need forty-five minutes to enter the Avium building, load their backpacks with Pulse—a drug with legitimate, though tightly regulated, uses—exit, and get kilometers away. They'd agreed to double the time span, to ensure ninety minutes of POTS invisibility to provide a healthy buffer for unforeseen circumstances.

Abbi's shields also disabled Avium Pharmaceuticals' private security. While the cops would know the system had been invaded, they wouldn't be able to trace it back to them. Not in a million years. Abbi swore the tech was that good.

His timer chimed and he surfaced with a start. Shaking his head to focus, he watched the countdown tick through the last seconds. When the counter reached zero, the shields erased themselves, gone forever, returning POTS to normal operation.

The tracking system reported that it still couldn't locate Abbi and Bridge.

Annoyed, he zoomed in on the park bench in Joseph-Louis Park, the agreed-upon rally point where he expected to find them. They'd chosen it because it was near a suite of community sensors, giving POTS plenty of tools to identify them. They weren't there.

Bridge was sometimes a fuckup, so Vincent wasn't too worried. He tickled POTS to perform a broader search, suggesting the system focus on the area up near Avium Pharmaceuticals. The search came back null, giving Vincent his first pangs of concern. He directed POTS to consider all of Deck 4. And then all of Demeter.

POTS finally located Abbi in the city's spaceport. Confused, Vincent donned his neural cap and chanted to the system, guiding it to access the flight-deck sensors so he could see for himself. He found her floating across the flight deck, positioned between two men, one of whom had a hand pressed against her back. He was propelling her in the weightless environment toward a space corvette, a smallish speedster named *Jaywalker*. When they reached the craft, he pushed her through the hatch and followed her inside.

She's being kidnapped!

In spite of being dosed with Pulse, Vincent felt a chill of fear pass through him. Where was Bridge? And why wasn't Abbi struggling and screaming for help? He tried to make sense of it but couldn't.

He spoke to POTS. "Back up ten minutes and show me a summary." He watched breathlessly as two men floated across the flight deck toward the *Jaywalker*, one with his hand out to the side in an awkward fashion. Midway across the flight deck, Abbi suddenly appeared, floating between the two men, two strangers. The one with his hand out was pawing her. No Bridge in sight.

Then POTS began pulling resources, shifting them to a situation unfolding in Avium's front lobby. It had found a dead body, tentatively identified as Darrell Hollenbeck, and was scrambling to understand the situation so it could call for help from the appropriate Community Patrol units.

Vincent shifted his view to Avium and received a punch to the gut. His missing partner lay on the floor at the base of a metal sculpture. He was on his back, arms at his side, eyes closed, as if he were asleep. Except his head rested in a pool of blood.

"Report his vital signs!" he barked.

"Pulse rate zero," replied POTS. "Respiration rate zero. Body temperature falling."

A wail of horror escaped Vincent's lips, the eerie cry of a feral animal caught in a trap.

POTS was preparing a series of alerts for the different Community Patrol units. Vincent intervened in a panic, manually canceling them and clearing the queue. Then he tried to think. But of all the different situations he, Abbi, and Bridge had imagined and prepared for, none were this crazy. Not even close. And he needed to allow POTS to take action *now* or this would all come back to him.

Then he remembered Abbi. Shifting his view to the flight deck, he saw that *Jaywalker* had moved into the massive airlock, queued to depart.

His wail became a cry of anguish. Every one of his options was bad. If he let the alarm sound for Bridge, he was screwed. If he didn't, Abbi was gone, spirited away by Bridge's likely killers. His Pulse high was crumbling, and he wished he had more of it to help him through, hating himself for having the thought.

"What should I do?" he cried in a plaintive voice.

"Do about what?" asked POTS.

"Oh, God." He had no choice. He removed his

manual blocks so POTS could send its alerts to Community Patrol.

Then he realized he should be stopping *Jaywalker*'s departure. "You idiot!" he berated himself as he scrambled to create a violation flag, a notification that would signal the deck master to hold the ship.

But he was too late. The craft was gone, Abbi with it.

Chapter 2

C uss Abbott rarely felt fear. Not like this. But looking out at the sea of faces, eyes fixed on him, expectant, impatient, his stomach roiled. A classroom of fourth graders, kids at Holsten Elementary, sat around him in a semicircle of desks waiting for him to talk about his job, that of Interworld Marshal.

It was career day, and he'd agreed to speak because he had been intrigued by their teacher, Deanna Robinson. It turned out that he and Deanna hadn't clicked; sometimes things can look promising at the beginning but not pan out. But he'd already committed to the visit and was a man of his word.

"Have you ever killed anyone?" asked a boy with curly hair sitting to his left, posing the question before Cuss had even started his presentation.

"You're interrupting," admonished Deanna. "And we talked about appropriate questions."

"Do you have your gun with you?" A freckle-faced girl sitting next to the curly-haired boy joined the interrogation.

Cuss needed to fill just ten minutes, but it already felt like an eternity. "I do have a gun," he began. "But I don't have it with me." He didn't address the question about whether he'd killed anyone. The answer was yes.

He looked at them stoically, trying to silence them by

quiet intimidation. He was a big guy, six foot one, two hundred twenty pounds, muscled torso, large hands, fit. Like a heavy-weight boxer. At forty-one, he was old to them. But like so many adult women, several of the fourth-grade girls found him dreamy, signaling so with their wistful smiles.

His Greek and Italian heritage combined to give him the classic features found on ancient Roman statues. Deanna had suggested Michelangelo's David. Cuss had heard similar comparisons in the past and never knew how to react to them, but appreciated they were intended as compliments.

He dove into his prepared speech. "You all know that Community Patrol officers are your friends, serving the people of Lagrange, making our cities safe for our residents." He pulled his badge wallet from his inside coat pocket and held up his six-pointed gold star, the words "Interworld Marshal" emblazoned on the front.

He handed it to the curly-haired boy. "Pass it around."

The children oohed.

He continued. "If a person commits a crime here in Lagrange and then flies off to another world, say Nova Terra on the Moon, Utopia on Mars, or anywhere on Earth, my job is to chase them down, arrest them, and bring them back to face justice."

The children ahhed.

"Have you ever arrested a little girl?" asked the girl with the freckles. She grinned when she asked.

"No. For girls *and* boys, I let their parents and teachers decide if they've done something wrong."

"Like interrupting," said Deanna. "Without raising her hand and waiting to be called on."

Cuss droned on, stressing how marshals worked as partners with Community Patrol on the different cases. And how Michael Belnick, Lagrange's very own governor, had been instrumental in establishing the Interworld Marshals Service. Their attention soon waned and he decided to end it. "Any questions?"

"What kind of ship do you fly?" asked a boy in back.

"A Starlane cruiser." Cuss's voice reflected his pride, like a teen on Earth bragging about his sports car. "Upgraded with twin Paulson drives, outfitted with the extended-range package, and customized with an ultra-reinforced hull." He'd finished the list but then added, "Cream colored, with gold trim. The *Nelly Marie*."

Cuss lived aboard the ship, sharing it with Ygo, his partner and friend. While Cuss occupied *Nelly Marie*'s three main levels, Ygo, an interworld marshal himself, dwelled in a private den in the ship's lower hold. The den was his permanent home, where Ygo, an enhanced human, lived in solitude, never emerging, a hermit in his lair. From there, he supported Cuss electronically using an AI network integrated into his brain. While they'd been partners for six years and lived as roommates, Cuss had met the man in person only once, the day Ygo moved into the ship's hold.

"Let's thank Marshal Abbott," said Deanna, starting to clap. Most of the kids joined in the applause.

With a broad smile, Cuss waved goodbye. Deanna walked him out to the hallway.

"That was great, Cuss. I'd love to pay you back. How

about dinner at my place? My chicken parmesan is to die for." She looked up at him through adorable blue eyes, her hopeful expression strengthening her pitch. It was his favorite meal and she knew it.

"It sounds delicious, Deanna, but new cases make it difficult for me to plan." He didn't say he *had* new cases. He was simply observing that *if* he had new ones, then planning would be problematic. So he wasn't lying. Technically.

Her face fell. "Ah, okay. Thanks for talking to the kids. I have to get back inside."

He gave her a peck on the cheek and started down the hallway. With class in session and the teachers and students ensconced in the classrooms, he was alone.

"That went okay," he said aloud, feeling guilty about his awkward departure. "It wasn't a disaster, anyway." When he spoke, Ygo heard him through a lens Cuss wore in his right eye, a proprietary contact lens packed with ultra-high-tech capabilities that enhanced sights and sounds.

"For Deanna or for the kids?" replied Ygo.

He smiled at Ygo's snark, knowing his good-natured ribbing was intended to cheer him up. That act of caring, no matter how lame, was the kind of thing that gave their partnership great strength.

He reached the front lobby. The administrative office was located on the left. As he approached the office door, he knew he was being assessed by the staff, who watched through a big window in the wall, keeping a sharp eye on their domain.

Unclipping the visitor's pass from his lapel, he stepped

inside to check out. A woman was ahead of him at the counter, and he used his wait time to view the students' drawings displayed on the wall. They had a wonderful innocence to them. Wholesome. Something he didn't see a lot of in his workday.

His favorite was a sketch by a fifth-grade student named Melinda, who had drawn a picture of herself with her mom, dad, and brother. The family mutt, a big black animal, sat in front of the group. Melinda had spent extra time on the dog's face, especially its smile. The result was a pooch with an oversize shit-eating grin, one that made Cuss laugh.

After returning his visitor's pass and exchanging pleasantries with the woman behind the counter, he made his way outside. As he descended the front steps, Ygo broke the news. "We caught a case."

His first reaction was an odd sense of relief. It meant his words to Deanna no longer hinged on a technicality. "Do tell."

"They found a body in the lobby of Avium Pharmaceuticals. That's here in Demeter on Deck 4. It's been classified as a murder, and it appears the doers escaped in a corvette."

"Where did they go?"

"Don't know. The *Jaywalker* left here with two men and one woman, but there's no record of it landing anywhere. POTS says the woman is Abbi Gillespie, who came to Lagrange a little over three months ago. But I can't match her to an exit visa from Nova Terra or Earth, and the *Jaywalker* is not equipped for Mars travel, so it's not that.

I have nothing on the two men. They arrived here two days ago, and all three left together early this morning."

As they talked, Cuss crossed the pedestrian thoroughfare, the grid of roadways used by those traveling the tube city on foot. On the other side, he got in line at a pod station. Lagrange didn't allow private carts or scooters on the thoroughfares. Instead, those who didn't want to walk could ride in pods: small, open-air cabins that carried passengers to any destination in the city.

"I just checked VICO and the plot thickens," said Ygo. "The *Jaywalker* isn't listed anywhere in the flight record. Nothing that matches that ship, anyway."

"Could they be flying from an off-book port?"

"They'd still be tracked during launch and reentry."

Cuss rubbed his neck as he considered possibilities. "Could they have changed the ship's identifiers midflight and landed under a different name?"

"That would explain it. Not a simple task, though."

Ships licensed for port use on any world carried a transponder that told the VICO flight control system who it was. Swapping that out with a second transponder was illegal but not technically difficult. The harder swap was the low-tech one—licensed ships had their name and registration code emblazoned on the hull outside the main hatch.

Changing it while the ship was underway required a spacewalk, signaling at least midlevel skills, a competency they could use to narrow the field of suspects. And if that's what happened, Ygo would need to search for the *Jaywalker* by inspecting the physical attributes of each ship in each port—the model, year built, exterior colors, custom add-ons. It was labor intensive and would take time.

"I've started a search. If they headed to the Moon, Port Collins is their only option and it shouldn't take long to find them. But if they've headed to Earth, there are *a lot* of places to look."

The line moved quickly and Cuss was next. A blue pod pulled up to the loading platform, and he stepped into a small compartment with the aesthetic of a carnival ride—utilitarian seat covers, floor mats, and decorative trim designed to resist the wear and tear of a carefree public. He slumped into the forward-facing seat, stretched his long legs, and rested his muscled arms on top of the surround. Pods had been designed to carry four average-size adults, but if Cuss had a twin, they'd do a good job filling the cabin all by themselves.

"So who's the body?" he asked as the pod got underway.

"Darrell Hollenbeck. Goes by the nickname 'Bridge.'"

"Bridge? Like spanning a river?"

"Yup. Twenty-six years old. Worked maintenance at Promenade."

Promenade was the theme park on Deck 2. "Are we on our way to the Avium building?"

"No. The scene has already been processed and the body moved to the morgue. We're headed for the Deck 4 Community Patrol station."

"Who are the leads?"

"Eve Boucher and Ferris McNish."

"Don't know either of them. What have you learned?"

"Ferris worked as a patrol officer for five years, passed the detectives exam last year, and has a few months left on his probationary period."

"Eve is his mentor?"

"That's right. Reluctantly. She's been on the job for nine years and just made detective first."

Cuss raised his eyebrows at that. While the rules were flexible, it typically took seven years for promotion from detective third to detective second grade. Then another five for promotion to detective first grade. Eve was doing well.

"Is she connected?"

"Nope. Competent and cooperative."

"Good for her. How far along are they?"

"On the investigation? They've fleshed out the basics. When they got to the part where the *Jaywalker* carried their suspects off world, they worked a few hours trying to figure out how to keep control of the case. Then they contacted the Marshals Service."

Ygo had begun assembling a case file—a chronology of documents, vids, and feeds—all cross-referenced and indexed. Cuss accessed it with his lens and sifted through it, fine-tuning the organization like a maître d' fussing with the silverware on a table set for important guests. He fiddled not because it had to be done his way, but rather as an avenue to get his head in the game. Going through familiar steps prepared him for the hunt ahead.

While he worked, the pod tooled along in its dedicated airlane above the pedestrian thoroughfare. It was early afternoon and residents were moving in and out of the buildings, living their lives in a city hovering in space. Real estate was incredibly expensive in the tube cities, and every square meter of land was exploited to the maximum. Buildings lined the way on either side, one structure pushed against the next so there was no wasted space. The buildings were eight to ten stories tall in this neighborhood, with shops and offices on the ground floor, and homes and apartments filling the floors above.

He felt the pod slowing and looked ahead to see a stately stone arch rising over a dark tunnel—the entrance to the interdeck shaft. Colorful banners across the top of the span gave it a festive appearance. His pod shuffled as it merged with other pods approaching from different directions, organizing themselves into a polite line as they prepared to enter the tunnel.

The four tube cities of Lagrange—Hermes, Athena, Demeter, and Apollo—were thirty-kilometer-long cylinders hovering in space between Earth and the Moon. Each had twelve internal levels—decks—created by arranging cylinders of different sizes one inside the next. Like Russian nesting dolls. Pods traveled between levels using the interdeck shaft, a pipe stuck in the side of the nested cylinders, piercing all the way to the center, creating a tunnel that provided access to everything in between.

His pod reached the front of the queue, glided under the arch, and entered a sorting room, a mechanical place where machines whirred and rumbled. A waft of grease and the smell of hot rubber tickled his nose. His body rocked gently as his pod was diverted to a chute labeled *Down*.

As he traveled the chute, the walls came alive with holographic displays advertising Demeter's major attractions: the Cyrus Sports Stadium on Terra Deck, Promenade Theme Park on Deck 2, Galaxy Performing Arts Center on Deck 3. He'd seen the adverts many times, and his brain filtered most of the onslaught. But then he caught mention of the Octavia Garden Museum on Deck 11, reminding him of a potential date-night option that had slipped from his mental list. He added it back.

The run through the chute lasted seconds, ending with a warning to keep hands and feet inside the cabin at all times. Then, as if being poured from a spout, his pod flowed out into a breathtaking chasm, an open abyss where the far side was two hundred meters away. Yawning pools of darkness loomed above and below him. His pod hugged the outer wall of the shaft, joining a line moving downward in a lazy spiral around the perimeter. A second spiral of pods moved upward, mirroring his. From across the chasm, they looked like strings of lights.

"Remind me of Bridge's priors." He remembered seeing a summary in the file but had skimmed the details.

"He got snagged in some small stuff five years ago when he moved to Demeter. Drugs for personal use. Ripping off the wrong street vendor. He appeared in court both times, but charges were dropped on the promise of good behavior."

"How did he land a job at Promenade? They don't hire trouble."

"His aunt is VP of marketing."

"That'll do it."

"And the job was in maintenance, stuff done by bots on Earth. Hardly glamorous work."

"Robbing a pharma house is a big step up for a punk. Either there were crimes along the way where he didn't get caught, or there are bigger forces at play."

"What are you thinking?"

"Not sure. But something's off."

Cuss felt his pod jostle from a push of air, a turbulent breeze that ramped in intensity. With a tremendous whoosh, a massive industrial elevator dropped through the center of the shaft, filling the chasm for a brief moment, a transport big enough to fit a dozen four-bedroom homes as cargo. The turbulence quieted behind him as he exited onto Deck 4.

His pod zigged and zagged its way to the center of town, dropping him off at the Community Patrol plaza. The station building, located toward the back of the plaza, was boxy, with lots of angles and edges and corners. It had big windows at the ground level that stretched across the front. The floors above were condensate composite formed to look like limestone block. Oxygen-producing vines clung to the building, their flowers white and blue, the official colors of Community Patrol.

At the entryway, a trickle of visitors shuffled in and out. He slowed at the door, waited a moment for an elderly man to exit, and then followed two ladies inside.

The patrol station lobby had an institutional feel, with a high ceiling, black-and-white-patterned stone floor, and faux-wood benches for visitors. Ahead, an officer sat at a window, assisting the public. A woman at the front of the line was explaining something that took a lot of hand movements to convey. The officer nodded as she spoke, showing he was engaged in her drama.

To the right, two uniformed officers were speaking with a half-dozen civilians, their laughter and nodding reflecting a lack of urgency. Cuss guessed they were discussing a community activity, perhaps planning a picnic or festival or athletic competition.

To his left, a man was working on the Heroes Wall, a display paying tribute to those who had fallen in the line of service. Curious, he crossed the lobby to have a look.

"Putting up a name," said the man when Cuss asked. He was an old guy in old clothes, a heavy canvas apron down his front, the material worn shiny near the pouches at his waist where his hands had snaked in and out over many years.

Resting an arm on his stepladder, the man motioned to the names of the officers who had made the ultimate sacrifice while serving the citizens of Lagrange. Each name was spelled with gold letters in raised relief. He pointed to Debra Gosling, the name at the bottom, the one he'd just added.

Seeing Debra's name on the wall caused Cuss a pang of sorrow. He'd been there when a bomb took her life, close enough that he'd ended up in the hospital himself.

"Looks good," he told the man, appreciating that all the names had received fresh polish so everything matched. He squared up to the wall and nodded to Debra, dipping his chin in a crisp movement, a salute. He turned to the craftworker and repeated the motion. Then he pivoted on his heels and made for the back wall and the door to Community Patrol's inner sanctum.

Chapter 3

As Cuss approached the door leading to the Community Patrol offices, a holographic projection of a uniformed woman appeared. "May I be of assistance?" she asked.

Before he could answer, the door slid open, she disappeared, and a man in his early thirties took her place. "Marshal Abbott?"

The man's skin bulged out from his round face, like he'd been inflated and was now under pressure. When Cuss shook his hand, it, too, seemed swollen. He was a couple of inches shorter than Cuss and had a quick smile. "I'm Detective McNish. Call me Ferris."

"Cuss," said Cuss. The man's handshake was firm, his eye contact strong. Cuss took it as a good omen.

"Come on back and I'll introduce you to Eve."

He followed Ferris down a brightly lit office corridor, brown doors spaced evenly along a beige wall. Halfway along, they passed a bulletin board crammed with postings typical for a work environment: memos, pictures, cartoons. They turned a corner and stopped at a door.

"This is us."

Cuss followed him into a conference room with ten chairs crowded around a table designed for eight people.

There was a gray metal cabinet on one wall, a fake fern on the floor next to a trash can, and little else.

A woman on the other side of the table stood facing away from the door. She was deep in discussion with someone not in the room.

From the back, Cuss saw a woman with brown hair contained in a loose bun, strands poking out rakishly as if she'd arranged it in a rush. The fabric of her blouse covered wide shoulders that dropped to a slender waist. A swimmer's build, a build he favored. He couldn't see her butt. An office chair blocked his view.

"Don't you dare," said Ygo.

He'd started to lean for a glimpse of her bottom. In a weak attempt at a save, he slid into the chair in front of him, as though sitting at the conference table was what he'd been about all along.

The woman said, "Let's touch base later this afternoon," to whoever she was speaking with, closed the call, and turned to face Cuss.

"Marshal Abbott? I'm Eve Boucher." She pronounced it boo-shay.

Cuss stood again, leaned over the table, and shook her hand. It felt cool. Nice. Blue veins showed through the skin on her arm, hinting at low body fat and a fit cardiovascular system. Her fingernails were trimmed short and buffed clear. He held her hand a moment longer than necessary.

"Uh-oh," said Ygo.

Eve was beautiful. Not cute. Not attractive. But stunning. Gorgeous. Perfect skin. Delicate features. Haunting green eyes. A smile men would make fools of themselves to see. Midthirties. She was dressed in a blue blouse, chaste neckline, half sleeves. No jewelry. Minimal makeup. Her khaki slacks were held up by an intricate belt, an interwoven pattern with a Celtic knot for the buckle.

As they sat, Cuss noticed she had blonde roots. He marveled that she dyed her blonde hair brown, the opposite of what so many women did. He figured it was an attempt to mute her appeal. It didn't work.

Skipping the normal chitchat, she launched a hoverview display, enlarged it, and directed it to float at the far end of the table where they all could see. She pointed to a clock ticking away in the lower corner of the image. "We're watching the Avium building starting this morning at one thirty."

The display showed a utilitarian building. Smooth gray-blue exterior. No windows. No decorative trim or other embellishments. The view centered on a black-metal sliding door on the front of the structure, a sturdy number with flanged seams for added strength. A sign above it identified the establishment as Avium Pharmaceuticals.

"That's in the manufacturing zone," said Ygo. "Deck 6."

As Cuss watched, the black-metal door slid open, paused, and then closed seemingly on its own. No one was visible near it. No one entered or exited. It was as if someone had spoofed an extremely sophisticated security system to gain entry but wasn't there to take advantage. That, or building security had suffered a massive failure.

The door stayed closed for half a minute, and then two people in nondescript clothes, hoods obscuring their faces, scurried up to it. The door slid open a second time and they entered.

Eve accelerated the playback, speeding through twenty-two minutes of the door staying closed, no activity beyond the light pedestrian traffic on the throughfare in front of the building. Then she slowed to normal speed as the same two people reappeared at the door. They now wore bulging backpacks. One held a hand out to the side as they hurried away, an awkward gesture, odd on the face of it.

"Doesn't it look like that one is escorting an invisible person?" Eve asked Cuss.

Cuss played with the notion in his head and decided he needed to see more before drawing a conclusion. He shrugged and returned his gaze to the display.

"We'll follow them for a while," she said. "Then we'll go back and watch again from inside the building."

As the thieves hurried down the street, they pulled back their hoods, revealing that they were two males, one maybe thirty-five, the other about ten years older.

"We don't have identities for either of them," said Eve as the action continued. She spoke in a matter-of-fact tone, but a lack of ID was a rare occurrence.

The thieves boarded a pod, stepping into it from the loading platform in a square dance that implied they were accommodating an invisible third person. The pod carried them down the interdeck shaft to Luna Deck. From there, they took a shuttle to Demeter's spaceport at the core of the tube city.

The spaceport didn't rotate with the rest of the

structure, remaining stationary to allow for the landing and takeoff of space vehicles. Since it didn't spin, it had no centrifugal gravity. That meant that everything not fastened down hovered in weightlessness.

They watched as the two men floated above the spaceport flight deck, drifting toward the *Jaywalker*. As they approached the ship, in an inexplicable feat of magic, a woman materialized, appearing from nowhere at the end of the one man's outstretched arm. The three reached the *Jaywalker* and boarded together.

"Whoa," exclaimed Cuss. "Where is this feed from?"

"POTS," said Ferris.

"The population tracking system," said Ygo.

"The woman is Abbi Gillespie," said Eve. "She's been here in Lagrange for about three months. Remember this timestamp. She becomes visible at two fifty-three." Eve made a swiping motion with her fingers, and the hovering display changed images. "This next bit is from inside the Avium building. It starts with a view of that same sliding door, but we're looking at it from their front lobby."

The image in the display started out pitch-black, and then slivers of light appeared, the silhouette of a doorway. The door opened, spilling light into the lobby. An overhead fixture lit up to reveal an empty room. No one was visible who might be driving the action.

A half-minute later, the front door opened a second time and the two guys from before entered the lobby. As soon as the door closed behind them, they began to shout and point and stomp about. With just the two of them present, it looked like improvisational theater. A war dance.

Then one of them stepped forward and, in a rapid sequence, punched the air twice, followed by a fierce karate-style side kick aimed at the emptiness in front of him.

The two halted their dance and, standing side by side, studied the ground. One of them crouched for a moment, continuing to look downward. Then they hustled through the lobby to the back of the building. The sensor feed followed them as they moved through an internal security door and into a large room with a high table and no chairs.

"This is Avium's product storage area," said Eve.

Cuss shook his head in wonder. "They've passed through external and now internal security doors. How?"

"That's what I want to know," said Ferris.

One of the two men approached a white cabinet and began fussing with it. After a few moments, he got the cabinet door open, and the two worked together to fill their knapsacks with fist-size bags of pills.

"They took ten thousand doses of Maramid."

"Pulse," said Ygo.

Cuss knew that Pulse was a growing problem. But drugs weren't his area of expertise. His specialty was solving homicides.

When the two men left the building, Eve said, "Now watch."

The display showed the empty lobby as the recording zipped forward. The lights dimmed automatically, and the image switched to an infrared view. Then, in the same magical style as when Abbi appeared floating above the flight deck, a body appeared on the ground near where the two thieves had been performing their war dance.

"That's Bridge?" asked Cuss.

"Yup. Darrell Hollenbeck," said Eve. "Look at the timestamp. Two fifty-three, the same time that Abbi Gillespie appears."

"Someone ran a filter," said Ygo.

"Someone edited the record," said Cuss. "But why hide Abbi and Bridge and not the two men?"

"Another good question," said Ferris.

"And if POTS is hiding people," Cuss continued, "it's possible more doers were at the scene, invisible people who participated in the crime. We saw Abbi appear only because we were looking at the two men she was with at just the right moment. But someone else invisible might have run in a different direction and we weren't looking wherever that was to see them reappear."

Eve leaned her head to the side and looked at Ferris as if this were a new idea to them. She bit her lip in thought, then she shook her head. "I understand it's a theoretical possibility. But I feel the four people we see can explain everything that happened. Nothing's hanging out there with a 'but how do you explain this?' uncertainty." She spoke with confidence but then added, "Don't you think?"

Cuss thought it through and decided he agreed. "Someone gave Abbi and Bridge access to the Avium building. Who and how are question marks. Once inside, one of them let the two men in. I'd guess Abbi since she left with them. The men fought with Bridge, killing him. Abbi and the men stole a haul of Pulse and escaped on the *Jaywalker* to destinations unknown."

"That's what we came up with," said Eve. "The 'killers escaped on a ship' part is where we reach the end of our line."

Cuss nodded absently. Chasing murderers across worlds was where his line started. "I'm confused about Bridge dying. That fight looked rough but not deadly, the half we could see anyway. Do you have a cause of death?"

"He hit his head on the artwork," said Ferris.

Eve manipulated the display to show a freeform metal statue near the wall. It looked like a grouping of lightning bolts. Sort of. She pointed to the base of the statue where a short, jagged piece poked upward. Bridge lay next to it, his head in a pool of blood. "The medical examiner matched his wound with this spike."

Cuss eyed the menacing projection. "Have you talked with his partner? His folks?"

"He lived alone, a bachelor enjoying his youth," said Ferris. "His parents live on Earth. Pittsburgh, Pennsylvania. They were shocked by the news, swore their boy would never do anything like this, are sure we have it wrong. Their lawyer will be here later this afternoon to explain it to us if you care to join in."

Cuss wondered if Ferris was teasing him because no one would subject themselves to that sort of situation voluntarily. "What does his aunt say? The one who's a bigwig at Promenade?"

"Wait. What?" Ferris paged through his personal log, looking for the reference, as if he'd recorded the information and then forgotten about it all in the past few hours.

"My brief from the Marshals Service included that tidbit. Apparently he has an auntie living here in Demeter who got him his job. I'll send you what I have." While Ferris updated his notes, Cuss continued with his list. "Have you been through his apartment?"

"Not yet," said Eve. "We're waiting for approval from the municipal attorney's office, which should come at any time. Until then, we're watching his apartment door to make sure no one disturbs evidence. Feel free to join us there as well."

"Thanks." He wanted to be in on that one. Then it hit him, the obvious question. "Who has the ability to erase people from a government tracking system? That's got to be a pretty select group."

"Good one," said Ygo, cheering on his thought process.

Eve must have thought so as well because she nodded and smiled, then issued a command. The hoverview image changed to a picture of a man sitting in a chair. Late twenties, long brown hair, soft features. Cuss could see he was in a suspect interview room, an off-white cubicle with bare walls and a small table with a metal loop on top to secure handcuffs. The guy wasn't cuffed, though. He was whispering to another person, Cuss guessed his lawyer.

"This is Vincent Rogalski," she said. "He contacted Community Patrol this morning at nine-twenty-two, all in a panic to report that his girlfriend, Abbi Gillespie, had been kidnapped."

"And?" Cuss could tell she was savoring the reveal.

"He's a security analyst for Community Patrol."

"And?"

Ferris spilled it. "And he provides technical support for POTS. I looked up his job description. Technical support means supervising updates, fixing bugs, customizing systems. Stuff like that."

"Bingo," said Ygo.

"He says Abbi was kidnapped?" Cuss looked at Ferris. "From what you saw, would you say she was being forced to accompany the men?"

"You mean like being taken against her will?" Ferris pressed his puffy lips together and shook his head. "There was a familiarity between the man with his hand out and the woman. They knew each other."

"That doesn't rule out abduction," said Eve, turning the question into a test for the detective still in his probationary period. "Which is the proper name for 'taking someone against their will.'" She made finger quotes for the last words.

"I know. Okay, I saw the man moving his hand up and down when she was invisible, like he was rubbing her back. He did it multiple times. So either they have some level of intimacy or the guy is creepy as hell." Ferris looked into the distance as he thought. "After she became visible, the look on her face was one of excitement. She was pumped up. And she looked at the backrub guy with a smile. I think they are a couple and she's part of their group."

"That's what I saw, too," said Cuss.

Eve nodded in agreement, winking at Cuss, bonding with him over their schooling of the probie.

Her wink hit him like an electric charge, stirring him.

He sighed.

As a rule, Cuss didn't become intimate with colleagues. With more than enough opportunity out in the civilian world, he didn't need to. And given how it could jeopardize a case and complicate careers, he didn't want to.

His sigh was an acknowledgment that his body desired something contrary to this rational mind. As Ygo had surmised, it was a shared problem because of their special relationship.

Ygo had been born disfigured, and as a youth learned to minimize his social pain by hiding from society. To combat his isolation as a young man, he underwent a surgical procedure to have a quantum interface embedded into his brain, one he used to connect with sophisticated AI that gave him remarkable abilities. Now approaching forty, he flexed his skills in support of Cuss, his partner and friend, doing so while remaining invisible to society. It was his personal comfort zone, and he asked Cuss to honor it by never mentioning his existence to outsiders.

Keeping Ygo out of the spotlight put Cuss in the awkward position of accepting credit for his contributions. To Cuss it felt dishonest, even immoral. When he understood it was a condition not only of Ygo's participation in the Marshals Service but also of their friendship, he relented, though even after half a decade, it still felt wrong.

Like a married couple, the circumstances of one directly impacted the other. And like a married couple, they faced challenges together, here the need to support Cuss's resolve.

Cuss asked Eve, "What does Vincent have to say?"

"When he called to report that his girlfriend had fallen victim to foul play, we asked him to come in and tell us about it. He arrived with a lawyer. By then we'd determined that it was an interworld case, so we've been letting him stew in the interview room, waiting for your input before we speak with him."

"Wow, thanks." It was an uncommon courtesy, perhaps the type of behavior that led to her early promotion. He rubbed the back of his neck as he distilled his request to the bare minimum. "My priority is to press him on who Abbi's two friends are. And where he thinks they went. A good lead would save a lot of time and effort. I'll leave it to you two to box him in on his local crimes."

"I can do that." Eve stood. "Want to watch?"

He'd expected to be in the room but replied without a hitch. "Absolutely."

"The room's not big enough for the three of us," she said as if reading his thoughts. "And I want to give Ferris the experience." She moved the display so it hovered directly in front of him. "I'll be listening, so if you have a must-ask question, say it aloud and I'll try to work it in."

She and Ferris disappeared down the hall.

"I may have found the *Jaywalker* in Port Collins," Ygo said to Cuss as they waited. "The ship *Salty Frontier* is a visual match. I'm gathering specs for a tech appraisal. More soon."

"Good work." Finding the missing craft was a critical step.

Eve and Ferris entered the interview room, and Cuss

turned his attention to the display. Eve introduced herself to Vincent and his lawyer, apologized for the delay, and sat on the cop side of the table.

She began. "Let's start by confirming that your attorney has apprised you of your rights."

The attorney had a long face and was dressed in a white suit with white ruffles at the neck and shirt cuffs.

"He looks like a poodle fresh from the groomer," said Ygo.

Cuss, who'd been thinking something similar, stifled a laugh.

"You think I did it, don't you?" cried Vincent, reaching peak agitation in an instant. "Cops always think the boyfriend or husband did it." He jabbed a finger at Eve. "Watch the feed, for Christ's sake."

The lawyer put a hand on Vincent's arm, calming him.

"Think you did what?" asked Ferris, being casual, like he asked it all the time.

"Made Abbi leave with them."

"Abbi is your girlfriend?" asked Eve.

Vincent nodded, a smug smile signaling he was proud of the fact. "For the past three months."

"How did you meet her?"

"We met at a club. The Gonzi on Deck 7. She was new in town, and I offered to show her around."

"Very smooth," said Eve. "Where's she from?"

"Kansas. Near Wichita."

"Did she talk much about Wichita? Tell stories about Kansas?"

Looking into the distance, Vincent tugged an earlobe

and then rubbed his nose. He shook his head. "Most of her stories took place in Nova Terra. I think she moved to the Moon when she was old enough to leave home."

"Why do you believe she was abducted?" asked Ferris.

"Because they forced her onto a ship and flew away." He said it like they were dumb not to see something so obvious. His cheeks flushed as he spoke, his agitation real.

"Are you talking about this?" Eve played the sensor feed from the spaceport showing Abbi boarding the *Jaywalker* with the two men.

"Exactly!"

"Does it look to you like she's being forced?"

"She's cooperating because she's scared. But she's under duress."

"Who are the men?" asked Ferris.

"Got me. Thugs. Kidnappers."

"Are they from Kansas?" asked Eve.

"I don't know."

"Where did they take Abbi?"

Vincent's hands squeezed the arms of the chair. "Believe me, if I knew that, I'd be there and not here."

"Do you think they flew to Earth?"

He sat back in his chair in a huff. "Are you going to help, or is this all just noise before you pin it on me?"

Eve studied Vincent for a moment and then ran the POTS feed stream showing Abbi Gillespie magically appearing over the flight deck. "Can you tell us what happened here?"

He shrugged and looked down, studying the tabletop. "Looks like a glitch."

"What do you know about the population tracking system, POTS?"

Vincent lifted his head, his eyes narrowing.

"It looks like the glitch fixed itself right here," she continued. "How could that happen?"

Vincent leaned over and whispered to his lawyer.

"My client came here to report a crime."

"That's what we want to talk about."

They whispered some more. "We've reported it. We've asked for your help. And now we're leaving."

"We have more questions."

"Sorry." The lawyer stood and Vincent joined him.

"I'd like Vincent to stay and answer them. Why won't he cooperate?"

"Is he being charged with a crime?"

"Not yet."

"Is that a threat, Detective?" The Poodle showing his fangs.

Eve shrugged, keeping her eyes on Vincent, her stare boring into his skull.

"We're leaving." The lawyer moved a hand to the small of Vincent's back, urging him toward the door.

"I came here for your help," snarled Vincent, "but you just want to do the easy thing and dump all over me. Ever wonder if that's why so many citizens don't support the Patrol?"

As the two exited the interview room, Eve called, "Stay close, Vincent. Don't leave Lagrange. We'll be talking more soon."

"Abbi played him," said Ygo as Vincent and his lawyer

disappeared down the hall. "But I can't tell if he knows and is angry about it, or if he's clueless and worried about her."

"Part of me wants him to chase after her so we can see where he goes."

Eve and Ferris rejoined Cuss in the conference room, and Eve moved the meeting into action phase. "We need to follow up on the POTS angle. Ferris, would you take the lead on that? Find out if one of Vincent's coworkers or supervisors can figure out what caused the glitch and if they can trace it to anyone."

"Can do," said Ferris, making a note in his private log. "Want me to talk with the aunt?"

Eve nodded. "Good idea." She looked at Cuss. "I'm going to Avium to see if someone can explain how their security was overridden. It seems whoever could do that is from a pretty select group as well. Care to tag along? I can take you through the crime scene while we're there."

"Sure."

But when Eve called to arrange the visit, she learned that Avium's head of security was in Apollo on business and wouldn't be back to Demeter for a couple of hours.

"I'll use the time to review the autopsy," said Cuss.

"The body is at Purity Hospital on Terra Deck," she said. "Both the coroner's office and the morgue are there in the basement. Farley Briscoe was the on-scene medical examiner. Tippi Swanson performed the autopsy."

"Dr. Swanson is at the hospital now," said Ygo. "He can see us in forty minutes."

Cuss arranged to meet Eve later at the Avium building and departed for the morgue.

Chapter 4

The Purity Hospital building had a series of arch elements up the front façade, each decorated with moldings and flutings and contrasting colors to create a modern twist on art deco. The courtyard continued the theme, with bold geometric benches and planters positioned to create visual interest.

In contrast to the modern architectural design elements, a stone statue of Demeter stood near the front entrance. She looked strong and wise in flowing robes, her outstretched hand beckoning to all.

Inside the hospital lobby, structural columns to the left and right were shaped like tree trunks. Overhead, a forest canopy rippled in the breeze, a lifelike holographic projection that included the faint sound of wind whooshing through leaves. The illusion gave Cuss a sense of outdoorsy health and vitality, undoubtedly the intended effect of the installation.

It was a busy morning in the hospital lobby, with visitors browsing the florist, gift shop, and café. Cuss weaved through the crowd to reach the central hallway and traveled its length to the stairwell at the end.

The basement was a drabber version of the corridor above. Lower ceiling. Fewer embellishments. Walls with dents and dings in need of a touch-up. Boxes stacked outside one of the doors as if that occupant was in the process of moving.

Ygo directed Cuss to a door that said *No Admittance*. It chimed as he squared up in front of it.

"My dad would call it a soup strainer."

Cuss had no idea what Ygo was talking about but knew it would make sense before long. "How's Pops doing?"

"Still driving Mom crazy. She's returning the favor."

Cuss smiled. And then a shadow appeared behind the textured glass in the door. Retrieving his badge wallet, Cuss held up his gold star.

The door opened to reveal a man in a white lab coat. A heavy man with a soft face, heavy black eye shadow, bold tribal artwork inked on his neck. A long drooping mustache hung over his mouth and down to his chin. When he breathed through his nose, Cuss could see rivulets forming in the hair. Like water flowing through reeds. And when he spoke, it was like watching curtains in the breeze.

"Welcome, Marshal," said the man, sending the drapes swirling. He ignored the badge, stepping back from the door to allow Cuss inside.

"Dr. Swanson? Thanks for meeting with me." He now understood Ygo's soup-strainer reference.

"Tippi. Please."

They shook hands, and Tippi's viselike grip caught Cuss off guard. He followed the man through a space that looked like a chemistry lab turned into a storage room. Lab benches down the center and along the walls were piled high with tools and boxes and binders and appliances, the different items seemingly plopped down at some point in the past and then abandoned forever to gather dust.

At the back of the overstuffed lab, they entered a small room, a repurposed office, empty but for four upholstered armchairs against one wall and facing across gray carpet to a smooth, shimmering surface on the opposing wall. Cuss recognized it as an upscale private theater. It looked and smelled new.

"Your message asked about the Hollenbeck autopsy?" Tippi's intonation made it a question. "You wanted to compare the feeds with the injuries to see if we can account for all the wounds?"

"That's right. I'm trying to confirm whether the one fighter did all the damage or if we should be looking for more people."

Tippi lowered himself into one of the armchairs, cushions hissing as air escaped from the foam inside them. He motioned for Cuss to join him in an adjoining chair. "Yours is an interesting request because it's unique. I've never had a case where an assailant is visible from all angles but the victim is invisible."

He spoke to the room and the lights dimmed. The projection area in front of the far wall showed a faint glow. "I had the system integrate the feeds of the fighter with a reconstruction of Hollenbeck standing where the blows were delivered. Here, let me show you."

He spoke quietly, and a holographic projection of Bridge materialized across the room. He appeared to be standing in the Avium lobby, arms at his side, neutral in stance and expression. The fighter was facing Bridge, crouching, arms raised, fists clenched, expression fierce. Bridge was shown in fluorescent green because he was a simulation, a guess as to his behavior during the altercation. The fighter looked real, as if he were there with them in the room, the image possible because it was created directly from the sensor record.

"Hollenbeck had four fresh wounds," said Tippi. "His solar plexus, his cheek, his temple, and the puncture at the base of the occipital bone."

"That spike to the head is what did it for him?"

Tippi nodded. "It slid under his skull in back and nicked an artery. He bled out from it."

"How did his head get off the spike? I mean, when he appears in the sensor feeds, his head is resting on the ground next to it."

"The blood spatter supports that he flexed up off it himself, his body instinctively recoiling in an attempt to minimize injury. He sits up, and then his injuries catch up with him and he slumps over." Tippi paused. "I can show you the sequence if you're interested."

"He's prepared a presentation for you," said Ygo. "He wants to show it."

"Yes, please," Cuss said to Tippi. "Show me what you have."

"Okay. First we'll watch it at full speed." Tippi sat forward in his chair and narrated the action like a sportscaster. "We know the kinds and sizes of injuries on Hollenbeck's body, so it's easy enough to position him."

Tippi pointed at the images frozen in place, one realistic and one an avatar, and like a film director called,

"Action."

In the span of perhaps two seconds, certainly no more than three, the fighter punched Bridge in the solar plexus. When Bridge flexed forward from the blow, the fighter delivered an uppercut that caught Bridge on the left cheek, standing him upright. The fighter then twirled and delivered a roundhouse kick to Bridge's temple, sending him down onto the statue, where he cut his head. The playback ended with the two men standing over the fallen man, looking down at him.

The spin kick was notable for two reasons. One, because its delivery was quite skilled. There was no leap, no drama. Just a quick spin and a foot that weaved inward to hit Bridge hard in the temple. A blow that would put anyone down.

The other reason was because the fighter's feet were wrapped and laced with corded sole. Nubku slippers. Footwear handmade by artisans in Nova Terra, who crafted the cord pattern to match the wearer's spirit as well as their feet.

"Did you see the Nubkus?" asked Ygo. The slipper was unique to the cliff dwellers of Nova Terra.

"Mmm," said Cuss, affirming Ygo's observation.

"As you just saw," said Tippi, "This man's actions account for the injuries. There's no damage left unexplained." He started a second showing, this time in slow motion, going blow by blow, using medical terms to describe the body parts and injuries sustained.

But with his question answered, Cuss stopped listening and returned to the silent conversation with his partner.

"I've confirmed that *Salty Frontier* is our ship," said Ygo.

Tippi reached the end of his second run-through and paused to see if Cuss had questions.

Cuss used the opportunity to wrap things up. "Thank you for the analysis, Dr. Swanson. It was very impressive. Full of insight." He stood. "You've answered my questions and helped me identify my quarry. Now it's time for me to chase them down."

Tippi beamed as Cuss lauded him. After a few more minutes of polite conversation, they said goodbye and Cuss was off to Deck 6 to meet Eve outside the Avium Pharmaceuticals building.

Chapter 5

The Avium Pharmaceuticals building looked different to Cuss, and it took him a moment to understand why. In the Community Patrol conference room, the display had focused on the front of the structure, framing it as if it sat in isolation. But in truth, Avium was one of a long line of utilitarian buildings that faded into the distance. All of them made products for the locals, and most exported their wares to help grow the wealth and independence of Lagrange.

Eve was waiting for him on the walkway in front of the building, sipping from a bottle of water. "How was Tippi?" she asked.

"He confirmed that it was just the one attacker, the doer we could see."

"Which is what I'd said."

Cuss nodded and then shrugged. "Confirmation is progress. It ticks a box." He gestured toward the Avium building. "I have a couple of boxes to tick at this place. The big one is learning whether the people who defeated their security are still here in Lagrange, or if I should be adding them to my pursuit list."

"We're meeting with Nels Hanssen. He's their security officer."

She tilted her head back and drained the water bottle. He watched, mesmerized as the flex of her throat muscles danced under smooth skin with each swallow. He closed his mouth when she started for the door.

Ygo briefed him. "Nels Hanssen was a lieutenant in the European Space Marines. When he got out, he wanted to become a detective, but before he could land a spot, opportunity knocked in the form of private security. This is his third gig in the business. He's been with Avium for six years and seems to be doing a reasonable job."

"Hmm," Cuss replied, conveying a "perhaps" about the reasonable job part.

Nels was waiting for them in the lobby. Late forties. Average build. Average looks. Ordinary clothes. Shifty eyes, a feature Cuss tended to project on all wannabe cops. He greeted them with a smile and handshakes, correctly referring to Eve as "detective" and Cuss as "marshal," a detail that civilians often got wrong. His official title was Chief of Security, Avium Pharmaceuticals.

The lobby was a small institutional space with beige floor tile, walls painted a darker beige, and an off-white ceiling with uninspired light fixtures. The only piece of furniture in the space was a single desk positioned toward the back, a substantial piece with a blue-gray metal finish. Cuss thought it would make a great guard desk. If only there were a chair behind it with a person sitting there.

"This is a manufacturing center, not a retail establishment," said Nels. He spoke to Eve, his eyes moving up and down her body. "We make medicines here and sell our products to retail businesses. We don't really serve individuals or walk-in customers."

He stepped over to the side wall and used an index finger to indicate a circle on the floor. "This is where one of the thieves met his demise."

Cuss scanned the tiles with his lens but couldn't find any evidence of the violence. No blood residue, even though Bridge's head had rested in a pool of it. No marks left by the statue's base. Since the floor was spotless, he asked the obvious, more as a way to start a conversation. "Cleaning crew been here?"

Nels nodded. "We got the okay from the medical examiner's office."

"Where's the piece now?"

"The statue?" Nels poked a thumb over his shoulder. "It's in back, locked under court order while lawyers fight over it."

When Cuss's forehead creased, Nels explained. "Supposedly the deceased's family is making noises like they're going to sue for negligence or wrongful death or something, and that has everyone running for cover. The artist who made the statue and the dealer who sold it to us have teamed together and are pointing at Avium as the responsible party. Meanwhile, the municipal attorney, who'd cleared the statue for release, changed his mind and wants to preserve it as evidence. The whole thing is a mess."

"Ask if we can see it," urged Ygo.

Cuss agreed with the suggestion but waited, letting Nels set the agenda for now.

"Come on back." He made a "follow me" motion as

he moved to the rear of the lobby. He squared up in front of a formidable door made of metal composite. The door confirmed his identity, a lock released with an audible click, and the gleaming slab slid into the wall.

As they passed through the opening and turned left down a hallway, Cuss paused to examine the doorjamb with its substantial works, wondering how the doers were able to get past such a sophisticated barrier.

Nels stopped at the end of the hall and opened an ordinary door. A light activated. He stood aside. "We were told to keep everyone away. But I'm assuming that doesn't include law enforcement working the case."

"A wise interpretation," said Cuss, stepping around Nels and into the small space: a storage closet with the shelves removed. The statue was as tall as he was, its broad base taking up most of the floor area, leaving just enough room for him to stand.

Reduced to its essence, the sculpture was a collection of jagged metal blades, their zigzag shapes suggestive of lightning bolts. The artist had them positioned in a loose cluster, tips pointed upward, like a quiver of celestial weapons.

Near the floor, a portion of a lightning bolt poked up through the base as if emerging from the ground to join the pack. It had a diamond-shaped cross section similar to that of a dagger. Its pointy tip reached as high as Cuss's ankle. But unlike the polished edges of a knife, this blade had the irregular edges of torn sheet metal. When it cut flesh, the serrations would tear more than slice.

Dried blood smeared the blade. A trail of drops led

across the statue's base. Cuss leaned to the side so the overhead light could reach the area and then used his lens to capture a nanoprint of the residue. While Ygo analyzed the result, Cuss stepped out of the closet and held the door so Eve could view the statue. Nels leaned in through the door to chat with her.

"I've confirmed the blood is Hollenbeck's," said Ygo.

Cuss took a few steps down the hall. "Another box checked."

"Except Bridge is a loser. When someone like him is involved in a slick operation like this, my first thought is that he's being used. A tool someone is manipulating." Ygo paused. "Could dear Abbi have been charming Bridge at the same time she was beguiling Vincent?"

Eve stepped from the closet and approached Cuss. "Tough way to go."

"Indeed," said Cuss in reply to them both.

From there, Nels led them to the product storeroom. White enameled cabinets filled the walls from floor to ceiling. In the center of the expanse sat a broad table, its work surface holding specialized appliances for sorting and counting and packaging pills. The floor was a spotless white surface with no joints or seams.

Cuss recognized it as the room where the two men had filled their backpacks with Pulse. He tugged on a random cabinet door. It was locked but his action caused a tiny light near the door handle to glow red, a visual tell that the system had recognized an irregular action. He tried another cabinet door with the same result.

Shaking his head in wonder, he asked Nels, "So they

stroll into your locked building, kill someone, pass through a fortified security door, and open these tamper-proof cabinets? How?"

"Don't forget that they edited themselves out of Avium's security feeds," said Eve. She motioned with a hand at the sea of white doors. "And they knew which cabinets to open."

Nels pressed his lips together in a sheepish expression and then tilted his head toward the storeroom exit. "We can talk in my office. It's just down the hall."

His office was a step up from a corporate cubicle. He'd filled the walls and shelves with photos and knickknacks and souvenirs, presumably from his travels. A desk like the one in the lobby faced the back wall, leaving room for two guest chairs near the door.

He invited them to sit while he grabbed his desk chair, one of those adjustable everything models, and rolled it over so the three of them formed a circle. He slumped into the seat, fiddled with the armrest positions, and began swiveling back and forth in a rocking motion.

"The obvious conclusion is an inside job," he said. "But the only people who have the means to defeat our security and edit our sensor feeds are Lizzy Freidman and me. And while I have the authority, honestly, I don't have the skill. Lizzy is our systems tech and looks after the company tools, everything from inventory to payroll to security. She has the skill to pull it off, but there's no way she did."

Eve sat forward in her chair. "Is she working today? Could we speak with her?"

"I called her in when you made this appointment." Nels checked the time. "She'll be here any minute. While we wait, why don't I show you the security summary I prepared for the company's executive team. It gives a pretty good overview of our practices and capabilities."

Without waiting for a response, Nels launched a display and started a virtual tour. Cuss recognized the presentation as a sales job by an underling trying to impress his bosses. But even correcting for that behavior, he was impressed with Avium's security features and methods. It was a company prepared for trouble. And that pointed all the more to an inside job.

A chime sounded and Nels stood. "That's her now."

The office door opened, and a woman poked her head in. "It's me," she said, hesitating at the entrance, her gaze flicking back and forth between Cuss and Eve before finding Nels. He motioned her in and introduced her.

Lizzy Freidman was a nervous woman, fiftyish, short brown hair, wearing a blue denim shift over a slight frame. Her face alternated between smiles and frowns as she digested the purpose of the meeting.

Nels invited her to take his chair. He sat behind her on the edge of his desk. As she settled in and answered questions, she proved to be friendly, unassuming, and gracious. Like someone's sweet aunt rather than a player in a murderous drug ring. Cuss knew that extenuating circumstances—threats, intimidation, desperation—could push people into atypical behaviors. He studied her, trying to decide.

"We're hoping you can help us," said Eve. "How is it

possible for the thieves to just stroll through Avium's security like it shows in the record?"

"Do I need a lawyer?" She looked back at Nels for guidance.

"You're not a suspect," said Cuss, pulling Lizzy's attention forward again. "Quite the opposite, we think you can assist with the case. But before we start, I must ask if you were involved in the drug theft here early this morning. It's a pro forma question for the record. You're entitled to a lawyer before you reply."

"Was I involved in the theft?" There was indignation in her tone. "Someone died!"

"I know. It's awful." He paused. "Were you involved?"

"No!"

"She's clean," said Ygo, who analyzed her mannerisms, facial expressions, vocal patterns, stress markers, and vital signs to assess truthfulness.

Cuss agreed, and when his gut instinct aligned with Ygo's science, the conclusion was historically reliable. He sought to reassure her. "We didn't think so. Did you watch the record? Did you see where the man magically appeared on the ground?"

Lizzy fingered the hem of her dress as she nodded.

"Doesn't that mean that someone edited your sensor feed?" asked Eve. "Or is there another way that could happen?"

"I need to look into it before I can answer. I do know that one of the men, one of the killers, somehow spoofed his identity as Mr. Rigney. It's why the security system gave them free access."

"Carl Rigney is Avium's CEO," said Nels from his perch behind Lizzy. "He's in San Francisco right now, has been for the past week, and wouldn't have a clue how to edit sensor feeds."

"If not Rigney, then who?" pressed Cuss.

"It's driving me nuts," said Lizzy, "because it requires system level changes, and those need my approval." She slumped back in her chair, gnawing on a thumbnail. Then she sat upright, eyes ablaze. "But maybe not."

"Explain," said Nels, forehead creased.

"Remember we gave a hook to Community Patrol a few weeks back? It was for their new partnership program."

Nels nodded slowly and then explained to Cuss and Eve. "Community Patrol invited us to participate in a pilot project. It was about integrating private sensor data from high-risk businesses with their own feeds to enhance monitoring and crime prevention. We agreed to participate, in part because we thought it might be a useful security enhancement. But we also wanted to be seen as cooperative by law enforcement."

"Who was your contact?" asked Eve.

"When the initial request came out, it was from someone high up." Lizzy looked at Nels. "The deputy chief, wasn't it? Once we committed, we were passed off to…" She pressed her lips together and tapped them with an index finger. "I worked with a PIA from Community Patrol's central services. Hold on." She consulted a private display.

"PIA is Lizzy-talk for 'pain in the ass,'" explained Nels.

"What's a hook?" asked Eve while they waited on

Lizzy.

"It gives them administrator-level access to our systems," said Nels. "Like they own it. From there they can do whatever they want."

"Vincent Rogalski," said Lizzy.

"Vincent, you idiot," said Cuss, shaking his head. "He thought he was being a clever thief, and now he's facing murder charges."

"At least we don't need to chase him," said Ygo.

"I wanted to keep Vincent's work separate from mine," said Lizzy, "so I gave him his own root function. It's called a handle. It gives him private access to everything. It's like duplicating the system and we each have our own. At the time it made sense because that way I wouldn't be distracted by his work and he, mine. While it stopped us from tripping over each other, it also meant I lost supervisory authority." She gave a nervous laugh. "If you can't trust the cops, right?"

"Is there any way to confirm what he actually did? To document his actions?" asked Cuss.

Lizzy shrugged. "I can enter the system using the credentials I gave him and try to reconstruct events. I might be able to figure it out. Some of it, anyway. Unless he set up some sort of picket. Then no, I can't."

"Will you work on it now and let us know what you find?" asked Eve. "The municipal attorney needs evidence in hand before he'll move on a suspect."

Chapter 6

When Vincent told the lady detective that he would chase after Abbi if he knew where to find her, he'd been responding impulsively to an uncomfortable question. But as he sat there on his couch, he considered the idea.

Yeah, their perfect crime had gone off the rails, their dreams dashed. But Abbi had made him into a different person over the last few months. Given him new purpose. When amped with Pulse, life with her was damned near perfect. Especially the sex. Long story short, he loved her and wanted her back.

If she'd been taken hostage by those two thugs, it fell on him to rescue her. The cops had made it clear that they didn't give a shit about any of it. And if she had run off with them willingly, as that one detective had suggested, he needed her to explain.

The problem with the first one, the rescue idea, was that he wasn't the hero type. Definitely not a fighter. Hell, just this morning he'd turned the wrong way down a corridor in his apartment building to avoid crossing paths with the local asshole.

The problem with the second one, that she'd run away with them willingly, was that he couldn't bear to learn that it had all been a sham. A cold calculation. That he was a pawn in a larger game and she had used him.

And it would mean that she'd stolen their big score.

That thought niggled in his brain as well, growing louder as he sat there, pushing him to act, raising his motivation. Being a hero might not get him off the couch. But toss a bucket of Pulse into the mix and his mindset started to change.

When the detective had asked whether Abbi told stories about Kansas, he'd thought it a dumb question. Odd, anyway. But he'd been pondering that one as well, dwelling on their past conversations, reviewing them in his mind.

And the answer was a resounding "no." Most of her off-handed comments related to the Moon, comparing and contrasting the food, architecture, lighting, clothing. It was always between Lagrange and Nova Terra. Never about Kansas.

"Cam would tell me if she was there." He said it aloud as if to persuade himself to push his luck. What little of it he had left, anyway.

Camillo Wilkerson was Vincent's counterpart on the Moon: a security tech on the civilian side of Nova Terra's police force. Like Vincent, Cam was responsible for maintaining the lunar implementation of POTS.

Vincent considered Camillo a friend. A work friend, anyway. They'd met a few years back while attending an annual conference of the Interworld Association of Security Professionals. Their friendship grew during time spent together at the POTS workshops, virtual gatherings intended to sharpen participants' skills with the population tracking tool. He and Camillo had spent hours together at these meetings, the intimacy of their connection augmented by neural caps.

The POTS workshops always included one segment on ethics, traditionally a case study where participants were challenged to recognize problematic behavior and formulate a response. A regulation hammered home during every workshop was that using POTS for personal matters was verboten. Always.

The case study at the most recent workshop was just like Vincent's situation: what to do when a colleague seeks help locating a lover. They all knew that with access to POTS, a stalker could invade a victim's world, watch their every move, track all aspect of their life to a frightening degree. The case study made it clear that Vincent would be crossing a line to ask Cam to locate Abbi. Cam would be crossing one to answer. And he'd be crossing another if he didn't report Vincent for the infraction.

Worried about how Cam might respond, Vincent toyed with spinning the facts to make the request seem work related, perhaps by using Abbi's involvement in recent crimes as the basis for an inquiry. Murder was about as big as it gets.

But if this were really about chasing a killer, why would one back-office analyst be asking another about it in a private communication? Cam was smart enough to know that detectives chased criminals. His natural response would be to get officers involved, and the last thing Vincent wanted was more cops nosing about.

In the end, he decided to stick with making it a personal request, mirroring the unethical behavior in the case study. He'd keep his ask to a simple yes or no: Is Abbi there in Nova Terra? No call for tracking. No request for personal details. Nothing creepy. It shouldn't be *that* big a deal. Hell, he'd do it for Cam if he asked.

Vincent opened a beer, chugged half of it, and as his face tingled from the alcohol rush, he placed the call. "Hey, Cam. Hope you're doing well. I've got myself a situation here and could use your input." He marked the message as urgent, sent it, then sipped his beer while he waited.

Forty long minutes later—time Vincent spent second-guessing the content of his message, wondering if he should have included more specifics—Cam called back. "Hey Vin. What's going on?"

Vincent got right to it, sending him feeds of Abbi. "I need help locating her."

"Who is she?"

"Abbi Gillespie."

"I mean to you. Who is she to you?"

Vincent caught Cam's gaze and put it out there. "She and I have been together for the past few months. Things were going great and then, boom, this morning she bolts. A total surprise. The thing is, she took something important to me with her. Something personal." He felt like a genius improvising the theft idea on the fly. "I'm pretty sure she went in your direction. I'd like to make sure she's okay, and I'm anxious to get my property back."

"What is it?"

"What is what?"

"What did she take that's so important?"

Vincent froze. He hadn't thought through that part of

the story and scrambled for a response. "My diary." It was the only item he could think of in the moment that might be personal, valuable, and small enough to carry. Except teenage girls keep diaries, not grown men. And even if he kept one, it would be buried in his record, it wouldn't be a book someone could take. His cheeks reddened as he scrambled for a save. "More of a ledger."

Camillo studied him for a long moment and then tapped and swiped where Vincent couldn't see. "I show her as Abbi Adamson. Yup, she's here."

"Wait, this is just a regular POTS question: How can she have a different identity in the two systems? I thought that was impossible."

"She's Indie, so she should be null in your system. If she shows a false identity, then she's broken a bunch of laws."

Vincent hesitated, but only for a moment. "Which is why I'm contacting you. I believe this woman is illegally using two identities and I seek to confirm it with you before bringing the issue to my supervisor." If Cam accepted his rewrite of history, they both would be ethically compliant.

"I confirm she's an Indie listed as Abbi Adamson here in Nova Terra." Cam played his part to perfection.

Relieved by the turn of events, Vincent stopped fretting about ethics rules and shifted to finding answers about Abbi. He was losing ground, though, because if she had a secret identity, his list of questions just got a whole lot longer. "I know about Indies, as in, they exist. They're the ones who live in caves, right?"

"Goddamn, Vin. I presented a whole segment on them

at the last meeting." Cam studied him with a scowl, then exhaled in a huff. He made an action Vincent couldn't see, and then a recording of Cam giving his recent workshop presentation began to play.

"Two decades ago, a group of people moved into an old muster station on Armstrong's east face. These are natural caves that had been outfitted for refuge in case of a dome breach. Designed to hold thousands, the caves are no longer part of emergency planning, replaced by local rally points distributed throughout the city. The group occupied the caves for many years, out of sight, growing in numbers. Independents with their own vision for Nova Terra. Eventually, their behavior drew negative attention and the government moved to clear them out. Their lawyer fought it, arguing that the caves fell outside the survey boundaries for the city of Armstrong, making the residents free of Armstrong regulations and oversight. Officials confirmed that the caves missed the city boundary by mere centimeters, and a judge ruled that they are an independent district outside Armstrong's control."

Vincent interrupted, shading the truth in an attempt to save face. "I know all that. But why aren't they in POTS?"

"The judge said that Indies—there's something like eight hundred of them living in the caves at this point—can be included here in our system but not in the feeds we export off world. Lagrange would have to negotiate with them directly to get their data, and there's no way they'll ever agree. The rulings are being appealed, but it will take years from what I hear."

"I should pay more attention during the workshops."

Vincent said it to lighten the mood but Cam didn't laugh. Then levers clicked and he remembered that POTS couldn't identify the two men who spirited Abbi away. They must be Indies as well, which would seem to add weight to the "she was with them" version of the story.

"If she really has different identities in the two systems," said Cam, "she's figured out the impossible. The POTS people say it can't be done." He gave a quick shrug. "At least we'll have something to talk about at the next meeting."

The conversation drifted from there, then Cam begged off with an excuse about another call.

Vincent stayed on the couch, sipping his beer and reflecting on what he'd learned, struggling to resolve the discordant pieces, struggling harder to reconcile his thoughts with his feelings. He knew Abbi to be a supportive, caring, soulful person. She'd said she loved him several times. "No one is that good an actress," he said, shaking his head.

He couldn't just walk away. Not from her. And not from ten thousand doses of Pulse. A haul Bridge had died for. They were rightfully his. Half of them, anyway.

His stomach growled and he move into the kitchen in search of food. His options were meager: leftover cheese pizza, peanut butter on a heel of wheat bread, an overripe apple, pickles in a jar. He slid the pizza slices from the box onto a plate, heated them up, and carried the dish back to the couch. As he noshed, he argued with himself, raising his level of agitation. He was soon pacing the living room carpet.

The old him wanted to sink into a pool of misery and self-loathing, where he'd hide from the world, licking his wounds, waiting for memories of her to fade enough that he could resume his life. But gathering forces—his desire for her, his need for Pulse, his fear of the cops—were pushing him to be proactive, to chase her to Nova Terra.

"Put up or shut up," he said aloud, goading himself yet again. The words were easy to say. But moving forward required that he overcome some significant hurdles. A huge one was how to catch a flight off Lagrange when the detective had told him to stay put. The moment she'd said "Don't leave Lagrange" with his name and everything, Community Patrol systems imposed broad travel restrictions on him. It was an automated action implemented by AI. He knew this from his job.

What he didn't know was how comprehensive those limitations would be. From his couch, he opened a display and tested his access to POTS. "Thank God," he said, relieved to find his credentials still worked. The restrictions hadn't spilled into his work. Yet.

Poking around his dashboard, he explored the parameters now in place to box him in, testing to see if he could bully past them with the administrator tools he could still access. After a good twenty minutes, he determined that the answer was no. His authority to modify POTS and a few subordinate procedures would let him weasel his way around some of the obstacles. But he couldn't even access systems like Visa Control or Off-world Banking, let alone modify them.

And that led to the next big hurdle: how to pay for it.

He checked flight costs and almost had a heart attack. Short-notice tickets were *expensive*. Then he'd need to pay for a place to sleep, food to eat, incidentals. "I didn't want an Immersion anyway." That was the new gaming system he'd been lusting after, scrimping and saving for months with his eye on the Pro model.

Stumped, he made for the kitchen to get another beer. But before he got to the refrigerator, he returned to the couch. He had an idea. Perhaps the answer.

When they'd first started planning the theft, Abbi had supplied Vincent with four identity shields to support the operation. She described them as intelligent payloads that would make a person invisible to society's automated systems. The person would still be able to function, seemingly unremarkable to everyone around them. But their actions would leave no permanent record. Like they were ghosts.

At first he was mystified by the claims of the shield's capabilities. It defied everything he knew about the systems he managed. But then his mind began imagining the mischief he and Bridge could cause as ghosts, and the titillation got the best of him. He stopped asking how the shields worked and instead concentrated on the opportunities they provided.

When Abbi had given him the four shields, she'd explained that one was for Bridge and one was for her. The other two were to be loaded for what she called contingencies. She spun a vague story of emergencies and adaptability. Her explanation didn't make sense to him, but she grew short-tempered when he questioned her.

After discussing it with Bridge a few days before the theft, Vincent decided that loading the two contingency shields was a waste of valuable resources. If something went wrong during the break in, a situation occurred where a backup shield would provide cover, then he could have one activated in seconds. And if nothing went wrong, they'd have two shields left over for a freelance adventure at another time.

He realized now that the extra shields were to hide Abbi's two companions. It's the only thing that made sense. "I wonder if that's what the fight was about?" The men could have been furious to learn they weren't hidden from POTS and reacted in anger.

And if that were true, it meant they were Abbi's partners. That she was with them.

The two shields he'd secreted away—if they still worked—might be the answer for circumventing his travel restrictions. He retrieved one from his data vault and reviewed the launch entries: Name, Start Time, End Time. No more complicated than pulling the trigger of a gun.

When Abbi had given him the contingency shields, the Name slot had been pre-filled with a cryptic code, a long string of numbers and letters. He issued a command to clear the field. It turned blank. Holding his breath, he entered his own name in the slot. The shield flashed his picture and he confirmed the entry. His heart began to thump.

The Start Time slot offered the option "upon activation," which he took to mean "start immediately when loaded." He chose that option. The End Time slot could be entered as a specific date and time, or as a shift from the start time. He selected +48 hours, meaning that he would be a ghost for the next two days once the shield was activated.

The shield was launched by moving it through the POTS portal, which on his display looked like a little round door. He could move the payload through the door using a voice command. Something as simple as "Launch the shield." If he were wearing a neural cap, he could launch it by thought.

He chose to use his finger, pointing at the shield and dragging it in a circle around the display. He'd bring it close to the POTS portal, tease moving it through the door, and then delay by swooshing it around again, a race car making another lap. It was his tentative nature pushing back against his bout of bravado.

A chime signaled an incoming call. The caller's ID was blocked. He paused his swooshing and used his administrator tools to explore. He could see that the call originated from someone associated with Community Patrol. But to learn their identity, he'd have to answer.

Whoever it was, whatever they wanted, it couldn't be good. His workmates never hid their identity. It had to be one of the detectives calling to hassle him about Bridge and Abbi.

He waited for the chime to stop. It didn't. Just the opposite, it became more incessant. Louder. His breathing quickened as his anxiety mounted. The chime became shrill, drilling into his head, edging his angst into fear.

Anxious to stop it, desperate for relief, he dragged the

shield into the POTS portal. It was an impulsive act driven by desperation. There was no reason to believe it would change anything. He wasn't sure why he did it.

The chime continued.

His fear became panic. He cast about for a place to hide. For something else to try.

The chime stopped.

He stared at his display. It just hovered there, waiting for his input.

He wondered if he were now invisible to the multitude of systems watching and guiding everything. That's what this was all about. The obvious place to test his status was with POTS. But it only covered public spaces, which meant he'd have to go outside to test it.

He did have security sensors in his apartment, a private feed only he could see. He accessed it and saw an image of his apartment. It was exactly as he saw it from the couch at that very moment. Only in the display, he wasn't there.

Shaking his head in wonder, he now understood Abbi's earlier behavior.

A month back he'd tried to impress her by freelancing a way into Axiom's security system. He'd pitched his boss on the idea of including the company in their ongoing data partnership trials. His boss had approved his suggestion and Axiom had accepted the invitation, giving Vincent access to their secrets.

But Abbi had responded angrily, telling him that he was putting everything at risk, that she had it handled, that he was hurting more than helping. The criticism stung, and he'd moped for days. Later she confided that the shield would spread across systems like a benign virus. It would get itself where it needed to be without damaging anything along the way and without drawing anyone's attention.

He considered himself a highly skilled technician. Community Patrol wouldn't have given him responsibility for POTS if he weren't. And what she said didn't make sense to him. Modern tech wouldn't let that happen.

Yet he couldn't deny what he was seeing in his display.

Chasing Abbi across worlds required balls much bigger than his. So in spite of his apparent success with the shield, he continued to waffle, focusing on his next big hurdle. "You still need a ticket."

If he could purchase a shuttle ticket in spite of the onerous travel restrictions placed on him, then the shield was working as Abbi claimed. And that feature was something he could test without leaving his couch. If the systems stopped him, then everything else became academic. It was out of his hands.

He found a tourist-class seat on a shuttle flight leaving in three hours and issued a command to buy the ticket. A *ding* signaled that his booking was confirmed. He examined the details of the reservation and found everything in order. His face tingled from the weirdness of it all. Next, for a place to sleep, he chose a two-day stay at the Starfall Hotel, a low-priced option out near the spaceport, a dive he'd stayed at on a previous visit. He prepaid for the hotel and shook his head in wonder when his reservation was confirmed.

With his stomach turning summersaults, he checked his personal account balance, expecting to see desolation and wreckage. But all his money was still there! He had a confirmed ticket on the Luna Express and a prepaid reservation in a hotel outside Armstrong, both in his name, both costing him nothing.

He continued to watch the display, wondering if maybe it took a few seconds for the transaction to register. But he knew it didn't work that way. Everything was simultaneous. Somehow, his ghost status made it so his purchases were free.

Vincent laughed, his natural greed swamping his caution. He canceled his reservations and rebooked a first-class seat on the same shuttle flight for ten times the price. Then he moved his stay to the Lofta Hotel in downtown Armstrong for a similar premium, this time adding the prepaid food-and-beverage option so nothing would come back at him after the forty-eight hours had expired. Hopefully.

When he checked his balance, he felt giddy. Free and clear.

On impulse, he opened his bookmark to the Immersion Pro gaming system, looked at it lovingly, and bought it. The system confirmed the purchase and asked about scheduling delivery. "Holy shit," he said when his account balance remained unchanged. His imagination ran wild.

As he worked on purchasing a bedroom set, something Abbi had told him he desperately needed, a worry grew in the back of his mind. A concern anyway. If the person who'd been calling was indeed a detective, could they have decided to pay him a personal visit? Maybe stop by his apartment and ask why he wasn't answering his calls?

That thought tipped the scale. Vincent was going to the Moon.

He stuffed a knapsack with a change of clothes, then threw in a light coat because it was cooler in Nova Terra. He scanned the apartment, trying to decide what else to take, shrugged, and made his way out to the pedestrian thoroughfare, figuring he'd buy whatever he had forgotten. As he walked to the pod station on the corner, he used a personal display to access POTS. He grinned when the system reported that he couldn't be located.

Chapter 7

The hot brew burned Cuss's tongue. But that didn't diminish the pleasure that followed from the full-bodied flavor of coffee from the Andes Mountains of Peru.

"So apparently the three I'm chasing are Indies," he said to Eve, who sat across from him, an espresso on the table in front of her. "Do you know of them?"

They sat outside a café a block down from the Avium building. A few tables outside were positioned to overlook the pedestrian throughfare. As they talked and sipped, they watched a steady stream of people move past, some hustling and others strolling, walking alone and in groups, talking and laughing and lost in thought.

Their table was shaded by a cloth umbrella, the kind you might see at a beach setting or perhaps on a backyard deck, this one red with white stripes. But it was purely for ambiance. Protection from the sun wasn't necessary in Demeter, or any of the cities of Lagrange, because the sun overhead was an artifice. An illusion. One that radiated heat, that transited the sky over the course of a day, that shone brightly and looked as if it were far away. But in reality it was only a hundred meters up, projected onto the massive cylinder overhead that was the back of Deck 5.

"Indies?" Eve nodded. "Sure. I've even visited the caves. Been in their homes." She rubbed a piece of lemon peel on the lip of her cup, dropped it into the dark liquid, and stirred with a small spoon. "Tippi sent me the simulation he created for you. Did you notice the Nubku slippers?"

Cuss looked at her anew, impressed by the observation but keeping his face free of expression. "It's what turned me to the Indies in the first place."

"I have a pair."

"Made for you?" He sat forward. "Cord pattern matching your spirit?" He thought about how that could be possible and connected the dots. "You have a relative who's one of them. An aunt or uncle?"

She nodded. "It's my great aunt's son on my mother's side. Mom says he's my first cousin once removed."

"Are you close?"

She shrugged. "Growing up, my mom would drag me along when she visited Johnny, who at the time lived just a few blocks away from us. He restored antique furniture, and Mom helped by hunting down period-correct knobs and pulls and hinges. Anyway, what made it interesting is that he is halfway in age between Mom and me. That perspective let him serve as a family ambassador, helping a mother and daughter understand each other a little bit better."

She smiled as she said it, remembering. "Johnny moved to Nova Terra eight or ten years ago, joined the Indies, and ended up marrying one of them. When I'm in town, we'll have dinner together. A couple of times he's invited me to his home."

"In the caves?"

She made a gesture that was a blend of a nod and a shrug. "That word conjures up visions of prehistoric living. But think that all of Nova Terra is a cavern dug out of the rock, a massive man-made hole covered with a clear dome. The homes inside the cave network are just as modern as the ones in Armstrong. Just as homey."

"How do I approach them when my intention is to arrest three of their members?"

She sipped her espresso as she thought. "Maybe start with their governing board? Explain the situation and ask for cooperation. Nothing official happens in the enclave without their approval."

"They call it an enclave?" It was the first time Cuss had heard the term.

"It's not an official name. At least I don't think it is." She smirked. "It's just easier than saying 'those people in caves just outside Armstrong.'"

"Are they reasonable people?"

"Johnny is. So is his wife. I met one of the board members, and she seemed pleasant. I've never appeared before them or worked with them in any way, so beyond that, I don't know."

"And when they come outside, they're free to enter Armstrong?"

She nodded. "They shop and socialize and even work in Armstrong. A lot of them, anyway. The times I've been there, there's been a steady stream of people coming in and out of the main gate."

"What about Johnny? Does he come out?"

"Oh, sure. He owns a warehouse out near Port Collins

where he sells reconditioned household items. Apparently space transport is hard on furniture and appliances, making no end to damaged goods in need of retail rescue."

Cuss shook his head. "I don't get it. How can they step across a line, enjoy the benefits of society, and then step back and say, now I'm free of responsibility? And they get to do it the next day and the next? It doesn't make sense."

Her face lit up. "I could act as your emissary. Introduce you around. I know them as well as any outsider. It'd be fun." She nodded, encouraging a positive response.

Cuss felt a flash of panic. Traveling together in the *Nelly Marie* meant he'd be spending time alone with her in his private sanctuary. It pushed hard on his boundaries.

Ygo came to his aid. "A professor at Conrad University studies the Indies and has published several academic articles on the subject. A Professor Stockard."

"Wow, thanks for the offer." He broke eye contact as he spoke, dropping his gaze to the tabletop, a tell he was lying. "I've already arranged for a proper guide."

Maybe she could read his tell. Maybe she could hear it in his tone. Maybe she took offense at his choice of the word "proper." Whatever the reason, she turned cold. Blue-ice cold. Deep space cold. "Fine, Marshal. I have to go meet up with Ferris. He can't get a response from Vincent and needs backup for a visit to his apartment."

She stood. "If possible, the MA would like to prosecute Abbi and her companions at the same time as Vincent. There'll be a lot of the same witnesses. Same evidence. Please keep us updated on your progress." She turned and started down the pedestrian throughfare toward the pod station on the corner, the stiffness in her step reflecting her annoyance.

"First Deanna and now Eve," said Ygo. "This isn't your best day, Buddy."

"No shit." He felt bad about both situations, especially about denying Eve a professional opportunity because he was hot for her. But she was interested in him in the same way. He could tell. And tempting fate could only lead to a different kind of trouble.

. . .

"Up and at 'em," said Ygo. "Landing sequence in thirty minutes."

Cuss opened one eye and checked the time. Ygo had let him sleep the entire five-hour trip while he'd piloted the *Nelly Marie* to Nova Terra, a straightforward journey complicated only slightly by orbital mechanics.

Lagrange hovered in space about sixty-five thousand kilometers away from the Moon. But traveling from one to the other was a longer journey. The Moon moved in orbit around the Earth, and together with Earth, moved in orbit around the Sun. Ygo had to guide the ship from where Lagrange was at the start of the trip to where the Moon would be after five hours of this celestial ballet.

During the trip, Ygo had helped Cuss sleep in comfort by maintaining a constant one gee acceleration, familiar Earth gravity. But in thirty minutes, he would be using the

Paulson drives to take the ship through a descent and landing sequence into Port Collins. The jolts and jostling that accompanied the maneuver required that passengers be strapped in or risk serious injury.

Cuss climbed out of bed and scratched himself. His bedroom was on the third level of the *Nelly Marie*, a midsize egg-shaped spacecraft. The room was large by Marshals Service standards because he didn't have to share with his partner. Ygo's den was located in the ship's hold at the other end of the vessel.

He yawned, pausing to appreciate the breathtaking field of stars visible through the viewport along the back wall of his bachelor pad. Making for the bathroom, he stepped around an overstuffed chair, one big enough to hold two people if they cuddled, and past a fold-down desk and a clothes closet. The mirror on the closet door showed the walls behind him, one holding framed pictures of his folks, his deceased wife, and his childhood dog, the other displaying posters from music acts he'd seen at venues across the worlds.

Cuss washed his face but didn't shave, a two-day stubble being his signature look. He dressed in sturdy black pants and a blue collared shirt, looped a shoulder holster harness around his back and through his arms, and covered it with a gray blazer.

Moving to the gun safe in the wall near his desk, he chose his Tosic 325 Hybrid. In a routine he'd performed so many times he did it in seconds without thinking, he pulled the magazine and verified it was full, returned it, cycled the slide to move a bullet into the chamber, then put the bullet he'd ejected the night before back into the magazine. The gun made a familiar *shlick* sound when he slid it into his shoulder holster.

He descended steep stairs to the middeck, an open area that could be configured a dozen ways: for dining, exercise, lounging, or deskwork. A corner could even be walled off as a temporary prison cell.

A kitchenette tucked under the stairway served most of Cuss's needs. As part of their morning routine, Ygo had started the coffee machine while Cuss dressed. Cuss filled his large cup and sealed the top so it wouldn't splash out during the landing maneuvers. From an overhead cabinet, he viewed an array of breakfast bars—lab protein manufactured into nutritious and tasty snacks—and selected one each of egg and cheese, and cinnamon crunch. With food and coffee mug in hand, he scrambled down another set of steep stairs to the command deck, the operations center of the craft.

The dominant feature on the command deck was the pilot's station: a chair positioned in front of an expansive display. Emergency controls lined a row beneath the display: levers and buttons, dials and gauges set in shiny metal and covered in clear glass, none of it ever used by Cuss but there just in case.

Ringing the deck, starting from his right, was a viewport similar to the one in his bedroom, the ops panel for the emergency life-support system, the stairway up to the middeck, another viewport, the ops panel for the emergency power system, and the oval-shaped exit hatch with its articulated hinges.

Snugging himself into the pilot's seat, Cuss took his first sip of coffee before speaking to his partner. "Good morning."

"De-orbit maneuver in one minute," replied Ygo.

"How did I get so far ahead of schedule?" It was a ritual joke. Cuss was known to slide into the seat mere seconds before the ride got too rough to be standing.

. . .

As a trawler pulled the *Nelly Marie* from the landing pad into Port Collins' huge pressurized hangar, Ygo said, "So I've reviewed the sensor feeds to see who got off the *Salty Frontier*. Whoever it is, they're invisible to all systems. The hatch opens. The hatch closes. No one comes out."

"Huh," said Cuss, still in the pilot's seat, waiting out the tow. "Is this technology they brought back with them from Lagrange? Or did they have it with them in the first place?"

"I'm leaning toward this being something they developed here and brought there. Anyway, while I couldn't see *who* got off the ship, I know *when* they did from the movement of the hatch. I calculated how long it takes someone to travel from Port Collins to the enclave, and I reviewed the public feeds near the cave entrance around that time."

The *Nelly Marie*'s command deck display came alive, showing a view down a roadway, a long perspective with buildings on either side, tall and tight, blocking the sun to create a tunnel-like effect into the distance. Pedestrians loped along the road and shuffled in and out of the buildings, moving in the long hop-steps that distinguished walkers in a low-gravity world.

At the far end of the roadway, the view opened up to a cliff face, a hundred-meter-tall, vine-covered wall of rock that was the edge of the massive underground basin containing Armstrong, the largest city in Nova Terra.

The display swiveled to focus on the first floor of the building to the right, the entrance to Gremond Market, a grocery store. Large windows along the front enticed pedestrians with attractively arrayed food. People on both sides of the window were milling about, most dressed in flamboyant clothes, pops of color in an otherwise somber world, dramatic outfits that had become the traditional garb for Nova Terrans.

The market's big double doors were fixed open, allowing patrons to move freely in and out. While Cuss watched, two teenaged girls exited, laughing and talking, sharing a bag of popcorn. A young woman holding the hand of a child followed them. An aging couple entered the market, moving slowly.

Then Abbi came out. It was her. No mistake. She wore rainbow pants with a red-and-yellow blouse, and carried a tote full of groceries in one hand. She was followed by two men, both also carrying groceries, both wearing backpacks, one eating a bright red tomato like it was an apple. Cuss recognized the two as the ones involved in the Avium robbery. Again, no mistake.

Abbi was a sturdy young woman with soft, pleasant features. Thirtyish. Brown hair just past her shoulders. Athletic. Appealing. She moved with purpose, her face communicating confidence and determination. She led the men as they moved in bouncing strides toward the cliff face with its cave entrance.

"This is Abbi and Barker Adamson," said Ygo. "The one with the tomato is Jaunty Gabala."

"When was this?"

"Yesterday afternoon."

"They made themselves visible after leaving the ship?"

"I can't find where it happened, but it seems it's a feature they can turn on and off."

"I'm going out on a limb and guessing Abbi and Barker are not brother and sister."

"They are not. They have a three-year-old daughter."

"We have Abbi leaving her husband and young daughter for three months, apparently with full hubby approval, to shack up with Vincent so she can steal Pulse?" Cuss shook his head. "Everything I learn about this case makes me more confused."

"Remember that governing board that Eve mentioned? The one she suggested you ask for cooperation? I believe Abbi is a board member."

"Perfect." Sarcasm dripped from the word.

"And some bad news. Professor Stockard, the sociologist at Conrad University who studies the Indies? I reached out to make an appointment for you and learned he's in Madrid as part of an academic exchange program."

"Madrid as in Spain?"

"That's the one. His call message says he's doing field work and will be unavailable for the rest of the week."

Cuss exhaled a sigh of annoyance.

"I'm researching possible substitutes. So far I have Stockard's grad student. She did a lot of the legwork for his studies. There's also the city attorney who's representing Armstrong in the case against the enclave. He's spent years studying his adversary."

"Have either of them ever been inside the caves?"

"I don't know."

Chapter 8

C uss struggled to outline a plan as he watched Abbi, Barker, and Jaunty march toward the main gate. Ygo elevated the perspective so they were looking down from above the buildings, giving a panoramic view of the cliff face in both directions. While the cliff had appeared as a straight, vertical wall when viewed from the roadway, this angle allowed Cuss to see a gentle curve as the wall turned inward to form a basin that encompassed the city.

The road Abbi and the men followed led straight to the main entrance. There, a broad forecourt of brickwork served as a funnel, narrowing the foot traffic from the street to a single line feeding a gate.

On either side of the main entryway, spaced at fifty-meter intervals, were a series of sister tunnels, a dozen in each direction, all the same size, all near ground level along the base of the cliff face. The two adjacent to the main tunnel were fed by entry ramps. The rest were capped shut with crude plugs of material, the entry ramps removed.

"The original installation had twenty-five refuge tunnels," explained Ygo. "After a judge granted the enclave its protections, the Nova Terra government capped all but these three, the ones claimed by the Indies, and redrew the city boundaries to bring them inside city limits. The judge wouldn't let them include the three enclave tunnels in the redraw, though. Not until the legal issues are settled. So for now, the city boundary juts out and in to exclude them."

Abbi, Barker, and Jaunty reached the forecourt, marched through it in a couple of purposeful strides, and disappeared into the tunnel. At that moment, a thump and a bump signaled that the *Nelly Marie* was secure in its hangar berth.

Cuss stood. "We need to set up surveillance on the forecourt. Those three will have to come out at some point. Officers can collect them when they do."

"It will have to be actual people standing there watching. Otherwise, they could use their invisibility trick and POTS would never see them."

Cuss's shoulders slumped. "Which brings us to the fun part of the job."

"Ah, yes. Begging the locals for help. Do you want me to see if Toni is available?"

Toni Carrabelle was Armstrong's chief of detectives. He would assign the local team to work with Cuss. He'd also be a good starting point to discuss the surveillance idea. While he and Cuss were on friendly terms, Toni was his own person, making decisions he thought were best for his city even if Cuss disagreed.

Cuss was about to let Ygo place the call but had a thought. "Where is the *Salty Frontier* docked?"

"It's here in the hangar about ten berths away. You want a look?"

"A quick one."

Since Cuss was up and moving about the ship, Ygo sent the feed to his lens.

Cuss hadn't known what to expect, but it wasn't this. The *Salty Frontier* was a rocket ship in the old sense of the word. Instead of the gentle egg shape of the *Nelly Marie* and most private vessels, it looked more like a jet aircraft, with a pointy nose under two narrow windows that gave the front a menacing frown. It had sleek lines, stubby wings, a jutting tail, and it sat lengthwise on its landing gear. Mostly cockpit and engines and built for speed, there would be no bedrooms, exercise areas, or kitchens in the *Salty Frontier*. At best a bathroom stall and a corner galley.

"Where is it sitting relative to us?"

"We're at the front of the hangar, and it's buried in back to the right. It's a ten-minute walk."

"I'm going to take a look on my way out. I can talk with Toni while I walk. After that, I want to stop in at Johnny's warehouse—Eve's cousin's place—and have a chat with him. She said it was out here near Port Collins."

"I've located the building but don't have any background on Cousin Johnny or his business. I'll see what I can scrape together."

Cuss worked the ship's hatch and pulled it open. The ground crew had pushed a mobile stairway into position against the side of the *Nelly Marie*. Feeling feisty, he stepped onto the stairway's top platform, paused to scan the bustle of activity all around him, and then leapt out over the dozen steps, straight onto the ground.

Cuss weighed two hundred twenty pounds on Earth, which translated to just thirty-seven pounds on the Moon. Jumping from the top of a twelve-step stairway on the Moon had the same impact on his body as jumping down two steps on Earth.

Arms out, he landed with knees bent onto the hard-packed soil. He remained upright and ready to move, for the briefest moment imagining himself a superhero.

"That grad student you mentioned. I'll meet with her. I'll skip the city attorney, though. He'll try to steer me to help his case."

"It's human nature."

As Cuss was getting his bearings, a tug truck—a muscular beast of a machine—beeped at him. Growling and rumbling, the machine pulled a fancy corporate craft toward the airlock. Cuss stepped off the roadway and started up its shoulder toward the *Salty Frontier*, moving back onto the roadway once he was past the ship and tug.

The hangar was organized like a yacht marina, but instead of a gridwork of docks over water, it had a gridwork of travel lanes lined with berths for small and medium-size spacecraft. The big stuff remained outside the hangar in the airless environment. The place was busy, almost chaotic. And like a yacht marina, the berths were filled with vessels of different shapes and sizes, many reflecting great private wealth.

As he walked, his lens came alive with the face of Chief of Detectives Toni Carrabelle.

"Marshal Abbott," said Toni, teasing him with the formal title. "What brings you to my city?" Toni was gender neutral in both clothing and physical characteristics, preferred male pronouns, and today wore an outfit swirling with color. In spite of the tease in his greeting, Cuss knew Toni was all business and tough as nails.

He gave Toni a thumbnail sketch of the situation: three Indies committed murder during a robbery in Demeter; they used new technology to hide from POTS during their escape; they flew here yesterday with ten thousand doses of Pulse.

Cuss moved to the ask, using "we" to strengthen his pitch. "We need surveillance outside their cave, someone to watch until they show themselves. And we need a crime team to process their ship."

Toni said nothing, instead looking pensive, as if deliberating.

"I'm sending you everything I have so far," Cuss added, knowing that as he made the promise, Ygo was scrambling to fulfill it.

Toni revealed what had been occupying his thoughts. "You'll need a warrant for the ship. And once the judge learns that Indies are involved, he'll probably want a warrant for the cave surveillance. Then he'll bring in the city attorney for a second review. It's going to be a hassle for everyone. I'll send someone to keep an eye on the ship until we can get inside, but it won't be today. Maybe not tomorrow." He paused before revealing the next issue. "Darlena and Hobby are up in the rotation. That work for you?"

Cuss's stomach twinged. "Perfect."

He'd worked with Detectives Darlena Washington and Hobby Bronson before. Both had trust issues when it came to the Marshals Service, fearing Cuss would have them do the heavy lifting and then steal the credit, leaving them empty-handed in the end.

To counter the fear, Cuss had been generous in the past, giving them full ownership of shared busts. It had helped in his relationship with Darlena, a hardworking, competent investigator. Hobby, a sullen and sloppy detective, hated all marshals and wouldn't piss on Cuss if he were on fire. It was pointless trying to win him over.

"Good," said Toni. "Give me time to make the assignment. They'll be working the warrant, so team with them to push it through."

"I can do that," he replied, feeling a hint of guilt at Ygo's growing workload.

After a quick exchange about lighter matters, Toni closed the call.

Cuss had reached the *Salty Frontier* at that point. It was parked in a corner berth, with an open lane in front and another to its left. While it was an older craft, it seemed in good condition. There was evidence of regular maintenance: matching parts, clean gear, new seals, service tags. He circled the craft, looking for anything on the outside that would spark a revelation.

He and Ygo had guessed that the ship left Lagrange as *Jaywalker* and became *Salty Frontier* along the way, the theory being that they'd switched transponders midflight. If Cuss could find the old *Jaywalker* transponder inside, it would prove the theory and provide crucial evidence at trial. The ship's name and registration number were displayed in black lettering above the wing near the ship's hatch. If the transponder had been changed, those had been altered as well.

The wing was big enough for him to stand on,

providing a perch he could use to study the lettering for evidence of a recent swap. It was a good three meters off the ground, though, which even on the Moon was too high for him to leap to and land flat on his feet. But with an easy jump, he could grab the leading edge of the wing with his hands, and then swing his thirty-seven-pound frame up without a problem.

Bending his knees, he pushed off, hands stretched up, eyes on the front of the wing. Everything went as he'd imagined in his mind, at least at the start. He gripped the leading edge. But when he closed his grip and pulled, he was surprised by a slick surface.

He wasn't sure what it was—oil, cleanser, degreaser— whatever the source, his hands slipped off and he smacked an elbow. Then his knees hit the underside of the wing, spinning him over. Stretching, he made a desperate grab at the wing, missed, and began a slow descent, one that took long enough for him to feel embarrassment on the way down. He landed on his back in the dirt, the superhero humiliated.

"Whoa there, buddy. You all right? We were told no one would be back."

Cuss swiveled his head to see a big man in a Port Collins maintenance uniform coming in his direction. The man was rolling a portable stairway like the one that had been pushed up against the *Nelly Marie*.

"You okay to stand?" A new voice behind him, another maintenance worker, hooked his hands under Cuss's arms and hefted him to his feet.

"I'm okay," he said, dusting himself off, protecting his

pride.

He acknowledged the man approaching from the front with a nod. A big guy. Broad. Sturdy. A huge round face that reminded Cuss of a scowling pumpkin. Not scowling like he was concerned for Cuss's health. More a face of determination. He wore the same coveralls as the other workers in the hangar. The same hard hat. But his hat looked small perched on his melon head.

Then Cuss's visual sweep reached the man's feet. Nubku slippers. He switched to a defensive posture just as Ygo called, "Behind you!"

The warning came too late. Harsh hands gripped his coat collar from behind and yanked downward, pulling the coat off his shoulders, twisting the material, tangling his arms in the sleeves.

"What do you want with the ship?" asked Melon Head. He stood in front of Cuss, a few steps away. The guy behind him jerked the coat, demanding a response.

Cuss struggled to free his hands, his mind racing to understand the threat. Melon Head stepped forward, right arm extended, reaching for Cuss's gun.

Cuss gave them a chance. It was his duty. "I'm Marshal Abbott. You are assaulting an officer of the law."

Melon Head seemed unimpressed by the declaration, barely pausing before continuing his advance. The guy behind him hissed, "Answer the question."

Losing a weapon to an attacker was unacceptable for a law officer. It was lore. Part of the code. The gun was a symbol of their power and authority. Even though it was IDed to him—Cuss was the only one who could pull the trigger—having it taken from him was beyond personal. Beyond unacceptable. It was failure.

It wasn't going to happen.

Cuss had grown up in Daytona Beach, Florida, where he had been an avid athlete in school. Ice hockey wasn't a big sport in the South, so he'd never played it competitively. But he'd watched it enough to know that game officials allowed fist fights between players.

A friend who had moved to Florida from up north— a hockey player with a penchant for fighting—had bragged about how he would pull the opponent's jersey up over his head to blind him and tangle his hands. It was a dirty move, one that provided a huge advantage in a brawl.

Cuss had logged the tidbit, filing it away in his bag of tricks. Though he'd been in far too many altercations in the twenty-plus years since then, he'd never found himself in position to tangle an opponent in his clothes. Cuss also had never considered that he might be the recipient of the move.

But decades of contemplation provided him a way to turn the tables. He used his jacket to fight back.

The guy behind Cuss was gripping the coat's collar. Cuss snapped his arms forward like he was hugging someone in front of him, flexing his muscles, pulling on the cloth with all his might. The move snapped the collar of his coat against his lower back, trapping the man's palms. He could feel the guy's fleshy hands pressing into him as he pulled. He willed the cloth not to tear, for the seams to hold, for the coat to keep the man in position behind him for just two seconds longer.

The action was violent enough to lift Cuss off his feet, the weak gravity depriving him of the firm purchase he needed to finish the move. Melon Head in front had hesitated when Cuss flexed. Cuss took advantage of the moment by attempting to wrap his legs around the guy's waist, a scissor hold that would join the three of them in battle, giving Cuss the leverage that the weak gravity wouldn't.

But the move had been optimistic. Perhaps naïve. While Cuss had long legs, Melon Head had a huge body. And he defended himself quite easily, swatting Cuss's right foot away with one arm while trapping his left foot under the other. The guy smiled as he squeezed the foot. Then he leaned to the side, giving it a twist.

While it wasn't the scissor grip Cuss had hoped for, as long as Melon Head squeezed, the arrangement provided him a solid fulcrum, the leverage he needed. He didn't hesitate. Bunching his shoulders, he snapped his head back, generating as much force as he could, planting the back of his head squarely into the face of the guy binding his arms.

He heard what sounded like the man's nose breaking. He imagined a split lip. Loose teeth. Some of it must have been true because the guy moaned and his grip loosened.

Melon Head's face registered surprise at the attack, and then anger. Still holding Cuss's foot with one arm, he took a swing at Cuss's head with the other, a roundhouse with a monstrous ham of a hand.

Because of the tangle of coat, Cuss had to shift his left arm behind his back to give his right arm enough slack to use it for protection. Even then, he needed to turn his torso to extend his reach, doing so in time to deflect the worst of the blow.

The swing left Melon Head's body twisted at the waist, a tight coil of muscle wound up like a spring, potential energy ready to be unleashed. When he snapped back, he unwound the coil, accelerating his arm as his body spun forward, converting the potential energy into kinetic energy. He directed all of that motion into his bent elbow, which he plunged into Cuss's trapped thigh, a brutal strike that sent flares of pain down his leg and up his back.

In turning his torso, Cuss's free leg was now positioned on top, level with guy's head. Ignoring the pain, he flexed his trapped leg, yanking the man forward with a jerk. He met Melon Head's face with his other knee, thumping him hard. It was a short stroke; he hadn't wanted to risk the delay of a windup before delivery. But it was enough to do the trick.

Melon Head cried out as his head snapped back, his hard hat flying. He brought his hands to his face, in the process freeing Cuss's trapped leg.

Cuss pushed off him, stumbling backward as he sought to regain his footing. He thrashed his arms and shoulders, trying to free his hands from the tangle of coat, finally lowering the collar under his butt and pulling his arms up and out of the sleeves.

Then he drew his weapon, a modern combination of an old-style Taser and a regular pistol. The ammunition looked and performed like traditional cartridges. The slugs would pierce most things, continuing until they came in contact with flesh. There they'd collapse on impact, leaving a bruise but not penetrating the skin. In the process of crumpling, they delivered one of three electrical charges—stop, dead, or drop—depending on the position of the gun's safety selector.

He thumbed the selector all the way forward, a hard push that moved it to drop, the easiest selection to find in an emergency, a nonlethal option most useful in the field. He shot Melon Head in the chest.

The guy gave a look of surprise, the trademark response often seen in the instant before a victim's muscles shut down. Melon Head slumped into the dirt, out for a good twenty minutes.

Cuss turned his attention to the guy behind, assessing him as a threat. The man was lying on the ground, on his side, curled in the fetal position. He held his hands to his face. Broken noses were notorious bleeders, and this one was sending blood flowing through the guy's fingers and onto the ground.

The *whoop-whoop* of an approaching siren told Cuss he had just a few seconds to gain information without a witness.

"Hey," he called to the bleeding man. He stood over him, prodding him with a toe, careful not to get blood on his shoe. He wiggled the gun when the man opened his eyes. "Who sent you?"

The guy didn't respond. Cuss glanced up to check that the approaching carts were still some distance away, then turned his toe prod into a kick. Not hard. Not to cause damage. But hard enough for the guy to grunt.

"Give me a name."

"Fuck off." The guy rolled on the ground, putting his back to Cuss.

"A name or I hurt you."

The guy didn't respond.

The man was fully subdued and under Cuss's control. He wasn't a threat. He wasn't trying to escape. And Cuss didn't care that much what the guy might say. But he shot him anyway. A slug to the back near his right kidney, dropping him for twenty minutes like his partner. Cuss did it to vent his anger. To punish the guy. A payback for his coat, his favorite. It would never be the same.

Shooting a suspect who does not present a threat, even with a nonlethal charge, was thuggery. Unprofessional. Likely criminal. His moment of pique qualified for review by the service board, a review Ygo could facilitate or one he could prevent. This not only made Ygo a witness, but if he did not submit the event for review, if he moved to conceal it, then he became a conspirator. Cuss had put him in this position without discussion. Without his consent.

Ygo conveyed his anger with his silence, a quiet so loud it dominated Cuss's thoughts. Cuss didn't regret shooting the guy, but he felt bad about putting Ygo in a difficult position. "He'll recover soon enough," he said. Not an excuse Ygo would accept, let alone a review board. But at least he acknowledged the situation.

Port patrol officers rolled up in dune-buggy-like carts, emergency lights flashing.

Ygo spoke tersely, his tone reflecting his unhappiness. "I've told them a marshal is on the scene. Hold up your badge so they can identify you."

Cuss had to reorganize his coat to find his badge wallet. Flipping the wallet open, he held the gold star high in the air.

Three officers took the attackers into custody and secured the scene while Cuss gave a summary of events to a fourth, the senior officer on the scene. Afterward, he limped over to the portable stairway that Melon Head had been dragging and sat on a step to wait for Darlena and Hobby. His left thigh throbbed and he probed it with a finger, locating the edges of the bruise where Melon Head had elbowed him.

Chapter 9

Abbi Adamson sat in her living room, her daughter, Lynne, in her lap. Three years old. Cute. They rocked back and forth, sharing time together, bonding. The child fidgeted every now and again, but Abbi barely noticed. She was traumatized. A combination of horror, hysteria, and fear.

Lynne squirmed in part because that's what three-year-olds do. But she was also fussing from discomfort, an affliction of her joints called Pernel's syndrome.

When she was diagnosed seven months earlier, they'd learned that her illness could be controlled with commercial meds. But since the disease was rare—Lynne was the only one afflicted in all of Nova Terra—the pharmacy didn't keep the medication in stock.

Lynne's doctor had submitted a prescription for the drug to PubHealth, marking it as "urgent" and "high priority." The PubHealth AI, as it had been instructed to do, flagged the request as a special order for an Indie. That triggered a notification to the mayor of Armstrong, who chose to use the drug as a weapon. The child would receive the medicine she needed the moment her parents ended their separatist drama.

The president of Nova Terra upped the ante, outright prohibiting the import of Ronolyx, the medication the child needed. He called for the Indies to move away from Nova Terra, to go to Earth where this drug and their fanatical agenda would be better served.

This put Abbi and Barker in a difficult position.

They would do anything for Lynne. But the situation was complicated by the fact that all eight of their grandparents had been early settlers in Nova Terra. Six of them had participated in the uprising, the workers revolt memorialized with murals and a statue in Citizens Square in downtown Armstrong. That lineage made the Moon their ancestral home. That history made the fight for freedom their fight.

And the fight wasn't over.

Their grandparents, like most early settlers, had migrated to the Moon for opportunity and adventure. The first settlement was a company affair. Corporations formed the government, made the laws, and enforced them to their own advantage. Forty years into it, with the settlement maturing into a small city, the lopsided priorities got the best of the people and they rebelled, demanding a larger say in governmental operations.

Their grandparents had risked everything to win the first concessions all those decades ago. Yet even today, many residents still chafed under a system that subordinated people to business.

The Indie movement was the beginnings of a new citizens uprising, a group dedicated to a more democratic Nova Terra. They felt optimistic about making lasting change this time around, in part because of shield technology, a tool only they had, a tool they believed tilted the playing field in their favor.

So, Abbi and Barker felt cornered. They needed to help Lynne. And they wanted to support the movement. But how to do both?

One solution was to bypass the government and find an alternate source for Ronolyx. When they explored the idea, they were excited to learn that Maramid—Pulse—could be converted to Ronolyx in a straightforward lab synthesis. Paulo Nang, an industrial chemist and fellow Indie, researched the procedure and tested it for them, claiming afterward, "Anyone who's taken a university-level chemistry course can follow the recipe."

Paulo warned that it was important to start with pharma-grade Pulse because the contaminants used to cut the street version could harm Lynne's health in ways unrelated to her disease. He also explained that it was an inefficient process, with six doses of Pulse required to make one dose of Ronolyx.

This was good news because while Ronolyx had but one manufacturer, a company located in Melbourne, Australia, Pulse was produced in a dozen locations, one being Demeter, just five hours away.

Using shield technology, they plundered the local supplies of Pulse, securing enough medicine to keep Lynne comfortable for a few months. Then they devised a plan for a score that would last her years.

"Abbi, love," said Barker, appearing in the doorway looking frazzled. "Vincent is outside the gate yelling your name."

"Who?" She didn't know a Vincent here in Nova

Terra.

"Your guy from Lagrange."

The blood drained from her face. If she hadn't been sitting down, she might well have fainted.

It had seemed straightforward. Three weeks in and out. The only questionable step was securing the cooperation of Vincent Rogalski, a man they'd identified as having both the skill and authorization to load shields into Lagrange's systems.

A key feature that made Vincent an attractive candidate was that he was unattractive. Beyond plain looks and slovenly personal grooming habits, he had an awkward tech-geek personality. The combination left him without companionship, without a woman. But he continued to prowl the singles haunts, oblivious to his failings, trying and trying again.

The plan was for Abbi to travel to Lagrange, beguile Vincent enough to secure his help with the tech, grab a load of Pulse, and be back home in a flash.

Simple. Easy. Safe.

But the plan had gone to shit from day one.

Vincent had needed more than just sexual teasing to get him involved. She'd done what she had to for her daughter, sleeping with him like a girlfriend. Then he began to drag his feet, making excuses, turning weeks into months, focusing on her body instead of planning the theft. She'd tried to keep it clinical, telling herself it was nothing more than an invasive medical procedure. It didn't work. Each time she felt violated.

And then Bridge fell on that statue. No one was

supposed to get hurt, let alone die. It was an accident. A tragedy. But the authorities don't ignore deaths, especially ones that occur during the commission of other crimes.

She was royally screwed. Her life was over. Same with Barker and Jaunty.

Their plan was to hide in the caves until they'd made enough Ronolyx to cover Lynne for a good year. Then they had to run.

"He did things to me," she told Barker, meeting his gaze. "Hurt me. Make him go away. I don't want to see him." Blinking back tears, she looked at Lynne. "Ever."

Chapter 10

Sitting on the steps of the mobile stairway, Cuss huffed a sigh of impatience. As the victim, he couldn't leave the scene. Not until the detectives arrived. But he was anxious to get on with it. Sitting around meant delay, and that gave the doers more time to prepare. More time to get away.

Three carts, white dune buggies with balloon tires and blue Port Patrol decals, were parked in a loose circle around the *Salty Frontier*, creating a perimeter of sorts. Melon Head and the guy who'd attacked him from behind had recovered and were now strapped into the passenger seats of two carts, hands secured behind their backs, also waiting for the detectives to arrive. A medic was attending to the one guy's busted nose.

"Any luck with cousin Johnny?" Cuss asked Ygo, testing the waters to see if they were back on speaking terms.

"His name is Johnny Prentice. His store, Prentice Showroom, is in the industrial district."

Cuss's lens came alive to show a lanky man, fiftyish, fair hair and skin. Johnny was bent at the waist, leaning over a wooden credenza with a distinctive retro look. He ran his fingers along the top of the piece as if evaluating its condition. Maybe to determine a list price. Or to decide whether he should feature it in the next advert.

Though the camera view showed a closeup of Johnny, Cuss could see additional furniture on display down the aisle, mostly dining room and kitchen pieces in this row.

"This live or archive?"

"This is live. He's there now."

"Do you think he'll talk to me?"

Johnny rose from the credenza and moved down the aisle, stopping at a dining table, where he repeated the examination process.

"My guess? Not in a million years. He'll chat with you. Smile. Nod his head. But his instinct will be to protect his home. His family. Which in this case is the whole enclave."

"Even if I drop Eve's name?"

"Maybe if she were standing there next to you. But even then, he'll be guarded. Careful. What would he gain by selling out his people?"

"Doing the right thing? Keeping the arrests from being more invasive?" Cuss shrugged. "I don't care about their political drama. But if they don't come out, we'll have to go in after them. You know that'll be messy."

"The moment the enclave learns of your intentions, they'll react as a group. A herd encircling the vulnerable, protecting them."

"We're here for murderers. They'll do the right thing." He said that last part to test the idea. But hearing the words spoken aloud, he knew it was bullshit.

A whine drew his attention to his right, a fourth cart tooling toward them. Hobby was driving. Darlena sat in the passenger seat, gripping the overhead handhold as the vehicle hopped and swayed as if moving in slow motion, a side effect of driving in one-sixth gravity.

The cart came to a stop near the nose of the *Salty Frontier*. Hobby clambered out and made for the cluster of officers gathered off to the side. He didn't acknowledge Cuss. Didn't look in his direction.

Darlena did the opposite. She walked toward him, making eye contact right away, grinning. A Black woman with a curvaceous figure, she had tall hair, a colorful outfit, and intelligent eyes. Cuss liked her spirit.

As she walked, he found himself wondering about her extra padding. Metabolic drugs had solved society's weight control issues decades earlier. That meant people who carried extra weight generally did so for one of three reasons: their physiology couldn't tolerate the medication, they preferred themselves that way, or their partners did.

Darlena had a big personality and perhaps sought a physique to match. Plus, in physical confrontations, bulk can strengthen authority, something important for cops. But since his relationship with her was strictly professional, he'd likely never know the answer.

"Cuss, as I live and breathe," she said, stopping in front of him. He'd stayed seated during her approach but rose to greet her with a quick hug. She flashed a wry smile. "We know that whenever you're in town, mayhem follows. But from what Toni said, we thought we had a day or two before it started."

"The Indies and I seem to have gotten off on the wrong foot."

"Toni mentioned them as well." She looked over at

Hobby, who was working through the scene, talking with everyone, documenting what he could. They'd combine his results with hers, add the feeds from the hangar's public sensors and the data from the crime scene microdrones now swarming the area, and pass it all to the city attorney, who would decide next steps. "Are you pressing charges?"

He nodded. "I need them off the streets until we're done. Otherwise, I'll be looking over my shoulder."

Ygo spoke with a sense of urgency. "If you become part of a legal action against the Indies, you'll have to step away from the broader investigation."

Cuss transitioned his nod into a shake of his head. "But I don't want to get sidetracked by lawyers and their games."

Darlena gestured toward Melon Head sitting in the cart. "Turns out the big guy has been in trouble before. We can tie him up for a couple of days." She shifted her gaze to Broken Nose. "But that one is a virgin. Without formal charges, we can't hold him for much longer than it takes him to get a lawyer."

"I'll take whatever you can get me."

"So walk me through it. The official account."

He was aware that when she said "official account," technology on the scene engaged to record his story. Choosing his words with care, and helped with the occasional prompting from Ygo, he gave her a more detailed version of what he'd told Toni, this time including times and dates and people and places.

He wrapped it up with, "We've got a strong case for murder against Abbi and Barker Adamson, and Jaunty

Gabala. I want inside this ship to look for evidence of the theft. Evidence that they changed the name of the craft. Given how those two reacted when I got close, I'm confident there are things to find inside."

"Toni initiated the search warrant but then passed it off to Hobby and me to finish. Can you help with the details?"

He nodded. "Send it along and I'll get it done." Then, "Do you have a handle on their invisibility trick? Can you break past it? See through it?"

Darlene shook her head. "We learned about it maybe six months ago, and that was a fluke. A tech was looking at a feed when a guy appeared out of nowhere. We've found only a couple of examples to analyze since then because you have to know in advance where to look to catch them. It's a challenge."

"If they can hide from sensors, we'll need actual people watching the tunnel entrance for when they come out."

"About that." She glanced over her shoulder at Hobby before continuing. "City leaders are convinced that if the separatists win the next round in court, it will be the end of the world as we know it. We've been warned up and down the chain to avoid doing anything that can give them a legal edge. That means we're by the book all the way. No shortcuts. Document in detail. Get advanced approval for *everything*, all the way down to permission to scratch your own ass. Even simple stakeout requests like you suggest are getting sidetracked while lawyers argue about how it could impact everything else."

Darlena's remarks suggested they wouldn't help him catch murderers. He waited for her to correct the misunderstanding. When she didn't, he felt his temper flare. Years of negotiation had gone into the formation of the Marshals Service. Agreements spelled out how they would work together. Procedures, expectations, shared responsibilities, the whole lot. Denying assistance wasn't among the options.

Before he could erupt, Ygo intervened. "She's boxed in by dictates from above and thinks you'll have greater success working outside the system. She doesn't want to be on record saying that, so she's being ambiguous. Still, she's trying to help."

After a calming breath, Cuss decided Ygo was right. They stood there in awkward silence, and then it occurred to him that the new rules of engagement meant he wouldn't be involved in the interrogation of his attackers, especially not as the victim of the crime.

"Maybe I'll poke around on my own while you process these two."

"I understand." She seemed relieved, nodding as if to encourage him. "Be sure to keep us updated. And reach out if you need backup."

"When you question them, dig for who sent them. Is there someone pulling the strings?"

"I'll try. But their lawyers will know we're being cautious, and I'll have a whole committee watching over my shoulder. Don't count on us getting much."

. . .

It was another two hours before Darlena and Hobby finished their investigation and left the scene, the delay caused by procedures associated with the discharge of a firearm by an officer. Cuss easily defended shooting Melon Head; the man presented an immediate and mortal threat.

But the shooting of Broken Nose was not straightforward given that Cuss did it when the guy was injured and lying immobile on the ground. Cuss stated that he believed Broken Nose was preparing to run, and that his injured leg limited his ability to stop the guy or engage in a chase. So he dropped the man to secure him until help arrived.

Darlena accepted his account, though he could see skepticism on her face. He was grateful she didn't pursue it. But she did ask if he would sit for a follow-up at the station if there were additional questions. He agreed.

Questions would arise only if Broken Nose filed a complaint. That would trigger a detailed review, one where the feeds would likely expose Cuss's questionable behavior. Eventually, the Marshals Service would get involved and he'd pay a price, somewhere between a verbal reprimand and suspension without pay. Certainly a write-up in his service file.

That was, unless Ygo intervened and guided the outcome. Cuss was confident Ygo would protect him in the end. But given his obvious annoyance, Cuss thought Ygo might let him twist in the wind for a bit, punishing him in his own way.

Limping to bolster the image of an injured leg, he walked back to the *Nelly Marie* to clean up, eat, and mull options for replacing the help he wouldn't be getting from the locals.

"Any ideas for backup?" he asked Ygo as he climbed up to his bedroom. He'd almost said "partner" but caught himself. Ygo held that position, took the job very seriously, and was sensitive about his performance because he couldn't be at Cuss's side in the field like a traditional partner.

"MFOD says the *Kelly Sue* is half a day out. They've offered us Miles for three days." Ygo pronounced it emmfod, which was the Marshals Field Operations Desk, a central clearinghouse with staff available around the clock to coordinate field actions for marshals in real time. As for Miles Burton, interworld marshal and certified asshole, Cuss wasn't that desperate.

"Anyone else?"

"You know who else."

He opened his mouth to deny it, but after a moment's hesitation acknowledged that he did know. He sought an officer of the law, preferably a marshal or detective. An outsider, not someone constrained by the intense local oversight. Someone who had been inside the caves. Who'd be seen as a friendly by the Indies.

"Jesus, Ygo. She's going to tear me a new asshole."

"Make it about the job and professionalism. Avoid explaining that you can't control your urges."

"What are you talking about? She has *me* in her crosshairs."

"Something billions of men and women across the worlds would kill for."

"Now you're the one being bad."

"Make the ask, eat some crow, ask again. She'll come."

"Shit." He imagined making the call, and the pit of his stomach dropped into free fall.

Reaching into his closet, he removed his second-favorite jacket: a gray blazer with a modern cut and casual styling. Sliding into it, he promoted it to his new favorite, the previous one so damaged from the fight that he'd recycle it.

Then, heart thumping, he called Eve. She didn't answer.

Panicked, he closed the call without leaving a message, feeling the sudden need to fine-tune his spiel. After practicing it in his head, he called again. This time she answered.

"How may I help you, Marshal?" she asked in a precise, formal cadence.

The ice hadn't thawed. Not even a little bit. She glared at him with leveled eyebrows, lips pressed together.

He gave it his best. "I need backup for this job, Detective. Someone from the outside. After reviewing the situation here on the ground, I conclude that you are the most qualified person for the role. I'm calling to request your assistance. Will you come to Armstrong for a few days to help out?"

"I have a job here, Marshal." Her words were clipped, testy.

"If you're interested in the opportunity, I'll have the Marshals Service make the request to your commander. It won't be an issue."

"I fear I'd just get in the way of your *proper* guide."

There it was. Hurt feelings poking through to the surface. "I'm sorry I pushed you away. But you must know why."

"I don't, Marshal. Please enlighten me."

"Oh, stop. I need you here, Eve. First class all the way. But it's going to be all business. Nothing but work."

"What else would it be?" Then she sat back, her mouth agape. She shook her head slowly. "Oh. My. God. Are you talking about *sex*? How vain are you?"

His face turned bright red. He had bad days. Real bad days. And then there was today. He scrambled for a save, choosing to gaslight her. "Jesus, Eve. Where did that come from? I simply meant that we would be working very long hours. It will be a blur of exhaustion."

She bit her lip in a way that made him think she'd bought his bullshit. Like she'd been the one out of line. "Tell me what you have in mind."

. . .

After wolfing down a late lunch, Cuss set out from the *Nelly Marie* for an appointment arranged by Ygo: a visit with Professor Stockard's graduate student to gather background on the enclave. Eve would arrive early tomorrow afternoon. He would hold off meeting with cousin Johnny until she could join him.

Conrad University was in downtown Armstrong, the

capital city of Nova Terra, four million residents strong. To get there from Port Collins, he took the tram, an open-top affair made practical because there was no weather under the basin's clear polymer dome. No wind. No rain. No changes in temperature. After switching lines at Pioneer Hill, he stepped from the car at University Station.

The campus took up one side of a city square. The other three sides held shops catering to students. Fast food, cheap drinks, games, music, clothing, sundries. It was busy, mostly young people milling about in brightly colored clothes of silk, cotton, and chiffon folded and draped with a dramatic flair. They reminded Cuss of the opulent garments he'd seen in both arid and tribal settings on Earth. But as a guy who wore black pants, a blue dress shirt, and a gray sport coat pretty much every day, he wasn't the best person to judge fashion.

The core of the campus was dominated by three medium-size buildings. Like every structure more than ten years old in the city, they were constructed of dark stone and covered with olive-green vines. The grounds were eye-catching, in part because of the beautiful plantings that gave the setting a luxurious feel. But the most impressive feature was the large field to the left of the buildings, a stadium complex with rare open space that could be configured for dozens of different events.

"Which one am I going to?" Cuss asked as he made his way across the square. No personal vehicles were allowed in the city, so it was a pedestrian paradise in that sense. But the younger crowd tended to walk in broad, energetic leaps, so he still had to pay attention to avoid a collision.

"The one to the right. Sixth floor."

Striding up the walkway toward the building entrance, he passed a courtyard set amid a cluster of bushes, a meeting area for students. He was surprised it was so busy given that education as he understood it was a virtual experience. He was also dismayed by the litter in the courtyard and along the walkway. There wasn't a lot, but any was unusual. It meant that either the students were committed slobs or the cleaning bots weren't functioning as they should.

Inside, the building lobby felt shabby, as if it needed more than just surface cleaning. The gray floor had chipped tiles. Dark stains marred the off-white ceiling. The state of the walls was difficult to determine because announcements were posted everywhere, a haphazard display of posts in a rainbow of colors: roommates wanted, tutoring services for hire, items for sale, rides needed.

A steady stream of people were moving up and down the stairway to his left, walking casually, preoccupied. Reaching that level of indifference took practice because the steps here were taller and broader than those on Earth. He joined the queue, concentrating while he matched his timing to the flow, and then he bounded up the steps.

"Right," said Ygo as Cuss stepped into the sixth-floor hallway. "Room 603."

The corridor was quiet. And unlike the lobby, surprisingly tidy. Room 603 was two doors down from the stairwell. He squared up in front of the door, faux wood made of a painted alloy, metal mined during basin excavation. A chime alerted the occupant inside that a visitor awaited.

"This is Tolly Vaughn," said Ygo.

The door opened. A young woman, late twenties, freckles, slight, maybe ninety-five pounds on Earth, looked at him with nervous eyes. Anxious. "Did Wallace report me?" She turned and walked into the room. "What an asshole."

Cuss followed her into a small, sparsely furnished office. No windows. A few pictures on the walls. A desk, three chairs, and a low-rise bookcase, all made in the same style of furniture found across the city, the early efforts of Nova Terra manufacturing. A binder stuffed with paper printouts, something rarely seen in the modern age, sat on top of the bookcase. The shelves held souvenir beer mugs from a dozen different establishments.

She dropped into the desk chair, motioned for him to sit in a visitor's chair across from her, and then folded her arms in a defensive fashion. "I'm confused why a space cop would give a shit either way."

"Can we back up?" Still standing, he flashed a winning smile and held up his Interworld Marshal badge. He chose not to correct her about his title. "I'm Cuss Abbott. I understand you're Tolly Vaughn?"

She nodded.

"Nice to meet you." He reached a hand across the desk. She hesitated and then shook it. Her tiny hand was lost in his huge mitt. She looked away. Shy.

Unlike the young people in the square, Tolly had a plain look. Straight brown hair to her shoulders. Pleasant face. Minimal makeup. No jewelry. No visible piercings or tattoos. A gray T-shirt with *Conrad University* emblazoned on the front in orange and blue. Khaki shorts.

"I'm not here about that asshole Wallace."

Her head tilted and her forehead scrunched. She waited.

"I'm involved in a police action with the Indies and am here to gather intelligence. I've been told that you and Professor Stockard are the gurus for insider information?"

She nodded slowly and then grinned, lighting up her face. "I know a few things. What do you need?"

He sat. "That's part of the problem. I don't know what I don't know and that makes it difficult to ask good questions. I've skimmed a few articles and watched some feeds, but it's all information from a distance. How about this: What's *your* perspective on these people? Who are they? What do they want? How far will they go to get it?"

To give her time to think, he changed topics. "I was surprised to see so many students here on campus. Aren't classes virtual?"

"Of course. Enrollment is something like a hundred sixty thousand from across the worlds. What you're seeing is a tiny fraction of the student population. Some are here because their degree requires a lab or field class they have to take in person. The rest just want to get away from home."

Cuss smiled, thinking back to his raucous time at the University of Florida. Then he steered the conversation back to the case. "What's your role?"

"My academic role? I'm a teaching assistant for

Stockard's classes, and I'm working on a master's in public policy."

"Studying the Indies?"

"Sort of. I'm analyzing the colossal series of fuckups that led Nova Terra to this point, that being the existence of a separatist society with legal status whose methods and priorities are at odds with the status quo. I mean, policy theory is well established and the leadership here followed the textbook of what not to do, just sleepwalking their way into this mess. Like waiting for cancer to really take hold before doing something about it. Dumb."

"How many Indies live in the caves?"

She sat up. "Wow. You asked the right question right out of the box."

"I'm not sure what she's talking about," said Ygo.

Neither did Cuss.

"For my work, I needed a demographic profile of the population. Get an accurate picture of who we're dealing with. So we coordinated with the mayor's office and got our hands on a government tracking tool."

"POTS?"

She nodded. "That's the one. I used it to track activity at the cave mouth, having it identify the people coming and going during a two-week window. I expected to see everyone at least once in that time except for maybe infants and the sick. Anyway, POTS logged a bunch of errors because there were people coming out of the cave twice in row without ever going back inside. Others were going in twice without ever coming out."

"Another entrance?"

"That was my first thought." She gestured to the binder stuffed with paper. "I borrowed the original geological survey from the library to see if I could figure it out. Turns out there's a whole warren of caves and tunnels in there. I thought that could explain the anomalies."

"I hear a 'but.'"

"But I also wondered if POTS could have a bug. So I started hanging out at Squally's Pub. They have an outdoor patio that overlooks the tunnel entrance. I've been sipping brew, studying the cave networks to see if I can find a back door, and whenever someone comes or goes from the tunnel, I check to see what POTS is reporting. On the second day of my stakeout—this is about a month ago—a guy walks out, comes into the pub, and sits at a table two over from mine. He's not showing up in POTS."

"What did you do?"

"What do you mean?"

"Did you approach him? Alert the authorities?"

"Hell no. I was *so* excited." She became animated as she relived the moment. "It gives my research a whole new dimension. Since then I've documented three more events. It means the city doesn't really know the population they're dealing with. And that means their strategies for countering the Indies could miss the mark."

"Four events total?" He thought about how the police investigators had found just three so far. Then he realized the implications of this revelation on his own case.

Ygo was right there with him. "You could breach the entrance and go in after them, create an interworld incident and everything, only to find out they aren't even in there."

"Yup, four," said Tolly, nodding. "For my thesis, I'm proposing a framework for making policy when there's imprecise knowledge of the target population, with guidelines that will minimize the fuckups our leaders have committed."

"Are a few missing people really enough to impact public policy?"

"Truthfully? No." She shrugged and then smiled. "But Stockard likes my theoretical framework. Thinks it's novel. Says if I write it up, it's enough for a master's. That's all I care about."

"How long before you share your missing-people discovery with the authorities?"

"Stockard wants our names attached to the policy idea, so we're scrambling to get that published. While we work on that, I'm supposed to keep watching for missing people. More data strengthens the work."

"Darlena is going to go ballistic if you delay telling her," said Ygo.

"We should have a draft ready in a couple of weeks," continued Tolly. "Then we're going to make a presentation to the city."

"They'll be upset that you waited."

"*Pffft*," she said in a dismissive fashion. "First, the Indies have been doing their thing for the better part of twenty years. How could a few weeks possibly matter? And I just told you all about it. Problem solved. I've done my duty."

"Now you *have* to tell Darlena," said Ygo.

Tolly checked the time and stood. "I'm following a

formal observation schedule that has me at Squally's in half an hour. Join me? See if we get lucky? We can bring the survey binder, and I'll show you the cave networks."

Chapter 11

Squally's Pub sat at the base of the perimeter wall, the towering cliff a facet of Moon living. The wall was a background feature, something people generally ignored as they went about their day. But in those moments when Nova Terrans lifted their heads and contemplated the soaring rock face, dappled by volcanic flows and asteroid impacts during the maelstrom of lunar formation, and carved by humans eons later using powerful explosives and huge machines, most found it awe-inspiring.

The pub itself was a local dive, a small place, a neighborhood watering hole plunked on the end of a street, the cliff across the way casting a shadow in the waning light. The pub entrance was a crusty red door. As they approached, Cuss glanced through the front window but was distracted by the dirt.

Tolly led the way inside, their feet *shlopping* with each step on the sticky floor. The place smelled of stale beer and old men.

The bar top ran from front to back along the wall to the right, a stained metallic surface long enough for eight stools. Three men were seated at it, glasses in front of them, empty stools between them, the youngest maybe sixty years old. They watched a game together on a holodisplay, sharing a vacant stare. Cuss figured them for the neighborhood regulars.

The bar was tended by a hairy guy, beefy, bored, leaning against the ice maker while he watched the game with the men. He turned to them as they entered. Tolly held up two fingers and wiggled them. He drew two beers in heavy clear mugs, put a lid on each—a necessity to control sloshing in weak gravity—and plopped them on the bar top in front of her.

As Tolly collected the drinks, she tilted a head toward Cuss. "He's paying." She left him there while she carried the mugs up a step and out the back door.

With a self-conscious smile, Cuss added a bowl of spugals to their order—a local snack that was something like pretzels formed into tortilla chips—started a tab, and followed.

The patio was a modest-size deck with four picnic tables, the kind where the bench seats were attached to the table itself. He and Tolly were the only customers out there.

"This is my spot." She walked to a table near the patio rail. It had a clear view of the tunnel entrance.

She sat with both legs under the table, facing the brick forecourt not thirty meters away. If he sat next to her in the same fashion, his back would be toward the pub door, creating a vulnerability that ran counter to his nature. So he straddled the seat, a long leg on each side, facing her, allowing him to see both the cave and deck with a sweep of his head.

The view was perfect. The entrance looked much like what he'd seen in the feed. But here he could feel the cliff on his face, a coolness radiating from the rock, a rich moisture from the veil of plants.

Tolly plopped the binder she'd dragged from her office onto the table, drank half her beer, let out a quiet belch, tucked her hair behind her ears, and looked over the railing. "There it is."

"Nice spot." There was a wall just inside the tunnel, a stone barricade about as high as Cuss was tall. A single opening, a gateway, allowed for scrutiny and control of those who walked through.

As they watched, a middle-aged woman moved out through the gateway and onto the forecourt.

"Oh!" said Tolly when she saw her, scrambling to open a personal display. She looked, said, "Nope," and then showed Cuss. POTS could see the woman, identifying her as Danette Fricano.

Tolly took another swig, and he joined her with a sip, pleasantly surprised by the beer's crisp flavor. He sipped again while Tolly prattled. She was an entertaining person, bouncing from topic to topic, using her hands to add drama to her stories, effusive in her speech, smiling a lot.

"What's up with Wallace the asshole?" he asked when she paused to take a breath.

She thought for a moment, sighed, and shook her head. "I'd been doing a great job keeping my mouth shut about the POTS anomalies. Then Wallace Baruchel, a grad student for a different professor, sits next to me at seminar yesterday. He's always bragging about his successes, making me feel bad about myself. I thought I could finally one-up him, so I spilled the beans about missing Indies. He was upset I hadn't reported the find to the authorities and became super self-righteous, threatening to report it himself if I didn't. I figured he followed through with his threat."

By the time they were ready for a second round, they'd seen four Indies pass through the entryway, all accounted for by POTS. When she stood to fetch the beers, Cuss said, "I'll have a black coffee."

"Baby," she teased before going into the bar.

She returned with a beer and a coffee. Sitting next to him, she pulled the geological survey binder in front of her, scooting closer to him so he could see, pressing her thigh against his knee as she did so. Opening the book, she spent a few moments turning pages back and forth, and then spread the book out, pressing down on the binding as she smoothed pages with the palms of her hands. "Check this out." She touched his forearm.

The page held a busy diagram showing a crisscross of underground passages, the result of volcanic activity during the Moon's primordial period. While Cuss tried to decipher the map, Ygo said, "If the Indies did a little digging, they could connect tunnels to access a half-dozen locations in Armstrong." He used Cuss's lens to show him possible routes leading under the city.

Tolly had puzzled through a couple of the routes on her own. As she traced her discoveries, Cuss watched her act the coquette, using his name, touching his knee, playing with her hair, leaning into him when laughing at a funny remark. She had switched to coffee as well, and they chewed up the evening talking and laughing. All thirty-two of the Indies they saw in that period were tracked by POTS.

"That's a wrap for tonight," she said eventually. "There's a great ice cream shop on the way to my place. Walk me home and I'll buy you one."

He studied her, pretty sure he knew where she was headed, trying to decide if he wanted to engage. He liked her. Found her appealing. And he couldn't deny his own needs. Eve had his libido twisted in knots.

"Can I ask how old are you, Tolly?"

"Old enough, Cuss. Twenty-six if you must know."

He delayed while he decided. "Where do you live?"

"Not far. Why, do you have somewhere else to be?"

He didn't. Not until Eve arrived. "No. And I like ice cream."

. . .

He didn't know what he'd expected from her apartment, but it wasn't the bold, industrial look he found. Exposed brick, beams, and ductwork all in one large room. Airy. Primitive paintings hung on the walls. Repurposed furniture gave the place a bohemian feel.

"This building was the original project management headquarters back in the early years of city construction," said Tolly.

"It's nice," he said as he took it in. "Impressive for a grad student."

"It's my uncle's. He bought it as an investment." She scanned the room as though seeing it for the first time.

"Lucky me. Care for a drink?"

"I'm fine."

"I'm going to have a nightcap." She took a bottle with a fancy label from a grouping in a corner cabinet and poured two fingers of a yellowish liquid—Cuss guessed a local brandy—into a tumbler, added one ice cube, and held it up to him. "Cheers." She paused with the drink at her lips. "While I'm still sober, I consent to whatever dirty deeds I hope you're imagining right now."

She tipped her head back and downed the drink. Her face twisted momentarily as the alcohol burned her throat. "Ahh. Mother's milk," she said with a grin.

He laughed.

She moved to stand in front of him. Her head reached only to his chest, her body so tiny he could nearly encircle her waist with his hands. She smelled faintly of lilacs.

She stood on her toes and lifted her face, inviting him to kiss her. He obliged.

"You taste like pistachio," she said. It was the ice cream flavor he'd had on the walk to her flat.

He picked her up. She clasped her hands behind his neck, her legs around his waist. He carried her through the living area to her sleeping space in the far corner and plopped her onto the edge of the bed. She lifted her arms over her head, and he pulled off her shirt. She was so skinny he could see her ribs, her breasts tiny buds. Her shy smile fed his growing ardor.

She was half his size. Less. He was concerned about crushing her. Hurting her. So he lay on his back and let her climb on top. She enjoyed herself, the uninhibited cowgirl riding her bronco.

He had so much fun he decided to stay the night, hoping for a reprise in the morning.

. . .

Cuss woke to the sound of a bell. It took him a moment to orient himself.

"Who the hell is that?" mumbled Tolly, cuddling against him in bed.

The bell chimed again.

With a sigh, she climbed over him, padded to her dresser, and used a viewer to see who was at the door.

Naked women were on Cuss's short list of favorite things, and he watched her the whole time, learning to appreciate her waifish figure.

"Don't know her," said Tolly. She grabbed a white terrycloth robe and threw it on as she made for the door.

"You're going to answer?" Most people would talk to a stranger electronically without opening the door.

"She's so pretty," Tolly called over her shoulder. "I want to see for myself."

That comment alone should have been enough to warn Cuss. Maybe waking up in a strange bed had disoriented him. Perhaps Tolly's pheromones had addled his brain. Whatever the reason, he was caught off guard.

"Oh," he heard Eve say when the door opened. "I was told Cuss Abbott was here? Marshal Abbott?"

"He's here. Come on in."

When he realized it was Eve, his face burned with the humiliation of a thousand suns. He knew instantly that Ygo had done this, created this incredibly awkward moment as punishment for his unnecessary shooting of Broken Nose.

"Eve," he called from the bed, rushing his words, gathering the sheets in case he needed to stand. "There's a restaurant across the street. I'll meet you there in twenty minutes."

"Oh, my goodness." Her face flushed red and she held up her hands, fingers spread like shields in an attempt to block the view. "I am so sorry. I was told to meet you here." She turned and scurried out the door.

"Go to Florentines at the end of the block," Tolly called after her. "They have the best breakfast in the neighborhood."

"She's a beauty," she continued as Cuss scrambled into the bathroom. "How is she in bed?"

"She's a colleague," he huffed as he shut the door. "I wouldn't know."

He spoke to Ygo as he stepped into the shower. "Good one. Please tell me you're done. That this is your pound of flesh."

. . .

Florentines was an automated eating establishment, everything cooked to order by bots. The décor was a testament to shiny metal: gleaming tabletops, countertops, ductwork, stools, cabinets. Posters on the wall showed aerial views of cities on Earth: Venice, Rio de Janeiro, Kyoto, Budapest.

Eve sat in the first booth, facing the door, waiting for him. She wasn't smiling. "I followed directions from your end, so I'm confused about what you were trying to say with that little performance. Were you trying impress me? To mock me?" She checked the time and continued before he could respond. "You know, it doesn't matter. I'm done here. There's a flight home in three hours and you're paying."

"I'm sorry for what you saw. I never asked anyone to direct you here. I'd been told you'd land later today. Did you catch an earlier flight?"

"Nope. I took the one your people arranged."

Ygo was more upset with him than he'd realized. He shook his head. "I intended to meet you at Port Collins. I wish this hadn't happened. Seriously. We're both victims."

"That child you were with is the biggest victim. Jesus, Cuss. Isn't statutory rape a thing on the Moon?"

"She's twenty-six." He could hear the edge in his voice. "Careful with the accusations."

They both went quiet. Calibrating their positions. Assessing their righteousness.

"You're self-absorbed, Cuss, so I'm picturing you interpreting my annoyance as jealousy. Know that's the furthest thing from the truth. This is about dignity. Respect. Decency."

"Now I feel bad," said Ygo. "And Tolly turns twenty-six next week. But close enough."

"I haven't done anything wrong, Eve, and I can't explain how you got directed here. It's a major-league fuckup."

She looked down at her hands.

"Bridge's killers are just down the road," he continued. "They may not face justice unless we do something about it." She seemed to be listening, so he bulled ahead, taking her through what he'd learned. He explained that the locals sought to stay an arm's length from the Indies out of fear it could affect impending high-stakes legal proceedings. They were using the fact that the murder occurred on another world to slow-walk the investigation. And as for POTS, the Indies could execute the invisibility trick at will. The local police were just starting to realize it could explain a number of unsolved crimes.

"On top of it all," said Cuss. "The Indies appear to have a backdoor tunnel system that adds to their potential for mischief. I'm not sure if the locals even know about it yet."

His flow was interrupted by his "urgent" chime. Darlena was calling. Excusing himself, he slid from the booth. As he did so, he heard a different tone behind him. Eve was receiving a call herself.

As he seated himself in an empty booth, back toward Eve, Ygo told him, "The locals found Vincent dead in a hotel room here in downtown Armstrong."

"No shit?" Cuss glanced back at Eve, who was deep in conversation. He answered the call. "Good morning, Darlena."

"Hello, Cuss. You know a Vincent Rogalski from down your way?"

"I do."

"A housekeeper at the Lofta Hotel found him floating in his bathtub about an hour ago. Fully clothed. Facedown. Like someone held his head underwater until he drowned."

"Vincent is an accomplice in my murder case. Has the scene been processed?"

"Crime tech just started. They'll be here for a couple of hours."

"Am I welcome on the scene?"

"You can come and watch, but stay clear of Hobby."

"I'm with a colleague from Lagrange. Detective Eve Boucher. Can she tag along?"

"She needs an official role. I'll have to explain her presence."

"That's not a problem." If Ygo was done with his games, he could hire Eve as a consultant to the Marshals Service in minutes. In fact, he'd probably done so already when he arranged to fly her here.

Eve was finishing her call, and he shifted back to join her.

"That was my commander," said Eve. "The locals found Vincent Rogalski here in Armstrong. Murdered. She asked me to liaise on the case."

"So you have an official role?"

She picked up her satchel, a handsome bag that served as both her purse and briefcase. Hooking the strap over her shoulder, she stood. "I'm here independent of you, Marshal. I have my own assignment and responsibilities."

. . .

There were seven of them crowding the hallway outside of room 321 of the Lofta Hotel. A uniformed cop stood at the door, controlling the scene. Darlena, Hobby, Cuss, and Eve huddled in front of him, watching the crime scene techs on a hoverview. A few steps away, the hotel night manager and the housekeeper who found Vincent waited to be questioned.

The display showed a spacious bathroom with lots of polished stone, cut glass mirrors, and ornate fixtures, opulence that justified the hotel's outrageous pricing. Two of the crime techs, identified by their white coveralls, were pulling Vincent out of the tub and placing him in a coffin-like body bag, a water-tight container they'd use to transport him to the morgue. A third tech guided Vincent's arms over the container to capture the water splooshing from his clothes.

Vincent's face was ashen. Lips blue. Eyes bugged out.

Eve zoomed the display and pointed at Vincent's neck. "He's been strangled. See these two thin bruise lines across his throat? They're perfectly spaced an inch apart all the way around, like you'd get from the edges of a strap."

"Maybe a belt," said Hobby.

Ygo zoomed Cuss's lens, showing him a closeup of Vincent's eyes. Broken capillaries had created ugly red splotches that were bright against the white sclera. "Subconjunctival hemorrhaging is consistent with strangulation," he said. A pause. "A belt around the neck is about as personal as it gets." Then, "Why is he dressed for church?" which was Ygo-speak for a person wearing dressier clothes. In Vincent's case, a collared shirt, cuffed slacks, and polished shoes. Plus, he was clean-shaven.

While two of the white suits sealed the body bag, the third, who Ygo identified as the medical examiner, exited the bathroom. Moments later he appeared behind the cop at the door. Pulling off his clear faceplate, he squeezed past the officer and joined them in the hallway. He kept in place the white hood covering his head, giving his face a round appearance as if he were peering at them through a porthole.

"Hello, Dr. Mackleberry," said Darlena. "Care to share a preliminary?"

Phillip Mackleberry was a somber guy, mid-fifties, tired. He looked askance at Hobby. "Last time I gave you a preliminary, someone blabbed it to the press like it was an official result. I looked like an ass when I had to correct it after the autopsy."

Darlena's face remained a mask, but Cuss imagined her reading Hobby the riot act when they were alone.

"When will you have an official COD?" asked Eve.

"There are a few things that I need to clear off my station. I should be able to start on him after lunch, and if it goes as I suspect, I'll have cause and time of death about three hours later. That's assuming he doesn't get bumped by a higher priority."

"Is the morgue at the hospital?"

Phillip looked at Eve for the first time. His face softened as he took her in. "That's right. Gleason Medical

Center. In the basement, down the hall from my office."
He smiled. "I'm Phillip, by the way. Come by later this
afternoon and I'll share what I've learned."

"I know the way," said Hobby, sounding like an
anxious teenager. "I can show you."

"Thank you, Hobby," said Eve. "I'd appreciate that."

Darlena rolled her eyes and moved down the hall to
interview the night manager and housekeeper.

Hobby faced Eve, shifting his stance so his back was
to Cuss. "Darlena and I are going to scan the feeds to learn
about the vic's last minutes. You have a good eye. Why
don't you tag along?"

Even though Hobby was clearly omitting Cuss from
his invitation, Eve was gracious enough to include him.
"Will you join us?" she asked, leaning around Hobby to
look at him.

"My boss is itching for an update," replied Cuss. "I'll
catch up with you later."

It was another one of those technical truths. In fact,
Girish Mannan wanted a report from him. But that wasn't
what he'd be doing. He wanted to dissect the feeds with
Ygo, and they would be far more productive if it was just
the two of them.

. . .

The Lofta Hotel had a café off the lobby. As he stood at its
entrance and viewed the setting—furniture, carpet, drapes,
lighting, decorations—he felt the individual pieces had a

cozy appeal that seemed warm and personal. Yet as he made his way through the room, the overall effect felt cold, institutional.

Hoping for privacy, he took a booth in the back and waited while the server brought him a grilled cheese sandwich and a carafe of coffee. After taking a bite and a sip, he sat back to learn what Ygo had found.

"What happened seems pretty straightforward," said Ygo as he queued up the first feed. "But because of the invisibility trick, the doer will be difficult to identify."

Cuss's lens came alive with a scene of Vincent standing in the forecourt at the mouth of the tunnel. He was bouncing on his toes in the weak gravity, yelling for Abbi to come talk to him. Far from a romantic gesture, his actions seemed deranged. At one point, a flash of anger and actual finger pointing added to the spectacle.

"He dressed up for this?" asked Cuss.

"Apparently. He keeps it up for twenty minutes," said Ygo. "Then this…"

Vincent stopped bouncing and yelling, and looked at the tunnel entrance, waiting. After a few moments, his head swiveled to the left and right. He was talking, gesticulating, but the sound was garbled.

"Why can't we hear?"

"I'm guessing it's a feature of their invisibility trick. That he's talking to people he can see but we can't. I've viewed the feeds from a few commercial establishments that have sensors pointed toward the forecourt, and they show what we're seeing here."

"*Aren't* seeing, you mean."

"Exactly. I can't figure out how it works. Whoever designed it is a serious genius."

Vincent began to walk, talking as he moved, making for the tunnel, disappearing through the gate.

"I've scanned the feeds from here until he's found dead. He never comes out."

"Because they made him invisible? Or did they take him out through a back door?"

"Not sure but I'm leaning toward a back door."

The scene changed to a different setting. Now Vincent was walking down a plush corridor. Cuss recognized it as the hallway outside Vincent's room in the Lofta Hotel. He was alone, moving with purpose, a determined look on his face. He reached room 321 and entered. The door closed behind him.

"Did you see it?" asked Ygo.

Cuss had. The door had just started to close when it opened again. Like a twitch. And then it closed for good. As if someone else had entered the room along with Vincent. Or right behind him.

"What time was this?"

"Last night at twenty-two forty-two. Sixteen minutes later, the door opens but no one comes or goes. Presumably Vincent is dead at that point."

"Did you follow him backward?"

"Vincent? I did." Ygo showed brief scenes as he spoke. "Here he is entering the hotel lobby. Here he is walking down Pismo Road toward the hotel. And here he is exiting Roust Escapes onto Pismo Road. I can't find where he enters Roust's."

Roust Escapes offered virtual holidays, vivid experiences you could enjoy from the comfort and convenience of their event rooms in the back of the shop. While their offerings were unique, their storefront was unremarkable, a door and a sign like the dozen other establishments along that street.

"Any chance the tunnel network leads there?"

"Don't know. This part of the city wasn't on the map Tolly showed you. And I can't find that book—the original geological survey—on any feeds."

"Where is it now?"

"The binder is in her apartment. Tolly is there as well. She's working from home today."

Cuss ate the rest of his sandwich in two bites, washing it down with the last of the coffee. "Let's go say hi."

. . .

Tolly was surprised to see him. "Don't tell me Miss Perfect turned you down?" She was leaning against the doorjamb in white tights and a tube top, arms crossed, shaking her head. Fresh out of the shower, her hair was wet and her skin pink. "The thing about a one-night stand is that it's for one night. I'd already started editing the memory of you in my head, elevating the good parts. Now you've jumbled it all up."

She turned and walked into her apartment, leaving the door open. He took it as an invitation and followed her inside. She went to the kitchen and resumed the task of slicing a tomato, dumping the pieces into a bowl of lettuce.

"I couldn't stay away," he said, scanning the room. He spotted the geological survey on the kitchen table where she'd dumped it the night before. He moved to it and opened the cover. "Your binder has me in its grip."

She paused in her meal prep. "I knew you weren't here for me."

"Why do you say that?"

"Because Miss Perfect is your speed. You were slumming it with me."

"Nonsense. I desire you *and* your binder. They aren't mutually exclusive needs."

She smiled. "I like how I morphed from a desire to a need."

"Yeah, but so did your binder."

She thought about it a second and shrugged. "Still, I'll take it." She joined him at the table. "You're after something. Tell me."

He told her about a possible tunnel exit inside Roust Escapes.

Her forehead creased. "Never heard of it."

"It's on Pismo Road." Ygo told him the address, and he passed it on.

"That's in the northwest quadrant, not far from the university." Squaring the binder on the table in front of her, she flipped over a fistful of pages and then did so again, moving deep into the book. She turned individual pages back and forth. "The maps are toward the front of each section."

"There," said Ygo.

"This one," said Cuss, putting his hand on the page to mark it.

Tolly pressed the book flat and studied the cave network shown in the diagram. She spoke a string of commands, and a hoverview opened above the table, the display showing a duplicate of the cave network in the book. A few commands later and a street map of the city appeared, superimposed over the cave network. They leaned forward to study the result.

Ygo highlighted where Roust Escapes was located. Working backward from there, he identified a series of natural channels and fissures and caves that could be connected to reach the main enclave. Cuss showed it to Tolly.

Tolly repeated the exercise, using a finger to trace from Roust Escapes through the passageways to reach the enclave, then forward again, following the route back to Roust's. "If that's a good tunnel sequence, then wouldn't this be one, too?" She traced a branch off the path Ygo had identified. It ended near the university.

"It could be," said Ygo.

Cuss could see the similarities as well. "Maybe so."

"I pass two blocks from there on my way to work." She zoomed in on that section, her face a mask of concentration. Then she nodded. "I know this place. It's an old building on the edge of the university property."

"What's it used for?"

"It was a pump station from the early days," said Ygo. "Now the university uses it for storage."

"Not a clue." She looked at him with a mischievous smile. "Let's go check it out."

Cuss's face tingled. If it was indeed a tunnel entrance, it would be monitored. Protected. Approach would be perilous. It wasn't something to do without planning. And it wasn't something for civilians, especially not for an impulsive grad student.

"I can't let you do that, Tolly. These people are killers. It's crazy dangerous."

"You can't *let* me?" she scoffed. It was a new Tolly.

"It's an expression. The message is the same."

"My sister likes to say, 'Give a man a taste and he thinks that puts him in charge.'" She moved to her corner bedroom and slipped on a pair of jeans. Looking in a mirror over her dresser, she ran a brush through her hair. "But from my experience, a more accurate version is, 'Men think they're in charge.'" She turned her back to him, pulled off her tube top, and replaced it with a T-shirt. "I'll cut you slack because you're trying to be chivalrous, which is cute and all, but know that bossy is a turnoff. Anyway, I need to go into the office. Instead of being a shit, why don't you walk with me?"

"This isn't going to end well," said Ygo.

"At least eat your salad before we go," said Cuss.

Chapter 12

Tolly didn't disappoint, taking a route to her office that "coincidentally" passed by the mystery building on the edge of the university grounds. And when it came into view, she continued with her predictable actions.

"That's it." She pointed, veering down a dirt path that led toward a low, dark structure. Built of stone block, much of it was buried in uncontrolled vegetation, a tangle of neglect so thick it looked as if the plants were eating the building from the rear.

On full alert, Cuss followed behind, brainstorming ways to dissuade her. "Look but don't touch."

"Bossy."

A small dirt parking lot in front of the building served a front door and two broad garage-style doors. There were no signs of life as they approached. No carts in the parking lot. No background thrum of equipment.

"I'm not trying to be bossy. Think it through. The Indies have killed. If this is one of their tunnel entrances, it's an incredibly dangerous place to be."

"Did they take away your balls when they gave you your badge?"

"This isn't about bravery, Tolly. They attacked me once already, so there's no question of danger. I also want to preserve this entrance for a proper breach. If we burn it now, it's useless to us."

She grinned. "We don't know for sure if it even *is* an entrance. We have to at least answer that."

"No, we don't." But he was speaking to her back as she leapt ahead.

The front door was chipped and scarred, the paint fading. In the top half was an insert of small windowpanes set in a three-by-three grid. Cuss blew the dust off the pane in the top-row middle, scraped it with the tips of his fingers, and used his lens to peer through the dirt and dark.

He expected to see a small reception area or front lobby, but instead he saw a large open space filled with old stuff, all of it coated in a layer of fine dust. Toward the back were cowlings for big equipment like pumps and compressors. In front of that, pipes and fittings. Machine tools. Buckets filled with smaller pieces. And at the very front, nearest the window, two old lorries, early model commercial buggies used for hauling equipment and people. Both carts looked clean and well-kept, perhaps destined for a museum if they survived a few more decades.

With his attention focused on the scene inside, Cuss didn't notice Tolly working her way around the outside of the building. But Ygo did.

"She's going to trip an alert. When the Indies see you out here, they'll know it isn't a false alarm."

"I'll bet they know I'm out here already. And I have no idea how to control her. I'm open to suggestions."

He gauged the height of the ceiling through the window and then stepped back from the door to view the exterior of the building. The roofline matched the ceiling inside, so there was no attic. Shifting his eyes downward, he examined the foundation but couldn't tell from the clues available if there was a basement.

Tolly was nowhere in sight, and he walked to the corner where she'd disappeared. He peered through the foliage there but couldn't see her.

"Tolly?" he called in a medium-loud voice.

The side of the building was a single, unbroken wall of dark stone. The terrain sloped downward from front to rear, exposing a lower foundation, confirming there was a basement level of some kind.

He squeezed into a narrow gap between the wall and the mass of vegetation, stepping over roots and pushing aside branches, making his way to the back. Barbs caught on his coat as he progressed, pulling at the threads, making him wonder briefly if he'd have to choose yet another favorite jacket from his dwindling collection.

"Tolly?" he called again, still controlling the volume of his voice.

Around back he found a recess in the foundation with a door to the lower level. A faint trail of footprints led from the door out through a break in the plant growth to his left. With his lens, he identified shoe impressions of different sizes and shapes along the trail, some leading toward the door and others leading away, old ones fading into the dust, new ones crisp and clear.

"It's possible they're from university employees visiting the storeroom," said Ygo. "Maybe students nosing about."

Cuss shook his head. "Double or nothing it's Indies

accessing a tunnel."

The back entrance was like the front, a battle-scarred door with a three-by-three grid of smaller windows at the top. Unlike the front, the lower right pane of this grid had been pushed in, dislodged from its framework by a solid blow. A hefty rock. The heel of a shoe. The fact that the pane hung inward—still whole because modern glass didn't break—meant that whoever hit it had done so from the outside. Fresh marks in the dust confirmed it was a recent event.

"Tolly?" he called through the open pane, louder this time. He couldn't see her.

"In here."

"Goddamn it," he muttered, trying to contain his fury. He was angry at her for ruining the place as a future breach point. Angry because she just told the Indies that the authorities knew about the tunnels. And he was furious with himself because he didn't have his gun with him. When he had left the *Nelly Marie* the day before, he thought he'd be chatting with a grad student. Maybe Darlena. Not this.

Peering through the window, he saw office furniture lining the side walls, with unorganized piles of junk in the middle of the room. Old rags and tarps and plastic sheeting gathered in a heap. A dozen boxes were scattered about, some open, everything covered in dust.

The trail of footprints continued through the room, a faint path weaving through the junk, disappearing behind a tall crate at the back. A hallway led off to the left behind the crate. He figured that's where the trail led.

"Hey!" cried Tolly.

A feature of Cuss's lens amplified soundwaves, letting him hear her muffled voice in the next room. She was surprised. Scared.

"Oof," she grunted. Then silence.

"Tolly! No games. Are you okay?"

No response.

"Goddamn it!" This time he shouted, smacking the foundation wall next to the door with an open hand. It was an impossible situation. He needed to move quickly to help her. But it was foolhardy to do so without backup or a weapon.

As quickly as he could, he called Eve but was rolled to her message system. Same for Darlena. In both cases he marked his call as urgent. They'd call back in the next minutes. But he couldn't wait. He'd delayed too long already.

"Cover me," he said to Ygo as he snaked a hand inside and touched the door controls on the wall near the damaged pane. The door opened.

"I have two patrol officers on the way," said Ygo. "They'll be there in four minutes."

"Send them in after me. And call for more."

As Cuss followed the path through the junk, he snatched a stick off the floor, a castoff leg from an old stool. Swinging it like a baseball bat, he gauged its weight, approving its heft. Then he tried to flex it, confirming it was strong and rigid.

As he approached the crate, he veered wide, concerned about a sneak attack from someone lurking behind. No one was there, so he leaned forward and took a quick peek down the hallway, snapping his head back in case of danger.

There was a doorway at the far end, maybe five strides away, open, light spilling out. No Tolly.

"That light is probably a trip wire," said Ygo. "When it activates, alarms go off."

"Help!" Tolly's voice was growing fainter.

Cuss rushed toward the light. "Can you see her?"

Ygo answered but his response was garbled. And then their connection failed.

Cuss stopped in his tracks.

The Marshals Service had paired Cuss with Ygo six years earlier. At the time, it had been a difficult transition for Cuss. His new partner rode along on his shoulder, always there, seeing the same things he saw, hearing all his conversations, witnessing his successes and failures, watching him negotiate every aspect of life. At the start he felt judged, crowded.

But he grew into it, learning that the arrangement offered benefits. Ygo was a good-natured soul. Accommodating. Fun. Professional. He nurtured and supported Cuss, a voice inside his head who helped with everything. After a period of compromise to establish boundaries, the unique arrangement let Cuss be more successful in both life and work. He began to rely on his partner for everything. To wield him as a tool when on the job. To share experiences with him as a friend at all other times.

So losing contact with him for the first time in six years was borderline traumatic.

"Whoa," he said, putting a hand on the doorframe to stabilize himself. Since it had never happened before, he presumed it was a blip. A temporary condition. That Ygo would return at any moment. "Are you there?"

Nothing.

Unsettled, he moved back to the front room. Ygo returned. "What's going on?" Cuss asked.

"The hallway is blocked," said Ygo. "I can't figure out how, though."

Tolly's first cries had been forever ago. Cuss needed to act, even if alone.

"If the Indies did this," Ygo continued, "it surely extends beyond the hallway. You need to wait for backup."

He couldn't. "Goddamn it," he muttered, rushing down the hallway, entering a weird silence. A singular existence that was normal for everyone else.

In the decade prior to joining the Marshals Service, Cuss had worked as a cop and then as a detective. Like riding a bike, the mindset he'd used back then reemerged. A hypervigilance. An awareness of his surroundings. He kept a mental image of his exit route in his head, adding to it as he moved deeper into the building, refining it with a running inventory of the things he passed.

The room at the end of the hallway, the one with the light, proved to be a private office, long abandoned, since filled with stuff. Desks, bookcases, and file cabinets were stacked against one wall. Tables and chairs along the opposing wall. Dust covered everything.

He passed a dead fly on the floor. Insects had made their way to the Moon in the early days of basin construction, stowaways during a time when the priority was to move as much equipment as fast as possible from Earth to the Moon. Like on Earth, they proved to be remarkably persistent and adaptable, annoying creatures that survived repeated attempts at eradication.

The footprints led to a sturdy gray metal bookcase set against the back wall. Squatting, he studied the floor next to it and found a track in the dust, two thin lines running parallel to the cabinet.

"It's a door," he said aloud, talking to Ygo as if he were still there. He tried to see behind the bookcase by pressing his cheek against the wall. When that didn't help, he pushed against the side of the bookcase, rocking it, thumping it with his shoulder. It wouldn't budge.

He turned to his stick, jamming the thin end behind the bookcase, hammering the thick end with the palm of a hand to wedge it deep. Then he placed a foot on the back wall and pulled, grunting while the cabinet groaned. Encouraged, he put both feet on the wall and heaved, his neck muscles bulging, his shoulders swelling.

Clunk. Something gave and the bookcase shifted, exposing a gap in the wall big enough to fit his fingers. Or his stick. He poked the fat end into the gap this time and pulled again, expanding the opening. After a few moments of effort, he had it wide enough to fit through.

Cuss poked his head inside and confirmed what he already knew: it was a tunnel entrance.

He'd imagined the Indies' cave network to be a dark and cramped labyrinth. But this tunnel was twice his height, plenty wide, and well-lit. The walls and ceiling were craggy, with sharp rock edges jutting everywhere, threatening those who weren't cautious. A pathway was cleared, a relatively smooth trail through the stone rubble.

Moving cautiously, he entered the tunnel. "Where's my backup?" he muttered to Ygo. The danger was through the roof.

The tunnel went straight for a bit, the distance difficult to judge in the circumstances. His best guess was thirty meters before it veered to the right.

Shadowy movements at the far end of the straightaway drew his attention. He zoomed with his lens to see a man carrying Tolly away. She was draped over his shoulder, her head and arms hanging down his back. Limp, like she was unconscious.

"Hey!" he called, hoping to slow the guy. To keep the confrontation near the exit.

The man looked back. The tunnel went dark.

Were it not for his lens, the blackness would be disorienting. Paralyzing. But the device in his eye processed wavelengths beyond the visible spectrum, giving him night vision that rivaled that of the daytime.

Fueled by adrenaline, he started after Tolly, taking a huge leap to close the distance. As he pushed off with his legs, his brain signaled a miscalculation.

He hadn't properly accounted for gravity, a momentary error in judgment that put him on an arc too high for the ceiling, a mistake with painful consequences. Ducking his head, he hit the top of the tunnel, absorbing the impact on his back and upper arms, jagged edges tearing into him. A sharp rock dug into the middle of his back, a serious gouge, but his amped state kept him from feeling the pain.

He fell to the ground and tumbled to the sound of laughter. When he righted himself and peered down the tunnel, the thug carrying Tolly was gone, replaced by two men. They wore augmentation glasses, sorry cousins to his sophisticated lens, and moved in his direction, his mishap the source of their amusement.

The one in front looked more like an accountant than a tough. Tall and skinny. Pinched face. Coiffed hair. He carried a shiny metal stick, a weapon slightly shorter than Cuss's stool leg. It had a ball affixed to the end the size of an apple. Perhaps a simple weight like you'd find on a medieval mace. Maybe a modern feature with dangerous capabilities.

Cuss glanced back the way he'd come, glad to see that a third tough wasn't crowding him from behind. They'd have a huge advantage if they boxed him in, forcing him to defend both his front and rear. He needed to end it before they figured that out.

Returning his attention to the threat ahead, he wondered which of the two was the leader. Removing him first would create uncertainty for the other, a moment of confusion Cuss could use to his advantage. But the path through the rubble was too narrow for them to walk side-by-side, so he had a good view of only the point man, the Accountant. The one behind was hanging back, giving his buddy space.

"I'm Marshal Abbott, here on official business," he called in a commanding voice as he rose from the ground.

He couldn't show them his badge because he was palming a rock the size of an egg in his right hand, the stick in his left. "I don't want any trouble."

Talking could influence the dynamics of a confrontation, especially if his assailants responded. His call was met with silence. Then his luck changed.

"It's too late for that," said the Accountant, who stopped his advance as he answered. The boss identifying himself.

Cuss dominated both of them in size and weight. He was strong, fast, fit, and skilled in hand-to-hand combat. All of that was irrelevant when a fight was decided by gun, but a huge advantage when it was decided with fists and sticks.

He couldn't guess what skills the two had and didn't dwell on it. When the Accountant spoke, Cuss reacted, pushing off from a rock outcropping, the move giving him flight, this time on a level trajectory, a missile cruising toward its target. He stretched his left arm out and pointed his stick at the Accountant's chest. In the darkness, a magic wand. A rapier. A rifle.

Cuss couldn't see the Accountant's eyes behind the augmentation glasses. But when the guy turned his head to follow the stick, Cuss made his move. As a ball player in his youth, he'd honed throwing skills that had served him well ever since. He whipped the stone at the man's head.

The Accountant's attention was on the stick only briefly, but it was enough to delay his reaction. The stone hit him in the temple with a dull *thunk*. His head snapped to the side, sending his augmentation glasses flying.

Still in flight, Cuss collided with the man before he

collapsed, grabbing his shirt, muscling him off the ground. He'd planned on doing the bowling trick—rolling the Accountant into the guy behind. But that guy was dancing about, thrusting the ball at the end of his mace toward Cuss, his movements making him difficult to target. Cuss kept the Accountant between them, positioning him like a shield, letting him take whatever it was the weapon had to offer.

What came next held little finesse, instead being determined by the physics of momentum. Cuss and the Accountant converged on the second guy, their bulk together giving them plenty of mass to overwhelm him. But their path was set. Cuss had no ability to adjust speed or trajectory, and the second guy's dancing had moved him out of the way.

Cuss improvised, sticking a leg out as he barreled past, delivering a glancing blow, one that spun his opponent around rather than knocking him down. The move sent Cuss tumbling.

The man righted himself and returned to attack mode, jabbing his mace at Cuss. It took Cuss a moment to untangle himself from the Accountant, a delay with unfortunate consequences. The ball grazed his thigh, the brief contact producing a searing jolt, a cross between white-hot heat and an electric discharge. It hurt like hell.

Desperate to avoid a second jolt, Cuss spun to get away. As he twirled, he slid both hands to the narrow end of his stool leg, gripping it like a baseball bat. His rotation brought him full circle. As he came around, he swung at the guy's hands, connecting, sending the mace careening off the wall in a shower of sparks.

With a guttural roar, the man threw himself at Cuss, who fell back, grabbing the guy's shirt lapels as he did so, pulling him up and over, delivering him headfirst into the cave wall. The impact sounded something like a wet mop slapping a tile floor. The guy collapsed in a heap next to the Accountant.

"Where's Tolly?" he asked, scrambling to his feet, knowing Ygo wouldn't hear him but finding that speaking aloud helped his focus. He started down the path after her. When he approached the point where the path curved, she came into sight. She was on her knees, arms out, hands probing the dark, her abductor nowhere in sight.

"Tolly, it's me," he said as he approached. He knelt next to her and put a hand on her shoulder. "Are you okay?"

She brought her hands to her face. "I can't see!"

"It's dark. Your eyesight is fine. Are you hurt?"

"I don't think so," she said, the frantic tone in her voice fading when she understood she was rescued.

Looking back along the path, Cuss decided that tripping hazards would make it difficult to lead her. "Let's stand you up." He held her hand as she rose. "All okay?"

"I think so."

"I'm going to carry you until we get to light."

She nodded. "Okay."

"Here we go." Stooping, he lifted her, one arm under her knees and the other behind her back. She was an easy bundle in the low gravity.

Moving slowly, he started back the way he'd come.

Tolly remained quiet as he walked. He slowed as he approached the Accountant and his partner, wary, studying them, wishing Ygo were available to provide a detailed assessment. They weren't moving and he went with that, scurrying past them before anything changed.

When he reached the opening behind the cabinet, he put Tolly back on her feet. The light from the office on the other side let her see, and she stepped through the gap on her own. When he followed, he was greeted by two patrol officers, a man and a woman. Both had a hand on their weapon, resting it there. Ready.

"I'm Marshal Abbott." He dangled his badge wallet for them to see.

"We were called for a break-in," said the man, relaxing his stance. He motioned toward Tolly. "Is this your prisoner?"

"No. She's the victim. Three men snatched her and were carrying her out through this tunnel. Two of them are still in there, unconscious last I saw." Cuss pointed with his thumb. "Maybe twenty meters along."

The other officer leaned into the tunnel and shook her head. "It's not safe in there without lights and more officers." She turned her back to them and started speaking to someone not in the room. The male officer poked his head in the tunnel and looked.

"I'm going to take the lady outside," said Cuss to the man's back. "Get some air."

"The detectives will need to speak with you," he replied over his shoulder. "Stay close."

"Understood."

He led Tolly through the office and down the hall. When they reached the front room, Ygo returned. "Give me a moment to review the record," he said to Cuss, accessing his lens and scanning recent events, adding, "I was worried about you."

Cuss and Tolly continued outside, where he led her through the break in the vegetation and onto a plot of grass at the edge of the university's stadium complex. A cop cart blocked the road. They sat on a park bench near it.

"That electric club looked like it hurt," said Ygo, done with the review.

Cuss nodded in agreement, watching a second cop cart approach. Hobby was driving, Darlena next to him in front. Eve sat in back, swaying as the cart bobbed and swerved to a stop.

As the three climbed out, another cart arrived from a different direction, this one carrying two more patrol officers. Hobby worked with them, helping them unload equipment—lights, microdrones, med kit—and carry it into the building. Eve and Darlena approached Cuss and Tolly on the bench.

Darlena started. "I hear there's been some excitement."

Cuss took them through it. "This is Tolly Vaughn. She's a grad student at Conrad. From her studies, she discovered that the Indies might have a cave network, tunnels they use to move about under the city."

Darlena's eyebrows shot up.

He told it straight, laying the break-in at Tolly's feet. He and Tolly had been walking to her office when she took it upon herself to see if a tunnel entrance originated in the old pump station, something her work suggested. It turned out that the answer was yes.

"While she was exploring inside, a guy came through a hidden door, grabbed her, and carried her into the caves. I didn't get a good look at the guy but assume he's an Indie."

"Where were you when this happened?" asked Darlena.

"Out here, calling for her to come out." He looked at Tolly accusingly, still annoyed at her impetuous behavior, her unwillingness to let him assert even the slightest bit of authority in their brief relationship. "I entered when she called for help."

He finished the story, downplaying the details of the battle. "I fought my way past two defenders to get to her. The third guy dropped her and escaped into the caves. We met two patrol officers as we were coming out."

A dull throb in his back demanded his attention. He paused his narrative and, taking off his jacket, turned his back to Eve. "Can you see anything? I smacked myself hard on a rock."

"Oh, Lord," said Eve, pulling his shirt up for a better look. "You cut yourself good. Darlena, does the cart have a med kit?"

Darlena retrieved a red-and-white satchel from the cart, and Eve dug through it. "I'll spray it and cover it, but you need to have it cleaned and closed by a doctor."

"Thanks," he said, trying to be cooperative to win her favor.

While Eve performed her ministrations, Ygo accessed

a security camera located on a pole behind Cuss and sent the feed to his lens, showing him a nasty gash below his left shoulder, a ragged tear maybe three inches long with a black-blue bruise around it. Blood trailed from it down to the waist of his pants, where it collected in a red blotch.

Hobby appeared through the break in the plant growth, stared at Cuss like he was viewing a cockroach, shook his head to show his disgust, and said to Darlena, "We have one dead and one unconscious." He turned back to the pump station building.

Darlena exhaled hard through her lips as if echoing Hobby's disdain. "Christ, Cuss. This will be the second day in a row I spend cleaning up your shit."

Turning away, she spoke in sharp barks, Cuss overhearing enough to know she was calling emergency medicine and the medical examiner. One to save a life, the other to learn why one had ended.

He waited for her to finish her communication before responding. "They attacked *me*, twice! Put the blame where it belongs."

Eve diffused the situation by changing topics: "The violence doesn't match what I've learned from my cousin. The protesters are angry, for sure, but not murderous."

"The violence started a few months ago," said Darlena, studying a hand display, perhaps tracking her request for assistance, maybe scanning updates from Hobby in the tunnel. "These people are bad news."

"We started it," said Tolly.

Darlena looked up from her display. "Excuse me?"

"Well, Scarpello and Gomez did."

Cuss turned to face her. "Juan Gomez, as in the president of Nova Terra?"

Tolly nodded. "And Haruto Scarpello, mayor of Armstrong."

"This I gotta hear," said Darlena.

"You know the story," Tolly replied, angry, judgmental, the tone carrying an implied finger jab. "Lynne Adamson?"

Darlena broke eye contact and looked at the ground, an acknowledgement of sorts.

"Is Lynne related to Abbi Adamson?" asked Eve.

Tolly nodded. "Her infant daughter. Lynne suffers from a rare disease, which apparently causes her pain. Lynne's doctor prescribed medication to control the illness. Mayor Scarpello, in all his brilliance, intervened, blocking Lynne's access to the drug, choosing to use it as a weapon, saying the Adamsons can't help their baby until they vacate the caves and the protests stop. Gomez supported the decision."

She went on to explain that their decision split Nova Terra. "Some feel it's the Adamsons' fault because all they need to do to help their child is step out of the caves and rejoin society. Others say that deliberately hurting a baby to solve a political problem is horrifying. Brutal. Completely unacceptable."

Tolly hugged herself before continuing. "It turns out that Pulse can be converted into Ronolyx, the medicine Lynne needs. The Adamsons chose to fight back by stealing Pulse from pharmacies across Nova Terra. A growing segment of the population cheers when we hear of their latest score."

Cuss imagined desperate parents trying to help their baby, and then a freak accident—in this case Bridge's death on a statue—sends it all south. His stomach twinged, and he looked at Eve. "I hate these kinds of cases."

She nodded, sparing him the lecture that they weren't judge or jury, that their job was to deliver the accused and let the system work out the details. Instead, she asked Tolly, "What's your source for all this?"

"I'm documenting the colossal public policy failures of the current Nova Terra leadership for my master's degree. Lynne's case is emblematic of how these people do business. My analysis of this one issue takes up two full chapters in my thesis." She smiled for the first time since the incident. "I'd love to have you read it. Maybe give me feedback?"

"Send it along," said Eve. "No promises."

"Get a copy for us," said Ygo. Cuss asked, having to speak over the siren from the emergency response vehicle swooping onto the scene.

Three minutes later, med techs brought out the unconscious thug. It was the Accountant. They loaded him into a cart and rushed away.

The medical examiner stayed in the caves for just over an hour. Documenting the scene proved to be a straightforward task given that they knew who did it and why. The one twist was that there were no public monitors in the tunnel, so there were no feeds to support Cuss's account. Or contradict it.

Cuss chose not to disclose that he wore a lens that had

recorded the incident. But he kept his report reasonably accurate, not wanting to upset Ygo, sure his partner supported him on this one.

Chapter 13

Abbi Adamson was glad she wasn't holding Lynne when she heard of Vincent's murder and Tolly's kidnapping because she might well have dropped her daughter in horror.

"What were you thinking?" she shouted at Barker, her mind struggling to digest the news. Jaunty Gabala stood to the side, indifferent to Abbi's outrage.

"I'm protecting my wife and child," replied Barker, his voice low but carrying an edge. "No apologies. No regrets."

"Except you've made things so much worse. Now we're an active threat to the community." She tried to control her fury. Her panic. She was shocked by Barker's actions, the behavior of a monster. Yet her situation was desperate, and she had nowhere else to turn.

"They have to find us to catch us," he said.

She shook her head. "We can't ask the community to protect us. Not from this. An accident is one thing. But cops will tear this place apart trying to get us now."

Barker stayed quiet, looking at the ground, accepting her wrath.

"We need to leave," she said, desperate to get them back on a righteous course. "And we have to be seen leaving to take heat off the others."

"If they see us, they'll chase us."

"That's the point. It makes it *our* problem and lets the community return to its original purpose."

"Pulse conversion just started," said Jaunty. "It'll take most of a month to process it all."

That quieted them. After a period of silence, Barker looked at Jaunty. "Then you and I go. We'll make it look like Abbi and Lynne are with us. She can hide here until the Ronolyx is ready and then catch up."

"Where are you going?" asked Abbi.

"Utopia." Barker looked like a little kid trying to be brave.

"Mars?" She shuddered. It seemed so distant. So foreign. So…primitive. A different kind of prison.

Barker shrugged. "They'll find us anywhere else. Utopia protects immigrants as long as we work hard and don't make trouble. They won't care why we're there."

"There's a freighter leaving at noon," said Jaunty. "The *Tomlinson*. I know the captain, and he's agreed to take us as crew."

"*Noon?*" She looked at Barker, eyes red, tears brimming, wondering when she'd see him again. When Lynne would. "How will I get there?"

"We've got time to figure that out."

Abbi began to sob. "Why is this happening? It's so unfair."

. . .

With the wound on his back cleaned and dressed, Cuss weaved through the crowd in the hospital lobby, continuing out the front entryway and onto a slate terrace. Rows of raised planters crisscrossed the space in two big Xs, with seating available along the edge of the planter stonework.

It was a busy morning, a good crowd, most of the seating space taken by people there on hospital business, and by diners, customers of a popular sandwich shop next door. He scanned the area, squinting because of the sun shining through the clear polymer dome. He found Eve off to his left. She saw him at the same time, waved, and started in his direction.

"All done?" she asked.

"All done here. Now I need to clean up." He rested a hand on his stomach. "And I'm starving." He looked around the terrace. "Where's Tolly?"

"They've admitted her. She was showing signs of emotional trauma, and they're addressing it while it's fresh."

He looked back at the door he'd just exited. "I want to check in with her, find out how long she'll be."

It turned out the hospital personnel wouldn't let him see her.

"They're all inside her head right now," said the floor nurse, a kindly older lady sitting inside a workspace, a fortress protected by a white chest-high countertop. "They'll let her have visitors tomorrow morning. Get in line, though. Detectives want to speak with her the moment the doctors clear her."

Back out on the terrace, Cuss's stomach rumbled. "I need food. Join me?"

"I've been called home." She gave a careless shrug, showing her mixed emotions about the order. "My commander says my work there is piling up. She has every confidence that the locals and the Marshals Service can wrap things up here."

"Stay." He blurted it out, his mouth moving ahead of his brain. They were reaching a critical juncture, and he still needed help. He tried not to sound whiny. "You're important to the effort. I can clear it with your commander if you want. Or the Marshals Service can."

She shook her head. "Short of active pursuit, I'm to return to Demeter. I don't like to make waves. If they want me there, that's where I go."

"When's your flight?"

"Boarding at fifteen forty."

"Today? Jeez." Cuss checked the time. "You have a few hours. Let's grab lunch on the *Nelly Marie*. You can relax there until it's boarding time."

. . .

Their journey took fifty minutes: a tram ride to Port Collins, a walk through the bustling spaceport concourse, a cart ride out into the massive hangar. Cuss led Eve into the *Nelly Marie* and up to the middeck where, with a few practiced moves, he configured the space with a table and chairs.

A selection of food was stacked in the kitchenette—healthy munchies, salty snacks, and sugary desserts—items

Ygo had ordered during their transit from the city. Cuss moved everything over to the table, chose a red apple from the fruit plate, rubbed it on the front of his shirt, and snapped a juicy bite. "Help yourself. Back in a flash."

While Eve sorted through the goodies, he climbed up to the third level and began to undress, his left shoulder twinging when he pulled the arm out of his shirt. Standing in front of the bathroom sink, he shaved, deciding a fourth day of growth would push his look from rugged to slovenly. He was stepping into the shower when Ygo said, "Whoa. Check this out."

Cuss turned off the water and rested his butt on the edge of the sink. His lens came alive, showing a scene from an elevated vantage point looking down: two spaceships sitting side-by-side on launchpads as if poised for liftoff. He presumed it was a local feed, probably from the launch facility just outside the hangar doors.

The focus shifted to the vessel on the left, a flattened cylinder, squat legs holding the vessel upright, engine pods attached at the bottom. Chipped paint, dents in the hull, and corrosion around the exterior ports all pointed to a working vessel. A service lorry was feeding air, water, and fuel into the craft's tanks through a trio of colored hoses.

The feed zoomed in on the ship's gangway. Barker Adamson and Jaunty Gabala were walking up it, making their way to the main hatch. Markings identified the vessel as the *Tomlinson*, an interworld freighter.

As the men walked, Barker had his hand out to the side, the same awkward stance he'd used when escorting an invisible-to-POTS Abbi through Demeter. When the two men entered the ship through the hatch, they shuffled a dance, again like before, as if accommodating an invisible third person.

Cuss's face tingled from the adrenaline flooding his system, a reaction to seeing his quarry within reach. He took a calming breath. "This is here in Port Collins?"

"It is. About two hours ago."

"Is the ship still here?"

"Unfortunately, no. It lifted off thirty minutes later, swung a single orbit, then made for Earth."

Cuss sighed as his excitement ebbed. The chase continued. "Any ideas where they'll land?"

"They filed a flight plan for Mexico City, but that could change at a moment's notice. We need to follow them down wherever they land or risk losing them in the countryside. If that happens, Girish will give us three days to find them before tossing the case to the locals."

The director of the Marshals Service gave Cuss and Ygo plenty of free rein. But he'd used the three-day rule on them in the past, so Cuss agreed with Ygo's assessment. "If they disappear into the neighborhoods, we'd need three weeks and a dozen cops."

"I've contacted Port Services. They'll have us ready for launch in about ninety minutes. We can catch that tub no problem."

Cuss began thinking through the logistics of having backup meet him at the landing site, a challenge because it could be anywhere on Earth, unknown until the last minutes. Then he remembered Eve was right there. He threw on a T-shirt and sweatpants and hustled down to the middeck.

"Check this out," he said to her as he launched a hoverview display over the table. He stood behind her, and together they watched the two men perform the mysterious charade up the gangway and onto the ship.

Eve sat quietly as she concentrated. "We presume that it's Abbi hidden from the feeds?"

"That's my guess."

"But why hide Abbi and not themselves? It's an odd decision. Like they want us to see them."

"Good one," said Ygo.

"Nice catch," said Cuss, now wondering the same thing, disappointed that he and Ygo had missed it.

He turned his back to Eve and spoke to Ygo in the same formal tone one might use when talking to an AI assistant. "What is the likelihood that Jaunty Gabala and Barker Adamson are onboard the *Tomlinson*? Use every available resource to confirm, and give me a confidence level."

Facing Eve, he explained to her while also speaking to Ygo. "I want to chase that ship. But as you pointed out, they're up to something. Let's make sure they didn't slip out the cargo bay in back or some other bullshit before we invest resources in pursuit."

Eve, who'd been nibbling on a cookie, popped the last bit into her mouth, dusted her hands of crumbs, and said, "Run it again. Can we tell if the child is with them?"

They watched the scene two more times but couldn't discern anything about daughter Lynne.

Then Ygo reported on his review. "Their invisibility

trick makes it impossible for me to be certain, but I don't think they slipped away. Ninety-five percent plus they stayed onboard. The two men anyway."

Eve was about to watch the boarding scene for a fourth time when a metallic *clunk* from outside the ship turned their heads.

Cuss began stowing the food. "Sorry but they're moving us out to the launchpad. You'll have to either debark or come with."

"Am I welcome?"

Cuss hesitated. After her earlier speech about being a loyal employee, he hadn't considered that she'd be interested. "Absolutely. It'll take half a day for the freighter to reach Earth, and then we land and makes arrests. You should be back in Demeter by tomorrow evening. Maybe the day after that, depending on how things play out."

Appreciating what a tremendous help it would be to have her along, he waved an arm at the wall behind them and sold the idea. "The back half of the middeck converts to a second bedroom, so you'll have a private place to crash. It has a sink, but there's only one full bathroom and that's up on three. We'll have to share."

After a few more *clunks* from outside, Eve said, "If I go, I want to be hired as a deputy marshal. It looks better than 'consultant.'"

He gave her a quizzical look.

"And if things go well, I want to list you as a reference when I apply next month."

"Wait. To the Marshals Service?"

"Why not? I like the independence. The lifestyle. And

my record is rock solid."

He agreed, choosing not to mention how insanely competitive it was to land a rare open slot. "Absolutely. Happy to."

Her face lit with a smile. "Let me call my commander and see if the 'active pursuit' option was real or just words." She rose from her chair and descended the ladder to the command deck, talking to someone as she went.

Three minutes later she was back. "Is the bathroom clean?"

He stifled a grin. "It will be."

. . .

Launching the *Nelly Marie* was a breeze for Cuss because he pretty much just sat there while Ygo did everything. But with Eve strapped in next to him, and with Ygo adamant that outsiders not know of his existence, Cuss began his own charade, pretending to take actions that influenced liftoff and the ship's rise to orbit. From there, he pretended to make a difference as they established a trajectory that would intercept the *Tomlinson* on its approach to Earth.

The escape freighter was a clunker traveling much slower than *Nelly Marie*'s normal cruising speed. As Ygo settled them onto a pursuit path, the slow acceleration required to match the *Tomlinson* meant they would be living with a ship's gravity that was about half that of Earth.

Things went quiet after that, the thrum of the twin

Paulson drives blending with the whirs and hums and buzzes from console fans, service motors, and rack electronics, creating a white noise that was a background staple of space travel. As Cuss unstrapped from the pilot's seat, he turned on music, a rambunctious piece from Chrome Grille.

"This okay?" He lowered the volume, trying to be considerate.

She nodded. "I like this song. Their whole first album is amazing."

Cuss added back some of the volume, then led the way up to the middeck. There he called to the air, "Peanut, clean the bathroom for guests." He took a moment to enjoy Eve's fascination as the ship's bot emerged from its cubby in the wall.

The machine looked something like an upside-down kitchen trash can that had been enhanced with a long spindly arm out the top and a short thick arm out the side. Once on deck, Peanut opened a closet and used its long arm to select accessories to place in its tool carousel. The closet was filled with attachments the bot used for maintenance and machining and assembly and, of course, cleaning. There were also special attachments it used when caring for Ygo, to keep him clean and his living space tidy.

With the bot working away on the third level, Cuss and Eve configured the middeck bedroom. They started by pulling a privacy barrier in place, a heavy curtain that ran across to create a partition. Behind it they lowered a cot from the wall, a space-age version of a Murphy bed. Cuss pointed out the drawer with bedsheets and then turned his attention to lowering a countertop that held a small sink, exposing a mirror on the wall behind.

While Eve emptied her kitbag into the drawers next to the mirror, Cuss dragged in a chair, interrupting her chores to show her the on-off control under the left arm that fixed the chair to the deck.

"We can't have things flying about during periods of weightlessness," he said, telling her something she already knew.

With her quarters squared away, they moved out to the common area. Cuss began a ship's tour, starting with the various features of the kitchenette. Her face remained stoic when he showed her his food stores—burgers, burritos, pizza, plus an impressive variety of protein and energy bars.

"There's only a couple of meals before we land," he said, suddenly self-conscious of his diet.

From there they descended to the command deck, where he took her through a basic safety review, something the Marshal Service required of outsiders when undertaking interworld travel on one of their ships. He could have used a canned presentation, an eighteen-minute thing done by a Marshals Service intern four years ago. But he chose to give it himself. It was an excuse to talk with her. To interact. Something he enjoyed.

Then, while Eve observed, Cuss worked with MFOD—Ygo contributing in the background—to arrange for additional backup forces when they landed. An analyst working the field ops desk noted, "The *Tomlinson* requires a class B pad to land. Class B or better. That limits them to maybe a hundred sites worldwide. Add in local politics—

operators willing to involve themselves with a vessel being tracked by us—and that drops to maybe eighteen. Twenty tops."

"Where are those located?" asked Cuss.

"Most are in Asia, with the rest sprinkled around the globe. All will be antagonistic to Marshals Service intervention. If that's how they play it, it'll be difficult to coordinate anything."

"Could we circle some jets? Spread them out and have the nearest ones chase 'em down?"

The analyst shook his head. "Maybe if your doers had killed a governor. That's a lot of resources and political capital to chase thieves who killed one of their own during the commission of a crime."

Cuss felt a tug of annoyance, the kind that could blossom into anger in a heartbeat. "They're also prime suspects in a second murder, plus a kidnapping."

"I put that in our update," Ygo told Cuss. "Though technically I only submitted it twelve minutes ago."

Cuss briefed the analyst about Vincent and Tolly. "It's all there in the latest report."

The analyst went quiet as he reviewed the information. "Let me send this up the chain and see if it changes anything." Then, after a delay, "Director Mannan is in a big meeting, so it will be a bit. I'll flag you as soon as I hear." He closed the call.

Cuss rested his head against the back of the chair and closed his eyes. Exhaustion flooded his awareness, calling to him, tempting him. He was running a serious sleep deficit, something his body would no longer let him ignore.

Standing, he said to Eve, "I'm going to my room to crash while we wait. Help yourself to whatever you need."

Chapter 14

"Uh-oh," said Ygo.

Cuss opened his eyes and waited, unsure how long he'd been out.

"They didn't cycle."

"What?" Rolling onto his back on top of the bedcovers, Cuss rubbed his eyes with his palms, working to clear his head of sleep and trying to digest Ygo's message.

A ship traveling to Earth began the journey with its engines pointing toward the Moon, the thrust pushing the ship ever faster toward its goal. Halfway along, the craft should cycle, flipping over in a somersault in space, pointing its engines toward Earth, the same thrust now slowing the craft so it could tuck into orbit at the end of the journey.

Ygo was telling him that the *Tomlinson* hadn't performed the flipping maneuver as expected. "They're still accelerating," he added.

Cuss sat up. "Slingshot?"

"It has to be Utopia. Nothing else makes sense."

"Can that crate take the gees?"

"No problem. Gravity assists are a staple for freighters."

"Shit." A hundred decisions needed to be made in the next hour, everything dependent on what they did in the next minutes. "Shit. Shit. Shit."

First, did the Marshals Service want to tie up Cuss, Ygo, and the *Nelly Marie* for a run to Mars? It was a good six weeks' travel time out and, because of the quirks of orbital mechanics, eight weeks back. Plus the time they'd spend on the ground.

"If they won't deploy aircraft for us on Earth," said Ygo. "I don't see them committing resources to send us to Mars."

But if they did, what would happen to Eve?

Outbound, the six-week travel time was achieved by using gravity to accelerate the ship. To perform the maneuver, instead of slowing down, the *Nelly Marie* must continue speeding toward Earth, the thrust of the ship's engine combining with the mighty pull of Earth's gravity to accelerate the craft to an extraordinary speed. At the last moment, Ygo would guide the ship to just miss a collision with the planet, to travel a path that would take them skimming past it.

But Earth wouldn't give up its hold. Not easily. Instead, its gravity would hug the screaming vessel, pulling on it like a string on a kite. In an action similar to a David-and-Goliath-style slingshot, the balance of forces would cause the ship to loop around the back of the planet, increasing its speed to the point where Earth could no longer sustain its hold. Relinquishing its claim, the planet would fling the ship back into the void, sending it on its way at speeds unachievable by drives alone.

The difficulty was that the slingshot stunt was incompatible with offloading passengers. They'd have to choose one or the other. Doing both wasn't an option.

Losing the gravity assist wasn't a horrible outcome. It would add nine days to their travel time to Mars—part of the previously mentioned quirks of orbital mechanics. But after six weeks of living in a tiny can, adding even one more day was a bigger ask than it might seem.

The other issue? Resupply.

The *Nelly Marie* wasn't stocked for a weeks-long journey to Mars, so if they were to go, the Marshals Service would need to start loading a robot supply ship on the Moon *now* and send it after them. The supply ship could take a more aggressive slingshot, with gee forces that would kill a human if they were aboard, allowing it to fly fast enough to catch up to them in just a few days.

But then, Eve again.

Should the supplies include her needs? Or should the supply ship travel slowly because there would be no slingshot, that she was being let off?

"Could you even live with her in these close quarters for a month and a half?" asked Ygo.

"Could be great. Could be horrible. But we'll need help at the other end, something that'll be hard to come by when we get there." He rolled off the bed. "Let's go talk to her."

He didn't see her on the middeck. When he peeked down the steps to the command deck, Ygo told him, "She crashed when you did."

"Eve?" Cuss called through the curtain. "We have a situation. Can you come out?"

He heard a rustle. A moment later she emerged, hair disheveled, eyelids drooping from sleep. She wore a light blue singlet, a garment that combined shorts and a tank top. Thin material. Form fitting. Tight everywhere.

Cuss concentrated on her face, determined not to stare. "The *Tomlinson* is headed to Mars, not Earth, and I need to coordinate with MFOD on our response. They're going for a gravity assist around Earth. We'll probably be called off. But if it's a go, we can either follow them with our own slingshot or stop to let you off."

She held up a finger and then ducked behind the curtain, returning seconds later wearing a black polo shirt, the hem covering her to midthigh. The shirt had a small Community Patrol emblem positioned over her heart, the word *Detective* beneath it. As she adjusted the collar, she asked, "If you let me off, do you lose them? Can you catch up?"

"It would make things challenging." He shrugged, choosing not to reveal the cost of time. "Can I persuade you to come along? I'll need help when I get there."

"It would be months, wouldn't it?"

"We could get there in six weeks."

"And then we need to get back." She bit her lip as she thought and then shook her head. "I can't walk away from my life for that long."

He tried to sell without pushing too hard, appealing to her sense of duty, the excitement of the unknown, capturing her quarry. It didn't work. He gave up.

"It probably won't matter, so don't sweat it. Let's see what Girish has to say." Climbing down to the command deck, he slid into the pilot's seat. He could talk to his boss from anywhere on the *Nelly Marie* but thought the image of him sitting at spaceship controls conveyed a strong message. Eve sat in the chair next to him.

It took ten minutes to connect with the same analyst as before, but Cuss thought it was worth the wait. It would take longer than that to bring a new person up to speed.

"Utopia, huh?" said the analyst. He looked at something they couldn't see. "He's wrapping up now. Should be just a minute. Ever been?"

"Utopia? No, you?"

The analyst shook his head. "No desire. It's too remote. Too insular. Too…Wild West."

Cuss started having personal doubts himself. He also had a life. A full one. Did he want to disappear for three months?

"Hold on," said the analyst. "Here he is."

It was another minute before Girish Mannan appeared. He smiled at Cuss. "Marshal Abbott. We have some decisions to make?"

Cuss took him through it. Two doers on board the *Tomlinson* with a possibility of a third. Two murders and a kidnapping. Gravity assist to Mars. Eve.

Girish listened, nodding a few times but not interrupting.

When Cuss was done, Girish looked at Eve. "Detective Boucher." He pronounced it boo-shay the way she did. His attention to detail was legendary. "It's a pleasure to meet you."

"Eve, please." She flashed her amazing smile. "The pleasure is mine."

He folded his hands as he gathered his thoughts. After

clearing his throat, he continued. "We'd like Cuss to go to Utopia. We'd like to get him there fast. But not because of these doers. Well, not only for them."

He sat back in the chair, shifting his hips like he was settling in for a long story. "The two marshals stationed there, Atepa Underwood and Jeremy Romesco, went dark two weeks ago. They'd been behaving a little wonky, pushing hard to modify their assignments, claiming it was necessary to accommodate the residents and their traditions. But from our end, it's seemed more like they'd started working for the locals. Like their loyalties were in flux."

He paused to sip from a coffee mug. "We don't know if their silence is voluntary, like we've lost their cooperation, or if something's happened to them that's keeping them from reporting. We reached out to a couple of local assets to see what they could learn, but their reports have been equivocal, like they're more interested in billing hours than getting us answers. Two days ago we got a cryptic message from someone claiming to be Jeremy, saying they're both okay. That he'd explain soon. Nothing since."

He looked off-screen, whispered, "good," then returned his attention to them. "The agency position is that the two are victims and need our help. We've been brainstorming ways to get someone there, preferably under the radar so the Utopians aren't on the defensive when they arrive. Your situation is perfect because it gives us a different reason to show up fast and in force."

Girish focused on Eve. "We'll happily hire you as a deputy marshal. We'll pay both a wage and a generous stipend that covers your back-home living expenses while you're away, rent and such."

"I don't want to be a bad person but the ask is too much. Three months?"

"Would a pay bonus make a difference? Encouragement from your commander? A nice vacation when you return? Tell us what we can do to make it attractive for you."

She stared at Girish for a long moment and then shook her head. She began to speak and then stopped. Started again and then stopped. Smiled briefly. Then looked him in the eye. "Make me a full interworld marshal. Not a deputy. A permanent job."

Cuss felt his eyes go wide.

Girish shook his head. "That's not how our hiring process works."

"Battlefield promotions have a proud tradition. That's what this is."

"No, that's when you jump people early who you've already vetted, already hired, putting them in line for the position."

"I'm not trying to back you into a corner, but it's my condition to continue. I'm asking a lot, but you are as well. You know that."

"It's a pretty aggressive stance, don't you think? Cooperation can enhance your career. A quite promising one, I might add. Recalcitrant behavior isn't a good look."

"You're seeking timid people to be marshals, Dr. Mannan?"

Eve had done her homework as well. Girish had a

Ph.D. in criminal psychology, though he didn't use the honorific on the job.

Faint lines appeared in Girish's forehead. "Give me a minute," he said curtly. His image faded.

"Do you play poker?" asked Cuss, impressed by her boldness, her confidence, her demeanor. She'd be a formidable opponent at the tables.

"Forgive me, but for all I know they're still listening. I'm going to stay quiet until this is over." She winked at him. Barely discernable. More of a nervous twitch than a close of the eyelid. "I've dabbled."

It took him a moment to realize she was answering his question, that yes, she played some poker.

It was a good twenty minutes before Girish returned, looking calm, in control. He started to speak, then held up a hand while he whispered to someone they couldn't see. Nodded. Spoke to someone else. Then turned his attention to Eve.

"You have us backed into a corner, which annoys me. But you're leveraging the opportunity well, which is to your favor. Your record is impressive. You have the qualifications on paper to be a short-list candidate. But hiring is a process. Here's what I can offer."

After another quick sidebar with someone on his end, he continued. "We will hire you as a full interworld marshal. Keeping the title, however, will be contingent on a list of things. Specifically, when this assignment is over, you must pass through the same gauntlet as your colleagues, same as what Cuss went through."

He ticked through a list, using his fingers to count. "It

starts with a formal psych test and a readiness test. If you pass those, you need the blessing of Governor Belnick, as it's a Lagrange hire as well. And if you make it past that, then you spend six months at Chaparral, the Marshals Service School in Seattle. Your grades there must be above the cutoff. Fail any step and your position reverts to deputy marshal, a temporary position."

She looked at him but didn't respond.

Then he began to sell. "We'll put your badge, service weapon, and uniforms on the supply ship. We're sending a pusher outfitted with a hab-pod—that's a sleeper and bathroom module—so you'll have your own small but private quarters."

A pusher told Cuss how serious this was. While most supply ships were designed to be offloaded and left behind for later salvage, a pusher would remain docked with the *Nelly Marie*, using its own drives and fuel to move them faster.

Eve stayed quiet, sitting there as if waiting to see if he had more goodies to add. He returned the stare, waiting as well.

Finally, she spoke. "Thank you, sir. I appreciate the vote of confidence. I accept. Well, I need to make a courtesy call to my commander and partner before I say so officially. But my acceptance will be forthcoming immediately after that."

"Welcome aboard, Marshal Boucher." His face relaxed. He seemed relieved.

Then to both of them, "The supply ship manifest will be sent to you in the next few minutes. Work with MFOD to add anything we've overlooked. Beyond food, fuel, sundries, and the habitat module, we've loaded it with crates of high-purity metals. Tungsten, chromium, vanadium, and molybdenum bar stock. A few others. Titanium billets. Platinum and silver. Gold in the form of Sols. These all are valued in Utopia. Materials the settlement needs to grow its manufacturing base, to become more self-sufficient. We're sending enough to give you serious leverage, hoping that will help things go smoothly. But in case things don't, we're also loading up a selection of firearms, everything from Marshal Boucher's service sidearm to some tactical weaponry. Review and modify as needed. Who knows what you'll find when you get there."

He glanced off-screen and returned to them. "It's a busy time. I have to run. We'll have plenty of opportunity to refine our strategy before you get there. I'll be back with you in a few days to start that discussion."

To Cuss: "Swear her in when you give her the badge and send us the record of it. Legal says she's not fully protected under the Marshals Service umbrella until then."

To Eve: "Cuss has the lead, Marshal Boucher. You are to follow his direction. Welcome again." He closed the call.

Cuss stared at where Girish's image had been, marveling at what had just happened. "Holy shit. Did you just do that?"

She turned bright red. "I don't know where that came from. My brain had these thoughts, and my mouth said them without any processing in between. People don't like being backed into a corner. Not the best way to start a dream job."

While she was speaking, the background hum grew in intensity, the ship's gravity increasing to match. Ygo had ramped the Paulson drives, beginning their sprint to Earth, the first step in a gravity assist maneuver.

"He's all about success. Deliver on this mission and he'll forget. Or at least forgive."

Eve bit her lip. "Not to be a prima donna but I didn't pack for this. I need clothes. Meds. Products. It's not a long list. But an important one."

"Don't hold back on your supply request. All the marshals have personal needs. Their own quirks. Mission Support is used to it. We only get this one shot, though, so think it through carefully. We can't ask them to send a second ship later." He hesitated and then made a decision. "The ship's AI is called Ygo. He can help you with planning."

He and Ygo needed to talk through how they would handle it in the longer term. But for now, Cuss would honor Ygo's desires. The man below their feet, the one connected to pioneering AI and feeds from multiple worlds, would be present as a machine.

Cuss unstrapped and stood. "For wardrobe, shorts and a T-shirt work pretty well. But in about four hours it's going to get rough. The slingshot is violent and the shaking will chafe your legs on the seat straps. I'm putting on long pants and suggest you do the same."

"Closer to three hours before the excitement begins," Ygo said in private.

Cuss heard but didn't correct himself to Eve.

"Got it." She followed him up to the middeck. "I'll need more than shorts and a T-shirt when we land. And prima donna again—can we lower the temperature in here a degree or two?"

Cuss feigned shock. "A woman asking to *lower* the temperature?"

"I'd like to cover up a little. Wear sweats without feeling hot."

"Of course." He tried not to sound annoyed. They were minutes into their partnership and she was already upending his routine.

They talked while they were changing, Cuss calling down from the third level to Eve, who was behind her curtain on the middeck. "We need to decide how aggressive to make the maneuver. Faster means more gees, the benefit being time saved on the trip. What's your limit, do you know?"

"Gees? I've done four a bunch of times. Takeoff from Earth. Reentry."

"How did you feel? Were you nearing your limit?"

"No. It was easy."

"For the slingshot, I would do ten gees if I were by myself."

Ygo lived on a special capsule-bed-chair contraption that alternately floated him in liquid, suspended him on dry netting, and levitated him on jets of air, all to ensure his skin remained healthy. While in his rig, he could handle ten gees with ease.

"Whoa. That's a serious number. Like, potential for injury." Her brow furrowed as she thought. "Is there a minimum to qualify at Chaparral? Is it something they test?"

"You'll be amazed at what they test. For acceleration forces there's a max test and a duration test. The max is for a brief period, like ten gees for ten seconds. The duration test is lower but harder. I think it's five gees for twenty minutes."

"Six," said Ygo.

This time he conveyed the correction. "Maybe it's six gees."

"How long will our maneuver take?"

Cuss decided to have Ygo speak to her. "Ygo, can you tell us?"

"From seventeen to twenty-three minutes, depending on how aggressive we take it."

Eve paused. "Not to get off topic, but if a supply ship can chase us down, why don't we chase down the *Tomlinson* and save the trip?"

Cuss knew this one but let Ygo explain.

"They loop behind Earth about four hours ahead of us. Since Earth moves through space, we'll be thousands of kilometers away from them when we do the same. The gee forces necessary to close that gap would kill us. An unmanned supply ship doesn't care."

"And don't forget," added Cuss, "We're going to Mars for our missing colleagues. The assholes are secondary."

"Can we compromise on eight gees when we go? We don't want me lying unconscious and six weeks from help."

Chapter 15

Jeremy Romesco sat on the edge of the cot, head in his hands, feet on the dirt floor, a chill creeping in from the rock walls around him. Though the room had the astringent smell characteristic of Martian soil, he also could smell himself. He'd been there about two weeks and he reeked. Overhead, a dim light from a single fixture let him see the door, a standard slider used all over Utopia, this one locked. He knew because he'd tried it dozens of times.

He was hungrier than he'd ever been in his life. They were starving him to secure his cooperation. One very small meal a day. He had free access to water, thank God. But at any moment, that could become a weapon as well.

He and his fellow Interworld Marshal, Atepa Underwood, had been serving in Utopia for just over two years. It was a nontraditional assignment in that the locals didn't support their mission. The reasons weren't complicated.

The bulk of the immigrants to Utopia were a mix of adventurers and offenders, people either seeking their fortune or running from justice. If those running from justice were wanted for a capital crime on another world, then the marshals' job was to collect them and send them back to face charges.

But to attract new blood, the locals started everyone

off with a clean slate and a fair shot. No matter their history, if a new arrival contributed more to the settlement than they took, they were desirables, people who could help Utopia thrive. As long as they behaved and kept contributing, the locals would protect them from the marshals. But if they were leeches, arrivals who ultimately consumed more than they produced, slackers who on balance were a drain on resources, the offenders would be delivered to the marshals' doorstep, bundled for a trip home.

Unfortunately for the marshals, there wasn't a local law enforcement agency they could partner with to strengthen their position. Utopia didn't even have an elected government. Quite the contrary, the locals belonged to one of two crime syndicates. The syndicate bosses *were* the government.

They'd sectioned Utopia into north and south territories using Broad Street as the demarcation line. Rory Gilcrest controlled north Utopia—the Hollow—so named because most of it was in a single massive cavern. Max Ironstone controlled the other half, called Southie, which was an assemblage of smaller hollows that had been connected by blasting and excavation. The Hollow had thirty thousand residents, Southie just over twenty thousand.

Syndicate rule was a dictatorship in the sense that there were no elections. No speeches with promises of anything. No town council. No votes. Yet it was democratic in that the majority of residents supported them. Many because they didn't want to be sent back to face the music. Others because they were treated with favor. The unhappy minority learned to keep their mouths shut.

In spite of the hurdles, Jeremy had been feeling good about their law enforcement efforts. He and Atepa were a strong team. Just two months ago, Girish Mannan had praised them for a high-profile capture. The operation had gone smoothly in part because they'd had the vision to open lines of communication with Gilcrest and Ironstone. They also had cultivated a handful of informants who provided vital last-minute intelligence for the mission.

It was around that same time that Atepa began carrying on with Zed Ironstone, a native Utopian and son of Max Ironstone, boss of Southie.

Jeremy raised the obvious concerns.

"I know what I'm doing," Atepa insisted. "He's not like you think." She swore she could handle it. That Zed wasn't a crook like his father. It was Romeo and Juliet all over again. Forbidden love. Zed cared for her. She looked Jeremy in the eye. "He wants to do the right thing for Utopia."

There were several men for every woman on Mars, so Atepa had her choice of suitors. But she claimed that Zed was the one who fulfilled her. He made her whole, was yin to her yang. She sang and laughed at work, clearly happy. Jeremy tried to be happy for her.

Then, two weeks ago, she learned a difficult life lesson, one Jeremy had feared.

Zed had been lying to her. Playing her. Using her. She'd told him confidential bits about Rory Gilcrest's operation, doing so to puff her own self-importance, to draw them closer together. Days later, the Ironstones used the information to launch a strike on the Hollow, stealing a load of fuel and a trailer full of mining explosives.

When she discovered what he'd done, when she understood he'd been using her, she felt betrayed and humiliated, furious to her core. She reacted badly, yelling, crying, pointing fingers. She made threats, saying crazy things to Zed. "The service is going to take you down. Your dad too. Say goodbye to Southie and hello to prison."

Jeremy learned of Atepa's meltdown when Southie enforcers came for him, dragging him out of bed. He hadn't seen her since. Didn't even know if she was alive.

After days with just one small meal a day, he'd become so weak he could barely stand. Then two big guys showed up at his door. His mouth watered from the savory aromas as they escorted him down the hallway, a man on each side of him, gripping him by the upper arms, holding him up as much as propelling him forward.

They escorted him into the room at the end of the hallway and shoved him into a chair at a table. In front of him was an empty plate. Just beyond it, a feast. A succulent roast with potatoes and peas. Gravy. Garlic bread. Beer.

He had to say six words convincingly. "Everything is fine. I'll explain soon." Drooling, his eyes teared with the promise of a meal.

He would have said anything.

Chapter 16

Two days after a trouble-free slingshot maneuver around Earth, Cuss and Eve watched breathlessly as the *Star Chaser* approached, the supply ship materializing behind them from the void of space, synchronizing with the *Nelly Marie*, and then attaching with a metallic *clunk*. Even though it was called a pusher, it connected to the side of their ship, allowing both sets of drives to work together to propel them ever faster through space.

A gray flexible conduit snaked out from the *Star Chaser* and clenched over the *Nelly Marie*'s main hatch, sealing around it and creating an airtight passageway between the two. The display on the wall near Cuss's shoulder turned green to signal that the conduit was holding pressure. He cracked the hatch and pulled it open.

They behaved like schoolchildren, laughing, jostling each other, competing to be the first one across. Cuss let Eve win. It seemed important to her. Lights came on when they entered the craft. It was cool enough that Cuss could see his breath.

"I've raised the temperature," Ygo told him. "It will take a few minutes to warm up."

Cuss didn't have any experience with supply ships. They weren't needed for short hops from Lagrange to Earth or the Moon, trips measured in hours. He did have experience with delivery vessels that would chase him down to transfer a package or person. But those were quick exchanges and then the chase ship was gone. He'd never left the *Nelly Marie* to visit one.

Star Chaser had the feel of a warehouse: open space dominated by a shelving system holding crates and cylinders and flexible sacks. But here, the shelves had a vertical organization, with everything accessed from a ladder that ran up the center of the ship.

There was gravity in *Star Chaser*, the same as in the *Nelly Marie*. It was created by the Paulson drives, which were accelerating both ships at just over one gee, creating a downward force on everything. On the *Nelly Marie*, that force held them to the ship's decks, letting them walk about. On the *Star Chaser*, it meant they had to climb the ladder to reach the different shelves.

Eve started up the rungs. "Yell if you find the pod."

He stepped onto the ladder, but instead of going up or down, he took a moment to understand what he was looking at. The shelves at this level held custom crates, storage units curved at the back so they could snug against the *Star Chaser*'s round hull. A tab on the outside categorized the contents. He found one labeled *C. Abbott*. Another for *E. Boucher*. Several were labeled *Misc.*

"Those are mine," said Ygo.

"Nice," Cuss whispered. The neutral labeling saved them from having to reveal Ygo's corporeal existence. The issue burned bright, however. Eve knew him as the ship's AI. And with every passing day, it became that much more awkward explaining why they hadn't revealed his presence earlier.

"This is it?" she exclaimed from above. "You're kidding."

Hearing the disappointment in her voice, he climbed up to see for himself.

Near the nose of the craft, Mission Support had installed a makeshift ledge, a small deck of sorts. Perched on it toward the back sat a white plastic box, its top about as high as Cuss could reach, its width maybe twice his height. The box had a door on the front with a decal identifying it as a Hawk Deluxe. Below that was written *Premium single habitat for sea, air, and space.*

"It's a premium model," deadpanned Cuss. "What more could you ask for?"

"I don't know what I expected," she said as she slid open the door. "But it was certainly bigger than this."

He looked over her shoulder. It was dark inside, but his lens let him see a molded composite interior. Off-white and empty. A single piece, formed with ledges and nooks and recesses for sleeping and storage. Like something you might find in a camper van. Or a prison. It had a new-plastic smell.

"Could use a few pictures on the wall," he said. "Definitely some bedding."

"There's no power," she said after fiddling with an electronic interface near the door. Stepping inside, she slid open the bathroom door. "I can't see." After a moment. "No water." She backed out and stood next to him, hands on her hips.

"I found the issue," said Ygo. "There are utility ports

on the side. None of them are connected."

"Let's see about hooking you up," said Cuss, moving around the outside of the pod.

Ygo highlighted a junction box for him when he turned the corner. A compartment made of the same white plastic, positioned on the outer wall at chest level. He opened the cover, looked inside, and read aloud the labels on the different taps. "Power, water, ventilation, drain."

"Found them," exclaimed Eve as she reached over her head and tugged on loops of cable and tubing that had been taped to the side of the pod. The *Star Chaser* resounded with harsh ripping noises during each of her pulls. Cuss helped her sort out the bundle, unspooling a wire cable, a flexible ventilation conduit, and a hose for fluids. They paired the fittings on the ends of the lines with the taps in the box, and did the same at a matching utility junction on the wall of the ship.

It all went smoothly, except they were missing a hose for the water connection.

"It's got to be here somewhere," said Cuss, walking around the outside of the pod, searching for the errant line. He completed the circuit, returning to Eve without finding it.

"Worst case is we fabricate one," said Ygo.

"Let's finish unpacking," said Cuss. "If we don't find it, I can make one in the fab."

"Really? I'd appreciate that."

"We have tubing in the hold, so we just need to make the connections on each end. Won't be difficult." He got back onto the ladder. "I'll bet we find the original anyway."

They started at the bottom of the vessel. It was a tight squeeze, the space filled with blue, green, and red flex tanks, bags the size of small swimming pools, each towering above them, the color codes indicating they held water, air, and fuel, respectively. Enough to keep the *Star Chaser* supplied, with extra to replenish the *Nelly Marie*.

"These tanks are designed to shrink as they empty," said Eve, reading an information plate on the red bag.

"Do we get extra room down here as they empty?" asked Cuss. "Space to spread out?"

She shrugged. "Got me."

"Some space will open up right away when we transfer fluids to the *Nelly Marie*," said Ygo. "More will come gradually as we use the fluids during the trip."

After poking around the tank area for a few minutes, Cuss started up the ladder. "Let's see what they sent for our trading leverage."

The shelves above the flex tanks held the canisters of valuable metals, the containers themselves made of heavy aluminum, the lids as thick as Cuss's hands. He snapped the latches on one, lifted the cap, and looked inside. Then did the same five more times, randomly choosing from among the two dozen canisters stacked around them.

Unlike the highly polished metals displayed in jewelry stores, the pieces inside had a dull finish. Cuss couldn't tell if they were tarnished from oxidation or just dirty. Maybe they'd come from old foundry inventory. Perhaps a government repository. Some canisters were filled with round bars. Others, flat billets. Without the labels on the canister covers, he wouldn't have known they were anything more than buckets of scrap.

The shelves above the metals held the tactical weaponry. Mission Support had sent a small armory. Pistols, shotguns, and assault rifles, all secured on racks that slid out from strongboxes, ammunition piled underneath. And explosives, from fragmentation grenades to shaped charges.

"How comfortable are you with any of this?" asked Cuss.

"I do okay on the range with guns. Score higher with pistols than rifles." She removed a Duluth Adapton from a rack, a pistol with a small profile that fired traditional 9mm rounds, the flex grip and trigger guard designed for use both barehanded and gloved. "I have one of these back home, but I've never used it in a live exchange. Never been in one. Not sure how good I'd be with people shooting back."

"Have you worked with explosives?"

"I threw two flash bangs at the police academy." She shook her head. "If things get to that point, I'm probably the wrong person to have as a partner."

Next to the strongboxes was a crate of drones, smaller models, as small as a fingernail up to the size of a dinner plate, potent tools for spotting, monitoring, and tracking. In a separate crate they found two Tigersharks, larger drones capable of carrying light weaponry.

From there they climbed to bins filled with supplies: items for the ship and products that Peanut used for cleaning and maintenance. Things Ygo thought they should have on hand for a long, lonely journey through space.

Cuss opened the bins one at a time and pawed through the contents so Ygo could get a look inside and create a master inventory. He said things like "Oh, good," and "Nice," and "That'll work" as Cuss explored, sending the message that they were in good shape for their journey.

As he rummaged the contents for Ygo's benefit, Cuss found a length of tubing that could be used for Eve's water line. They'd still have to fabricate the connections for each end, but at least they wouldn't need to raid the *Nelly Marie*'s modest inventory for the project.

The shelves above the bins of supplies held their personal stuff. They began shoving each other again, laughing as they jostled for position so they could access the bins with their names on them.

"You're like kids at Christmas," said Ygo, laughing along with them.

Cuss's first bin held a stack of colorful boxes, five across and five high. He knew what they were from the logo on the packaging: protein and energy bars. Twenty to a box. Twenty-five boxes. Five hundred bars in all.

"Yum," said Eve when she saw the cache.

Cuss knew she was being sarcastic and responded by opening a box, removing a cinnamon crunch bar, taking a bite, pretending to appraise the flavor, and nodding in approval. "Good batch."

After more exploring, Eve identified the items she wanted to move up to her pod and began lugging loads up the ladder. After three trips with more to go, she sat on the edge of the ledge to rest. "There has to be a better way," she called down to him. "Did you see a rope? Maybe I can winch loads up."

"I have an idea," said Ygo. "I'll kill gravity and you float everything to her."

Gravity came from the constant acceleration of the Paulson drives. By shutting the drives down, everything would become weightless, allowing them to move things about with minimal effort.

"Hold on to something," Cuss called up to Eve. "Ygo is going to shut off the drives to kill gravity. I'll float your stuff up and you catch it."

"Is it safe?"

"I'll try not to hit you. Are you a bad catch?"

"I meant turning off the drives. They'll restart no problem?"

"They will," said Ygo.

"No problem," Cuss reassured her.

When the drives shut down, three things happened. Cuss felt his stomach lift, like riding a rollercoaster over a crest and plunging down the other side, only the giddy stomach feeling continued as the new norm, not just a momentary thrill. Next, the deep thrum omnipresent in the background disappeared. The silence was jarring. But as Cuss's awareness adjusted, subtle hums and buzzes filled the quiet.

And last, moving Eve's stuff up the ladder changed from a test of endurance to one of precision and skill. Like playing darts, Cuss would send each item with a gentle toss, aiming carefully, watching it drift up the shaft toward her outstretched hands. He had a good arm and good aim. After hooking a leg in the rungs of the ladder to hold himself steady, he launched a parade of items in her direction.

Eve's hand-eye coordination wasn't the strongest, and she missed her catch a couple of times. Fortunately, they bounced off the nose of the ship and rebounded back, giving her a second chance at securing the item.

When they were done and Ygo had restarted the drives, Eve worked to organize her space while Cuss went to *Nelly Marie*'s hold to fabricate the water hose connections.

"You can't be an AI for the whole trip," Cuss said to Ygo as the fab unit chugged away.

"I can if we can keep her from poking around down here in the hold."

"She's going to think I have debates with the ship's AI. That I argue with it."

"I'll be entertained."

"That's part of my worry."

. . .

They were on the middeck of the *Nelly Marie*. Cuss was shuffling cards for his favorite poker game: Texas hold 'em. Already seated, Ygo was participating as a holographic projection, a trick he could pull off when they were inside the ship. He chose a lighthearted look, a clean-shaven man of forty wearing a colorful Hawaiian shirt and a Panama hat. He puffed on a virtual cigar.

Eve joined them at the table. With a pensive look, she set a small handbag on the floor at her feet.

Today was the fifth day of their journey, and things were going well. Cuss enjoyed Eve's company, and she seemed to enjoy his. She was a diligent worker. Conscientious. The separate spaces helped, keeping friction to a minimum, allowing escape if tensions rose.

"We're playing for chips?" she asked as Cuss put the cards down and began organizing colored tokens into stacks.

"Unless you want to play for articles of clothing." He'd said it to be flippant. As a goof. Being silly with a colleague.

"Is that an option?" She bent to her handbag and retrieved a silver pen. She fit a clear plastic cap over the end, held it to her lips, and blew for five seconds. Then she sat still, forearms resting on the table, the pen in her right hand, looking at him, waiting a long thirty seconds, not saying anything.

Caught off guard, Cuss struggled to divine her intentions.

A small display projected above the pen. She looked at it.

He knew about the pen. It was a bioanalyzer. He'd used one in the past for two reasons: a couple of times at the scene of an accident to determine compatibility with someone needing an emergency blood transfusion; and dozens of times since then to compare transmissible viruses and bacteria, a common step when two people were considering swapping fluids. Like during sex.

In rough numbers, there were one hundred fifty

distinct "bugs" that could be identified by the bioanalyzer and that could be transmitted during sex. One hundred of them were completely benign. Some so virulent you could catch them off a toilet seat. But in the end, they had zero impact on the recipient. One more hitchhiker in the symbiosis of life. People usually set the pen to ignore these.

Of the remaining fifty bugs, forty-one had varying health consequences, from annoying to debilitating. Modern vaccines provided full protection, and as law enforcement officers, both of them were kept up-to-date to protect them on a job where searches and scuffles heightened random exposure. The pen should find them clear of these bugs.

There were no vaccines for the final nine. Not yet, anyway. Seven were chronic conditions, meaning medications for life. Sometimes invasive procedures. If you weren't already infected, you should take great measures to avoid becoming so.

The last two were death sentences.

Eve put a new cap on the pen, and with her results still displayed, handed it to Cuss.

She was clear of infection. He was confused. "What's going on?"

"We're adults. Are we going to spend the next six weeks sleeping alone in our own rooms, doing whatever to relieve ourselves in private? Or maybe we help each other. Build on our attraction. Relieve some boredom. Get some exercise. Have some fun." She sat back in her chair, arms folded in front of her. Biting her lip. Looking down at the tabletop. Nervous, like she'd been thinking about this speech for a while.

He waited for her to look up, but her gaze remained fixed on the table. He spoke to the top of her head. "Seriously?"

"What?"

"Christ, Eve. Think how embarrassing this is for Ygo."

Ygo took a puff on his cigar and grinned. "I don't mind."

Cuss shot him a death stare. "We're colleagues on assignment. Hell, I'm your lead. It's inappropriate."

She turned red and finally looked up. "Am I that unappealing? There's just the two of us, all alone, no other choices, no one to stumble upon us. Like we're on a desert island. And I'm not good enough?"

"Of course you are. That's not the point."

She showed the hint of a smile. "So you do want to."

He let out a gasp of frustration. "Again, that's not the point. We'd have to follow certain rules. Like ensuring it's consensual."

"I consent."

"It has to be documented."

"Ygo, please record this: I consent."

He was having trouble keeping up. "What did you have in mind?"

She shrugged. "Maybe Mondays, Wednesdays, and Fridays at my place. Tuesdays, Thursdays, and Saturdays at yours. You do all the work when we're at my place. I return the favor when we're over here."

"On the seventh day you rest?" said Ygo, still grinning, still puffing.

She tilted her head and looked at Cuss. "That. Or we could do one of each."

His brain churned with possibilities. He didn't know what to say.

She continued. "The beauty is that neither of us will fall in love and complicate things. I know something of your reputation, Cuss. People talk. You've been there. Had to deal with the lovelorn. I have too. It's uncomfortable."

He felt simultaneously hurt by the certainty that she wouldn't fall for him, and relieved knowing things wouldn't get complicated later on.

Her voice took on a slight edge. "I wear extra clothes because of your lecherous gaze, and still you stare. Don't pretend you're some innocent being cornered by a horny colleague."

"Ygo, what's today?"

"Thursday."

He looked at Eve. "According to your schedule, we'd stay here and you'd do all the work?"

"That's the proposal."

He stood and held out a hand, inviting her to join him. "Ygo, please record this: I consent."

"Slow down, cowboy." She pointed to the pen.

He blew into the cap. The next thirty seconds were among the longest of his life.

Chapter 17

With little to occupy them, the days dragged. Ygo had organized the case file into volumes for Abbi Adamson, Barker Adamson, and Jaunty Gabala. He had moved the information they'd collected for Vincent Rogalski out of its own volume and made it a subsection for their three suspects. They opened a new file to organize what they knew about marshals Jeremy Romesco and Atepa Underwood. But data was sparse. They needed current, insider information to guide decisions and plan actions.

Eve asked MFOD for a whole laundry list. "We need street maps, population demographics, summaries of the commercial industries, information on local customs, details of the syndicates, their goals and motivations, organizational charts, favored weapons…"

They were dismayed at the sparse results from that request, much of it old, incomplete, or mere speculation.

Periodically they used the ship's sensors to locate the *Tomlinson*. While it was too early to predict with precision, based on the freighter's current course and speed, the *Nelly Marie* would arrive seven days ahead of it.

"We'll be able to rescue the marshals," said Cuss, "and still have time to waste before they land."

Beyond that, Cuss exercised every day, usually with a

few bouts of Street Fighting Full Contact where he fought against a projected opponent controlled by Ygo. It was a visual and tactile fighting game where Ygo would slap and punch and kick him, forcing him to fight with everything he had, honing his practical skills while providing him a thorough workout. Cuss believed Eve exercised as well, but she did it on the *Star Chaser*, so he didn't know her routine.

At Eve's encouragement—insistence really—they ate dinner together. Cuss was a snacker and rarely sat for formal meals on the ship. But it was a different time with different routines.

They played a few games. Watched some vids.

And they had their regular romp.

She started out a little bossy. Giving suggestions. Guiding his ministrations. As per her proposal, he let her do all the work when they were at his place. Contrary to the agreement, he also let her do most of it when they were at hers.

Among his favorite parts of their lovemaking was when he'd pause to look at her. Stare, really. She was visually stunning with her clothes off, and he couldn't get enough of studying her form, from head to toe and everything in between. He confirmed her natural hair color was blonde, not the brunette on her head. And her fitness level was a turn-on. While she looked soft and cuddly when she was lying there, every time she moved, muscles rippled beneath her skin.

She didn't seem bothered by his inspections, something other lovers had found uncomfortable, intimidating, embarrassing. But in Eve's case, she was too busy returning the favor to notice. Cuss was a natural beefcake, with broad shoulders, strong arms, a powerful chest, and a muscled stomach.

On the job, she was hardworking and competent, showing ingenuity, asking great questions, willing to tackle whatever Cuss put in front of her. And she compartmentalized perfectly, never mentioning their sessions. She didn't behave lovey-dovey. No lingering gaze. No suggestive comments. No unnecessary touching. Nothing at all. She was like a female him in that regard.

And in their downtime, she was entertaining as hell, creative, making him laugh. Today was no exception.

He was on the middeck fixing a snack when he heard her climbing up from the command deck.

"The Great Drone Race starts in ten minutes," she said when her head appeared at the top of the ladder.

"The who what?"

She had a drone in each hand and placed one in front of him, joining him at the table. "I thought about calling it a regatta, but that didn't sound right."

He picked it up and examined it: a tiny flying saucer whose plain exterior belied the amazing technology inside. It was a high-speed model, a beige disk that was big in her hand but small in his. "I imagine this will make sense at some point?"

She spoke a string of commands, and two hoverview displays opened, one in front of her, one for him, showing piloting functions and interfaces to their machines. She wiggled her fingers and her drone floated off the table, her display showing the view from the saucer's camera. "I'll lead the way through the circuit. You follow so you can get a feel for it."

He understood they were going to race, thought it was an amazing idea, and felt his competitive spirit awaken. "Go. I'll catch up."

It took him a moment to familiarize himself with the controls, and then he launched, chasing her drone. They flew down to the command deck, across to the *Star Chaser*, and up the central shaft to her pod. There, they circled behind the module, zipped down to the bottom of the ship and around the back of the flex tanks, then back up, with a return to the *Nelly Marie*.

"The winner is first to land on the tabletop." She patted the surface.

"How many laps?"

"You pick."

"It's called the *Great* Drone Race, so ten?"

She nodded. "Good."

"What's the prize?"

"I don't know. Breakfast in bed?"

"No. Neither of us even eat breakfast."

She bit her lip as she thought, then snapped her fingers. "Winner gets to sit in the pilot's seat during our next meeting with Girish."

He felt a tingle. It was a bet he didn't want to lose, and that made it exciting. "Done."

They recruited Ygo as the race official, and he took them through the circuit a last time, pointing out the different things they were required to go under or around or behind. "Miss one and you have to loop back to get it.

Any questions?"

Cuss was ready, his heart thumping.

Ygo started the race. "On your mark, get set, go!"

Cuss took an early lead, feeling supremely confident, sure he'd dominate. And he did, maintaining a comfortable margin through the first nine laps. On the last pass behind the flex tanks, he used the same maneuver he'd used in the previous laps. But this time he went wide, as if his drone had slipped. He passed behind a crucial support pole, one he needed to be in front of, requiring him to circle back to correct the mistake. Eve took the lead and won by two seconds.

Her victory dance was a sight to behold. While he suspected that Ygo may have had something to do with his flying mishap, watching her laugh and gyrate made losing worth it.

He didn't fall in love that day. But the event turned his head. Her energy was so beguiling that over time he found himself thinking about her in emotional terms. A tug on his heart. A stirring that was outside his norm.

Ygo found him staring off into the distance. "Are you okay?"

Normally, Cuss would respond with something arcane, like, "No, I'm not Oklahoma." Or perhaps he'd go wiseass, "Why, are you writing a book?" Instead, he responded wistfully, "I'm fine."

"Oh no," said Ygo.

. . .

Girish Mannan checked in on the ninth day. "We've received another communication from Jeremy Romesco."

He tapped something on his end, and after a pause, they heard a weak, raspy voice say, "Atepa and I are undercover on a case and we can't risk making contact."

When Cuss realized that was the whole message, his forehead creased. "I'm assuming you've verified that it's him."

"Yes, Marshal." The question was insulting, one of basic competence, so Girish's annoyed tone was understandable. "In the original communication, he sounded upbeat and confident. Our techs determined that the signal had been manipulated and used their magic to tease this out of the transmission."

"Is this his normal reporting protocol?"

"It isn't. Because of distance, Utopia comms suffer a half-hour delay. Combine that with a settlement governed by corrupt syndicates, and I admit I came to accept reporting from him that deviated from what I expect from the rest of you. With that said, this is way outside his norm."

Every time Girish spoke, they had to wait several seconds for the transmission to travel from Earth to the *Nelly Marie*. Their response back to him had the same annoying lag, a problem that would only get worse, the beginnings of the thirty-minute delay Girish referenced.

The reason for the delay? Because on a cosmic scale, the speed of light was painfully slow.

All electromagnetic transmissions—radio, the visible spectrum, x-rays—traveled at the speed of light, the fastest speed in the universe according to physical laws. A comms transmission took fifteen minutes to travel from Earth to Mars. The response back took the same. This meant that communications with the planet nearest to Earth had a frustrating half-hour delay. Science missions to Pluto and the edges of our solar system took half a day for a single comms exchange with Earth.

The *Nelly Marie* was still early enough in its journey that the delay was manageable, each side compensating by speaking a bit longer than they would in an ordinary conversation, guessing what the other might want to hear in the hope of saving an exchange. Before long, though, the seconds would grow to minutes, adding to the challenge. It was a contributing factor for why the intelligence from Utopia was so thin.

Cuss and Eve tag-teamed Girish, complaining that they didn't know who they were chasing, what crimes had been committed, who they had as potential allies, or what the place even looked like.

"I'll shake the trees and get you whatever we have. I can tell you now, though, that it won't be what you need, what you have every right to expect. When you're close enough, we can guide Ygo to feeds we've identified, and hopefully he can backfill the holes."

They discussed strategies for doing that, and then Girish signaled they were almost finished by asking, "How is everything going otherwise?"

"We're fifteen-thirteen," replied Cuss.

"I saw the consent forms. I guess it's no surprise."

Eve must have deduced that a fifteen-thirteen was the internal code for consenting sexual relations between colleagues, because she blushed.

"Both of you are allowed to change your mind at any time. Please update your status immediately if that happens. Ygo, can you get access to Chaparral's Work Life course?"

"I can," said Ygo.

Girish looked at Eve. "You'll be taking the whole sequence when you're there, but I suggest you sit through the third and fourth units now. They explore relationships between marshals, define consent, explain procedure, all of it."

"Yes, sir," she replied.

He shifted his gaze to Cuss. "It might be a good idea for you to take a refresher yourself. There have been a few tweaks to the rules since you took it."

Cuss nodded, groaning internally. This was another reason why he avoided relationships with colleagues.

. . .

Just past the two-week mark, Cuss crawled over to the *Star Chaser* to grab a box of snack bars. He was on the ladder when he heard Eve, who was in her pod up by the nose of the craft, giggle. Then she laughed. He amplified the conversation using his lens in time to hear her say, "You're silly."

Curious, he strained to identify who she was speaking with, but he couldn't tell. She continued with her giggling, this time saying, "You behave, young man."

When he heard that, he froze, pangs of jealousy derailing his other thoughts. He climbed higher, moving quietly, anxious to learn about his competition. As he drew closer, he could hear a muffled male voice.

"Who is she talking to?" he asked Ygo.

"Me."

"*You?*" He pondered that for a moment. "Have you told her who you are?"

"Still an AI. Just an entertaining one."

. . .

Recognizing that his feelings were becoming a problem and failing to see a solution after days of reflection, he decided to confront the issue. "Eve, I have something to confess."

"You're pregnant."

She delivered the line so seriously that he paused, trying to understand, his misery clouding his thoughts. When he realized she was teasing him, he continued. "No. But I'm finding that our intimacy is messing with my emotions. I'm starting to think about you in ways that could detract from our mission."

"Thinking about me positive or negative?"

"Definitely positive. I'm like a high school kid with his first crush."

"Are you saying that the famous womanizer of Lagrange, immortalized in gossip and graffiti, has a crush on little ol' me?"

"Is there really graffiti about me?"

"None that I've seen. Just the gossip. But it sounded dramatic in the moment." She got serious. "Tell me what's on your mind."

"I was thinking maybe we should cool it for the rest of the trip. Let me get my head right before we get there."

She nodded. "Maybe we should see other people."

He hesitated before realizing she was still teasing. "I'm serious, Eve. I need to get it under control."

"Is 'it' me?"

"No. Getting control of the thoughts that are distracting me."

"If we stopped having sex, would you stop thinking about me?"

He was about to say yes but knew it would be a lie, that he would mope about, become unpleasant to be around. Before he could answer, she continued.

"If I stay over here and you stay over there, not even seeing each other, would you stop thinking about me?"

He broke eye contact. "Probably not."

"Truth is, we can't do anything about it until we get off our island and return to society." She moved closer to him and put a hand on his arm. "I have a way that some good can come of this."

"Really?" His heart lifted, anxious to hear.

"We'll continue our sessions. But now that I know you love me, you're going to be doing a lot more work. I mean *serious* effort."

He snorted as he belly laughed, a response to her humor as well as an expression of relief that she was taking the awkward situation in stride.

It made him care for her that much more.

Chapter 18

Over weeks of travel, Ygo painstakingly collected feeds from an array of sources on Utopia—public space cameras, home links, industrial sentries—and stitched them together with the bits MFOD had supplied to create a tour of the settlement. Chattering with excitement, Cuss and Eve sat in front of the large viewscreen on the command deck while Ygo used image casting to insert them into his simulation, as if they were on an excursion through the town.

"The sights are accurate," he told them. "But I simulated the sounds. I didn't add scents but can assure you it's not going to be flowers in the springtime. I'd guess more like livestock in the summer."

Eve's nose crinkled.

"We'll start with the Hollow and then visit Southie."

The lights dimmed and Cuss was floating down a street in the Martian settlement, Eve by his side. It appeared to be a primitive version of Nova Terra. Not in the rustic sense. More like Stone Age primitive.

Rather than a clear polymer dome high overhead, the Hollow was a massive cavern with an uneven ceiling of dark rock, low in spots, and only medium high at its peak. And instead of a convincing sun like the one simulated in Lagrange, the ceiling was covered in a web of lights, tens of thousands of them, uniformly bright, like a perfect grid of stars shining from all directions, the effect muting shadows on the ground.

"What are they doing for power?" asked Cuss, looking up at the glow.

"They have fourteen generator modules on the surface. Mobile units wired together, positioned below the rim of a nearby crater in case things go wrong."

"Sounds safe," said Cuss.

"I've learned that nothing about Utopia is safe. It's a frontier town, a mining settlement focused on the production of penelopite. You've heard of it?"

Cuss shrugged. He'd heard references to it over the years, but the core of his knowledge could be summarized with two facts and a rumor. Penelopite was a mineral mined on Mars. Sketchy people ran the mining operation. And the discoverer of the mineral supposedly named it after his daughter, Penelope.

"It's a mineral used in the production of electronics," said Ygo. "Quite valuable. Mining on Mars is a dirty business. Dangerous. Too remote to manage from Earth. So a trade consortium purchases product from syndicates—criminal organizations really—two of them because competition works to maximize production. Syndicate management has its benefits. It keeps costs down for things like workplace safety, environmental responsibility, employee rights. And as customers, the trade consortium maintains an arm's length from the liability, which is significant from what I've seen."

"And the wheels go round and round," said Eve.

"But I digress." Ygo returned to his tour. "A mining outpost needs most of its people to dig and process what they call pay dirt, soil with high concentrations of the mineral. The rest work to support those doing the mining. Food service, equipment repair, medical care, spaceport operations, a few school teachers. Like that."

As they moved along, Cuss saw that the streets were little more than dirt paths that meandered around outcroppings and over rises, following natural formations in an efficient fashion. People were out and about. Not a lot. Mostly men. A few were walking, others standing and talking. One was using tools on a machine. Two stacked material in preparation for a stonework project.

"They don't look like criminals," said Eve. The people wore either jumpsuits or canvas overalls, rust colored as much from a veneer of Martian soil as the dye in the material itself. "I suppose that doesn't make sense. They look like workers. Hardy. Tough. People with a purpose."

A vehicle tooled down the road in their direction, a buggy that was all truck bed, its bucket-like body holding lengths of pipe. People moved out of the way but continued with whatever they'd been doing, a subconscious response to a familiar event.

"Buildings are constructed mostly from clay brick. It's an aggregate harvested from a pit on the surface. They fire the bricks in a kiln up there as well."

The structures along the road were narrow one-story boxes that, like the road, undulated with the landscape. Some were built in the dips, others perched on rises, some even balanced on ledges hacked from the rock face. It reminded Cuss of indigenous archeological structures he'd seen excavated on Earth.

"This is typical housing. Inside are three tiny rooms: bedroom, kitchen-living area, and bathroom. The kitchen is a few simple appliances. The toilets back up because the sewers were installed as an afterthought. It's spare living."

"No wonder they're so desperate for immigrants," said Eve.

"Most use image projection to make the insides homey. Wallpaper, windows, plants. Pictures on the wall."

"No vines?" asked Cuss, realizing that the exterior of the structures were bare.

"No need. They've tapped into a nearby ice pocket. Melting it gives them plenty of water, and splitting the water molecules gives them all the oxygen they need."

As they approached an intersection of two meandering paths, Cuss saw a largish building with wide doors and a broad porch on one corner. A sign on the front identified it as the General Store, with the words Liberty Street written beneath it in stylized script. Diagonally across on the opposing corner was a building of similar size, this one labeled Lucky Tavern. A dozen people moved about in the dirt square between the two.

"It's a classic company town," said Ygo. "Workers make good money but then turn around and spend most of it to live. The food and lodging come from the syndicates. No outside vendors allowed. They spend the rest of their wages trying not to be bored. Drinking. Gambling. Entertainment. Also supplied by the syndicates."

"Poker?" asked Cuss, his voice hopeful.

"I knew you were going to ask that," Ygo said to him inside his head. To both of them, "Yes, poker."

Ygo moved them onto a different street, where they passed a cluster of bigger homes. Up ahead was another general store, this one identified as the Highland Street outlet. Across from it was a tavern called the Frontier Pub.

"These are the homes of the inner circle," said Ygo. "The locals call them associates. It's like being a made man in a criminal family. Rory Gilcrest is the boss, so they do his bidding. Loyalty above all. In exchange, they live well and enjoy a certain status in the community. Respect."

"Fear?" asked Eve.

"It's the root of everything else. But Rory and Max are both smart enough to minimize social discomfort, to instead focus on building community. They need people to want to stay. It's much more effective than force or fear."

"What community?" asked Eve. "I don't see garden parks or theaters or anything else that gives the place warmth."

"The biggest driver for this population is the promise of riches. The locals dream about a big score the way some do winning the lottery. Beyond that, it's little things, like the syndicates tolerating a certain level of individual initiative. People make stuff in their homes and trade with others who are doing the same. The workers get a sense of control over their destiny from it. A relief valve from other pressures. As long as they keep the scale small, the syndicates look the other way."

They slowed in front of a structure roughly the size of a general store, this one with a covered porch, big windows on either side of a rust-red front door, and a roof of sheet metal, ribbed to give it strength, dusty with Martian soil. The house was set back behind a natural ridge of stone that rose head high like a protective fence. A guard stood on the front porch. He wasn't wearing a weapon that Cuss could see.

"This is Rory's home," said Ygo.

"Does he spend his day here?" asked Cuss.

"He's usually at the mine site, micromanaging everything. He earns fat bonuses if he beats quota and will be replaced if he falls short, so he's motivated. Same arrangement for Max Ironstone."

"Is that his real name?" asked Eve. "It sounds contrived. Like Big Hard."

"Don't know. Hold on." A pause. "He was born Maxwell Thomas Ironstone."

"Still sounds fake."

Ygo laughed. "I made a clip of Rory leaving the house. Have a look."

The simulation blipped, and the guard was suddenly in a different position. The front door slid open, and a man exited. He was shorter than the guard. Slight build. Somewhere in his early fifties. He had bushy light brown hair. A full reddish beard. Round, friendly face. Dressed in a rust-colored jumpsuit. Soiled, like a working man. He walked out to the street, and a cart pulled up. He climbed in, and it drove away.

"How long has he been here?" asked Cuss.

"Eighteen years as a resident. Eight years as a boss. That's a lifetime in this business."

Resuming their tour, they followed a road toward the craggy cavern wall. An airlock door came into view when they topped a rise. It was a sturdy metal number built into the rock face, with straps, ribbing, and rivets, broad enough to allow passage of small trucks. The road they were on led right to it.

"The mine is on the other side. They keep it sectioned off to protect the air in case the machines punch through to a rift that vents to the surface. It also keeps the noise and dust from invading the town. I'm still working on the mine simulation, so we can't go through the airlock door yet."

To their left near the cavern wall was an open area stacked with old equipment. Digging machines, feeder belts, sieve stacks, drive systems. A tangle of add-ons and extras. Everything crusty and corroded, bent and dented. All organized in haphazard piles.

"Nothing gets discarded. If it's too far gone to be used in the mine, they stack it here. Then, when something inside breaks, this becomes their supply store. Scavenge whatever might work—a belt or bearing or pulley—hack together a bush fix, and get back to processing paydirt as fast as possible."

In a clearing past the scrapyard, Cuss could see light seeping out from what looked like a tent of black plastic. A big thing. Much larger than a general store. Ygo elevated their view so they could see that it was one of several tents stretching a good distance along the wall.

"These are the food factories that feed Utopia. It's mostly manufactured fare, but the populace seems content. The syndicates provide a free communal breakfast and lunch every day so people can work with a full stomach. It helps them focus and saves them time on shopping and meal prep. It's a generous spread, a huge contribution to the community-building effort we were talking about."

They traveled another street, this one with a metalworks factory and a lubricants plant on one side, and an industrial-sized air-handling installation on the other, equipment that ensured Utopia's air had the proper oxygen content, temperature, and humidity.

At the end, Ygo turned south and crossed over Broad Street.

Everything looked the same as they crossed. But Broad Street was a boundary road, one that defined territory the way they can in cities on Earth where rival gangs compete. Cross it and you move from the Hollow to Southie, from one syndicate's control to the other.

Broad Street also served as a geological dividing line of sorts. To its north, the huge cavern of the Hollow. To its south, just a few hundred meters along, smaller caverns that had been joined together by breaking walls and digging tunnels, providing space for the underground settlement to grow. Southie's modular nature made it impossible to stand back and take it all in the way you could with the Hollow, and to Cuss that made it seem less grand.

"You can see overhead that they have the same starlight ceiling," said Ygo. "They share the same mobile generators on the surface. Same air and water systems. The buildings are the same brick construction. They even operate the same food factory together."

"Makes sense," said Eve.

"Where they separate is what I call daily life. They work different mine sites. They have their own communal meals. Their own taverns and shops. Who wants to mingle with the enemy? Oh, and they wear blue clothes instead of red."

"Uniforms?" said Cuss. "Is this a friendly rivalry like competing sports teams, or is it more serious?"

"It's both. It's an artificially created rivalry stoked by Skyline. That's the trade consortium. They do it mostly with incentives. An example is the ongoing contest where the most productive mine each month gets a bonus, money that trickles down to the workers, making them care. Or Skyline will include a load of sweets along with a shipment of equipment from Earth, and award it all to just one syndicate based on a 'who can mine the most in three days' challenge. And when new mineral veins are discovered, they'll play the syndicates against each other, having them bid before deciding who gets control of it."

"I can see that creating tension," said Cuss.

"As long as everyone is playing fair, most workers view it as a friendly competition, though there are arguments and the occasional fist fight. But the bosses expect to get their bonus and won't allow anyone or anything to stand in the way. They also make money by skimming, the time-honored tradition of taking a bit for yourself before passing the loot up the chain. And they get a sizable chunk from the workers: alcohol and gaming and rent. It's as serious as can be to Rory and Max. People who are problems disappear."

Cuss and Eve sat quietly, taking it in, digesting the

challenges ahead, watching the scenery of Southie. The multi-cavern geography made traveling through it feel like a theme park ride, where each turn revealed a new sight. They'd just left a large chamber holding a few hundred homes clustered around a neighborhood store and pub, and were entering a smaller chamber that held Southie's equipment scrap pile. The airlock into the mine was on the cavern wall next to it.

After that was a bubble-shaped cavity that held a small school and a smaller interfaith church. Then they arrived at a chamber with a high ceiling and smooth ground. Desirable features, features reserved for the privileged. In it were ten well-appointed homes similar in size to those of Rory Gilcrest's team.

"The ones in front belong to Max Ironstone's associates." Ygo elevated their view, allowing them to see to the back. "His is the one against the far wall."

Max's home was easily identifiable because it was as big and fancy as Rory's. Cuss couldn't see a guard. But the structure's position at the back, surrounded by the homes of associates, made any sort of surreptitious approach all but impossible.

"I have a scene of Max leaving the house with his son, Zed," said Ygo.

The simulation blipped and the door slid opened. A man in his late fifties stepped out, followed by a younger man, maybe thirty. Both were tall. Broad. Big, like Cuss. They both had bushy eyebrows and matching pencil mustaches. Their heads were triangular: broad forehead tapering down to a pointy chin. Max's chin was clean shaven. Zed had a goatee. They wore similar blue jumpsuits. Max's was smudged with Martian soil. Zed's looked clean.

"Max seems unhappy about something," said Cuss, watching the man's cheek muscles ripple and flex from grinding his teeth. His forehead showed the furrows of a frown as he stared into the distance. Next to him, Zed studied the ground, biting his lip, avoiding eye contact.

"Do you think this is their normal father-son dynamic?" asked Cuss. "Or is something going on between them?"

"Hard to say," said Ygo.

"Could be as simple as Zero grabbing the piece of toast that Big Hard had his eye on," said Eve. She sat back and crossed her arms. "The real question is, how do we proceed once we get there? I don't see anyone answering our questions. Or showing us around. Or doing anything useful to help us find our missing marshals. Why would they risk it?" She looked at Cuss. "How do we conduct an investigation in such a foreign and antagonistic setting? And even if we confirm a crime and identify the doers, how do we go about arresting them?"

"Good questions," said Ygo.

Cuss felt a tension in his neck and shoulders, and rested his head on the back of the chair, seeking relief as he struggled for answers.

Chapter 19

Preparations for arrival began earlier than necessary, reflecting both excitement at the conclusion of their long isolation, and their boredom. With a bump and a shudder, the two ships separated in their final approach to Mars. They swooped around behind the planet, slowing until they settled into orbit. Then, with the *Nelly Marie* leading the way, they began their descent.

Cuss didn't pretend to pilot during the landing sequence, instead letting Ygo manage the details for both ships. The thin Martian atmosphere provided little resistance to the plummeting craft, so they weren't buffeted in a fiery maelstrom the way they would be on Earth.

He used the time for a look-see. "Can you show us the spaceport?"

Ygo cast the image onto the large viewscreen so Eve could see as well. "They call it the shipyard. I can't find any formal name for it."

The shipyard was archaic by modern spaceport standards. There were twelve landing pads in a symmetrical three-by-four grid. The pads themselves were little more than circles bulldozed smooth on the surface, with a thick layer of stone powder on top to harden them. Cuss could see gantries at each pad, simple structures providing ship services. But given their small size and spindly nature, he didn't expect much in the way of port amenities.

Five pads were occupied, one by a cruiser—a corporate craft that could carry three or four people on the long journey back to Earth. The other four served cargo ships, purpose-built freighters transporting equipment and supplies to Utopia in support of the mining operation, and ore to Earth to pay for it all. Cuss saw that the freighters were at pads with larger gantries, which made sense, as they would need specialized equipment for loading and unloading material.

"I don't see the *Evalina*," said Cuss. That was the name of Jeremy and Atepa's ship.

"Neither do I," said Ygo. "I'll contact MFOD and let them know."

The shipyard was located on a table of land, a flat area surrounded by craters and hills. A well-used road led from the landing pads over to a sturdy building with a smooth mortar surface. Dull gray, evenly shaped, angular. The road sloped down into a channel as it neared the building and disappeared beneath it, dead ending at a formidable airlock, the surface entrance to Utopia.

The image shifted to zoom in on two landing pads halfway back in the grid. "We've been assigned these two."

Cuss watched them grow in size. Another roar, more thumps, and the *Nelly Marie* was safely on the ground, the *Star Chaser* next to it.

As they stood and stretched, Ygo said, "I've linked with the airlock and am learning their procedures. It will take a few."

"So, why are we here?" asked Eve. They'd discussed

several options to explain their visit to the populace but hadn't finalized one.

He was digging through a drawer and paused to respond. "We're here as replacements in the normal assignment cycle. We're surprised and disappointed that our predecessors left before we arrived." He returned to his task, pushing around the contents until he found a small box, the target of his search. He removed a sheet from the box, peeled off a tiny clear plastic dot stuck to it, and examined it on the tip of his right index finger.

"Surprised how? Comms still work. We'd be in contact with them if it were true."

Cuss smiled. "Play dumb. The Marshals Service director is furious about their behavior, is handling them personally, and has asked us to stay out of it. He wants us to focus on building relationships in our new home."

"I imagine they would see dumb as a positive trait in a law officer. It might buy us a day or two until someone with sense thinks it through."

"A day or two is a start." He took her by the shoulders and turned her so she stood sideways to him. He pulled her hair back and stuck the clear bit on his finger behind her right ear, pressing firmly until it adhered. The device provided boost to keep her linked with Ygo when they were underground, something his lens did for him. "Give it a try."

She looked into the air. "Testing, testing. One, two, three." She laughed, reacting to something Ygo said to her privately. "You are so bad." Apparently it was something suggestive. Either way, Cuss had confirmation that the boost was working.

Standing there, he began to feel his impatience festering. "How much longer?" he asked, a kid complaining on a family vacation.

"A transport is on the way. Should be ten minutes. You can move out to the gantry now if you want."

Cuss pulled on his gray sports jacket and then moved his left elbow up and down like a bird flapping a wing, squeezing his armpit each time, unhappy because of what wasn't there. "I hate going in naked."

Ygo had told them that weapons weren't allowed, that they'd be searched, and they would have to surrender whatever was found, probably losing it for good. Cuss had compromised by secreting a knife in the sleeve of his jacket, a special Marshals Service weapon with circuits designed to defeat electronic detection. Still, it wasn't a gun.

"At least you have your size." Eve hugged herself, looking small in her gray blazer with matching slacks.

Seeing her worry, Cuss reacted. "I'll be right back." He scrambled up to his bedroom and dug his compact ankle gun—a Pittsfield Slim in a tuck holster—from his locker. Hustling back to the command deck, he held it out for her. "Wear this in your waistband in back. If they find it, we give it up with apologies."

"You sure?" She took the gun from Cuss, pulled it from the holster, worked the action, checked the load, and snugged it back into place. The gun's small profile fit her hand well. "Ygo, what do you think?"

"They won't be happy if they find it. But if you give it up freely and let them keep it, I imagine it would be okay."

With a shrug, she tucked it inside her pants at the small of her back, seeming to relax a bit as she did so.

Excited to finally depart, Cuss worked the ship's hatch and stepped out onto the gantry platform, a space big enough for four people if they knew each other well. New smells filled his nostrils, primarily off-gassing from the ship combined with the sharp scent of Martian soil.

The gantry structure was assembled from metal tubes and flat plates tacked together in a less-than-inspiring manner. A translucent shroud covered the structure, flexible enough to mate firmly against the *Nelly Marie* to provide a habitable environment for those inside. The shroud eliminated the need for space suits on the gantry, though a safety officer would likely suggest they wear one anyway.

A stairway led to the surface. He leaned over the railing to look down and saw more features than he expected to. Hoses to supply the ship. A winch for moving goods in and out of the cargo bay. A simple airlock at the bottom big enough to accommodate a small vehicle.

Their feet clanged on the steps as they descended, the firm sound somewhat reassuring. At the bottom, he saw a shadowy blur approaching them through the translucent walls. There was a rumble, the whine of pumps, a whoosh of air, and the veil lifted to reveal a Martian trawler, a brown box on wheels with windows all around. It had a single door on the side that slid open as the cart came to a stop, revealing two bench seats that together could fit four people with some comfort and six in a squeeze. Space in back had room for luggage and gear.

They climbed in and sat together in the front seat, facing forward, taking in the desolate views as the transport trundled across the barren reddish soil surface. To his left, Cuss could see factories of some sort in the distance. Straight ahead he saw the smooth gray bunker. He turned in his seat and inspected the *Star Chaser* receding behind them, assuring himself that all was secure.

"We'll be fine," said Ygo, who would guard both ships and himself while they were away, able to draw on everything from electric shock to a ship-mounted laser gun for defense.

The roadway leading down under the bunker was longer and went deeper than Cuss had perceived from the air. But soon enough they arrived at the door leading from the Martian surface into Utopia, an imposing metal barricade covered in a layer of fine dust.

Traveling on tracks, the door rumbled to the side, its weight causing vibrations he could feel inside the trawler. When it had cleared several meters, the vehicle advanced to enter a brightly lit airlock chamber deep enough to accommodate large vehicles. The door reversed itself and rumbled closed behind them. The air cycled, and a matching door opened in front, sliding like a curtain on a stage to reveal the stone paradise called Utopia.

It also revealed two men standing next to each other on the other side of the door, positioned right in front of the cart, blocking forward progress. Both wore dusty coveralls, one rust red, the other navy blue. Both had a serious expression. Not glaring. But not welcoming either.

"The trawler stays here," said Ygo. "It's for travel onto

the surface. It isn't for driving around inside."

Cuss slid open the trawler door and stepped out.

The one wearing blue moved toward him, the other following close behind. "You the new marshal?" said the leader in a voice pitched higher than Cuss expected.

Both were middle-aged men, medium height, medium build, shaggy hair, beards. The one who spoke had a gap between his two front teeth. The one wearing rust red had a full beard but no mustache, leaving a clean upper lip.

Cuss squared up in front of them, a good head taller than either. "That's right. I'm Marshal Cuss Abbott." He tilted his head toward the trawler. "Inside is Marshal Boucher. We're the replacements. Our colleagues get to go home."

"You have a weapon?" Gap Tooth didn't bother to introduce himself.

"I do not."

"We'll have to search you."

"I don't think so."

"Have to. Orders."

"Go ahead and try." Cuss didn't feel threatened by them, though if either produced a weapon, that could change.

They looked him up and down and then turned and began to whisper.

"Tell you what," offered Cuss. "I'll let you search me if one of you will show us to the Marshals Service building."

He knew Ygo could guide them through the town. But he made the offer to see if either would respond in a positive way. Volunteer to be helpful.

They stopped talking and turned back to him. Gap Tooth said, "Good decision," and proceeded to pat Cuss down. Quick, nervous, doing a poor job. Then he nodded at the trawler. "Your partner too."

Cuss motioned to Eve, who stepped out of the van.

When the men saw her, they froze. Eyes wide. Silent.

"You're not going to touch her," Cuss warned. "I don't care about your orders." He turned to Eve. "Would you open your jacket? Show them you don't have a weapon underneath?" He spread open the front of his own coat to demonstrate.

Eve unbuttoned her jacket and spread the material. Both men's eyes riveted to her breasts, staring hard. Gap Tooth licked his lips.

Cuss imagined Eve's humiliation and instinctively moved in front of her, blocking her from their view, motioning for her to close her coat. "Thank you, Marshal." He faced the men. "Now, which of you is going to show us to our office?"

Clean Lip turned and pointed to a building just four doors down the street. "It's there. With the green trim." His rust-red overalls meant he was from the Hollow. Perhaps one of Rory Gilcrest's associates. And he was cooperating with the new marshals.

Cuss gave a nod to acknowledge the information and started Eve forward, maintaining his position between her and them. As soon as they were out of earshot, he whispered, "I hadn't meant to put you on display like that."

She clucked her tongue. "Men have been reducing women to their body parts since the dawn of time. It's behavior I see daily, pathetically so." Then she smiled. "Anyway, I want extra clips for the gun, and now I know how we're going to get them inside."

He laughed, resisting the urge to throw an arm around her and give her a squeeze. They were already the focus of attention by the handful of locals out and about. He didn't want to add more grist to the mill.

They walked slowly, taking in the unfamiliar world. While Ygo's simulation had been an accurate visual representation of Utopia, being inside felt different. Like a wonderland theme park. The Hollow was huge. Truly massive. Big enough to hold thirty thousand people with room to spare. The grid of lights overhead made a dramatic display. The buildings were stark. Dirt and dust everywhere. The hum of the air-handling equipment bounced off the cavern walls, filling the space with a low resonant growl.

A freight depot sat to their right, a big installation with easy access to the airlock. Cuss needed to turn his head to see it all. While they watched, a tall crane lifted a shipping container from a stack on the ground and swung it onto the bed of a surface truck. The shipping containers were big silver-colored casks designed to fit into spaceship cargo holds and carry bulky material. A second truck waited behind the first for a turn at the loading station.

On the left side of the street, across from the depot, he saw a line of midsize buildings. Nearest the airlock was an emergency rescue station next to a utilities maintenance building, then a field bureau for the Skyline trade consortium. And finally, the Interworld Marshals Service building.

"This is Broad Street," said Ygo, reading Cuss's mind. "It's the boundary road, so neutral interests tend to collect on it."

The people they passed seemed to be walking with a purpose. Focused. Busy. Still, they gave Cuss a long look. Eve even longer. Cuss smiled and nodded in greeting, trying to adapt to the unfamiliar social structure of this strange world.

He studied the building as they approached. The front door was painted the same green as the building's trim and had a brass nameplate affixed at eye level engraved with the words *Interworld Marshals Service*.

"I assume you can unlock it?" Cuss asked Ygo as he examined the door.

"Good news, bad news," replied Ygo. "Yes, I can unlock it, but I have to contact Earth for the code. You'll need to cool your heels for a bit."

Cuss put his face near the access panel and said, "Marshal Cuss Abbott requesting entry." The door opened. He looked at Eve and smiled. "Let's cool our heels inside."

The interior was more impressive than he had expected. It had two floors. The first floor had a reception area in front, with chairs and a side table to meet and greet people. To the left, a seriously disorganized storage room. Next to that, a side room that could be adapted to become a small conference room, or an interrogation room, or even a detention cell. And in the back, an office with a single desk that the two marshals appeared to share. Tables along the office walls held a collection of technology, devices used for communication, tracking, forensics. Some of the equipment looked new, other pieces outdated.

They climbed the stairs to find a central living area with a couch, a couple of armchairs, and a dining table. Two small bedrooms were off the living area, one on either side. There was a bathroom in the corner, and a modest kitchen in back.

A thin film of dust covered everything. No one had been there in weeks.

"Do we leave this place untouched in case it's evidence?" asked Eve.

"What, and live on the ship?"

"I don't know. Is there a hotel?"

"A few of the taverns have rooms for rent," said Ygo.

Cuss shook his head. "We *are* the forensics team. There's no help coming." He twirled in place, scanning the living area. "How about if I start up here? You take the main floor. See if we can figure out what happened. When we're done, we'll switch."

She nodded and started down the steps.

He began in the bedroom with men's clothing. The bed was unmade, the cover pulled partway off and hanging onto the floor. Clothes were draped over the back of a chair with more scattered on the floor. The wastebasket was tipped over.

He spoke to Ygo as he moved, though he didn't really expect an answer. "Is he a slob and this is normal? Or is he neat and something made him leave in a hurry?"

Working methodically, he opened the closet door and pushed aside jackets and shirts, tapped on the walls, lifted shoes. He rifled through the dresser and bedside table, pulling out drawers, looking underneath and behind them for anything hidden. He lay down on the floor and looked under the bed.

He continued the search in the living area, a room that reflected a mix of comfort and utility. Wall art was a collection of wildlife pictures taken at heritage parks on Earth. The furniture was simple, functional, and unattractive.

A potted fern on a table was desiccated, the leaves brown, a scatter of them arrayed on the tabletop like a pixelated shadow. He lifted the pot and confirmed from the stain underneath that the plant had been sitting there for a long time. Someone had taken care of it for years and then let it die.

He checked the drawers of the side tables, lifted the cushions, searched the bookshelves, looked behind pictures, finding nothing that gave him pause. He processed the bathroom and moved into the kitchen, opening cupboards and drawers, looking inside the refrigerator. He dumped the contents of the trash can onto the countertop and poked through it.

The only items of interest from his search so far included a potato in the pantry with eyes growing wild—making it into a spooky Medusa—and an ancient plate of macaroni and cheese in the sink, hard and off-colored but not coated in mold the way it would be on Earth. The sterile environment on Mars combined with Utopia's efficient air scrubbers kept the place free of microscopic life.

Finishing in Atepa's bedroom, he had little luck until he reached the bedside table. On top was an ornamental frame with digital pictures that cycled through on a timer. While he was looking in the table drawer, the picture shifted to a closeup of two people. Atepa and a man with a goatee. It was a face shot, their cheeks pressed together, grinning for the camera.

He picked up the frame, and as he studied the picture, it shifted to a new one. This was of the same two people. He now recognized the man as Zed Ironstone.

In the second photo, Zed was standing in front of a wall of red rock, facing forward, expression fierce, his legs shoulder-width apart, his hands on his hips. Atepa was crouched next to him, also facing forward, an arm around one of his legs as if she were hugging it. She, too, wore a fierce expression, but she hadn't quite pulled it off the way Zed had.

The picture shifted to a family shot: old folks and a cat. Cuss fussed with buttons on the back until he figured out how to shift the pictures manually. There were dozens to look through, but only the two pictures of Atepa with Zed.

Carrying the frame, he descended the steps, calling to Eve. "Check this out." He handed it to her, showing her how to view the two pictures.

"That's Atepa with Zero." She shook her head. "I wonder how old the pictures are?"

"They were taken here on Mars, so relatively recent. I wonder if Zed has had that goatee the whole time? That might narrow the time frame some more."

"Didn't Vincent Whathisname tell us it was always the boyfriend?"

The front door chimed, alerting them to a visitor. The

person announced himself, "Michael Mangual."

They exchanged quizzical glances, and then Cuss walked to the door, signaling for it to open.

Clean Lip stepped inside.

"I'm here to welcome you on behalf of Rory Gilcrest and the Hollow." His delivery was fast and without inflection, like he'd practiced the line.

"Thank you," said Cuss, extending a hand to shake. "I didn't get your name."

"I go by Mamba." He shook Cuss's hand, squeezing hard. Cuss loved that game and squeezed back, crushing the man's knuckles, grinding them together, smiling innocently the whole time. Mamba's forehead creased and he released his grip, pulling his hand back before Cuss did permanent damage. Then he tried to act like it hadn't happened. "What's yours again?"

"I'm Cuss Abbott, and this is Eve Boucher."

Mamba nodded a greeting to Eve. "Ma'am, if you ever need a tour of our fair town, I'd be happy to show you around."

"Thank you, Mamba. I'd like that. But only if you stop calling me ma'am." She gave him a dazzling smile. "I could use some lunch. Can you show me some food options?"

He nodded, avoiding eye contact with Cuss. "Be happy to."

Cuss interrupted the man's fantasy. "Would you know when our colleagues left? We expected to find them here."

Mamba pressed his lips together. "We had nothing to do with it. Look to Southie for answers."

Cuss frowned and played dumb. "Had nothing to do

with what?"

"I'm here to welcome you and deliver that message—look to Southie for answers. I'm not to say anything beyond that." His face softened as he turned to Eve. "We can have a community lunch with the workers, or we can sit at a private table and eat pub food."

"Both sound intriguing." She moved toward the door. "Tell me more about the community lunch." She gave Cuss a wink and a finger wave and then led Mamba out of the building.

Watching them go, Cuss wondered if she still carried the gun or if she'd ditched it here in the office. Either way, he was glad they were gone because he wanted to poke around on his own.

Killing time to give them a head start, he took a moment to look through the storage room. It was filled with junk, much of which predated Jeremy and Atepa, stuff that should have been recycled long ago. Old clothes. Random kitchen pans and dishes. A big Marshals Office sign for the front of the building. Pamphlets promoting the Interworld Marshals Service as a dependable and cooperative partner. Prisoner restraints still in the original shipping package. A metal box with a random collection of hand tools.

He saw an awl in the box, a tool shaped something like a screwdriver except the handle was round to fit in the palm, and the blade was a sharp point for punching holes. He slipped it into his left jacket pocket, worked the knife out of his sleeve, and moved it to the right jacket pocket. He practiced retrieving them, ensuring they wouldn't get hung up in the cloth if he needed them in a hurry.

Then he made for the door. Eve and Mamba had enough of a head start.

Outside, he turned away from the airlock and headed into the Hollow, wandering up and down streets in a manner similar to the way they'd moved on Ygo's tour. He saw actual people this time, so he tried to smile. To be open. For the most part, people seemed friendly. Several nodded an acknowledgement. A few said "Hi."

When he felt he had the rhythm of the Hollow, he crossed over Broad Street so he could "look to Southie for answers."

Things seemed to change on the other side. The streets were quieter. Fewer people strolling about. Two men seemed to be paying too much attention to him. He ran a simple evasive maneuver, turning, backtracking, watching to see if they adjusted their course along with him.

"They're tailing," confirmed Ygo.

Then he made a careless mistake, turning down a road that proved to be a dead end, an alleyway between buildings, brick walls boxing him in. The back of the alley was strewn with junk—casks for liquids, broken shelving, a box of electronics—and he turned to find the two men who'd been following him now standing at the mouth of the alley, blocking his exit. He walked in their direction, hands at his side, trying not to be threatening. Three more men appeared from around the side of the building, joining the others, making it five against one.

They were big men. A couple as big as Cuss. Wearing blue, the Ironstone crew. All five were carrying clubs that looked like short baseball bats, prompting Cuss to wonder if there was a Martian sport that used them. Or perhaps they were a tool employed in mining.

Either way, clubs were deadly weapons if used correctly. But in Cuss's experience, few knew how. Most swung away, trying for the big hit, the fight-ending connection. If they missed, they presented Cuss an opening as their body turned to complete the swing.

Three of them rested the clubs loosely on their shoulders, a batter approaching the plate, reinforcing Cuss's belief that they were unskilled fighters. Beyond that, five was a crowd in the narrow alley. They'd get in each other's way. He could use that to his advantage.

Cuss stopped a few paces from them and spread his arms out, hands open. "I don't want any trouble."

The men looked tough. Rugged. Calloused hands. Broad shoulders. Determined expressions. One in back hocked up saliva and spit on the ground.

"Then go home," said a man in front. His clothes were cleaner than the others. His grooming nicer. They seemed to defer to him.

"Okay. Step aside and I will."

"I mean home to Earth."

"But I'm from Lagrange."

Boss Man didn't answer, apparently done with talking. He tilted his head to one side and then the other, signaling for his men to spread out.

"Does Max know that Zed sent you?" Cuss spoke to them as a group.

The men stopped and looked at each other in a way

that told him he'd hit close to home.

He slipped his hand into his jacket pocket and fingered his knife.

"If you cut them up," said Ygo, "you're done in Utopia."

Cuss understood that a fight that led to black eyes and split lips could be rationalized by a populace. But cutting men open, sending them to the infirmary with punctured organs or gaping wounds, was a whole other level of violence, especially in a place that had only a field hospital.

In response to Boss Man's head signal, one of the men began drifting to Cuss's left, while another moved to his right, working to surround him, straining his peripheral vision. Cuss chose to act before he lost sight of them.

Though his hand was empty, he pulled it from his pocket, closed as if wrapped around an object. He mimed like he was throwing it up in the air, stretching his arm high, spreading his fingers wide, looking up to sell the ruse. Three of them looked up as well, including the guy to his left.

The moment that happened, he acted, swinging his arm down and around in a continuous movement, building momentum that he accelerated by turning his shoulders and shifting his hips. Spinning on one leg, he moved like he was going to extend the other foot up high in a kick to the man's head. But big guys shouldn't be lifting a leg high in a street fight. He was too slow, they were too many, making it a horrible gamble.

The feint gave him the opening he needed. The guy readied for a kick, and Cuss caught him with his elbow, a devastating blow to the temple, one that snapped the man's head back. His eyes rolled up in his head, and he slumped to the ground.

Cuss snatched the bat from the man's hands and squared up in front of his four assailants. "I don't want any trouble," he said again.

"You started it, asshole," said Boss Man. "We get to finish it."

The biggest of the four was next to Boss Man. A monster of a man. Thick arms. Beefy hands. Huge beer belly. He gripped the bat in his right hand, holding it down by his hip. It looked like a toy next to his massive torso, a toy that was positioned a long way from where it would need to be in about two seconds.

Cuss rushed Boss Man, raising his bat like he was going to hit him, howling a war cry to unnerve the group. Boss Man stepped back, ducking and then jabbing his club at Cuss, who accepted a knock to the ribs in exchange for the opportunity to deliver a blow to his intended target, a thrust kick into Big Guy's knee.

He had cocked his leg to start his lunge forward. When he raised his bat overhead, it lifted him into position to deliver a clean blow. Just as he felt Boss Man's club hit his ribs, he snapped the heel of his boot into Big Guy's knee from the side, hitting the fragile joint hard, following through.

Big Guy howled to the sound of tearing ligaments and twisting cartilage. With his body's support structure damaged, he crumpled to the ground, a huge mass of flesh groaning, rocking back and forth, holding his injured knee with both hands.

Cuss had been driving his body forward to deliver the blow, and his momentum carried him into the thick of it. He took hits on a thigh, shoulder, and forearm but kept charging ahead, using his elbows as much as the club, swinging, parrying, and chopping, catching the guy who had spit on the ground with a somewhat lucky blow, sending him down.

His rush had put him on the other side of his assailants. He was no longer trapped. Boss Man and his last henchman backed away, holding their clubs in front, waiting.

Cuss glared at them. "Tell Zed that I want to meet him, that he should come by the Marshals Office first thing tomorrow morning."

He threw the bat at their feet, turned, and started toward Broad Street, his back to them, projecting the image of a fearless lawman. In contrast to his bravado, Ygo sent a feed to his lens the whole time. Together they watched the Southie crew, looking for any signs of threat, ready to respond if one appeared.

Chapter 20

"Bueno," Abbi Adamson said to the old woman as she searched the table for the correct form. "Uno momento."

She was living outside Caracas, Venezuela, helping at a medical clinic for campesinos, poor farmers determined to survive in an increasingly mechanized world. It was not the life she'd envisioned for Lynne or herself. But she was slowly coming to terms with it.

She'd hidden in the caves of Nova Terra, waiting the weeks it took for their stockpile of stolen Pulse to be converted to Ronolyx. During that time, she scoured the feeds and spoke with other Indies, learning what she could about Utopia. The social dynamics. Daily life. Amenities. Or, as she soon learned, conveniences and comforts they would have to live without. What it would be like to raise a child in such a rough-and-tumble society.

After much contemplation and soul searching, she concluded it wasn't going to work. It wasn't an appropriate environment for either of them. No way they would become amusements for lonely men who worked hard, drank hard, and wanted to play hard.

And truth be told, she hardly recognized the man she'd married. Barker had turned to Jaunty Gabala for help back in the early days, when stealing Pulse meant hitting local pharmacies in Nova Terra. Jaunty had an unstable streak, a mental disorder doctors could control with medication. But only if he took the pills, which he didn't. It left him with the kind of brazen crazy that Barker needed to pull off the thefts.

Then the friendship took on a life of its own, blossoming into the idea of robbing Avium Pharmaceuticals in Lagrange. When the man died in that awful accident with the statue, Jaunty had gone full-on psycho, thinking more death was the solution to their problems. And to her alarm, Barker didn't seem shaken by the violence.

He had called every day from the *Tomlinson*, encouraging her to start the journey, rationalizing Vincent's murder by claiming he'd been fueled by jealousy knowing the man had been with her. "I did it for us, babe."

"Bullshit," was her reply, but only after closing the call.

She struggled with the decision. Really struggled. And then decided to go dark. To ghost him. To escape.

Using the Indie's shield technology, she and Lynne left Nova Terra and flew to Earth, showing up at the South American field clinic and pretending there was a mix-up, that she was a proper volunteer. In the end, the medical team was grateful for the extra pair of hands. She'd picked the location as randomly as possible. She didn't know anyone in Venezuela. She didn't know anyone who knew anyone. This made it impossible to track her by habits or relationships.

She latched on to the idea of medical clinics because they were loosely run organizations staffed by workers from all over the world. This one would be closing up shop next week, but there were others coming to the region. They always needed help. She was learning how to sort the patients, a triage that got them in the right order at the right stations inside the clinic's tent. It was a skill she could offer to similar operations.

And if Lynne's condition were to deteriorate, she could turn to the clinic and its medical professionals for help, a priority in her planning.

Meanwhile, Lynne spent time in a play group, seemingly happy. She slept well, was growing like a weed, and if Abbi stuck it out, would end up learning Spanish along with her English. Abbi was using an autotranslator on the job but thought she might learn the language as well.

The setting outside the city was beautiful. Hills and greenery and dramatic vistas. Real sun, wind, and rain!

Abbi couldn't say she was happy. But she wasn't sad, either. She felt fulfilled, helping people who desperately needed it. She and Lynne were safe.

For now, that would have to be enough.

. . .

"How is that possible?" Barker Adamson asked Jaunty Gabala, worry crowding his thoughts.

They were a week out from Mars when they learned that the marshals who had been stationed at Utopia had gone missing. Disappeared. There were all sorts of rumors about what had happened. Who was responsible. But neither he nor Jaunty really knew the players, so the names didn't mean much.

"We're home free," Jaunty promised. "We'll be there for a month before any new marshals can get there. Maybe more. We'll have time to earn loyalty with Ironstone, make some friends, get lost in the crowd."

"Make some friends" was a Jaunty euphemism for learning who they'd need to pay off to gain protection. The payments would come from money they'd stolen on their way out of Nova Terra.

They'd robbed an old couple, friends of Jaunty's parents, before boarding the ship. Last year, Jaunty had overheard the man tell his father that he kept Sols, gold coins minted right there in Armstrong, in a safe in their bedroom. Jaunty had clung to that tidbit ever since, visualizing the treasure, imagining having it for himself.

Wearing masks and gloves, they had broken into the couple's home. Jaunty held a knife to the old man's neck, terrifying him, forcing him to open the safe. When the blade had pricked the old man's skin and a drop of blood oozed out, Jaunty had grinned.

It was a weakness for Pulse that had drawn Jaunty into their world at the start. But over time, his fascination with violence clouded the picture. Barker had no control over the man. Never really had.

Rather than dwell on the catastrophe his life had become, he imagined a new beginning. Becoming a provisional member of the Southie syndicate. And perhaps most important, being joined by Abbi and Lynne.

The *Tomlinson* carried supplies destined for Southie. The captain knew Max Ironstone personally and had arranged job opportunities for Jaunty and him, positions in the mine. They'd paid him for the lead, a handful of Sols from their stash, and were grateful.

They didn't know that the captain was getting paid twice, taking their money as well as a finder's fee from Max Ironstone for recruiting workers. And in truth, even if they had known, it wouldn't have mattered. They needed the introduction, and the captain could provide it.

Then, just days before their arrival, things went to shit.

First, Abbi had stopped communicating. It had been more than a week since they'd spoken. He talked to friends at the enclave, and they all claimed ignorance. No one would admit that they knew why she wasn't calling or where she was staying.

And worse yet, new marshals had landed on Mars, a presence that defied physics. Even a Starlane cruiser that had been muscled up by the Marshals Service and then run hard the whole way took six weeks to complete the trip.

That meant that the new team had gotten underway before the Utopia marshals had disappeared. Which meant they'd probably been sent for a different reason. Like arresting double murderers on the run.

He couldn't help but feel he was being carried to his doom in a tin can, and all he could do was watch, wait, and fret.

. . .

260   DOUG J. COOPER

As Cuss made his way back to the Marshals Service building, Ygo critiqued his decisions. "That's the third time you've tried the 'look at my hand' trick."

"And it's worked three times."

"Someday, someone will ignore your nonsense, and when you stick your arm out, they'll chop it off."

"Let's hope not."

He nodded a greeting to three men coming his direction on the street. They stared back but didn't respond. When they passed, Ygo asked, "You took a few good ones. Any damage?"

"Don't think so."

But when Cuss reached the Marshals Service building a few minutes later, his right shoulder felt stiff. He worked the arm in circles as he stepped through the door, hoping to stretch it out before it set up on him. The deltoid muscle in that shoulder howled in protest at the movement, pain he ignored as he continued stretching for several more turns.

"You here?" he called to Eve as the door closed behind him.

"She's still out with Mamba," said Ygo.

He spun his arm the other way, turning his hips at the same time to check on them as well. As he twisted and turned, his eyes fell on a door near the entryway. He'd been distracted by the excitement of finding the images of Atepa with Zed, and then by Mamba's visit, so he hadn't opened it yet. He presumed it was a closet.

Inside, he found a cleaning bot. From the look of it, the Peanut from Jeremy and Atepa's ship. He fussed with the controls on the jury-rigged setup until the bot woke up, and then he gave it an assignment: "Clean the bathroom and kitchen. Launder the bedsheets and towels." He stopped to look across the room. "And clean the dust off everything. A full top-to-bottom."

While Peanut selected its tools and attachments for the job, Cuss had a thought and asked Ygo, "You'd tell me if Eve was in trouble, wouldn't you? If she was being threatened in any way?"

"Of course."

"Did you tell her that I was being threatened? In a fight?"

"I didn't. It hadn't even occurred to me. Should I have?"

"No. Not unless I needed help."

"That's how I saw it."

He climbed the stairs, undressed, and stepped into the shower, in the process interrupting the assignment he'd just given Peanut. Under the mist, he examined his shoulder as best he could and then checked the welts on his torso and legs. Four of them were already ripening into ugly bruises. None of them needed medical attention.

After toweling off, he dug through Jeremy's bedroom dresser. Cuss borrowed laundered skivvies and socks, but Jeremy was an average-size man, and he couldn't come close to fitting into the other clothes. He put his own back on. As he finished dressing, he heard a commotion on the first floor and descended the stairs to find Eve, alone, carrying two bags of groceries.

"Have you eaten?" she asked, handing them off to

him.

"No, and I'm famished." He led the way back up the stairs, carrying the sacks into the kitchen. "Thanks for thinking of me."

While they talked, he unloaded the items onto the counter and assembled a sandwich of crusty bread, sliced cheese, and sliced meat that, although grown in vats, looked and tasted like deli beef.

She watched him act the chef from the end of the counter, at one point taking a small corner of meat and tasting it. As she chewed, she tilted her head to the side in a "not bad" gesture.

Then she updated Cuss on what she'd learned. "Rory Gilcrest is worried that Zed's misdeeds are going to reverberate across all of Utopia. He's playing defense with us, trying to make sure the fallout doesn't come his way while also trying to preserve some sort of relationship with Southie. They share tight quarters here, and even though they compete, they need to work together."

"What does he think Zed did?"

"He wouldn't say. But when I suggested murder, he shrugged and looked away."

Cuss filled a glass with water from the kitchen sink and grimaced at the chemical taste. He looked in the refrigerator for something drinkable. Failing there, he searched the cabinets and found a filtering carafe. He filled it from the tap, and when it had processed enough water, he poured a glass. It tasted better but still had a faint plastic flavor.

"Did he hint at where they might be? Or where their ship is?"

"After he reinforced the message about looking to Southie, he spent the rest of the time trying to win my favor." She shook her head. "With so many frustrated males on the prowl, this place could be a mega-ego-boosting existence for women, or an intimidating and even scary one. It's not the place to come if you want to be left alone, that's for sure."

"Sorry to interrupt," said Ygo. "But I have some news about the *Evalina*. MFOD couldn't detect its beacon, so they reached out to ships in transit, asking them to scan for it. No luck there either. The consensus is that if it's not in space, it must still be here."

"On Mars?" Eve spoke up to the ceiling the way people sometimes do when talking to a disembodied voice.

"It's a big planet with lots of craters and crevices and chasms. Plenty of places to stow a ship where it would be difficult to find."

"You have any ideas?" asked Cuss.

"Skyline has a mapping satellite in orbit that's scanning the surface for new penelopite deposits. I've tapped into its data link and am monitoring the feed. If it flies over the *Evalina*, I'll see it."

The front door chimed as Cuss was about to ask how long a search would take. The visitor announced himself. "Max Ironstone."

Cuss looked at Eve with raised eyebrows. She scowled back. "Big Hard?" Turning, she made for the stairway. He stuffed the last two bites of his sandwich into his mouth and followed her down.

Max was a large man. A working man, or so the

smudge of dirt on his cheek would suggest. Steel-gray eyes. Salt-and-pepper hair. Blue jumpsuit. Up close, Cuss could see fine lines around his eyes and mouth, badges earned by age and stress.

"Marshals." His voice was deep, gravelly. He reached out a meaty hand. "I'm Max Ironstone."

Cuss shook it. A firm handshake. No squeeze games. Good eye contact. Phony smile.

Max shook hands with Eve, the smile now an honest grin. After holding her hand a moment too long, he addressed them both. "I'd like to welcome you to Utopia, and to Southie, my home. I assume you're aware of our friendly competition with the Hollow. It's my privilege to lead Southie in that rivalry." He paused, projecting a solemn expression for drama. "One that can become heated at times. One that can become personal."

Cuss waited, glad that Eve did as well. Let a subject talk for as long as he's willing. Let him say what he came here to say.

Max looked at him. "I heard that some of my men gave you a difficult time today. Threatened you."

Eve's eyes stabbed at Cuss, a glare packed with questions and concern.

"I apologize for that," Max continued. "They weren't operating under my instructions." He gave a careless shrug. "If it makes you feel any better, I lost two workers in that exchange. I don't know if either will ever be of much use in the mine again."

Cuss continued to wait, though he felt the urge to toss out a sarcastic, "Sorry for your loss."

Max finally got to it. "I hear you're looking for Zed. That you think he's involved in something nefarious?"

"We do need to speak with him," said Eve.

"Perhaps I can help. What would you like to know?"

She shook her head. "That's not how it works."

He didn't relent. "I heard you believe he had something to do with your colleagues. That perhaps there was foul play."

They returned to listening. Waiting.

"I have sources that say that Mickey Montoya was the last to see the two. It seems that Mickey and Jeremy Romesco had some sort of disagreement that spun out of control." He took a viewer from his pocket and showed them a picture of a man holding a mining shovel over his shoulder, a smile on his face.

Cuss recognized Boss Man from the fight in the alley. "Doesn't he work for you?"

"Mickey? He did but doesn't anymore, not when I learned about his outrageous behavior with you, about his involvement with your missing colleagues. Wouldn't surprise me if he's up in the Hollow sniffing around for a job."

"Where are Jeremy and Atepa right now?" asked Cuss. "Are they safe? What did Mickey do to them?"

Max acted coy. "Talk to him yourself. I know an eyewitness who saw it all."

"Saw what?" asked Eve.

Cuss interrupted before Max could answer. "Why would Mickey come here and confess to anything?"

"Maybe he won't. Makes the witness that much more

important, don't you think?"

"Not really," said Cuss. "It turns out we have our own way of learning what happened." He looked at Eve, nodding to encourage her support. "Our colleagues had sensor implants that recorded everything they said and saw and heard. That data is stored on their ship and can be accessed through a link on the pilot's console. As soon as we locate the *Evalina*, we'll have all our answers." He flashed an aw-shucks smile. "We are marshals, after all."

"That's great news," said Max, though his tone didn't reflect even a hint of enthusiasm. "But you won't have to wait. I'll send Mickey over first thing tomorrow. You'll have this wrapped up before you finish breakfast."

"If you want to help us," said Cuss, his voice firm, seeking to exert control. "Send Zed."

Max moved toward the door and signaled for it to open. "I am helping you, Marshal. Saving you from wasting time. Getting you your answers so you can move on." He paused, his bulk filling the opening almost as effectively as the door had. "Friends help each other. I'm happy to do my part."

He stepped onto the front porch, looked both directions, and continued into the street. With long, deliberate strides, he walked away, never looking back.

"I didn't know about the implants," said Eve as the door closed. "That makes finding the ship an imperative."

Cuss looked at her from under his eyebrows.

She frowned in confusion, and then her face relaxed. "There are no implants. You were bluffing."

"I was."

"You want to see if Zed will go to the *Evalina* to destroy the recordings."

"Zed or Mickey or whoever." He smiled. "It was spur of the moment. Do you think it will work?" Before she could answer, he said, "Ygo, are you able to monitor the airlock? Let us know if Zed or Mickey leaves?"

"I have the airlock covered. Tracking them once they're outside might be a bit of a challenge, depending on where they go and how they travel."

"We have a few hours, so do what you can. Let us know how we can help."

Chapter 21

Evening was approaching, and before it got too dark, Cuss and Eve made a trip out to the *Nelly Marie* for a load of personal items, plus some firepower. When they returned through the airlock, Cuss had been prepared to resist any attempt to paw through their stuff. Perhaps word of the alley fight had spread, because they received unfriendly glares but nothing more.

When it came time for bed, Eve took Atepa's room, making no mention of their prior intimate arrangement. Cuss dawdled until she closed the door and then took Jeremy's bed, the mattress requiring that he sleep with his knees bent to keep his feet from hanging off the end.

He'd been out for a few hours when Ygo woke him. "They're dumping Mickey Montoya's body out front."

Cuss sat up. "Here? Can you see who it is?"

"No, their faces are covered. Two males. Average size. Dark clothes. They're having trouble with the body, so they're not strong men."

"Is he dead?"

"Hold on." A long pause. "He is."

"That was predictable. Obvious, even."

"I suppose in retrospect."

"Did you wake Eve?"

"Not yet."

"Good. Don't." Cuss lay back down and closed his eyes.

"You're going back to sleep?"

"Will the body still be there in the morning"

"I'd bet on it."

"Will he still be dead?"

"Got it. Sweet dreams."

. . .

Wiping sleep from his eyes, Cuss stepped from Jeremy's bedroom. He was barefoot and wore only a T-shirt and skivvies. Eve was in the kitchen making coffee, already dressed for the day in a long-sleeve forest-green shirt and beige canvas pants.

"Get it while it's hot," she said, placing a white mug of steaming liquid on the counter and pushing it in his direction.

It smelled better than it tasted. But it was rich in caffeine, something his body craved.

He foraged for food in the refrigerator while he sipped, and finished his first cup in minutes. Pouring his second, he asked Ygo, "What does morning look like in Utopia?"

A hoverview opened at the edge of the counter. Like a slideshow, Ygo switched from camera to camera, showing them different scenes from outside their building: a view up the street toward the airlock, a scan of the freight depot, a look down the street into the heart of the city, and then a view from the depot showing the row of buildings across from it.

"What's that?" asked Cuss, pointing toward the one with green trim, their building, pretending he didn't know anything about his conversation with Ygo a few hours earlier.

Ygo zoomed in on their porch, on a body, a man on his butt leaning back against the green door, his head lolling to the side, face gray, lips blue, eyes bulging, staring lifelessly out into the street. Ygo homed in on the man's face, on a nasty red line on his neck showing drips of dried blood, a horrific necklace produced when choked by a wire.

"That's Mickey Montoya," said Cuss.

"Oh my God," said Eve. "This is out front? Now?" She rushed down the steps.

Cuss stopped in Jeremy's room to throw on pants before joining her on the first floor.

She stood at the front door, staring at it. The door was still closed.

"Is it broken?"

"Just waiting for you."

Cuss triggered the door and it struggled to open, sliding in fits and starts on its track. And then Mickey Montoya, rigor mortis keeping him in a sitting position, fell onto his side across the threshold, blocking the door from closing. He was dressed the same as when they'd fought in the alley, making Cuss wonder if he'd been killed soon after.

"What the hell?" said Eve, moving so she could see Mickey's face.

"It looks like Max delivered his star witness as

promised," said Ygo.

"Max?" asked Eve. "Or Zed?"

Cuss stepped into his boots. "What are we supposed to do with him?"

"There's an emergency rescue station a couple of doors up," said Ygo. "Maybe bring him there?"

Mickey was a big man, and Cuss considered enlisting workers passing by for help moving him. But as he scanned for likely candidates, his attention was drawn to the freight depot across the street.

"I'll be right back." He stepped over Mickey and made for the installation in long strides.

The depot grounds weren't protected by a fence, security being unnecessary in a closed society. It was a busy place. Lots of hustle and bustle as people and machines responded to a truck pulling out of the airlock with a half-dozen shipping containers on its flatbed. Motors whined as the crane and a pair of forklifts moved into position and began sorting the load.

With the attention of the ground crew on the truck, no one was paying attention to Cuss as he wandered onto the property at the other end of the yard. He spied a handcart alongside a battered metal shed. Something like the cart gardeners drag about when they care for their yard on Earth.

With nobody around to object, he wheeled it across the street.

Lifting Mickey into it was awkward. Since he was frozen into position, they tipped his upper torso onto the bed, muscled him into the middle by sliding him on his back, and then spun him up on his butt to get his legs aboard. But when they began to pull the cart up the street, he rocked back and forth, threatening to topple out. Cuss suggested breaking a knee joint to flatten a leg and stabilize him, but then Eve tipped the body so Mickey's chin hooked over the side of the handcart, bracing him enough to complete the trip to the rescue station.

They announced themselves at the door. After most of a minute, it opened. A woman of indeterminate age, anywhere from late forties to early sixties, answered. Wrinkled face. Weary eyes. Salt-and-pepper hair. Wearing a coat and cap that had been white at one point but were now dulled by the tint of Martian dust.

She began to speak, and then she caught sight of the handcart and its load. "Mickey Montoya," she said, shaking her head in a knowing fashion. Stepping out of the building, she pulled a device from her coat pocket and pressed its probe against his skin. She bent over to read the display. "What happened?" she asked, standing upright.

"He was left on our doorstep as a house-warming gift. I'm Marshal Cuss Abbott, by the way. This is Marshal Eve Boucher."

"I'm Clarise." She bit her lip as she thought, staring at Mickey. "I need to call Mr. Ironstone."

"I'm pretty sure he knows."

"Either way, it's procedure." She exhaled in a huff and shook her head. "Given how he's been acting, this is no surprise."

"'He' meaning Mickey?" Cuss glanced at Eve.

Clarise looked up and down the street. "That's right.

He was a wannabe in Southie. Mr. Ironstone had given him the title of junior associate to shut him up. Then Zed comes along and tells Mickey he's organizing a crew, that he's his number one. Gets him involved in his dirty work." She motioned to the body. "And this is his reward."

"Would Zed have done this?" asked Cuss.

"I don't think so," said Clarise.

"What kind of dirty work?" asked Eve.

She shrugged. "You'll have to ask Zed."

"We heard he stole supplies, altered mining reports, stuff like that." Cuss let the silence develop, hoping to pressure her to respond.

She didn't. No confirmation. No details.

He used his viewer to show her the pictures of Zed with Atepa. "She's missing. So is her partner, Jeremy. We're worried that they're victims. Would you know what happened to them?"

She frowned. "Their ship took off more than a month ago. Probably two months by now."

"Their ship is missing. No one can find it. Was Zed around when they left? Do you think he knows where they are?"

Her face was a mask, but she wrung her hands like she was washing them. "I wish I could help, but I don't know anything." She motioned to Mickey in the handcart. "Would you help get him inside? It's just myself and Figgie here at the moment, and he's a big guy."

As the three of them muscled Mickey into the building, Eve asked, "What happens with the body? Do you send it back home?"

"This *is* his home. The brick kiln up top has become the semiofficial disposal method for biologicals. It's big and hot and will turn him to ashes in a flash."

. . .

Back outside the rescue station, Cuss looked up and down the street. "I'd say it's time to follow Mamba's advice. Let's look to Southie for answers. Pay Max and Zed a visit. Ask about Jeremy and Atepa. About Mickey."

They started down Broad Street, heading into the heart of the settlement, keeping pace with pedestrian traffic.

"Do you know if they're home?" Cuss asked Ygo.

"Max is there," replied Ygo. "But his routine is to leave for the mine at any minute. Zed is already out and about, likely at the mine but I don't know for sure."

They reached Roxbury Ave and turned toward Southie. As they walked, Eve said, "I'm getting an uneasy feeling thinking about a kiln used for the disposal of bodies."

"Same here," said Cuss. "It's hard to imagine the two being held prisoner in this small community for months. Half the town would have to be in on it by now."

"If they ended up in the kiln," said Ygo, "we may never learn what happened. There *should* be a record of activity at the main airlock. It's basic security. Comings and goings and such we could use to piece it together. But the data archives are empty. I don't think anyone has maintained those systems for years."

"Feeds showing who they last left with would be pretty compelling," said Cuss. "Keep digging."

The general store on Roxbury Ave came into view, and Eve pointed to it with a tilt of her head. "The one I was shopping at earlier had groups of people standing around talking. Might be a good place to ask about Jeremy and Atepa. See if we can detect reactions that hint at community knowledge."

Cuss hesitated until Ygo said, "Could be an interesting experiment."

He stepped onto the store's porch. "Let's ask about Zed, too."

The place seemed bigger than he'd imagined from the street. Organized with a traditional floor plan, the bulk of the room was filled with rows of tall shelves. To the right was food. To the left, dry goods. The front held tables of produce. The back, a cooler for meat and dairy. The ends of the aisles featured standalone displays of popular items, the one nearest offering replacement filters for water purifiers.

In the produce area at the front, Cuss saw three men picking through a pile of potatoes and onions heaped on a table, focusing more on their conversation than the produce they handled. Two men and two women did the same at a table of fresh greens to his right. Near the cooler at the back, the proprietor, identified by his white apron, unloaded packets from a box and arranged them on a display bin. Three lone individuals were actually shopping, wandering the aisle, carrying baskets, selecting items from the shelves.

All wore Southie blue. All stopped their activity to view the interlopers. Most eyes on Eve, though a couple were giving Cuss the once-over.

"Hello," he said in a loud voice, addressing the situation head-on. "I'm Marshal Cuss Abbott, and this is Marshal Eve Boucher. We're new in town and wanted to do a little shopping. Don't mean to be a bother."

The two groups resumed talking, watching Cuss and Eve, gesturing more than before.

He continued to project his voice. "We're also looking for Zed Ironstone. Would any of you know where he is? Seen him recently?"

The talking became a buzz. One of the lone shoppers set his basket on the floor and slipped past them, avoiding eye contact, hurrying out the door, either because he didn't want to get involved in anything or, more likely, because he wanted to be the first to tell Max.

The proprietor stood and wiped his hands on his apron, studying them from across the shop, deciding. Then he started toward them. As he approached, he, too, spoke so everyone could hear. "Don't know about Zed. But the Marshals Service has an outstanding balance that's sixty days overdue."

He stopped a few paces away, pulled up a personal display, and fiddled for a few moments. Biting his lower lip, he continued his search, finally said "there," and then showed Eve, using it as an excuse to stare at her face.

Cuss moved so he could see. It was an itemized list of goods bought by Jeremy and Atepa.

"Sorry. It's not my decision," he said. "Company policy is that after sixty days, no new purchases until the account is cleared."

"We'd be more comfortable discussing finances in private," said Eve. "Would you have a place we could do that?"

Cuss loved the idea of moving somewhere where they could question the man without the pressure of witnesses. He loved it even more when the proprietor said, "There's a storeroom in back. Would that work?"

Eve rewarded him with a smile. "Lead the way."

The storeroom was a modest space with shelving around the perimeter. The shelves were surprisingly empty, making Cuss wonder if there were shortages. Or perhaps they were at the end of a weekly cycle and this was normal before the next delivery.

A crate in the corner had a stool in front of it and a scatter of paper on top—his makeshift desk. With no other chairs, they remained standing. He introduced himself as Lance.

"His real name is Lasse Nettleton," said Ygo. "Wanted for questioning in a jewelry theft in Phoenix two years ago. Wanted more by the organization he stole from than by the cops."

Lance was a small man. Early thirties. Wiry. Nervous. Blonde fuzz on his face instead of a beard. He showed them the list once again.

Cuss viewed the invoice. The most recent purchase was eight weeks earlier. The oldest, twelve weeks. "This invoice includes purchases from three different stores?"

Lance looked at the display. "That's right. All purchases in Southie are consolidated on this one bill. You'll have to ask in the Hollow for anything up that way."

"Why would they shop in three different stores? Why not just the one nearest their place?"

"No idea."

"Did you ever see Zed with Atepa? The woman?"

Lance shrugged and looked down and away. "I don't remember."

Cuss studied him for a long moment. Back in Lagrange, he would use the system to force cooperation. Drag him to a Community Patrol station, sweat him in an interview room, get in his face, let him get hungry, use technology to catch his lies.

But here, it was just Eve, Ygo, and him. After considering his options, he turned to a method that was equally effective, though it went against his grain. Pained him, in fact.

Bribery.

Sliding two fingers into a small pocket at the waist of his pants, Cuss pulled out three Sols. He displayed them in the palm of his hand.

Lance stared at them. "Are those real?"

"Yup. I'm going to ask you three questions. If you answer all three correctly, you get the gold. Miss one and you get nothing."

"What kind of questions?"

"The kind I'd pay for. Here's the first one: Tell us about the relationship between Zed and Mickey Montoya."

"That's not a question."

Cuss raised his eyebrows. "You're a lawyer now? Okay, *would you* tell us about the relationship between Zed and Mickey? Their treatment of each other. Their treatment of everyone else."

"How many questions is that?"

"It's one."

"Bullshit. It's at least two."

Cuss exhaled in exasperation and made a show of returning the coins to his pocket while saying to Eve, "What he doesn't understand is that we'll tell everyone he cooperated. He'll be both broke and an outcast."

"Why are you being an asshole?" Lance snapped. "I'm just trying to understand this transaction."

"It's simple, Lance," said Eve. "Tell us what you know and earn a nice payday. Continue being difficult and we'll hang you out to dry."

"You'll want to talk fast," said Cuss. "Otherwise, the people out front will think this is more than a discussion about an overdue invoice."

Lance huffed and shook his head. "You're a dick."

Cuss and Eve remained quiet. Waiting.

"Look. I saw Mickey with Zed a few times. Saw him without Zed way more. Mickey spends more time bullshitting about how he's Zed's right-hand man than actually doing anything. Blah. Blah. Blah. He has diarrhea of the mouth, I swear to God."

"What sorts of things did Mickey talk about?" When Lance's eyes flicked down to the pocket with the coins, Cuss added, "This is still part of the first question."

"It's not a conversation with him. He yaks and blabs

and I pretend to listen. Lately he's been jabbering about how he's going to recruit a crew that he'll be leading for Zed."

Cuss wanted to ask more about Mickey but felt he had to move on to maintain Lance's cooperation. "Question two. Would you tell us about Zed and Atepa?"

Lance scratched the back of his head. "First, let me say that Zed is an asshole. He's the kind of guy who treats all women bad." He looked at Eve. "The prettier you are, the worse he is. And for some reason, a frustrating fraction of women respond like it's a challenge and they'll be the one to tame him." He shrugged. "Anyway, she made a run at him with some success. But then she went back to Earth with her partner. That must have been two months ago."

"She's missing, Lance. So is her partner, Jeremy. So is their ship. Could they still be here in Utopia? Maybe hiding in the Hollow? Or being held prisoner somewhere?"

He stroked the fuzz on his chin. Then he shook his head. "Hard for me to imagine. Almost impossible. Why do you think that?"

"I don't know." Cuss waited, and when Lance remained quiet, he moved on. "Question three. Would you tell us about Zed and Max? Their relationship?"

"I don't know Max at all, and Zed only from seeing him around. Anything I know is what I heard from Motor Mouth Mickey." Lance laughed. "That's a great name. I'm gonna use it." He laughed again. "Anyway, my spin is that Zed keeps trying to show his dad that he's ready for a bigger role. But he's really a fuckup, causing more problems than solutions. Mickey thinks he can help Zed be more strategic.

Grow their power together."

"What has Zed done recently to make his dad proud?"

"Got me. Ask Mickey. Or better yet, ask Max."

Cuss fished the three Sols out of his pocket and handed them to Lance, who beamed as he stuck them in his own pocket.

"I'm going to pay the invoice now." While Ygo made the payment, Cuss waved his hand in the air like a magician performing an illusion. "Done."

When Lance saw the outstanding balance on the display reset to zero, he said, "Wow, how did you do that?"

"It's much less impressive when you know the trick," said Eve.

"I'm going to give you cover now," said Cuss. He raised his voice and yelled, "That's outrageous!" In a normal voice, he said, "Just ignore the next minute." Then he yelled, "I want to talk to your supervisor!"

He winked at Lance, looked at Eve, tilted his head toward the door, and stepped out of the storeroom. Holding the door open with one hand, he said in a loud voice, "We aren't paying *anything* until we can talk to our colleagues!"

Turning, he stormed out of the shop, hoping that Eve was close behind.

Chapter 22

Outside the general store, Cuss paused to let Eve catch up, and then they resumed their trek into the heart of Southie toward Max and Zed's home. But just a few steps along, Ygo stopped them. "I found Zed. He's at the airlock. They're readying a surface truck for him."

"Alone?"

"He is."

"How far can those things go?"

"They're good for maybe a hundred kilometers."

"Can you follow him?"

"I'll launch a drone. Should have video for you in a bit."

Cuss looked up and down the street for a place to sit and view the feed. "Let's head back and watch from the office."

. . .

From his den in the hold of the *Nelly Marie*, Ygo linked with *Star Chaser*'s worker bot, a beefier version of Peanut, guiding it to unpack a Tigershark drone and prepare it for launch. The craft was made of a glossy light-shifting material. Its top was dome shaped, like the canopy of a handheld umbrella. The bottom was flat except for two slots underneath, fixtures for mounting an assortment of specialized attachments.

He had the bot insert a long-range camera into one of the fixtures, and a high-powered laser rifle into the other. After swiveling the components on their spindles to confirm proper function, he had the bot move the drone into the launch tube and seal the hatch. Prep work completed, he detached from the bot and gave it final instructions to police the area and stow the tools.

Linking to the drone's controls, he brought the craft to life and monitored the data stream while the motor purred. After confirming a "systems go" status, he launched the nimble craft into the thin carbon dioxide atmosphere. He flew away from the airlock, staying low and weaving to avoid projections of rock sprouting from the ground, using the vessels and gantries of the shipyard to screen the drone from Zed in his truck.

Ahead, the morning sun rose behind mountain peaks. Dust in the atmosphere gave it a brown halo, as though struggling to penetrate city smog on a bad day. Or maybe smoke from a forest fire. A half-kilometer out, the drone reached the rim of a crater, craggy hills ringing the lip, the material ejected when a meteor slammed into the planet a billion or so years earlier. Ygo flew the craft up between two spires of fractured stone and down into the crater.

Once in the bowl, he tacked north, staying below the lip, out of sight of any observer on the planet surface. He followed the rim for about three minutes, and then rose out of the crater, sprinted across an open area, and ducked into the next one, this one with a much bigger bowl and bigger piles of rock around the lip.

Plotting a course across the valley, he began a sprint that would put the drone well ahead of Zed and his truck. As he waited for the drone to traverse the distance, he daydreamed.

About Eve.

He'd never been in such a situation before, one where he could interact with a woman over an extended period of time, having her full attention, giving him a chance to reveal his personality in stages. He loved talking with her. Interacting. Came to cherish it. She shared secrets with him. Traumas from her past. Hopes for her future. He could make her laugh, almost at will. And when she did, it was a moving experience. She was absolutely beautiful in her mirth. Breathtaking.

The past month had been an awakening. Emotional. Treasured. But he wasn't delusional. He knew it was lose-lose for him. She thought he was an AI. If she were ever to learn of his deceit, it would end badly. But if he had been honest from the start, if she had met the real him, a misshapen, pasty-skinned, bedbound blob connected to machines, he felt certain it wouldn't have begun.

Still, it was the closest thing he'd ever come to an intimate relationship with a woman. He liked it. He liked her. He wished the circumstances could be different.

The far edge of the crater loomed, a steep wall of rock with a jagged lip, like the teeth of some mythical beast. He followed the terrain upward, passed through a gap in the rock, and banked toward a tall spire to the left, the highest peak in the area.

Hiding behind the rise, using it as cover, he sprinted for the summit. As he neared the top, he opened the throttle wide. The drone accelerated above the crest, soaring high over the land, climbing until he could see a dozen craters below. Then he hovered, confident that he'd completed the maneuver without revealing his presence to Zed.

Beneath him, he saw mountains and craters, rock and sand. And tire tracks. Lines in the soil made from the passage of vehicles, all starting from Utopia's airlock.

"Check this out," he said to Cuss and Eve, linking them to the camera feed.

He showed them a wide, well-worn road from the airlock out to the launchpads. He showed them smaller roads out to the brick factory, power generators, and other works in the area. He showed them trails to more distant spots, places used on occasion by the settlement.

Then he panned along several fading lines out to distant locations, tracks made by lone vessels, perhaps on an excursion to sample penelopite deposits. Or to stage instrumentation for a scientific study.

Or to hide a body.

Ygo shifted the focus to Zed's truck. It was traveling cross-country, following one of the fading lines in the sand.

"If he continues on this trail," said Ygo, "it should be easy to see where he's going." He swiveled the camera to look ahead. The line Zed followed faded into the horizon. He accelerated the drone in that direction.

Eight kilometers out, the line in the sand stopped at

the edge of a square blur on the ground. A blur that masked what lay beneath.

"That's an EM camouflage blanket," said Ygo.

"How big is it?" asked Eve. "I can't judge its size."

"Not huge. But big enough to cover a Starlane cruiser," said Ygo. "It would explain why we couldn't see it from orbit."

"You think the *Evalina* is under there?" asked Cuss.

Ygo took a moment to verify that Zed was a good distance out, and then he directed the drone down near the blur. "MFOD couldn't figure out how the ship just disappeared. How its ID beacon could go offline the way it did. This would explain it."

"There has to be a big hole under there."

"There is. I just checked the geological survey for this spot. There's an underground silo."

"Man-made?"

"No. From a small meteor. Lots of iron oxide all through here. A straight-on impact melted the iron, and when it cooled, it left a metallic silo. It's not a common feature on Mars, but it's not unheard of, either. This one is deep enough and wide enough to hold the ship."

The drone moved around the edge of the blur and stopped at a post stuck in the ground, a thick pole with a bowl on top, the hollow of the bowl pointing out over the EM blanket. The camera panned the edges of the blur and located four such poles in all, one on each corner of the square.

"Do you have a way to disable it?" asked Eve.

"The drone has a gun. I'm sure if I blasted a couple of

these cups, the electromagnetic field would collapse."

"Let's not do that," said Cuss. "Let's wait for Zed. Let him hang himself by shutting it off while we watch."

"Do you think Jeremy and Atepa are under there?" asked Eve.

"If we find the *Evalina*," said Ygo, "my guess is that we'll find them, too."

. . .

Back in the Marshals Service building, Cuss sat with Eve on the upstairs couch, watching the feed from Ygo's drone. Zed's truck was creeping toward the camouflage blanket. The camera zoomed in through the front window to show him in the front seat, bouncing along as the truck's suspension battled the demanding terrain.

Zed wore a full-body pressure suit on his lower half. The top part was gathered at his waist, the sleeves and helmet hanging behind him. In the span of two minutes, he rubbed a hand on the back of his neck, tapped his feet, and tugged his bottom lip, all classic fretting behaviors. If the truck had been big enough for the man to pace, Cuss felt certain he'd be doing so.

Progress over the rough Martian surface was slow, but the truck finally reached the edge of the blur. As Zed slipped his arms into the sleeves of his suit, Cuss said, "The fact that he's aware of this spot proves he's involved in whatever is hidden here."

His helmet sealed, Zed stepped from the truck and strode toward the nearest pole. No hesitation. No looking around.

"He's not talking to anyone," said Ygo.

Eve's eyebrows scrunched. "There's no one with him."

"I mean, I've been monitoring his comms for the past half hour. He hasn't talked to anyone. No 'I'm almost there' or 'I see it' or 'I'm here.' No comms at all."

"You think Big Hard is in the dark?"

Cuss shook his head. "Max knows everything that happens in his empire. It's a requirement for survival. He wouldn't have dumped Mickey on our front step if he didn't think Zed needed cover."

As he spoke, Zed fiddled with the pole in front of him, and the camouflage cover vanished. In its place was a round hole in the ground, surprisingly cylindrical for an impact crater. The steep walls were dark, with a rough, porous texture similar to pumice. A number of good-size boulders littered the lip, though the edge wasn't piled high with material like more traditional craters.

But the feature that riveted their attention was the nose of a spaceship just visible in the center of the void. Cream-colored finish with distinctive gold filigree trim. Just like the *Evalina*.

Ygo moved the drone so they could see down into the cylinder. He zoomed in on the name appearing on the side of the craft next to the main hatch, confirming what they already knew.

As they digested the discovery, Cuss saw a shape at the

bottom of the hole. "What's that?" He pointed to the spot.

Ygo had already noticed and was shifting the drone to better see the shape. It was a body. He homed in.

A man lay on his back at the base of the silo, his shoulder pressing on a support leg of the *Evalina*, staring upward through milky eyes. He wasn't wearing a pressure suit, which meant he'd been exposed to the Martian atmosphere for some time, which meant he was dead. His face was gaunt, cheeks sunken. Tiny cracks in the pale skin formed networks of crevices that ran along his forehead and around his eyes. His hair was falling out in patches.

"That's Jeremy Romesco," said Ygo.

"Goddamn Zed." Cuss clenched and unclenched his fists a half-dozen times. It was unacceptable to lose a marshal in the line of duty. Losing one to a piece of shit like Zed Ironstone boiled his blood. "Goddamn him. Can you see the woman? Atepa?"

The drone rotated so they could view the bottom from all angles. They didn't see another body.

"There are no life signs from inside the *Evalina*," said Ygo. "Wherever she is, odds are she's dead as well."

"One of them had to fly it here," said Cuss. "The ship wouldn't respond to an outsider."

"Zed could have forced Jeremy by threatening Atepa."

"That works."

Eve said, "Zed would need help once he got here. Help getting out of the hole. Help setting up the electronics. Someone to give him a ride home."

"I'm not seeing Max in that role," said Ygo. "It was Mickey Montoya."

"Now I'm wondering if Max knew at all," said Cuss.

Ygo pulled back on the view to show Zed walking to the truck. He leaned into the cab, lifted out a rucksack, tucked it under an arm, and returned to the lip of the silo. There, he unfastened a flap on the sack, held the whole thing out at arm's length, and waved his hands up and down as if shaking a towel, unfurling what proved to be a rope ladder.

After a few moments of sorting through the lines, he tied one end around a tall boulder sitting at the edge of the silo. He dropped the other end into the hole, fiddled with it until it was hanging to his satisfaction, and swung himself onto the top rung.

Bristling, Cuss wanted blood. "How fast can you get me out there?"

"Not fast enough," said Ygo, his voice grim.

Zed had worked his way below the top lip, battling the frustration of descending a light, flexible ladder that wanted to bend in ways he didn't want it to.

The camera focus drifted away from Zed, moving to the tall boulder near the edge, the one being used to anchor the ladder. Cuss wondered if the drone was malfunctioning.

Before he could ask, there was a brilliant flash. The *pop* of a small blast. When the light faded, the rock was leaning inward, teetering on the precipice, balancing between Newton's first law of motion—a body at rest stays at rest— and gravity, the relentless attractive force of a massive planet pulling downward.

After a moment of uncertainty, gravity won. The rock shifted inward, moving slowly at first, Zed's weight on the ladder causing it to topple faster. As the rock rotated, the ladder fell loose. Zed started to tumble, flailing his arms, attempting to right himself. He hit the bottom of the silo near Jeremy, landing on his back, the impact severe but not deadly.

Then the rock, at least ten times Zed's weight, fell squarely on top of him, crushing his chest and lodging against the side wall of the silo in a way that prevented it from shifting off him.

After a period of silence, Cuss said, "Nice. Except I wanted to do that." A pause. "Is he dead?"

"I have no way to access his vital signs to confirm. But based on the visual evidence, there's little doubt."

Eve seemed dazed. "What's going on?"

"What's going on," said Cuss, "is that Zed just learned a hard lesson called, 'Don't fuck with the Marshals.' It's a motto you'll come to embrace after your time at Chaparral." In a slightly louder tone meant to include Ygo, "My only problem is that it was too quick."

"Yeah?" Eve's tone was aggressive. "Well, *my* problem is that an AI just made a decision to kill. To perform an execution. Without asking? Without direction?" She shook her head. "Even the Ministry of Defense doesn't have anything like that in their arsenal. And for good reason. And Zed was our lead to Atepa. What the hell?"

"Atepa is dead," said Ygo. "Ninety-nine percent plus."

Cuss couldn't think of a way to shield Ygo. He'd warned the man repeatedly that his deception would backfire. He tried anyway. "You heard me call him 'partner' a bunch of times during the trip. Even 'Marshal' a few times. That's because he is."

"Is what?"

"A marshal," said Ygo. "An officially badged interworld marshal who did what needed to be done."

She shook her head. "Giving an AI a title doesn't change its nature."

Cuss struggled to keep his frustration in check. "What you're saying makes sense. But let's circle back to this *after* we clear the scene." Then his annoyance got the better of him. "Anyway, what do *you* think should have happened here? There are no jails or judges or juries. No justice system at all. We've been sent here to make this right. Hell, I would have done it myself if Ygo hadn't."

She folded her arms and shook her head. "You and I should have discussed it and reached a decision together, and *then* we delegate."

She was right given the facts as she knew them. He tilted his head to the side in a yes-no motion. "Ygo can make it make sense. But later. Now we need to focus."

Eve started to talk and then stopped. She looked up to the ceiling. "You will explain the moment this is over."

"Understood," said Ygo, sounding despondent.

Cuss returned them to task. "Is there any evidence that Max can use to tie us to this? Like maybe burn marks on the rock?"

"The laser shatters rock, so there are no burn marks," said Ygo. "An excellent forensic team *might* find shards at the rim of the silo and figure it out. Not a chance anyone in Utopia could. The whole point was to make it look like an accident. An error in judgment on Zed's part."

"Anything else you can think of that might point our way?" asked Cuss.

"Max's gut will scream that you killed Zed, but Mickey blocking your front door last night and you being at that general store this morning gives you some level of cover."

"How long before he learns that Zed is gone?" asked Eve.

Ygo didn't answer.

Cuss shrugged, his mind racing. If Max blamed them for Zed's death, their lives were in danger. If Zed had been working with accomplices beyond Mickey, people who would kill marshals, the threat was imminent.

Chapter 23

Max Ironstone worked through his morning rounds at the mine, a routine that took a couple of hours to complete. Not because of distance, but because he took his time, checking progress on the new cut, listening to the concerns of the dozer crew trying to keep up with the tailings, bullshitting with the old-timers. When he finished the circuit, he picked his way through the rubble to his office pod.

Inside, he sat at the big table and drank coffee while he reviewed the mine reports from the day before. Behind him, a young man was putting the last touches on the lunch buffet Max provided his associates every workday.

Skimming the task summaries, he saw that the assembly of the new drill rig was running days behind. Zed's project. He let out a sigh.

"Have you seen Zed?" he asked Holt Yavarone, his shift boss, who had just arrived to review the work schedule.

Holt shook his head. "I'm not his nanny." He took a plate from a stack on the countertop, shoveled a serving of meatloaf from a covered casserole onto it, added a scoop of mashed potatoes and another of cooked greens, ladled gravy over everything, and joined him at the table.

"Mary!" Max used his viewer to call to his home

helper. When she appeared in the display, he asked, "Where's Zed?"

"He was gone when I got here. His suit is missing from its hook, so maybe he's up top?"

Max tried to stay calm. Tried not to jump to conclusions. They had been playing poker at the tavern last night. A private table. Just him, a few of his associates, plus Zed and Mickey. At some point in the evening, he'd told the group what he'd learned. That the missing marshals had sensor implants that recorded everything about their lives; that the data was stored in *Evalina*'s console; and that if the new marshals gained access to it, they could learn exactly what had happened, and who did what.

Mickey had been unperturbed. Even flippant. "I'm not worried."

Max was, though. He was furious over their stupidity. Their impulsive behavior. It could end his run. Everything was at risk.

That's when he resolved to deliver Mickey to the marshals in a condition where the fuckup could never fuck up again. The decision felt good. Decisive. He started winning hands after that.

He'd called an early evening. After saying goodbye to the boys, he'd pulled Zed aside. "Let's talk it through onsite tomorrow. Right before lunch. Figure this out."

Now, sitting at the lunch table, watching Holt shovel food into his maw, he prepared for the worst. That his idiot son had gone off to implement his own half-assed "solution." The kind that so often made everything worse.

With an impatient flip of his fingers, he switched his

viewer from Mary to the airlock. He huffed as he waited for a response. Taking a calming breath, he picked up his coffee cup, realized it was empty, and set it back down.

Valentine Newsome, Southie's man in the airlock this shift, joined the call.

"Is Zed up top?" Max was abrupt. No "Good morning." Not even a "Hi."

"Sure is. He rode the big rover out..." Valentine paused to check the time. "...just over four hours ago."

"Where was he going?"

"Didn't talk to him. And he didn't file an itinerary."

Max caught the dig. He and Rory Gilcrest had agreed that everyone going up top should file a time and destination itinerary. The decision was motivated in part by safety concerns. But a bigger issue was preserving resources. They'd sent crews out in the past to rescue people who were late and not answering their comms, only to find they were safe, just careless in their procedure. Valentine was making it clear that his son was in violation.

"Tommy Everson was coming in when Zed was going out. Saw him tracking northeast. Open country."

"Hold." Max hadn't wanted to call Zed directly, because his son complained whenever he did. Common refrains were, "You don't believe in me" and "Let me do my job" and "Give me room to breathe."

Max called him anyway. When Zed didn't respond, he asked Valentine, "When did he last check in?"

"He hasn't. But I'm tracking the rover." Valentine made a motion, and a map appeared in the display. It showed the surface of Mars near the settlement, detailing the various craters and hills and ridges and trails. Utopia and the shipyard were displayed prominently in the center. At the far edge of the map, in the upper right corner, an avatar showed the location of the rover.

Max leaned forward and studied the spot. Zed had told him about a cylindrical crater where he and Mickey had stowed the *Evalina*. At the time, Max had been listening with one ear, his mind in a daze, fighting back fury and fear and disbelief, trying to understand how killing marshals made any sort of sense. And with it done, how to proceed.

He was pretty sure this was the place Zed had described.

"I'm headed your way," Max told Valentine. "Get the Dash ready."

. . .

Cuss was eating lunch over the sink in the kitchen when Ygo said, "We have movement."

A hoverview opened at the end of the countertop showing a view down Broad Street, looking away from the airlock. Cuss saw normal pedestrian traffic, people walking alone and in groups, some moving toward them on the street, others moving away. Some excited and animated, others quiet, looking tired from the job.

Then he spotted an anomaly. A mote coming their way. Growing. Three men walking fast. Like a bullet cutting through the air, pushing oxygen and nitrogen molecules aside, sending them spinning, creating a wake behind it; the three men's intimidating approach moved pedestrians aside, shoulders bumping as men and women shifted over, crowding each other, and then filling in behind, returning to their previous state, a disturbance settling out.

Ygo zoomed in on the group. Max Ironstone was marching in the lead.

"Any idea what's up?" asked Eve, who stood next to Cuss.

"Just observation," said Ygo. "He seems upset, he has his suit over his shoulder, and he's rushing to the airlock. I'd say he's going to look for Zed."

Cuss didn't recognize the two men marching with Max. "Who's that with him?"

"Security. Southie muscle."

The three men drew even with the Marshals Service building. Max, pressure suit draped over his shoulder, was staring straight ahead. Taking long strides. Scowling. Determined. The two toughs were swinging their arms and stretching their legs to keep up.

When he was past, Cuss stood. "Let's follow him to the ship."

"Why?" asked Eve.

"To gauge his behavior when he finds Zed, use it to assess his involvement. To guide the narrative while it's forming, that it wasn't us, that we were in town the whole time. To learn about Atepa."

"It's going to be brutal watching him find his dead son's body."

"Zed killed two marshals. I need to know if his dad is

involved, and I can't think of a better situation than this to find out." Then to Ygo, "Any idea how he'll be traveling?"

"Give me a bit." And then, "They're pulling a hovercraft out of the service lot right now. The chatter I'm hearing is about prepping it for him."

"Do you think he'll let us hitch a ride?" Cuss looked at Eve when he asked, signaling he was open to all opinions.

She shook her head. "If he has even a hint of what he'll find when he gets there, I'd say not a chance."

"I agree," said Ygo.

"What options do we have? Are there other hovercraft?"

"If I'm reading it right, the vehicles parked on the north side of the service lot belong to Rory Gilcrest, which means he owns one, too."

"Think we can we borrow it?"

"Not without his permission. Or a gun."

"I wish we'd had a chance to meet him before asking for a favor."

"Do you want me to call him?" asked Eve.

Looking at her, Cuss got lost in her eyes. Rory Gilcrest didn't stand a chance.

"Where is he now?" asked Cuss.

"At his mine," said Ygo. "He's finishing lunch."

Eve moved to the back office and sat at the desk that Jeremy and Atepa had shared. "Can you show me our barter inventory? I don't want to promise something we don't have."

Ygo displayed it for her. As she reviewed it, Cuss said, "Don't give away the store. We still need to deal with the assholes on the *Tomlinson*."

"Barker Adamson and Jaunty Gabala," said Ygo. "They arrive in four days."

"Have faith." She checked her reflection and organized herself at the desk. Cuss watched from the office door.

Ygo placed a call using Rory Gilcrest's private link. He answered.

"Who the hell is this?" he snapped, his mouth twisted in annoyance.

"Hello Mr. Gilcrest. I'm Eve Boucher, one of the new marshals."

Rory was sitting in a chair, fork in hand, chewing. He chewed while he studied her. Did so for an uncomfortable amount of time. It was probably twenty seconds but it seemed like minutes. Then he took a swig from a cup to clear his mouth.

Finally, he spoke. "Mamba was right. You are classic."

"Mamba is quite the gentleman. I enjoyed my time with him."

"Would you like to spend time with me?"

"What I would like, Mr. Gilcrest…"

"Rory. Please."

"What I would like, Rory, is to rent your hovercraft."

"My what?"

Ygo told Eve that it was called a Dash, and she corrected herself.

He still looked confused.

"As you may know, our colleagues are missing. So is their ship. Well, two hours ago, out of the blue, we picked up the ship's broadcast beacon. It seems to be coming from a crater a few kilometers away."

"Here? On Mars?"

Eve nodded. "It appears so. We're anxious to get there as soon as possible in case the marshals are with it and need help. We don't have a Dash of our own." She bit her lip in a hint of a pout. "Can you help us?"

Rory scratched his chin. "You mentioned rent? How about dinner?"

"That's not the way to come at me, Rory. Anyway, I was thinking more in the way of currency. Or maybe specialty metals?"

Rory sat up. "You have any molybdenum? Or vanadium?"

"I might have a few kilograms." Tiny amounts of molybdenum and vanadium are used in the steel-hardening process, among other applications. Prized in Utopia, MFOD had loaded quantities of each into the *Star Chaser*.

"What purity?"

"Pure, Rory. It comes from the Marshals Service private stock."

"A thousand kilos of molybdenum and a thousand of vanadium."

Eve laughed. "I wasn't asking to buy a fleet. Just rent one used Dash for a few hours." She stared at him for a long moment. "Twenty kilos of each."

"I guess you'll be walking."

Eve didn't say anything. She just waited. She'd made an offer and it was his turn to counter.

"Five hundred."

"You're not going to solve your metal shortage with this one transaction. Fifty kilos of molybdenum, fifty of vanadium, and dinner with me, here in the Marshals Service office, along with my partner, Cuss Abbott."

"One hundred of each plus a game of poker with you and your partner. Tomorrow evening at the Appaloosa Tavern. Bring buckets of metal."

"Poker is a lot of games."

He laughed. "Good for you. We play Texas hold 'em."

Eve looked at Cuss, who was nodding vigorously, giving her a thumbs-up.

"Done. I'm way overpaying and know it but we're in a hurry. We're right here near the airlock. Could you call your man and get us underway?"

"He'll have the craft ready as soon as you show him the metal."

"Time is important here, Rory. Can we pay when we return?"

"Your pals have been missing for two months. They can wait another hour."

She began to say something and stopped. "Fair enough. Thanks again."

"See you tomorrow." Rory was chuckling when the hoverview closed.

"Ygo?" prompted Cuss.

"I'll send the metal on a surface wagon. It should be at the airlock in thirty minutes."

"Send our suits, too," said Cuss, realizing they'd left them on the *Nelly Marie*.

Chapter 24

The airlock was really three rooms: a big pressure vault, a medium-size staging area, and a small control room. The big pressure vault had matching doors front and back, heavy metal barricades that allowed the passage of vehicles in and out while protecting the settlement's precious reserves of air. A third door on the side led to the staging area, a chamber where vehicles and goods could be readied before being loaded into the pressure vault. And next to that was a control room, a small space filled with displays that let men like Valentine Newsome from Southie, and Iggy Rosen from the Hollow, keep an eye on everything. Let them monitor the flow of people and goods. Let them make sure their respective bosses got their rightful share.

When Cuss and Eve arrived at the airlock, Max, his two goons, and Valentine were in the staging area, fussing with the Dash hovercraft. Iggy, dressed in a rust-red jumpsuit, stood in the doorway of the control room, arms folded, shoulder against the door casing, watching.

"Did you hear?" Cuss said in a loud voice, talking to no one but talking to everyone. "The *Evalina*'s beacon started broadcasting a couple of hours ago. It's right here on Mars, just a few klicks away!"

All conversation stopped, and every eye turned to Cuss, though they then shifted to Eve.

"Is one of you Iggy?" he said with feigned excitement. "Rory Gilcrest says we can borrow his Dash to get there. To see if Jeremy and Atepa are still alive!"

The two goons and Valentine looked to Max, who held up a hand to them, flat, palm forward, like a traffic cop saying stop. He walked over to Cuss and Eve, smiling. "Marshals! Did I hear you say you've discovered a ship's beacon?"

"Not just any ship," said Cuss, continuing his act of innocent enthusiasm. "The *Evalina*. That's Atepa and Jeremy's ship. This is amazing news." He turned to Iggy. "The metal will be here in just a minute. Maybe we can start prepping the Dash?"

Iggy didn't move. "Can't happen until I'm holding the metal."

Max interrupted. "Do you have coordinates? Can you show me where it is?"

With Ygo's help, Cuss showed Max the spot a few kilometers to the northeast. He thought Max paled. He certainly hesitated before speaking.

"That's exciting news, Marshal. I wish I could join you, but I have my own emergency."

"Oh?"

"Nothing to bother you with. Mining is a constant string of challenges. Boring stuff. Anyway, best of luck. I sincerely hope you find them well."

As Max returned to his craft, another Southie crew member, this one carrying a pressure suit, entered the staging area and joined him.

"That's Eddy Clayton," said Ygo. "He's one of Max's

associates."

While they watched, Max and Eddy climbed into the Dash, and Valentine and the two security toughs pushed it into the pressure vault. The staging area door rolled shut. They all stood there listening to the sounds of gas hissing, then rumbling, from the big barricade door. A moment of silence. Compressor whining, more hissing and rumbles. The staging area door rolled open.

Like a magician's reveal, the Dash behind the door was gone, replaced with a small buggy. A motorized wagon. Dirty. Dusty. Carrying two shiny sealed containers and two pressure suits.

Iggy issued a command, the wagon rolled forward into the staging area, and the big door closed. He opened each container, reached into one and pulled out a short, thin rod, a piece of molybdenum somewhat longer and thicker than a traditional chopstick, and waved it around like it was a knife. He put it back, checked the second canister, and called to someone outside the room. A minute later, two men rolled Rory's Dash into the staging area and departed.

"It's been serviced recently," said Iggy. "Has air and fuel for twenty hours. It drives itself. Just tell it where you want to go."

The Dash had one door, and it was at the back. Cuss opened it, tossed their suits inside, and with the door still open, began pushing on the frame, rolling it toward the big vault. As Eve moved to help, Cuss signaled for Iggy to roll open the staging area door.

"Mr. Ironstone asks that you wait until he returns before you go."

Max's two toughs and Valentine were standing in front of the Dash, blocking their progress. The guy speaking was one of the men Ygo had called Southie muscle. Big. Strong. Cheeks pink from rosacea. Broken capillaries on his nose, perhaps exacerbated by overdrinking, made it red. Like Rudolph the reindeer. Valentine stood at one of his shoulders. The second tough, this one shorter but with bulging arms and a thick chest, stood at the other.

Cuss immediately regretted a decision he and Eve had made not a half-hour earlier. Since it was a short walk to the airlock from their building, and, once there, they would be putting on pressure suits that would make any weapons they carried inaccessible, they'd decided to leave them behind.

"You are about to interfere with marshals in the line of duty," said Eve in a loud, firm voice. "It's a serious charge. If you continue, the charge will be on your permanent file, waiting for you when you return to Earth or wherever home is. Even if it's a decade from now."

The three burst out laughing. Deep guffaws.

Ygo said, "Rudolph and Muscles are both wanted for home invasion and assault in Miami, Florida. Valentine for grand theft and assault in Dallas, Texas."

"Oh no," mocked Rudolph. "Will someone shake their finger at us and give us a stern warning?" Then he leaned forward, like his eyesight was failing and he needed help focusing. He leered at Eve. "Goddamn, you are tasty."

Cuss, seeking to change the dynamic, projected his words so everyone would hear. "That's what your mother said when she was sucking my cock."

Rudolph shook his head quickly like his hearing was broken. "What?"

"She swallows, by the way. Your mom."

His whole face turned as red as his nose. "I know what you're doing." He made a big show of reaching into a pocket and pulling out a glove. A ritual act. He worked it onto his right hand. "You're trying to get me angry so I'll do something stupid." He pulled out a second glove and continued the show, putting this one on his left hand.

Cuss recognized them immediately. Scrapers. Gloves that fit tight like a flexible second skin that padded the hand while toughening the blow. And the exposed surface, the back of the fist, was covered with tiny hooks. They looked fuzzy from a distance, like the hooks that make up one side of a Velcro strip. But these were stiff. Each one designed to dig into the skin, cling tight, and hold on as the fist completed the blow, leaving behind an angry abrasion. A wound welling with blood. Painful when it happens. Painful while it heals.

The palms of Rudolph's scrapers were a whiteish gray. The part covering his fists, the part covered with miniscule hooks, was a splotchy brown. The color of dried blood.

Cuss moved away from the Dash and into the open, giving himself room to maneuver. "Make you act stupid? You don't need my help. You're doing a fine job by yourself."

Out of the corner of his eye, Cuss saw Eve reach into the molybdenum container. He heard the sound of scraping metal. When she rose, she held two short, thin rods of molybdenum. The ends weren't pointy, but the stock had been cut at an angle so they had a certain sharpness to them.

She held one rod in each hand, gripping them like daggers. Her right hand near her chin, sharp end of the makeshift knife pointing forward. Her left hand was lower, close to her waist but out from her body. Sharp end again pointing forward.

Cuss didn't recognize her stance from any martial arts form he knew and wondered if she was faking it. But she looked fierce. Determined. Intimidating.

"I'm going to ask you to move into the control room," she said to Iggy.

He complied, leaving Cuss free to focus on the Southie toughs.

Valentine and Muscles seemed happy to leave the heavy lifting to Rudolph, who was rolling his shoulders, making a show of limbering up.

Rudolph was big, experienced, confident. Dangerous. He acted like he expected a fist fight. But Cuss had no intention of boxing like a gentleman. Not when it was three against one. Not when an opponent wore scrapers.

Using his lens, he studied Rudolph's body, looking for warm spots that might indicate healing from recent injury, or scars that pointed to older problems, or twitches in movement that hinted at joint or muscle issues. He found nothing he could use to his advantage. Neither did Ygo.

"We asked you politely," said Rudolph, who shadow boxed a few swings, demonstrating his prowess. He had good form. Excellent power. A little slow. Heavily focused on his fists.

The door from the staging area into the vault was

closed behind the three men, the barrier causing them to group closer together than they otherwise might. Cuss, believing that more delay was time they could use to their advantage, launched without warning. He rushed at Rudolph while bellowing a warrior's cry, cocking his right fist back, winding up to deliver a devastating blow.

When caught by surprise, a small fraction of fighters will respond with immediate aggression of their own, advancing on instinct, seeking to blunt the strike and overwhelm their opponent with a whirlwind of fury. Cuss counted on Rudolph to behave like everyone else. And he did, taking a step and a half back to give himself room, to gain extra time to raise his own fists, position his feet, and prepare for battle.

And when Rudolph stepped back, he did so without consulting his buddies. They remained flat-footed and were now standing out in front.

The act of cocking his fist had put Cuss's arm up and back. As he closed on the group, he turned and accelerated his raised elbow, increasing its velocity, putting his full weight behind it. Kinetic energy is proportional to mass times velocity squared. He directed the devastating results of that equation toward Valentine's temple.

When his elbow connected, Valentine had his hands at his sides. The force of the blow snapped the man's head, straining muscles, stretching tendons, tearing ligaments. The rapid acceleration and deceleration of his skull sent his brain bouncing off the sides of his cranium. Bruising it. Causing a severe concussion. Valentine slumped to the ground.

Cuss immediately disengaged and danced back, re-establishing his footing. When Rudolph stopped his shadow boxing to watch Valentine collapse, his inattention made Cuss wish he'd gone for a two-fer.

"If you surrender now," he called to Rudolph and Muscles, "we won't hurt you."

"Fuck you, cop," said Rudolph. He advanced, fists raised, ready to box. Muscles moved to the side and raised his own fists, showing he wasn't going to get caught flat-footed like his fallen comrade.

Cuss was worried. He didn't want to box a guy wearing scrapers. One blow, by skill or by luck, could end the fight. Could hurt him severely. He glanced at the ground around his feet for something to use as a weapon. No luck. He lifted his head just as Rudolph began his assault, a flurry of blows. Cuss bobbed and weaved, struggling, deflecting.

He stumbled.

Rudolph pressed his attack. He didn't bother with jabs, the quick punches used to keep an opponent back, to pace the fight. Instead, he went for powerful crosses and hooks and uppercuts, big blows that could end it all at once.

Cuss, struggling to right himself, threw a defensive swing that missed. Rudolph, hand cocked, seemed to smile as he started his shoulder forward, the weight of his body behind his fist, the beginning of a crushing blow.

Cuss turned away, hoping to take it on a shoulder. He winced at the moment he expected impact. But it never came. Instead, he heard a *whoosh* and a *schlop*.

When he looked, he saw Rudolph with a metal bar poking out of his right eye, a short rod shaped something like a chopstick. Molybdenum.

A rivulet of blood began to drool from the wound. Rudolph lowered himself to the ground, moving slowly, sitting on his butt. He brought a hand up to the bar, touching it, acting as if he might pull it out.

Cuss vetoed that idea. Lifting his foot, he thumped the rod with the bottom of his boot, pushing it into the man's head, sending it deep into his brain.

Rudolph's whole body began to vibrate as if he were being zapped with electricity. The ghastly dance continued for a good ten seconds. He let out a final gasp and slumped on his side to the ground.

Muscles, watching in horror, turned away. He bent at the waist, put his hands on his knees, and started to retch. Before he had a chance to make a mess and stink up the place, Cuss grabbed him by the belt and collar, and slammed him head-first into the heavy staging area door. Muscles collapsed with a groan. Cuss kicked him in the side of the head for good measure, ending the confrontation.

. . .

Adrenaline triggers a fight-or-flight response: a racing heart, quick breaths, prickly skin, the slowing of time. As Cuss and Eve skimmed above the bleak Martian surface, seated side-by-side in the Dash, they experienced the aftereffects of an adrenaline rush, their bodies processing the remnants and restoring their systems to baseline chemistry.

It left Cuss exhausted. His skin was covered in a thin layer of sweat. His mouth was dry. His muscles twitched.

Eve responded differently, chattering nervously. "I'm standing there guarding Iggy when Ygo yells, 'Throw the bar! Throw the bar!' It took me a moment to understand what he meant. When I did, he guided me. 'Elbow up. Step and release. Snap the wrist. Follow through.' It was crazy."

"It was an amazing throw."

"I was aiming for his chest. Center of mass. I was hoping to buy you a few seconds." She rubbed her hands on her knees. "But I'll take it."

They rode in silence for a bit, and then Cuss spoke to Ygo. "Thanks, pal."

Eve shifted in her seat to face him. "Do all the marshals have an Ygo? Or access to him?"

Cuss waited for Ygo to answer. Hell, it was his mess. She was asking an obvious question, though neither of them had thought of this issue back when they'd been arguing about hiding Ygo's true nature. If he was in fact an AI, he should be duplicatable. And all the Marshals Service ships would have their own copy.

"The short answer is no," said Ygo. "As to why, I'll explain when we have our chat."

Eve didn't respond at first, instead taking the time to spread her pressure suit on the floor in front of her seat. She began working her feet into the suit's legs. "Is this more of your 'good explanation' that you won't just tell me? My mind is spinning trying to understand. I swear, whatever it is, it better be epic."

An uncomfortable silence followed. Ygo broke it by changing the subject. "Max is going to be angry about losing more workers."

"Fuck him," said Cuss. "It was self-defense all the way."

"Of course. But in his head, everyone would be alive and healthy if we had just waited as he'd asked. So that makes it our fault."

"Yeah, well, he didn't ask, his goons did. And they made it a demand. Anyway, when he finds Zed, I think his priorities will change." He began pulling on his own suit. "How long before we get there?"

"Just over twenty minutes." Ygo showed them the view from the drone. Max's Dash was parked near the lip of the crater.

For the remainder of their ride, they watched Max and Eddy work. The two got out of the Dash and looked into the hole, and then responded with a flurry of activity, running from the crater to the Dash and back three times, gathering supplies, stacking them at the lip, talking and pointing, working through a game plan. Eventually, Max dropped a line into the hole and climbed down. Eddy remained up top, providing support.

Chapter 25

Cuss and Eve parked their craft next to Max's, exited together, and approached Eddy, who toggled his comms to the line-of-sight setting so only the three of them would be included in the conversation. He didn't seem surprised by their arrival. "Zed is down there with a boulder on his chest. We need help moving it."

"Oh my God." Cuss rushed to the edge and looked down the near-vertical wall. "Is he okay?"

"No." He sucked in his breath as if fighting back tears. "He's dead."

Cuss turned to him. "Dead? What happened?"

"We're trying to figure it out ourselves. Best I can tell, Zed saw your marshal friend lying at the bottom and started down to help him. The rock holding his rope ladder gave way and fell on top of him."

"Which one? Jeremy or Atepa?" asked Cuss.

"The man. Sorry to say that he's dead, too."

"Oh my God!" cried Eve.

Eddy bowed his head. "This is going to be so hard on Max. What a mess."

Cuss toggled his comms to include Max and called down to him. "Max, this is Cuss Abbott. I'm up here with Eddy and Eve. How can we help?"

After a longish pause, Max answered, "A rock is sitting

on top of Zed, and it's too big for me to push off him by myself. If I tie a line around it, maybe the three of you can pull while I push?"

"Can we pull with a Dash?" asked Eve.

Eddy shook his head. "Hovercraft float. You need something gripping the ground if you want it to pull. Something with traction."

Cuss returned to the lip of the crater and zoomed with his lens. The boulder was as tall as Max and twice as wide. It was sitting upright on Zed's chest, the top end leaning against the cliff wall, wedged into a notch that locked it in place. They needed to muscle it out of the notch before they could tip it off him.

"The *Evalina* has a portable winch," Ygo told Cuss. "Secure it up here at the top and we can use it to pull the rock off Zed. After, we can use it to lift Zed and Jeremy up out of hole. Max, too, for that matter."

Cuss passed the idea along, and it was accepted as the plan of action.

Getting to *Evalina*'s hatch turned out to be a challenge. The smooth surface of the ship's exterior made it impossible to climb down freehand, especially while wearing a pressure suit. They ended up stringing a line across a portion of the crater, positioning it so it passed near the ship's hull. They hung a second line from that, and with Eve and Eddy belaying, lowered Cuss into position.

Dangling in front of the main hatch, he asked the ship for access. The ship's sensors identified him, the hatch opened, and he climbed inside.

The winch was stored in the hold. Unhooking himself,

he moved to the trapdoor in the floor, climbed down, and turned about, orienting himself. The ceiling wasn't much taller than he was, and the space was packed with tech. The top of the Paulson drives poked up in the center. Positioned around the circumference were fuel pods, stores of air and water, a life support system, a waste-processing and recycling unit, a variety of electronics racks, and a power generator. He knew that the spaces in between held storage for food, drink, clothes, entertainment, tools, supplies, a med kit, pressure suits, and everything else one might need to journey through space.

"It's spacious down here," he said to Ygo. The *Nelly Marie*'s hold was cramped compared to this because of Ygo's private room.

"They pay the price with small crew quarters," said Ygo. "Wait till you see how tight it is up there."

Cuss worked his way through the hold, lifting lids, opening doors, pulling back covers, looking for signs of Atepa. No luck. He gathered the winch and more line from a closet, carried the bundle up to the command deck, and left it there while he searched the remainder of the ship. She wasn't on board.

He hooked the bundle to the line dangling outside the hatch and waited as Eddy and Eve pulled it up. When they lowered the line again, he attached himself to it and climbed out of the hatch, and they helped with his ascent.

It took some time to anchor the winch. But when it was secure, it pulled the rock off Zed with ease. And then, one at a time, they lifted Zed, then Jeremy, and finally Max up out of the hole.

The mood was grim at the top of the crater. They worked together to load Zed into Max's Dash and Jeremy into theirs. Cuss knew he didn't want to be there in the airlock when Max learned of his other losses.

"You two go ahead," he told them. "Eve and I need to secure the ship."

"Have you screened the recordings yet?" asked Max. "Do you know what happened?"

Cuss shook his head. "The record is blank. Like it had been erased. We may never know the details of what happened here."

"I told you already," said Eddy. "Zed died trying to rescue Jeremy. He's a hero."

Cuss nodded. "It's certainly a tragedy."

After an awkward goodbye, Max and Eddy drove away with Zed.

"What a load of crap," said Eve as they drove away. "How do they think Jeremy got out here in the first place? Why is the ship in a hole? Why was it camouflaged?"

"Do you think Max killed Jeremy or Atepa?"

"No. It was Zed both times."

"Zed and Mickey Montoya. Both have been brought to justice, the scales balanced. By accepting Max's fiction, we can have a working relationship with him for however long we're here."

"That all sounds good until he reaches the airlock," said Ygo. "Then his goodwill will vanish."

Cuss shrugged.

. . .

The surface of Mars didn't support life, and with no microbes to decay flesh, Jeremy wasn't decomposing in the traditional sense. But the extreme temperature cycles, low atmospheric pressure, and background radiation of the planet had taken their toll in other ways. Jeremy looked bad. And as he warmed in the hovercraft, he smelled worse.

"We should have packed a body bag," said Cuss.

They settled for an emergency pressure suit they found stowed in the Dash. Fitting a desiccated body into a flexible suit was an awkward task, especially when they were trying to be gentle. They persisted, and after twenty minutes of effort and an impressive string of expletives, they finally had him secured.

During their labor, Cuss thought through the logistics with Ygo. "We need to get Jeremy to Earth, and the assholes from the *Tomlinson* to Lagrange."

"You're thinking of contracting?"

"Any candidates?"

"A pretty good one. Freddie Keyes on the *Swallowtail*. He was a tech sergeant in the Space Guard, retired twelve years ago after serving twenty, been running freight ever since. He's taken contracts from the Marshals Service in the past."

"When is he due to depart?"

"Five days."

"Perfect. Where is he now?"

"On his ship."

Cuss looked at Eve. "Let's swing by the *Nelly Marie*, grab a pocket full of Sols, and pay Freddie a visit. See if we can contract with him to transport Jeremy and the prisoners."

"Anything that keeps us away from the airlock until Max is gone."

They'd been underway for a good twenty minutes before she made the connection. "Why do we need Sols? Freight companies don't deal in hard currency."

"We'll be dealing directly with the captain. Freddie won't be asking his company for permission, and he won't be sharing his fee. It's a side hustle for these guys."

Cuss had experience dealing with freelancers, but the cold reality of Utopia changed the game. "We're operating under different rules out here. Girish isn't going to send a ship on a three-month round trip just to pick up the assholes. And where would they stay until then? If we don't find a solution, though, we risk having him tell us to bring 'em back ourselves."

After riding for a bit more, he added, "If you ever find yourself dealing with a freelancer in the future, only pay half up front. At a maximum. They need an incentive to complete the transfer. There was a case years ago where a marshal paid in advance and the prisoners somehow 'got lost.' They were found weeks later floating in space back near the starting point."

"Without suits, I take it."

"Without clothes, if I remember right."

· · ·

The *Swallowtail* was a tub. A sixty-year-old beater that looked something like a mammoth bullet held upright by four sturdy grasshopper-style legs. Flexed. Crouching. The dents and scrapes and corrosion and crud covering everything on the outside served as fair warning of what to expect on the inside.

They hailed Freddie as they climbed the gantry, a beefier version of the one supporting the *Nelly Marie*. This one had dual cranes, a conveyor system, transfer buckets, and an airlock spacious enough for surface trucks, all necessary for a ship loading ore. They'd reached the *Swallowtail's* main hatch before Freddie responded.

"Marshals, how may I be of service?" His voice had a phony sweetness. Solicitous. He smelled money.

"Hello, Captain Keyes." They pulled back their flex helmets, and Cuss made the introductions. "We do have a bit of business to discuss. Something you might find profitable."

They heard a brief high-pitched whine, a *clunk*, and then the ship's hatch cracked open in front of them.

"Come in. Up the ladder to your right."

Cuss pulled open the heavy oval door and entered first, stepping into a cheerless metal-composite vestibule. There was a ladder going up to their right, a ladder going down to their left, and straight ahead, a line of three doors in a row.

The vestibule area was as disgusting as the exterior. Old things can sometimes look dirty because of wear on the finish, parts with surface indentations from constant use, hinges that show grease lines at the seams. This wasn't that. Cuss saw squalor from dirt and goo and bits of trash, as if no one had taken a mop or sponge to the place in a good decade.

"Yuck," said Ygo for both of them.

The hatch sealed behind them as they climbed. They chose to keep their suits on to protect themselves from the filth.

The ladder led up to the bridge, an electronic setup that had been modernized a few times, but not recently. The trash was pushed to the outside of the room, a donut around a form-fitting captain's chair. The personal grooming of the man sitting in it matched that of his ship. He smelled so bad that Cuss had to fight the impulse to put his helmet back on. His clothes hadn't been washed, perhaps ever. His face was covered in a scraggly beard, the hair on his head hanging down to meld with it. He was missing a front tooth, which showed every time he smiled.

He was smiling as they approached. They didn't get close enough to shake hands.

"How may I be of service?" he asked.

"We have a body that needs transport to Earth, and two men and possibly a woman and baby who need transport to Lagrange."

"We aren't sending a baby on this vessel," said Eve. "No offense, Captain."

"None taken. I don't take kids, anyway. So, we're talking four bodies, three of them alive?"

"That's right."

"Whose are they?"

"What do you mean?"

"Southie or the Hollow? Max or Rory?"

"The deceased is a marshal, so he's ours. The two men and possibly a woman are arriving in three days on an incoming freighter, so they don't belong to anyone."

"Yeah, they do. What ship is it? I promise you the captain has arranged that part if they were coming unclaimed, which is pretty rare."

"The *Tomlinson*. You know it?"

Freddie shrugged.

"I guess we don't know who's claiming them. Either way, we're taking them."

Freddie swiveled his chair back and forth in a rocking motion, pulling on his beard, thinking. He seemed to drift off and then shook his head as if trying to wake up. "I need to maintain relationships or I can't do business here. So, you'll either need to pay enough for me to retire, or we'll have to do the transfer in orbit where no one can see."

"Sounds expensive."

Freddie nodded. "Very. I'm guessing the retirement one is a no-go. You have a ship that can pull it off?"

Cuss turned his back to Freddie and whispered to Eve and Ygo, "We could intercept the *Tomlinson* in orbit and take the assholes before they land. We avoid confrontation with the locals. And it's harder for the captain to resist in space."

"It's tough to board a ship in flight if the crew resists," said Ygo.

"We'll fire a shot across their bow."

"If things go wrong, if either ship gets damaged or innocents get hurt, it will be a huge black eye for your career."

"Okay, then if he doesn't cooperate, we'll follow him down and take them in front of everyone, which is our other choice either way."

Cuss turned back to Freddie. "A hundred Sols. Half in orbit and half upon delivery."

"You came here to mock me? To make fun of a working man?"

"What?"

"A thousand Sols. Per passenger. A third right now. A third in orbit. A third upon delivery. And I'll make only one transfer on my approach to Earth. You take 'em all at once and distribute 'em however you want."

When Cuss hesitated, Freddie said, "Would you like a tour of the quarters?"

Cuss accepted to give himself time to work through his sticker shock.

They descended the same ladder they'd climbed earlier and faced the three doors. Freddie opened the one to the right and the one in the middle, stood back, and swooped a hand, inviting them to inspect the rooms. A cloud of disgust wafted off him as he did so.

They were spartan accommodations. All composite metal. Stark. Cold. Small. The first room had a bunkbed on one wall. A bathroom stall in the back. A sink. Perfect for two men. The middle room was smaller, a single bed with the toilet and sink built into the corner. Perfect for Abbi. Both were cleaner than much of the ship, perhaps from lack of use.

"This meets code," said Cuss after stepping inside each. "Barely."

The Marshals Service had a long list of rules and regulations for prisoner transfer that applied to Earth, the Moon, and Lagrange. Utopia had flexible guidelines because of the distance and lack of options, with "humane" being the guiding adjective.

"No," said Freddie. "This is for crew. Next door is for prisoners."

They shuffled over, and Freddie opened the second door. The room was tiny. Crusty. No beds. Filth everywhere. A bucket in the corner for a toilet. A bottle for water. A wretched smell.

"You're kidding," said Eve.

"What a weasel," said Ygo. "This is a negotiating tactic. He's going to bump you up knowing you'll need the proper rooms."

As if on cue, Freddie said, "This one is the thousand per. Double rate for those rooms."

Cuss felt his face flush, tried to calm himself, and spoke anyway. "Fuck you." Then to Eve. "Let's go."

He turned to the hatch, lifting his helmet into place as he did so.

"No need for dramatics, Marshal. Make your offer."

Cuss stopped and swirled. "They need potable water, three meals, and exercise. You've seen the guidelines."

"All the way home. Why do you think it's so expensive?"

"A thousand per for the good rooms."

"No. Goodbye."

"Twelve hundred."

"I'll make you one offer, Marshal. I hope you'll take it." He went silent, stroking his beard. He kept it up for a long time.

"More negotiating tactic," said Ygo. "That was some nice drama yourself."

Cuss struggled not to smile.

"Fifteen hundred. A third, a third, a third."

Cuss shook his head. "Fifteen hundred per head. A hundred Sols now so you can enjoy yourself over the next few days. Of the remainder, half in orbit, half upon delivery."

Freddie flashed a gap-toothed grin and stuck out a hand. "Done."

The man seemed smug, causing Cuss to feel he should have bargained harder. Then he shook Freddie's hand, glad the pressure suit had gloves.

Chapter 26

"The *Evalina* is a significant asset," said Girish Mannan. "Something we can't afford to lose." He'd approved the funding to hire a transport contractor. He'd even taken responsibility for arranging the prisoner transfer and final payment during Freddie's approach to Earth. In exchange, he'd tasked them with retrieving the ship. "If you can't do it without damage, though, leave it. I'll send a follow-up crew."

With that as their charge, they sat on the couch in the Marshals Service building while Ygo guided the drone around the *Evalina*. They studied the feed together, agreeing that Jeremy's piloting had been exceptional. The ship had not been damaged during its descent into the narrow crater. There were no obstructions restricting upward flight. The ground was level enough to support a vertical liftoff.

They then worked through the sequence required to fly out of the hole without a fin or leg hitting the side, or having the launch blast stir up a rock storm that would pelt and damage the ship. That assessment held nothing but concern.

"The big problem comes right after the drives fire," said Ygo. "The moment it's clear of the ground, the craft shifts its tail to maintain balance and keep its nose up. Think how your hand moves about when you're balancing a pole on your palm. The ship does the same thing, making small, precise moves. If one of those moves puts a leg against the crater wall before we can get them retracted, it's all over."

"Could we lift it out with a crane?" asked Eve.

"Possibly," said Ygo. "But that's a huge project for a small settlement. Weeks of planning. Moving big equipment. Assembling structures. Lots of local politics."

"If Jeremy could fly it in," said Cuss. "I can fly it out."

"That sounds like bravado," said Eve. "We don't want you or the ship hurt because you're proving your manhood." She caught his eye and winked, the first intimate outreach since they'd landed. "Trust me. You've nothing to prove."

Hearing it from her made him tingle, inspiring more bravado. "I like challenges." Then he admitted the truth. "And Ygo will be helping."

"Before you get too invested," said Ygo. "Let's get you out there, onboard, and running system checks. We won't know for sure if the ship is even capable until then."

"We left the rigging in place," said Cuss. "That'll get me inside."

"But it'll foul the ship on liftoff," said Ygo, "and clearing it is a two-person job. Right now, with you inside the ship, Eve is alone at the top. And we still need a way to get you both out there."

"I could ask Michael Mangual to drive us," said Eve.

Cuss's face scrunched. "Who?"

"Mamba. Rory's associate. The guy who took me to lunch. He'll help clear the line, too."

"Why would he help?"

She shrugged. "I just think he would."

Looking at her, Cuss thought so too. "Ask him to bring a rock rake. I'll rake under the drive nozzles. Try to reduce the rock storm."

. . .

Late that night, Cuss climbed into Jeremy's bed, exhausted. He lay his head on the pillow and closed his eyes but became fully alert when he heard the bedroom door open. Framed in the faint light, he saw Eve's silhouette. She was naked.

She came to the bed, lifted the sheets, and slid in next to him. She snuggled her warm body up against his.

He hesitated and then adjusted his position to become the big spoon. Wrapping an arm around her waist, he pulled her against him, making her the little spoon. They took a moment to adjust their pillows. He kissed her on the shoulder and then pulled back her hair and kissed the side of her neck.

Dropping his head on the pillow, he closed his eyes and celebrated inside his head. He'd missed her.

"You're a good man," she said after a bit.

Ygo heard her.

Cuss was already asleep.

. . .

Mamba had readily agreed to help. And when they arrived at the staging area the next morning, they found a Dash hovercraft being prepped as he had promised. Except it wasn't Mamba doing the prepping. It was Rory Gilcrest.

"Hello, Rory," said Eve. "Are you joining us?"

"Mamba couldn't make it," he said with a smile. "I'll be your helper today."

"This is a menial task for a mine boss."

"I'm a sucker for pretty scenery. And I want to get to know you before we play poker. It takes me awhile to learn to read people."

Cuss took Eve's pressure suit from her, bundled it with his, and tossed them both into the back of the vehicle. He leaned inside. "Did you bring a rake?"

"Brought two so you can choose."

Cuss found them on the floor under the front seat, a steel garden-style rake and a claw rake, both with heavy tines and sturdy handles, well worn. A canister with a pump spray handle sat next to them. "I take it this is the foam?" The plan was to rake the stones beneath the *Evalina* into piles and then spray the piles with a sticky foam that would keep them from swirling in the liftoff vortex.

"That's what Mamba told me." Rory put a hand on Eve's back and escorted her into the craft.

The ride to the crater was chatty, with Rory asking Eve endless questions.

She was good-natured about it, answering most of them, sometimes reflecting the same question back to Rory.

While at one level Cuss found the inquisition annoying, he learned several things about Eve that he hadn't known, even after having lived alone with her for six weeks.

She was born April 18, making her an Aries. She was an only child. Her favorite color was forest green. Though she didn't have a pet now, when she was young she had a dog, a mutt named Barney. She didn't see being a marshal as a courageous choice. She saw the work as more procedural, more technical. That you could go your whole career without ever pulling a gun. She enjoyed eating way more than cooking. She'd taken piano lessons as a kid but hadn't played in years.

She had a boyfriend.

While they talked, Rory was overly solicitous. Laughing too much. Too loud. Trying too hard.

It made Cuss think that an unfortunate feature common to frontier towns throughout history was an imbalance between men and women. It made life problematic. In the American Old West, some towns would post signs saying "women welcome," and even "wives wanted." He tried to imagine the longing. Craving. Tensions rising. Fights. He shuddered, glad it was not his life.

After what seemed like an interminable ride, they arrived at the crater. There, everything went mostly to plan. Eve and Rory used the winch to lower him to the bottom. While he raked the rocks from under the ship, Rory continued to engage Eve, now talking about himself, his achievements, his dreams, his wealth. After a few minutes of listening, Cuss turned him off by switching his comms to "urgent only."

As he raked, Ygo pressured him. "You should wait up top and let me fly it out. There's no need for you to be onboard. It's reckless." After a bit, "Please don't." And then, "Don't be an ass."

Cuss had a couple of reasons why he would be in the pilot's seat. One was that, while Ygo was enhanced with remarkable AI, he still made mistakes. They were rare. But it happened. The only way Cuss could intervene in the launch sequence was if he were there at the controls.

The second reason, perhaps a bigger one, was friendship. Loyalty. If Cuss were standing on the rim of the crater and things went bad, that meant Ygo had been the fuckup. He alone would be blamed for the loss. Cuss wouldn't let that happen.

It took two hours to rake the small rocks into four piles, about three times longer than he'd estimated. He was breathing hard and sweating when he finished, his suit working overtime to process his body's output.

Using Rory's canister, he sprayed foam onto each pile to glue the rocks together. But he ran out of goop as he was finishing the third pile, forcing him to scramble, humping the rocks from the fourth pile onto the other three before the foam set up. He succeeded for the most part.

Then, as he held the rakes, Eve and Rory winched him up to the main hatch. He pushed the tools in ahead of him, climbed through, and sealed himself in.

"Enable pilot functions," he said to the ship as he took the pilot's seat. The large viewscreen in front of him came alive with a summary report of the ship's various systems. The craft was healthy and capable of flight.

"I've got all green," he reported to Eve and Rory. "I'm gonna warm the drives."

He began the soak cycle on the Paulson drives, preparing them for ignition. While he waited for the process to complete, he paged through a detailed health report for the vessel. He found a few minor issues, but nothing he wouldn't find in a similar deep dive on the *Nelly Marie*. Jeremy and Atepa had taken good care of their ship. Then he worked though the preflight checklist with Ygo, finishing moments before the viewscreen displayed *Drives Ready*.

"You can clear the rigging and pull back," he called to Eve and Rory. "Let me know when you're sheltered."

While he waited for them to shield themselves behind a ridge, Cuss activated the seat safety options and chose the highest setting, something he rarely did. Flaps extended from within the chair to wrap his legs, secure his pelvis and torso, brace his head and neck.

"How are we looking?" he asked Ygo as he adjusted his position in the seat, trying to get comfortable.

"It's calm at the surface, so wind shouldn't be an issue. We just need a tiny bit of luck."

"Piece of cake."

"We're secure," Eve called. "Be careful."

"Always." He took a deep breath, exhaled slowly, and said to Ygo, "Whenever you're ready." He rested his right hand next to the emergency dump plate, ready to slap it if things went bad.

There was a fighter pilot from World War II named Pappy Boyington, who Cuss would occasionally quote:

"Flying is hours and hours of boredom sprinkled with a few seconds of sheer terror." The saying surfaced in his mind just moments before fear obliterated it from his thoughts.

While he'd launched a Starlane cruiser hundreds of times before, he'd never done so from within a silo, a liftoff where the smallest mistake could spell catastrophe. His normal resting heartbeat was fifty-four beats per minute. As the *Evalina* roared to life, his heartbeat soared, thumping hard at one hundred sixty beats per minute.

When the drives fired, it took four seconds for the craft to clear the rim of the crater. Two and a half of them were spent on the ground, the drives ramping up, reaching the critical point where their thrust exceeded the weight of the ship. The last second and a half was spent on the ascent, the ship reaching three gees of acceleration by the time it cleared the hole.

Reverberations off the crater walls shook the vessel, a thunderous resonance that penetrated the ship's hull. Vibrations rattled everything around him. A hum grew into a buzzing whir, angry hornets in a kitchen blender.

The craft shuddered. The growl outside became a shriek. His vision blurred from the shaking. The seat pressed into his back.

An alarm blared. Red lights flashed on the viewscreen. He lifted his hand, hovering it over the dump plate.

And then...quiet.

The ship was out of the silo. The vibrations stopped. The roar diminished. The alarm silenced. Everything returned to normal.

"All clear!" called Ygo as Cuss lowered his hand.

Cuss laughed, an expression of joy and relief. "I knew you could do it," he crowed as the *Evalina* arced across the sky on its short hop to the shipyard.

He released himself from the seat restraints, calling to Eve and Rory. "See you at the airlock."

As he shifted focus ahead, it hit him that Eve was now riding alone with creepy Rory, and would be doing so for the entire trip back to the airlock. She'd been comfortable with Mamba. Rory was an unknown element. "My comms will be open until I see you," he told them, information for Eve, a warning for Rory.

"No need for that," said Rory. "We'll call if we need help."

"It's not personal," Eve said with a laugh. "We're partners in the Marshals Service. It's standard procedure."

. . .

Eve made it back without incident, with Rory dropping her off at the *Evalina*. She reported her view of the man. "Talkative. Tedious. Harmless."

They worked together after that, spending the afternoon assessing their prize, looking for clues. They were digging through the storage lockers positioned around the perimeter of the middeck when Ygo said, "We heard back from Girish."

"Is he happy?" asked Eve, standing, dusting off her hands, talking to the ceiling.

"Ecstatic. He wants to know if you would be comfortable piloting the *Evalina* on a return trip to Earth."

"Me?"

"You."

"What do I know about Starlanes?"

"Your record shows you have almost two hundred hours piloting spacecraft."

"That's from flying my dad's company transport from Lagrange to Earth and back. Or Nova Terra. I worked for him part-time while I was in school."

"Since we're leaving the *Star Chaser* here for the next crew," said Cuss. "We can link the *Nelly Marie* and *Evalina* together. That way Ygo can help us both. We can share resources. And we can keep each other company."

"You'll arrive home with over thirteen hundred hours on a Starlane in your pilot's log," said Ygo. "That should help you stand out in your application to Chaparral."

"Hell, it took me two years to reach that," said Cuss.

"A real bunk," said Eve, seeing the possibilities. "No more sleeping in a plastic box."

"I'll tell Girish you're excited to help," said Ygo. "On a different note, I spoke with the captain of the *Tomlinson*. Inquired about the woman and child. He says he doesn't know anything about them."

"Thank God," said Eve. "I've been worried sick trying to figure out what to do if they show up with a toddler."

"Do you believe him?" asked Cuss.

"Yeah. He admitted to carrying the two men. I offered big money for the woman and child. Enough to turn his head. When he heard my bid, he said he could deliver for me next trip, which is a whole different concern. But he insists he doesn't have them to sell this trip at any price."

"Did you tell him who you were? Did he think he was dealing with a marshal?"

"I told him I was inquiring on behalf of Zed Ironstone. I stressed that this was a private conversation, that Max didn't need to hear about it. I think he bought it."

"Until he learns that Zed is dead."

"Yeah, well. I also learned that Barker and Jaunty are already committed to Max. Since I was supposedly working for Zed, it wouldn't have made sense for me to try and buy their contracts. I asked if Rory had tried. He didn't answer that but confirmed he'd promised them to Southie. That Rory knew to talk to Max if he wanted to change the terms."

"I've wondered about buying their contracts from Max ourselves," said Cuss. "It would ensure a peaceful transfer, something that doesn't seem likely if we try and arrest them here in front of everybody."

"We've cost him five workers," said Ygo. "And he'll be looking for someone to blame about Zed. He's going to lash out. I say stay far away."

"Could we persuade Rory to buy them?" asked Eve. "And then we buy their contracts from him?"

"That's another reason why I'm interested in poker tonight. That, and I want to learn what he knows about Atepa. And does he agree that Max wasn't involved? The whole 'look to Southie for answers' business means he knows something."

"Speaking of poker, I should probably just watch

tonight."

Cuss looked at her with a frown. "What are you talking about?"

"You've seen how bad I am."

"Ygo will be your secret partner. Don't worry."

"With you in the game," said Ygo, "we have more flexibility to manipulate. It's important to have you at the table."

"It will be the same game we played on the ship? Two cards in my hand. Five community cards face-up on the table. We make the best five-card hand from that?"

"That's right. Straight, flush, full house. Regular poker."

"The betting is like we did, too," said Cuss. "Bet after you get your two cards. Bet again after the dealer flops three of the community cards. Again after the fourth card. Again after the fifth."

He drifted over to the kitchenette, opened cabinets until he found a stash of breakfast bars, pulled out a cinnamon crunch, and began to nosh. "Rory wants us to bring metal to bet with. Will he be pushing nuggets of penelopite into the pot?"

"I'm sure they'll use chips during play," said Ygo. "Different colors buying different amounts of metal."

"We need to bring enough to buy the two assholes," said Cuss, "and to pay for information on Atepa's whereabouts and Max's involvement."

"I bet he's going to charge us for using the Dash that second trip," said Eve.

"He will if he's losing. Maybe four canisters with a mix

of metals?"

"Make it six," said Ygo. "Gives us a margin for error."

Chapter 27

To Cuss's amusement, the Appaloosa Tavern had Old West style swinging doors at the entrance, the half-height kind. He pushed them open, hinges squeaking as he stepped through, leading Eve into a large, dimly lit room.

Forty pairs of eyes turned to them. The sounds that had filled the room when they entered—loud laughter, clinking of glass, shuffle of chairs—died all at once. For a few moments, the background music, an upbeat piano instrumental, was the loudest noise in the pub.

To his left, a bar top stretched the length of the room, its gray metallic surface scarred and stained, the stools along its length filled with men wearing rust red. To his right, a row of booths lined the wall, packed with more drinkers wearing Hollow colors. The walls above the booths held mementos collected from the founding years of Utopia: old mining tools, images of the early settlers, original survey maps. In the middle of the room, a cluster of tables was crowded with drinkers, the tabletops laden with glasses and plates, the surfaces sticky from spilled beer.

Cuss took a quick count. Eve was one of six women in the room. The other five were receiving overwhelming attention and appeared comfortable with the situation.

"Marshals! Back here."

Rory Gilcrest motioned to them from an alcove at the

rear of the tavern, a small back room that opened wide to the main one, giving the boss private space while letting him revel with his workers. Cuss could see three other people sitting at the table with Rory. There were two empty chairs, the ones with their backs to the big room.

If this were a date, Cuss would let Eve lead the way across the floor. But they were working. And the rapt attention focused on her gave him the creeps. He decided to walk next to her, close but not touching, blocking the view from one side of the room, reducing the leering by half.

They made it to the back room without incident, Rory gesturing them into his private space with a wave of his hand. "Marshals. Please, have a seat. This is Buddy. This here is Chek. The bald fuck is Eppers." Buddy and Chek laughed at that. "Boys, this is Marshal Cuss and his partner, the beautiful Eve."

They shook hands all around while someone pulled a heavy curtain behind them, closing off their space from the big room, secluding them. The din on the other side of the curtain resumed, though now dampened by the barrier. Cuss felt himself relaxing a bit in the private setting.

"What are you drinking?" asked Rory, getting everyone settled. They made small talk while orders were filled, Cuss with a coffee, Eve with a beer. The three associates were respectful of Eve. Not staring, not trying to capture her attention. They left that to Rory.

As Ygo predicted, everyone had a stack of chips at their seat. A quick glance let Cuss see they all had the same. On the way into the settlement, they'd been invited to inspect four barrels of penelopite in the airlock's staging area. Cuss had declined, having no intention of taking it even if they won. They left their crates of metals beside the barrels, together representing everyone's buy-in for the game.

Rory began a longwinded explanation of how they'd valued the metal and how they'd associated it with the different colored chips. Cuss nodded occasionally but didn't question any of it, hoping to encourage a genial environment.

When Rory paused to take a breath, Cuss said, "Sounds good. Let's play."

At that point, the only people in the room were the six players.

Rory put three decks of cards in front of Eve. Red, yellow, and green. "Visitor's choice."

Eve tapped the green deck, the least used cards in the group.

While Rory shuffled, everyone threw their antes into the pot, small pre-bets following the rules of the game.

The strategy they'd settled on was for Cuss and Eve to work together, guided by Ygo, winning chips from the three associates, and losing them to Rory. By tradition, if someone busted, they'd leave the room. With a bit of luck and a few hours, they should be able to reduce the crowd to just the three of them, with Rory still in possession of what he'd brought to the table. They hoped that would create a situation conducive to sensitive conversation.

Rory started as dealer, a position that rotated around the table with each hand. He was comfortable with the deck, dealing everyone their two private cards with a smooth efficiency.

Cuss drew two kings, the beginnings of a powerful hand.

"Eve has junk," Ygo told him. "Nine and a seven."

Chek started the betting. "All in," he said with a smile, pushing his entire stack into the pot.

Players will do this in the first hands to intimidate outsiders. No one wants to lose everything right at the start. And since there had been no opportunity to learn the players and read the table, most visitors would fold, giving the pot to the brazen gambler, choosing to live another hand.

"He's bluffing." Ygo zoomed Cuss's lens tight on the beer mug in front of Chek, focusing on a streak of condensation, cleaning the reflection, filtering a blur, revealing the image of a jack and a ten.

Eve folded, making it Cuss's turn. He took a long time studying Chek, pretending to read him, looking for tells. After an uncomfortable half minute, Chek rubbed his nose. "Call," said Cuss, pushing his stack in next to Chek's.

A couple more folds, and Cuss and Chek were alone in the hand.

With everyone else out, and with no more chips for Cuss and Chek to bet, they both showed their cards. The table "oohed" when they saw the hands.

Rory dealt the five community cards, one after another, face-up for all to see. Chek got a second jack early on, raising the tension. But he didn't get a third and that was it, Cuss's two kings beating his two jacks.

"One down, two to go," said Ygo as Chek drained his drink. Gracious about the loss, the man wished everyone good luck and left the room.

Cuss kept Chek's pile of chips separate, dividing them into two roughly equal piles in the center of the table.

"Which one holds more?" he asked Rory.

Rory took a moment and pointed to the pile to Cuss's right.

Cuss pushed it toward Rory. "We owe you for renting the Dash the second time. This is probably three times what we paid before, so I trust it's enough." He didn't want the issue hanging out there, muddying the waters at some crucial point later in the evening.

Rory looked at him in wonder and then gathered the chips and added them to his stack. "You are a true gentleman, Marshal."

Play continued, chips moving back and forth over a series of hands. Eve hung in by folding most of the time. She bet only when she had a strong hand, something the table quickly learned. But with Ygo's help, the strategy worked well enough to let her replenish her chips every so often, keeping her at the table, a tool for Ygo and Cuss to use as they managed the game.

At the two-hour mark, they pushed out Buddy, his three tens losing to Cuss's three queens.

But after four hours, Eppers was still hanging in. He was a strong player. And without the right cards, even insider knowledge couldn't force a win.

Rory had a big pile and a big smile at that point. Cuss's stack included his original chips plus a small pile he had yet to lose to Rory.

He could sense that they would soon be stopping for the night, that these were working men who needed sleep. He put it out there. "Eve and I were hoping to have a private talk with you."

"What can I do for you?" asked Rory, arranging his chips into neat stacks.

"We'd be more comfortable talking in private."

"Eppers is my right hand. Think of him as my Zed, only he's not my son, he's not a fuckup, and he's not dead." Rory was the only one who laughed at that. When he saw the stony faces, he said, "Ah, fuck you guys. That was funny." Then, "I'll tell him whatever you say to me the moment you're gone, so tell us both and save me a step."

Cuss accepted his request, telling them both about Barker and Jaunty. Who they were. What they'd done. That the Marshals Service was determined to bring them home. "The thing is, they've already been contracted to Southie. Instead of us arresting them and risking violence, we'd like to buy out their contracts and take them peacefully. But since we're not Max's favorite people right now, we wondered if you would make the deal with him and then transfer them to us?"

Rory shook his head. "While I appreciate your dilemma, I'm not about to ask a man who just lost his son to engage in business that can wait. It's not how we do things in Utopia."

"What about minimizing the potential for violence?"

"That's on you. Don't even hint that I'd be responsible in any way."

"With everyone refusing to work with us," said Eve, "I don't get why they even station marshals here at all."

"Simple," said Eppers. "It's a cynical ploy by the Skyline trade consortium. 'Law and order' gives them cover with their customers. I've heard that people think we're criminal gangs, but we're really just a bunch of hard-scrabble folks trying to make a living. Your presence lets Skyline tell investors that the marshals are on the scene. And the best part? When someone isn't working out, you're our disposal system. We bring them to you so you can pay to transport them home."

Cuss was frustrated by the situation. But their timing was shit, and they'd have to live with it. He moved on, asking about Atepa's location and Max's culpability.

"I have some answers," said Rory. "No proof other than a witness, one I believe, one I vouch for. You can hear his story, question him, and judge what you think for yourself. It's what I have. And it will cost you your buy-in whether you believe him or not." He tipped his head in a form of shrug. "I want that metal."

Cuss looked at Eve, who bit her lip and nodded. He sighed and pushed the rest of his chips into the center of the table. "Deal."

Eve moved hers in next to his.

With all the chips, Rory retained ownership of his barrels of penelopite and gained possession of their six canisters of metals.

The curtain pulled back near the wall, and Iggy Rosen, Rory's man from the airlock, the one Eve threatened with daggers of molybdenum, the one who watched Rudolph the red-nosed tough guy die, stepped into the room. He was a man in his mid-forties. Shaggy brown hair. Somber demeanor.

"Have a seat," Rory said to him. "Tell the marshals what you told me."

Iggy sat in Chek's empty seat. Nervous. Clearing his throat.

"Take your time," said Eve. "Say what you came to say."

Iggy placed his hands flat on the table and tapped them a few times. "I was working the airlock. It was like three in the morning. Zed and Mickey Montoya come in, all in a hurry. They have a tote, a kind of flexible bucket we use in the mine."

"When was this?" asked Cuss.

"About three in the morning."

"I mean how long ago? Do you know the date?"

"A couple of months." Iggy frowned and looked into the distance. "The day before the marshals' ship left. I can get you the exact date if you need it."

"Was the tote big enough to hold a body?" Cuss continued. "Could you tell?"

"It was bulky enough and shaped right for it to be a small person."

Cuss nodded. "Go on."

"Tommy Everson was Southie's man in the airlock that night. Zed calls him over, acting all important. Tells him to help Mickey load the tote into the back of a trawler. After, Tommy asks them how much fuel do they need 'cause the trawler was low. Zed said they were just going to the kiln and back, that they were fine."

"Did Tommy see what was inside the tote?"

"That's the thing. I asked him what it was after they left. He gets all serious. 'Can't say.' He never acted like that before."

"Were you there when they got back? Was it the right amount of time for a trip to the kiln? Was the tote empty?"

"I was. It was. It was."

Cuss paused a moment to digest that Iggy was saying "yes" to all three. Then he realized his mistake. "I shouldn't be leading you. Please, tell us what happened in your own words."

"Okay. Back to Tommy. After I asked what's in the tote, I ask him what he thinks Zed and Mickey are doing at the kiln at such an early hour. He looks away and says he don't know nothin', ain't seen nothin', don't ask him nothin'. I've known the guy for years. He was upset."

Iggy stopped to lick his lips, his eyes dancing around the glasses at the table. Eve had a mostly full beer in front of her. She pushed it in his direction.

"Thanks." He downed half of it, sighed as he relaxed, and continued. "They get back about fifty minutes later, the right amount of time to drive to the kiln, dump something into it, and get back. And now the tote is lying all flat, meaning it's empty. Zed climbs out and yells at Tommy to service the trawler and park it."

He paused to drain Eve's beer. "I'm in the control room and they're standing right outside the door while Tommy's working on the trawler. Zed says something like, 'That sucked,' or 'I hated that.' Then Mickey says, 'The bitch deserved it. The planet is better off without her.' Something close to that, anyways. Then they leave."

Cuss waited, and when Iggy didn't offer any more, he asked his questions. "Who were they talking about?"

"I don't know, but I was sure they'd killed someone. But then later I thought I was wrong. When someone goes missing, it's obvious. This is a small community. People will notice and start asking questions. But over the next days, no one was gone, especially no women. Not in the Hollow. Not in Southie. Now, the marshals had supposedly left the next day, and I never connected that it might be Atepa they'd dumped. But now that her ship is still here and she's missing, I'm thinking it was her they dumped in the kiln that night."

"Did they mention Max at all? Did you get a sense that he was involved?"

Iggy nodded. "As they were leaving, Zed says, 'My dad will shit when he finds out.' Something like that."

"Will her ashes still be in the kiln?" asked Eve.

Iggy shook his head. "They clean it out every week or so, so they'd be on the ash pile on the surface. That pile is a big hill at this point. Good luck finding her there."

"Do you think Tommy will talk to us?" asked Cuss.

"No way. He's loyal. He wouldn't be on the airlock otherwise."

Chapter 28

Digging through the food stores on the middeck of the *Evalina*, Cuss worked on assembling a burger, passing time as he waited for the big confrontation. He was frustrated because the only bread he could find had a soft crust, and there were no spicy peppers anywhere.

"Who lives like this?" he complained to Ygo.

While he was marking time on the *Evalina*, Eve was on the *Nelly Marie*, serving as pilot under Ygo's close supervision, about to join Cuss on one of the wildest rides of their lives.

Lacking better options, they'd decided to intercept the *Tomlinson* while it was in orbit above Mars. They would collect Barker Adamson and Jaunty Gabala, either through cooperation or by intimidation, transfer them to Freddie Keyes on the *Swallowtail*, and then head for home.

Like so many undertakings in space, the goal was easy to state: intercept the *Tomlinson* while in orbit above Mars. But bringing three spaceships traveling from different directions at thousands of kilometers per hour into a formation so tight that they were just a few hundred meters apart was a maneuver fraught with peril.

The *Tomlinson* would be coming in hot, blistering along at interplanetary speeds, bucking and kicking as its drives struggled to slow it down. It would swoop around behind the planet, brushing against the edge of the thin Martian atmosphere, using friction as an additional braking mechanism, slowing the ship. When it dropped into orbit, it would begin descent maneuvers, bringing it to the shipyard on the planet surface.

To intercept the vessel, Cuss and Eve needed to fly a loop out into space, come around, and return, their own ships accelerated by the planet's pull. As they screamed back toward Mars, they would follow a precise path that tucked them into orbit near the freighter, matching its exact course and speed. Imagine three marksmen targeting a flat washer at a hundred paces, all shooting so accurately that their bullets passed through the disk's center hole in a straight line separated by just millimeters.

The smallest miscalculation could have the vessels arriving fractions of a second too early or too late, enough to miss the intercept completely. Or worse yet, arrive at the exact same instant, multiple craft trying to occupy the same space at the same time, a disaster in the making.

The reason Cuss was eating and not preparing was because he was waiting out the approach loop, as was Eve. The distances required to make it work were big. Tens of thousands of kilometers. A journey that took more than a day. Twenty-seven hours, sixteen minutes, fourteen seconds, to be precise.

He'd passed the time sleeping, eating, and exercising. Brooding about Jeremy and Atepa with Eve and Ygo. Contributing reluctantly to mission reports.

They had three hours to go.

He ate his burger in four bites and then paced. Played

air guitar to raucous music. Found himself getting wound up. Tried to relax.

When they were forty minutes out, he climbed into the *Evalina*'s pilot's seat and strapped in. Eve had been seated at the control of the *Nelly Marie* for more than two hours. The ride was growing increasingly violent, with Ygo making course adjustments to align their approach.

Cuss watched their progress on the main viewscreen, three vessels converging from different directions. With Ygo guiding the ships, Cuss was unconcerned, assuming they would complete the maneuver successfully.

They did. Putting the *Evalina* in orbit next to the *Tomlinson*, with the *Nelly Marie* trailing right behind, Eve ready to take out the *Tomlinson*'s drives if Cuss made the call.

Which ushered in their next challenge. This one unexpectedly difficult.

Dealing with Rikel Taliaferro, captain of the *Tomlinson*.

"How do I know that you're marshals?" Rikel complained. "For all I know, you're bandits with ships trimmed to look like marshals."

Cuss watched him on the front viewscreen, a young man, baby-faced like a teenager but in his late thirties according to Ygo. Small frame. Thin. Longish hair floating up around his head from lack of gravity. He sat in a tidy space, the equipment around him old but not ancient like they'd found on the *Swallowtail*.

"Does this look like a pirate ship?" In the same way that Cuss could see Rikel's surroundings, the man could see a portion of the *Evalina*'s command deck behind him.

"It's easy to spoof that."

"What does your ship's nav say? Doesn't it identify us as marshals?"

"My nav is shit."

"Didn't you get an official communication from the Interworld Marshals Service detailing our mission and your responsibilities?"

"I get lots of messages. Who listens to 'em?"

"Maybe listen now. Get your confirmation. We'll wait."

Rikel swiveled his chair around so his back was to them.

"He's calling Utopia," said Ygo.

"Blanket him."

"Done." Ygo used equipment on the *Nelly Marie* to cast an electromagnetic envelope around the *Tomlinson*, a cover much like that used by Zed to hide the *Evalina* in the crater. This isolated the ship, blocking Rikel's communications in and out.

"We need you to work with us, Captain," said Cuss. "Cooperate and you can be on your way."

Rikel swiveled back to face them. "What do you want?"

"Two of your passengers. Barker Adamson and Jaunty Gabala. Give them to us and you can go."

"Anything else?"

"That's it."

Rikel shook his head. "My problem is that they're under contract to Southie."

"You'll just have to explain what happened."

"Yeah, but who's going to reimburse me?"

Cuss groaned. Boarding a ship by force was fraught with peril, something he wouldn't consider if there were other choices. That meant accepting the alternative, dealing with freelancing freighter captains on their terms. The process was like being at a bazaar. Everything was a negotiation, prices were seemingly made up on the spot, and, of course, cash only.

"How much are we talking?"

"We have their transportation from Nova Terra to Utopia; food and lodging for the trip; fuel, air, and water use; maintenance charges; incidentals; plus the finder's fee from Southie." He pretended to calculate in his head and then gave Cuss a number.

It was absurd. Eve gasped.

"His only real loss is the finder's fee that Max promised him," said Ygo. "The rest is nonsense."

Cuss knocked a zero off and counteroffered at ten percent of Rikel's opening bid.

The man acted insulted. Outraged. Saying things like, "No, no, no," and "That won't work." Cuss saw him move his hand in a way that suggested he was making selections on a display they couldn't see.

Cuss warned him. "Try and run, Captain, and we are within our rights to disable your drives. I don't need to tell you what happens then."

What would happen is that the *Tomlinson* would become stranded. Without drives, it couldn't land and it couldn't return home, a derelict in orbit until repaired. And repair work in Mars orbit was a very slow, very expensive proposition.

"No need to get testy." Rikel's hand returned to the armrest. He quoted another price, almost as high as his first.

Cuss bumped his offer to fifteen percent of what Rikel had initially asked. "That's our last and best. We have Sols and will pay on transfer. We'll even make it look like bandits snatched them. Leave a few marks on the ship and such. No charge. You'll have a jingle in your pocket and a foolproof excuse."

Rikel groused some more, continuing to negotiate.

Ygo said, "Offer to let him keep whatever the two are carrying. Surely they have a stash. Between our price and what he finds, he'll do well."

Cuss passed along the offer. Rikel saw the possibilities and accepted the terms.

"Who else do you have aboard?" asked Cuss.

"It's me, my two crew, and your two prisoners. That's it."

It matched what Ygo had guessed. "Sit tight. We're going to approach and latch."

"Got it." Rikel closed the call.

While seemingly hovering side by side, the two ships were traveling at thousands of kilometers per hour in their orbit above Mars. Ygo made small, precise maneuvers as he edged the *Evalina* up near the *Tomlinson*. Eve maintained her position trailing behind, on alert for the slightest signs of life from their drives.

When the ships were close enough to connect the passageway between the ship's hatches, something that normally involved both parties, Cuss hailed the *Tomlinson*.

Rikel didn't respond so he hailed again. "Captain Taliaferro. We won't renegotiate. If you don't respond, we will breach your ship."

"Stand down. You do not have permission to enter."

"What is he doing?" asked Eve.

"That's not him," said Ygo.

The main viewscreen came alive. Rikel was sitting in the pilot's seat, strapped securely the way he would be during takeoffs and landings. A man was behind him, his feet floating off the floor, a thick arm around Rikel's neck, lifting his chin. The man's other hand held a knife against Rikel's throat, a sinister-looking folding blade with a razor's edge. He was bigger than the captain by a good bit. Physically able to deliver on his mortal threat should he choose to do so.

"That's Jaunty Gabala," said Ygo.

With a Southie-blue bandana tied around his forehead and an untamed beard that had grown wild during the long trip out, Jaunty flaunted a renegade look. Barker Adamson was hovering at Jaunty's side, an observer, at least so far. His trimmed beard and washed hair suggested a man who was less eccentric, perhaps less dangerous.

Cuss tried to imagine what could have led to this outcome. Maybe the two had overheard Rikel agreeing to sell them out. Maybe Rikel had become excited by the promise of a money stash and had gone looking for it on his own.

"Everyone relax," said Cuss. "No one needs to get hurt. And Mr. Gabala, be aware that you need the captain to fly the ship. The tech is linked to him. If he's gone, you're stuck, waiting for your food or air or water to run out. Not sure which will go first. I hear water is the worst. Or maybe your orbit will decay and you'll land the hard way."

"Fuck you," said Jaunty. "You are going to fly away and leave us alone. You do not have permission to board."

"We aren't going anywhere. Neither are you."

"Tell Barker that if he cooperates," said Ygo, "the Lagrange MA won't charge Abbi. She'll be a free woman, able to care for their daughter."

Cuss didn't know if it was a bluff or if Ygo had learned something. Either way, he liked the idea, trusted Ygo, and made the pitch.

Barker stayed quiet. But Cuss could tell they had him thinking.

"It's bullshit," Jaunty told Barker. "Why would that even make sense? They're trying to divide us, my friend."

"How do I know you're telling the truth?" Barker wasn't asking Jaunty. He was asking Cuss.

"Don't you dare," yelled Jaunty. Still holding Rikel around the neck with one arm, he swung the knife toward Barker, pointing it at him. "Don't you even think about it for a second."

"When I made you the offer," said Cuss, "that put it on the record, made it official. Your child needs her mom. I forget her name?"

"My daughter? It's Lynne. Mom is Abbi, my wife."

"Let's keep Lynne with her mom."

While they were talking, Jaunty bent forward and whispered into Rikel's ear, giving a slight jerk to his throat as he did so. Rikel moved a hand, and the viewscreen went dark.

"They are denying service," said Ygo. "I can't do anything about it."

"Oh, for God's sake," fumed Cuss. "Why is nothing ever easy?" He spent a moment feeding on his exasperation before asking, "Can you get me inside?"

"That's a big risk for a couple of assholes."

Ygo's concern was that Cuss would need to suit up, float through open space to the *Tomlinson*, and enter using tools and time. Once inside, he'd need to navigate through an unfamiliar ship to confront armed killers.

"We get to go home when it's over. Let's get it done."

Ygo and Eve tried to dissuade him. When he remained insistent, Ygo became supportive, researching possible entry points. He found an access panel near the thrusters on the ship's tail. The ones Eve was targeting if they showed the slightest signs of activity.

"If they power the drives while you're back there, Eve can't shoot them out without killing you. Which means the drives will fire, and that will kill you."

"How long will it take me to get inside?"

"Not completely sure. I can't find build plans for the *Tomlinson*, so I'm working off plans for a sister ship they built the next year. I don't know what changes were made in between. Assuming these are good, an access panel on the tail is held shut with a row of fasteners. You use a wrench to turn them, open the panel, and climb through. From there, you reengage the fasteners so they hold pressure, cycle through a service hatch, and you're in."

"So how long in minutes?"

"If the fasteners have been used in the last year or so, they should turn freely and you'll be inside in ten minutes. If they're frozen in place from a decade of corrosion, then we might need a plan B."

"This sounds crazy risky," said Eve.

"The captain and his crew are being threatened because of me. I need to help them."

"Because of *us*," said Ygo.

Cuss smiled. "You're right. *We* need to help them."

"Some good news," said Ygo. "I have a clean angle from the *Nelly Marie* and can see the access panel. It's where the plans say it should be, so they're at least that accurate."

"I'm going for it, then." He took off his jacket and strapped on his shoulder rig, tucked his Tosic 325 Hybrid into the holster, and struggled his way into a borrowed pressure suit, the largest size he could find on the *Evalina*, still barely big enough for his outsized frame.

Suiting up was hassle enough when there was gravity to help. It was thoroughly frustrating when floating in a weightless environment, the limbs of the suit folding, twisting, and doing everything but cooperating. He kept at it, and soon enough he was ready. Cycling through the main hatch, he moved out into the cold vacuum of space.

His objective was the *Tomlinson*'s tail, maybe twenty meters away from where he was floating outside the *Evalina*. The plan was to shoot a dart—a small harpoon with a self-attaching mechanism on the front and a line trailing out the back—at the hull.

He aimed the dart gun and fired, the projectile vanishing into the starfield, the thread-thin line unspooling and unspooling. And unspooling. The way it kept going reminded him of the time he'd dropped a rock into the well behind Tubby's house when they were kids, and marveled at how long it took to hear a distant splash deep underground.

Though it seemed like forever, in truth it was only four or five seconds before the dart hit its mark. The line tightened. He tugged on the lead to confirm it was firmly anchored. Then he hooked his tether to it, placed his feet against the hull of the *Evalina*, and pushed off.

His transit took twenty seconds, enough time to observe the rust-red planet turning slowly below him. On a different day, he might find the view awe-inspiring, even soul moving. But he lifted his gaze to the approaching hull of the *Tomlinson* and concentrated on getting to the assholes before they hurt anyone.

He arrived with a light thump, absorbing the impact with his shoulder and hip. Untethering, he pulled himself hand-over-hand along a landing strut, working his way down, around, and inside the *Tomlinson*'s drive bay. The access panel was where Ygo had said. It was a small door on a huge assembly at the base of one of the main thruster nozzles, a black cone the size of a house.

Fishing the wrench out of a pocket, he teased Eve, "Don't shoot. It's just me."

Luck was with him. The fasteners turned easily, and he was past the panel and through the maintenance hatch in nine minutes. "So far, so good," he reported as he stripped off his pressure suit and pulled his gun.

Then he began a frustrating collaboration with Ygo,

who, watching through Cuss's lens, did his best to provide directions to the bridge. The build plans they were using were good but imperfect. Twice, Cuss was forced to backtrack and seek alternatives.

Through perseverance and a bit of trial-and-error, he reached the door to the ship's bridge. A smooth surface of gray composite, it was positioned at the end of a clean but aging passageway.

"Can you see inside?" he asked Ygo.

"Not until I get access to the ship's feeds."

Using the noise-amplifying capabilities of his lens, Cuss listened for any sounds coming from within that might indicate human presence. He heard hums and whirrs and clicks, noises he associated with normal ship operation. But nothing that suggested people.

"Can you force the door?"

"Maybe. You passed a maintenance display back a bit. That might do it."

Cuss floated along the corridor, returning the way he'd come, and stopped in front of a glowing spot on the wall, a circle the size of his palm that radiated a faint white light.

"Tap it," said Ygo.

Cuss hit the spot with an index finger. The glow brightened, changed to red, and then returned to white.

"Again."

He tapped again. The same white-red-white.

"Tap it three times in a row. I'm trying to associate your tapping with a signal back to central."

Cuss tap, tap, tapped.

"Got it. Authenticating."

A display projected in front of Cuss. Ygo guided him through a lengthy sequence of selections, having him tap and swipe until he opened a direct link to the ship's systems.

"I'm in," Ygo announced after a longish pause.

Cuss floated back to the door leading to the bridge, drew his gun, and secured a foothold that would allow him to maintain position as he swung his weapon across the room. After practicing, he said, "Cut the lights and open the door."

"On three." Ygo began a countdown.

Cuss was plunged into darkness, and then the world around him took on an ethereal glow as his lens pierced the gloom.

A chime dinged in the distance, the sound of a low-level ship's alarm.

The door opened.

He flexed the leg of his anchored foot, canting his upper body into the room. At the same time, he swung his gun from left to right, his shoulder braced against the jamb for added stability.

The bridge was empty.

Unhooking his foot, he floated in through the door, spinning, clearing the space, and confirming that no one was hiding under a counter or behind a console. Ygo brought up the lights, and Cuss drifted across the bridge to the only other door he could see.

"It was designed as a captain's ready room from back in the day," said Ygo. "Not sure how it's being used now."

The door looked identical to the one he'd just passed through. They repeated the previous entry sequence, with

Cuss anchoring his foot, and Ygo dropping the lights and opening the door.

Inside was a small conference room. It had a table with four chairs. Star maps as art on the ceiling. Neat blue storage cabinets covering the back wall.

Jaunty sat in the far chair, staring across the table at Cuss.

A sinister-looking folding blade protruded from his chest. A little bit to the left of center. Over the heart. A huge red blotch stained his shirt.

"He's dead," said Ygo.

"It's not the worst outcome I could imagine."

"I've found Barker and Rikel in the ship's galley. It's back around the corner."

When Cuss reached the two, they were in a daze, staring at nothing.

Barker was the first to respond, turning his head to look at Cuss. "You better not be lying about my girls."

· · ·

It took most of a day to wrap things up. They paid Rikel fifty percent of his original outrageous bid for a modified deal. He would release Barker Adamson to them, and he would deliver Jaunty's body to Utopia for disposal.

They transferred Barker to Freddie Keyes on the *Swallowtail*, who demanded full payment even though he was now transporting just a single live prisoner. His deal also included delivery of Jeremy Romesco's body to a transfer point near home.

They linked the *Nelly Marie* together with the *Evalina*.

Cuss, Eve, and Ygo began their eight-week journey home.

Chapter 29

Ygo watched as Eve stepped through the door and into his den. His home. The first person to visit since he'd moved in six years earlier. That tally included Cuss. It didn't include the equipment specialist who'd visited a couple of times for maintenance and upgrades. Those weren't social calls.

He'd dimmed the lighting around the perimeter of the room but kept a bright light shining over his bed. Over him. Like a spotlight. So she could see. Using feeds integrated into his brain, he studied her face from a dozen angles, looking for her brow to crease. Her mouth to twitch. They didn't. He did see her nose crinkle, a natural reaction to the cleansers and disinfectants used to keep his skin healthy.

"Hello, Ygo," she said, studying him. "A man and not an AI."

"Hello, Eve."

He generated a feed that showed him what she was seeing: a white blob in an oversized recliner, the current configuration of his capsule-bed. He could see his head and arms and hands. The rest was covered with a white sheet, a shapeless, bulging mass. His head was oversized. Smooth. Shiny. No hair anywhere, including no eyebrows, making his puffy, round face look even more odd. Thankfully, he couldn't see the quantum link trailing out the back of his neck, so she wouldn't either as long as he didn't turn his head. His features were small, lost in his fleshy face. Tiny nose. Tiny ears. Tiny lips. His arms were short. His hands had webbing between the fingers, almost like flippers.

She took a step forward and then stopped, still near the door. She folded her arms in front of her, her face a mask. "You know what I'm going to say."

"I believe so. That I am a liar."

"It's a poison to any relationship. Any of mine, at least."

"I like that you use that word. Relationship."

Her eyes flared, warning him that deflection wasn't his best approach.

"Eve, I have sinned. We both know I can't apologize it away. In every conversation we have from this point forward, you will be wondering if I am being truthful. You will second-guess me. Question my motives. And rightly so. I made an unforgivable, unrecoverable mistake. I am sorry, for what it's worth. But the damage is done."

"Then why did you do it?"

"You know."

She took another step forward. "Because you believe you're a monster who could never be accepted, let alone loved."

"Ouch."

"I'm sorry. Then tell me."

His way would be through a long story. One of hardship, pain, and betrayal. Humiliated. Rejected. Despised. But the summary of it all, if he were to reduce it down to a single sentence, was what she had said. "You are accurate. It's a good summary. And now you're going to insist that I didn't give you a fair chance. If I had, I would see how wrong I was. That I wouldn't see pity in your eyes. In your face. Or revulsion."

"What you are seeing is me not letting you use the sympathy card to excuse the lying."

He didn't say anything for a good half minute. When enough time had passed that he felt he could introduce a new topic, he motioned her forward. "Please. Come into the light so I can see you."

She stepped up next to his chair and rested a hand on the silver rail that ran down the side, a reminder that it was a medical device. She looked around, taking in the room. Then she looked at him. "You're Cuss's partner, yet you never leave here."

"Yes."

"And he hides the fact that you're helping him. That you're a person contributing to his success."

"Yes."

"How is that ethical, him taking credit for your work?"

"Because he is a generous person. To me. To the agency."

Her brow creased.

"It's my precondition for being involved, for helping the Marshals Service. I choose to keep my contributions private. I want to be invisible. I'm more comfortable that way. He hates taking credit for my work and has nagged me from the beginning to reveal the truth, occasionally threatening to do so himself. But he understands that I will resign if he does, so he doesn't. Girish Mannan knows who

I am and what I do. The folks at MFOD. That's enough for me."

He paused, smoothing the sheet covering him. After giving her a moment to digest his words, he continued. "When I was first introduced to you, you were to be on board for a short hop. Calling me an AI was an efficient cover. Then it turned into this months-long journey, and I was too embarrassed, too far down the liar's path to see a way out. I thought I could pull it off. And then you took to me in a way that was so exciting. So fulfilling. I'd never had a woman share with me like that. To confide in me. Ask my opinion. Listen to my stories. Tease me. Laugh at my jokes. I feared that revealing myself would jeopardize everything."

She nodded in a way that said "I hear you" more than "I understand." Then she asked, "So why Cuss?"

"What do you mean?"

"You could choose anyone to work with. You chose him. Why?"

"To be fair, he chose me as well. It was a mutual pairing. We get along. We like each other. I admire who he is."

"Who is he?"

Ygo could feel himself becoming animated. "He's different from anyone else I know. He's a guardian. A sentinel. I am in awe of him."

She frowned.

"Think that most people are just trying to get by in life. Innocents wanting to enjoy their day. To have a sense of community. To be safe. Have a full stomach. The comfort of friends and family. Unfortunately for them, society also is sprinkled with aggressors. The sinister. Abusers, thieves, oppressors. Murderers. Not just misfits, but defects. Broken people who threaten the rest. And then there is Cuss. An avenger who doesn't just keep evil away from good. He pursues it. Chases it down. Battles it head on. And damned if he isn't good at it. It's an honor to help him. A privilege to be part of it."

"Which makes him judge and jury?"

"That's the thing. Almost never. He sincerely tries to bring them to justice."

"Like you? Judge and jury for Zed?"

"Not like me. That was one of the toughest calls of my career. If you two had tried to arrest Zed, I saw high odds that one or both of you would be killed. That would lead Girish to sending gunships in an expensive, slow-motion disaster. Our realistic choices were to leave Utopia with Jeremy and Atepa unavenged by society, or for me to be not only judge and jury but also executioner. While most of me is horrified, a small part is proud. Enough so that I would do it again."

"You aren't just in awe of him. You love him. I can tell."

"Cuss?" He nodded. "I do."

She looked away. "I do too, in my own way."

"What would your boyfriend say about that?"

"My what?"

"You told Rory you had a boyfriend."

She laughed. "It's a standard response to unwanted attention. I'm taken. Leave me alone."

"Are you going to tell Cuss?"

"That I don't have a boyfriend? He's been around way more than most. I'm pretty sure he's familiar with the tactic."

She leaned against the rail and traced her eyes up and down his body. Then she reached over and stroked his hand, the one nearest her. Rubbed it. Ran her palm up and down his arm.

He stared at her hand. It felt so good he couldn't believe it. Pleasure and intimacy swirled inside him. It was overwhelming. Like she'd reached into his soul. Literal magic.

"How long has it been since you've been touched?" She gripped his hand in hers. Like lovers.

It had been forever since anyone had touched him. Longer. He started to cry.

She kept his hand in hers, waiting for him to finish.

After a bit, when he'd cried himself out, he pulled the edge of the sheet up to his face and wiped his eyes. Dabbed his nose.

She moved her hand back up to the rail. "This is where you watch over Cuss?"

"Twenty-four seven."

"Do you sleep?"

"Of course. A couple of hours a night, always while he's sleeping. Even then, though, I have proxies watching for me, programmed to wake me at the slightest anomaly."

"Do you watch over me as well?"

"I do, and will for as long as you're teamed with him."

"You watch him. You watch me. Do you watch us?"

For a tiny fraction of a second, he thought "us" meant

her and him. Eve and Ygo. Then he understood and was mortified. Humiliated. He could feel his face flush with embarrassment, a tell more visible than a theater marquee.

She was asking if he watched while she and Cuss had sex.

To protect Cuss, to have his back, he had to watch him. They were partners in every sense of the word, which meant his vigil never ended. And blanket monitoring was how he compensated for not being out in the field with him, for not being at his side.

So watching was his job. His life.

He was embarrassed because when he watched them making love, he did so at a level beyond that necessary to provide for Cuss's safety. Or hers.

And after he'd fallen for her, he'd watched her in her cubicle.

He hated himself for it. Like so many people who suffer from compulsions, he'd sworn over and over that each time would be the last.

Rationalizations were plentiful. He was bedbound. She was exciting. And it wasn't as simple as closing his eyes. The feeds went right into his brain. What choice did he have?

"Does Cuss know?"

He answered that question the same way he'd answered the last. No words. His face becoming a deeper shade of crimson. Of course, he'd never discussed it with Cuss. He would die first. But Cuss seemed to know he was there. He'd talk to him on occasion, ask him for things.

"I'm not going to judge you, Ygo. Trust me, I carry

baggage you wouldn't believe. Volumes of questionable decisions."

Her words gave him an odd sense of relief, like receiving forgiveness in a confessional. He studied her face, taking her in, desiring her more if that were even possible.

She noticed his stare and blushed, and then headed for left field. "Do you think I'll qualify for Chaparral? That I'll be admitted?"

Her chaotic thought process made him smile. "You clear every hurdle with ease except for Governor Belnick. He typically has one open slot per year, if that. And he's a politician, so he has things to balance. Requests from donors. People who have done favors for him in the past and now want payback. The upside is that he needs the Marshals Service. He uses us, calls on Cuss when things get tough, especially when all of Lagrange is watching. Add that Cuss has twice protected the governor from aggressors, an assassin in one instance. His recommendation will go a long way. Mine will as well, though for different reasons."

"I'd appreciate your support when we get home. You and Cuss. I really want to go. To serve."

"Of course. I predict the governor will nominate you, and you will become an amazing officer."

She grinned and changed topics again. "What do you do for fun? Down-time? Your life has to be more than supporting Cuss."

"My AI can cast worlds inside my head for me to enjoy, places so vivid I get lost in the wonder of it all. In just a few minutes of real time, I can live for what seems like days in these places. I have worlds where I can fly, or be a star athlete, or a sex symbol. Sometimes I'm an artist or musician. Fashion designer. Chef. Gunslinger. Comedian. Craftsman. Some of them are personas I visit often, like other lives. It's fulfilling in its own way. Certainly entertaining."

"It sounds amazing. Especially the creative experiences."

There was an awkward silence. He could tell she was about to wrap up her visit.

"I'm going to let you go," she said, giving the room a last look.

"I've enjoyed having you. You're welcome to visit anytime."

She moved to the door, stopped, and turned back to him.

"It's okay for you to watch me when I'm alone. I hope my permission will relieve some of your guilt. But the rule is that you have to be talking to me. I treasure your company, treasure you as a friend, and snooping is creepy. As for Cuss and me—I'm okay with it, but you need to ask him, too."

He didn't respond, his mind swirling from her forthright attitude. Her support for their friendship.

"Let me add that you do *not* have permission to watch me in the bathroom. That's gross. And when we arrive home, it ends. You won't follow me around. Stalk me. I hope we'll be friends, but the watching will end."

"Okay." He didn't know what else to say.

"Swear to me. Convince me you're not lying."

"I swear, Eve. No snooping. No toilet. No stalking."

"Keep talking to me, though. I like it." She winked. "I like you."

The door opened and she was gone.

Chapter 30

It was the second day of their return trip. Cuss and Eve were lounging at a table on the middeck of the *Nelly Marie*. Eve was finishing making a pot of orange pekoe tea, an item that, for whatever reason, was wildly overstocked on the *Evalina*.

She poured. He took a sip.

"Not bad." He liked it okay but preferred coffee. Fortunately, his ship had that item in good supply.

She sipped, looked at her cup, tilted her head, and nodded.

He interpreted it as her saying, *Not bad.* He waited until she looked up. "So, how does it feel to captain a Starlane cruiser?"

"Am I pilot or captain?"

"Ygo, what do you say?"

"I'd claim both. Who's going to argue?"

"Not me." Cuss started to sip, and then he paused and looked up. "I've been meaning to ask, what is it that you'd learned back there about Abbi Adamson? When we promised she wouldn't be charged?"

"That the municipal attorney's office has her as a suspect in just one case: the robbery of Avium Pharmaceuticals," said Ygo. "It's a big charge. Bridge Hollenbeck died and ten thousand doses of Pulse were stolen. But for evidence, all they have is POTS showing Abbi in the vicinity, disappearing from the system before the incident occurred, and reappearing some distance way in the company of the doers afterward. There's no evidence that she was ever in the building. That she participated in the robbery. That she was involved in Bridge's death. If they'd caught her with the Pulse, that would have changed things. But they didn't. That leaves them with weak circumstantial evidence. And the only people who could provide first-person testimony of her involvement are Vincent Rogalski, Bridge Hollenbeck, and Jaunty Gabala."

"Dead, dead, and now dead," said Eve. "Don't forget Barker."

"As long as hubby keeps his mouth shut, the MA doesn't have a case. Oh, and it turns out that Abbi and Lynne have disappeared. There's no sign of either of them in Nova Terra or Lagrange, which puts them somewhere on Earth. So even if they made a case against her, they'd still have to find her."

Hearing Eve and Ygo interact prompted Cuss to ask about their much-anticipated tête-à-tête. "Did you two work out your differences? Are we all friends?"

"What happens behind closed doors is none of your concern," said Eve, speaking before Ygo could. "But I will observe that it was actually *you* who first said that Ygo was an AI. His desire to be supportive of you forced him to maintain the fiction. If I were to be upset at anyone, it would be you."

"What?" Cuss stared at her, incredulous, knowing something was off, realizing it when a corner of her mouth twitched up. He confessed. "You're right. It was me."

She grinned. "Word of warning. When I graduate from Chaparral, I'm going to invite Ygo to be my partner."

Cuss raised his eyebrows. "Really? Good thing I misplaced your recommendation. And I'd written such high praise for you."

"Don't worry," said Ygo. "I know where the letter is. And I know his signature better than he does. It'll get submitted."

Eve carried her cup to the kitchenette, cleaned it, and stowed it. "I'm going back to my captainage, or whatever it's called. I want to search that ship from nose to tail. See what new toys we have to play with for the next couple of months." She started down the stairs to the command deck, speaking louder so he could hear. "I'm anxious for a project. Something that takes weeks to do, that can capture our attention, keep our hands busy."

She paused at the passageway connecting the two ships. "Come over for dinner?"

"Sure." He heard shuffling noises as she climbed into the tube.

He sat for a bit, finishing his drink, and then he stood and cleaned the pot and his own cup. "It sounds like things went well between the two of you. Maybe better than expected?"

"I confessed and begged for forgiveness. She was very understanding. Gracious."

"It sounds like you hit it off."

"It was pretty spectacular, I must admit."

"Do you want me to step aside? Give you a clear

runway? I'm happy to oblige."

"Oh, stop it." A pause. "She was put off by the fact that in protecting you, I watch everything. I see the good and the bad, the public and the private. She thinks I need to be more discerning about my coverage."

"All I know is that you've saved my life more times than I can count. Whatever you're doing, please keep it up. I'm asking you to. It works. It's proven. Why fix it?"

"I agree with you. But I agree with her. I'm a work in progress."

"Good people struggle their whole lives trying to be better. Stay with it. I'm proud of you."

"She thinks you need to inform the women you are being intimate with."

"Inform them of what?"

"That another is watching."

It took a moment for him to digest Ygo's message. "Holy shit. I'll never get laid again."

"I'm just telling you."

He gnawed on a thumb, thinking. "All the marshals have some sort of passive coverage. Cameras and such. What do they do?"

"Blur."

"Why can't we do that?"

"We can, but it's postprocessing. The actual image is blurred after the camera captures it. The way I'm wired, I'll see either way."

"Goddamn, pal. I'm hating this conversation." It was like a choice between having a life, or having Ygo as a partner. And beyond that, it felt like Ygo was being slandered for doing his job, that his surveillance was somehow prurient. Then he thought about Eve's desire for a project. "Do you think you could work with Eve to develop a protocol that would give my guests privacy and that lets you protect me? Be thoughtful about it. Set lofty goals. Take your time."

"I'd enjoy working with her. We'll give it a go."

"Good." He felt like he'd dodged a bullet.

. . .

Later, when Cuss went over to the *Evalina* for dinner, Eve had a white plastic box on the table. He got a beer and sat down, waiting for her to show him.

"It's a seed bank," she said, opening the lid. "Forty-five super-fast-growing hydroponic-friendly choices. I've picked out lettuce, green beans, cucumbers, onions, tomatoes, radishes, and a mix of herbs. All producing harvestable fruit in three to four weeks."

"Any hot peppers?" Cuss leaned in to read the labels.

"A serrano-habanero hybrid." Eve showed him.

"Perfect. Let's add that. And let's grow small cukes that I can pickle. Then I can make *great* burgers."

Eve grinned. "So, you're in?"

"We're talkin' food. Of course I'm in."

"I'm thinking a container garden using the tubs that are at the bottom of these tall storage closets." She opened the closet behind her, ducked down, and pulled out a black bin holding the odd bits that hadn't been stowed on a shelf. She dumped the contents back into the space where the tub had been and held the empty container up for him to see.

"I figure we can put eight of these at the back of each middeck." She pointed to where she had in mind. "It's hydroponics, so we don't need dirt. We fill these with fluffy packing material I found in the hold. That becomes our soil to plant seeds in. Then we drip nutrient-rich water over the top of the packing to feed the roots and keep them from drying out." She sketched the idea with an index finger on the deck. "The nutrients need to circulate, so each tub needs a drain at the bottom. We gather those drains using a hose over here and send them to the recirculating pump."

She looked up. "Ygo, you said we could control the lights?"

"That's right. I can manipulate the spectrum and focus the beams, so each plant will get what it needs while keeping the overall brightness down. Reduce the annoyance factor."

"I'm hungry now," said Cuss. "I can't wait three weeks."

"Good things come to those who wait," said Eve, patting him on the shoulder.

· · ·

Over the next few days, Cuss mostly watched as Eve worked. He tilted back in a chair and sipped orange pekoe tea. They'd learned that if you brewed a strong batch, cooled it, and served it over ice, it was a tasty and refreshing beverage. One of his jobs was to make sure her glass was full.

Another was to keep her company. She was drilling drain holes into the bottoms of the tubs. Piled at her feet were lengths of tubing and a jumble of fittings.

He made idle conversation. "Now that it's behind us, what are your thoughts on Utopia?"

"I'm glad for the experience but I have no desire to go back."

"It is pretty stark. I think they need other drivers beyond penelopite to mature. Maybe if a different company discovered new minerals to export, or if they started making products the other worlds wanted. Something to broaden and diversify the flow of immigrants."

"Until they attract women and families, the future looks bleak."

She bent over to connect a drain plug.

Looking at the top of her head, he saw blonde roots peeking through.

"Can I ask why you dye your hair? Your natural color would be pretty stunning."

She stopped working, sat back on an upside-down bin, and picked up her drink. Sipping her tea, she studied him over the top of the glass, crafting her answer. "It started when I was twelve. All of a sudden, men wouldn't leave me alone. I mean, like guys in their thirties and fifties and seventies. Cousins. Even an uncle. There was this hunger in their stare. A lust that they projected onto me. It never stopped, and it was scary."

She looked into the distance, remembering. "In high school, when my friends would go on and on about their plans to attract boys, all I could think about was how to make it stop." She grabbed a lock of hair and wiggled it at him. "This is one of a hundred things I tried to reclaim my life, one of the few things I've stuck with."

"So it worked?"

"Not really. But it's symbolic. Something I control." She took another sip. "What finally worked was a realization. I was maybe eighteen and decided I wasn't going to worry about their feelings. Why should I be gentle with their egos when they impose themselves on my world, acting all entitled, making me miserable? I was exhausted, so I hardened myself. I learned to push them away, to not listen, to say no. That's how I got my life back." She shrugged and shook her head. "Of course, now that makes me the bitch."

. . .

They were halfway home. Cuss sat at a table on the middeck, building a burger. He stacked lettuce, tomato, onion, hot peppers, and dill pickles—produce grown in Eve's container garden—on the meat patty. Eve had helped him with pickling the baby cukes.

He positioned the bun on top, the capstone to his masterpiece, and was about to take a bite when Ygo said,

"You just got a message from Tolly."

"Who?"

"Tolly Vaughn. The graduate student from Armstrong? Tiny person. Spirited."

"Oh, Tolly." He pictured her, recalled her waif-like figure, and felt a stir. "I wonder what's going on?"

"Geez. If only there were a way to find out."

Cuss smiled. "Okay, show me."

Tolly appeared in a hoverview. She looked fresh, smiling, happy.

"Hi Cuss. You'll never guess where I live now. That's right. Apollo!"

The four tube cities of Lagrange were Hermes, Athena, Demeter, and Apollo. Because he was a marshal who lived on his spaceship, he could park in any of them. So Tolly was now a neighbor, and could be a very close neighbor if he chose.

"I'm looking for jobs after graduation and couldn't find squat. Who would have guessed that the demand for public policy specialists was so limited? Anyway, I got a callback for a research analyst position I had applied for with Governor Belnick's office. Had a great interview, and now I have the job!"

She smiled. "I may have let on in the interview that you and I are really close. Best buds and whatnot. Which I hope we will be." The smile became a grin. "Anyway, when I dropped your name, it was like opening doors. So, thanks for that. Look me up. Let's get together. It'll be fun." She bit her lip. "Hope you call." The hoverview closed.

"Oh, lord," said Ygo.

From the Author

Thanks for reading. If you enjoyed the book, please consider telling others about it with a rating or review on Amazon. Reviews are the lifeblood of an author, and reader excitement motivates us to write!

Also by Doug J. Cooper

The Crystal Series

The Crystal Series is four books of action and suspense involving AI, spies, romance, and battles in space!

Crystal Deception (Book 1)
Crystal Conquest (Book 2)
Crystal Rebellion (Book 3)
Crystal Escape (Book 4)

Readers' Praise for The Crystal Series (Amazon Reviews):

★★★★★ "Characters that feel like real people, who behave in ways that make sense and you can empathize with."

★★★★★ "It has all the features of Anne McCaffrey 's Dragon Riders of Pern series. Strong characters, sentient improbability and interesting plots."

★★★★★ "Nicely done hard sci-fi. I am a fan of this kind of story line so it sucked me right in."

★★★★★ "A tale of intrigue, action, a touch of romance and heartbreak."

For info and purchases, visit: crystalseries.com

Free Story!

Crystal Horizon – Prequel to the Crystal Series

The Crystal Series is four full-length books where the emergence of self-aware AI and alien first contact occur at the same time.

Sample this popular space opera for free by downloading Crystal Horizon, the prequel.

In book 1 of the series, Crystal Deception, Cheryl is captain of the military space cruiser Alliance, and Sid is a covert warrior for the Defense Specialists Agency. We learn that the two have a shared history, and in particular, a romantic relationship that has somehow gone awry.

In the prequel, we get their backstory. We join Sid and Cheryl on the day they first meet, and experience that shared history with them.

Crystal Horizon is offered free to newsletter subscribers.

To obtain this free book, visit: crystalseries.com

Have you read Lagrange Rising?
Cuss Abbott book 1

The bodies of wealthy seniors are being dumped in Lagrange, their ID implants cut from their skulls, their bank accounts emptied. Authorities learn that the elderly victims were snatched from Nova Terra on the Moon. Lagrange is a sovereign nation, a massive space structure orbiting between Earth and the Moon, so the chilling crimes fall under the purview of the Interworld Marshals Service. Cuss Abbott, a resourceful and tenacious investigator, starts the case with few clues, a rising body count, and politicians demanding answers. The criminals are seemingly invisible, disappearing after each heinous act. Shadowed by his partner, an enhanced human named Ygo, Cuss corners the butchers, setting in motion a confrontation with tragic results. Distraught, he bulls ahead, pursuing the killers across worlds to a suspense-filled showdown.

For info and purchases, visit: crystalseries.com

Adventures in Time
With an Evil AI

Bump Time Trilogy

On his twenty-fifth birthday, Diesel Lagerford is visited by a twenty-six-year-old version of himself. His look-alike spins impossible tales of their shared future, claiming they have dozens of "brothers" from parallel timelines who can visit each other using a T-box, a machine they bankroll with lottery winnings. He introduces Diesel to the incredible Lilah Spencer, the T-box operator, and Diesel falls head-over-heels in love. But during his travels across timelines, Diesel learns that Lilah will soon die under suspicious circumstances. Devastated, he joins his brothers in a race to save her. Can they solve the mystery of her death before it's too late? And will their unusual solution play out over time in the ways they had anticipated?

For info and purchases, visit: crystalseries.com

56890599R00221